RAIN WILL FALL TRILOGY 1

FOREVER

Rain

Cindy Lou Moldovan

PUBLISHED BY CINDY LOU MOLDOVAN

Copyright © Cindy Lou Moldovan, 2014

Date of first printing: June 2014

Cover Design: Victorine E. Lieske
Editor: Lea Ellen Borg, Night Owl Editing Services
eBook Formatting: Guido Henkel, www.guidohenkel.com

OTHER BOOKS BY
CINDY LOU MOLDOVAN

RAIN WILL FALL Series

FOREVER RAIN – book 1

RAIN OVER ME – book 2 {coming July 28, 2014}

SEASON OF RAIN – novella {coming August 25, 2014}

RAIN EVERLASTING – book 3 {coming soon}

Non-Fiction

GROWING UP THIRD WORLD

CHAPTER 1

I LAY ON MY SIDE WITH MY BACK TO MY LOVER, MY ASS snug against his pelvis, his chest pressed against my back and our legs a tangled mass of limbs. His strong arms hugged me into him possessively. Sensing that I was awake, he ran his hand over my abdomen in a circular motion. Slowly, his large hand that I've become accustomed to on my body paused at my rib cage, then made its way up between my breasts and back down again. My nipples beaded into tight knobs, begging to be touched.

Knowing just what I wanted, his hand cupped one of my breasts that was heavy and needy for his touch. He palmed the globe in his hand; two fingers reached my nipple and squeezed firmly, sending a rushing heat between my legs.

I gasped and he repeated the action again. I covered his hand with mine demanding that he stay there and continue the erotic play on my skin, which he does. I squirmed against him, my ass rubbing against his cock that's now steel hard and pushing against my back. Not to be ignored, he paid homage to my other breast as my body continued to move against him.

He chuckled behind me and pushed his face in my neck, inhaling the scent of my skin. My earlobe was pulled into his warm mouth as he sucked gently on it, emitting a needy sound from my throat. With one swift motion, he rolled onto his back and flipped me to lie on his chest. My breasts pressed against him. I straddled him with both of my legs and bent my knees causing my wet, puffy folds to rub against his steel hard erection.

His hands cupped both of my breasts now and he rubbed and squeezed the dark pink areolas, bringing his fingers to the knobs of my nipples that were elongated and deliciously sensitive. I moaned and held onto the rumpled bedding beneath us. My long auburn hair tumbled over my shoulders as I leaned my head back and rubbed my wet core onto his manhood.

He lifted my hips, and in a slow motion, lowered my moist slit onto his cock. I sank down on his long shaft that was rippled with veins, showing the power of his need. I bit my lips and moaned as I started to move above him. Knowing just what he liked when I'm on top, I circled my hips slowly on his pelvis which caused his massive cock to move inside me. The feeling of fullness lay low in my abdomen sending a shiver of pure pleasure up my spine.

I repeated the motion again and again, then leaned forward and braced myself on his broad shoulders, lifting my hips slightly to better accommodate his length. I put my weight on my knees and lifted my hips as I moved him in and out of me. My hair fell onto my breasts now, my grey eyes staring into his brilliant blues. His pupils were dilated and his breathing increased.

The sounds of our bodies mating with our combined fluids of pleasure made an erotic sound in the room. He pushed his hips up to meet mine and soon we were moving in perfect unison. The motion of our bodies together moved as one. I looked down at our joined bodies, the lips of my labia spread onto his cock as my juices glistened on his skin. I looked up at him and he was looking at us as well. His jaw was clenched as he gripped my hips with big hands. My body succumbed easily to the throes of our passion.

I pushed up from his chest and rode him harder and faster, my breasts jiggling now; he moved his toned body below me matching my rhythm. I moaned his name as my breathing become choppy. My body was feeling the need to let loose. The point of explosion was dangling right in front of me. I wanted to free-fall into the abyss where I knew he would soon follow.

I was chanting his name begging for release. It was right there, building fast, sending my body in a frenzy, seeking the promise of fulfillment. He pushed my hand to my clit and I felt the wet swollen knob of my pleasure. My fingers swirled in the warm juices of my pleasure as I rubbed my clit, enjoying the incredible feeling that was sweltering in my core now. My hand flew over the pleasure knob again and again. I screamed his name as I shattered around him, my folds clenching rhythmically as it milked his cock, demanding his release as well. He followed with a shout as his own pleasure crashed into him.

My legs were shaking from the incredible orgasm that I'd become accustomed to by the only lover I've ever known. He pulled me down to him and took my mouth in a scorching kiss. Our breath came in spurts as we descended from the moments of incredible pleasure. Our skin was moist with perspiration that mingled with the musky scents of our desire. I lay my head on his chest, his arms like a vise around my body. We stayed in the cocoon of each other's arms, breathing each other's air until his cock eased out of me.

~ ~ ~ ~ ~

The digital alarm clock on the nightstand rudely interrupted me from my blissful state of sleep. I reached my hand between my legs and it was sticky from the orgasm I'd experienced in my dream. He still had this power over me; even when my conscious mind is at rest, my body seeks his. When will the dreams stop? When will I know such pure unadulterated pleasure again? I peeked at the time on my bedroom ceiling projected from the LCD of the clock. Yup, 6 a.m. Ungraciously, my hand reached the clock and silenced the alarm. Not one to snooze, I got up and out of bed. Like my alarm, this part of my day was necessary.

After using the bathroom, I hopped into my workout clothes and I make my way to one of the two spare bedrooms that I'd converted into a small home gym. I attached my iPhone into the small speaker and turned the music to my Pandora app. After finding Coldplay on my music list, I got on the treadmill and walked for five minutes while my foggy brain cleared. After that, I took off on a full-out jog for thirty minutes.

My phone rang as I stepped off the treadmill. I slid the indicator across the flat screen of the iPhone to see who it was from. Andre—an early morning call from my assistant wouldn't be good news.

"Good morning, Andre," I greeted him as I made my way to the kitchen to grab a cup of coffee. The coffee maker was on auto timer set for 6:30 a.m.

"Good morning, Zoe. Sorry to bother you so early, but I wanted to inform you that Gail Haas was in an accident this morning."

"How is she doing? Were others involved?' I asked, as the coffee cup paused at my mouth and I listened to the report about one of my agency nurses.

"Apparently someone swerved in front of her in traffic and hit the driver side of her car. An ambulance is taking her to the hospital and her car is being towed," Andre reported.

I wanted to breathe a sigh of relief that the accident was not as bad as it could have been, but would have to wait for further evaluation from the ER physician and other test results before fully exhaling.

"I covered her shift with another nurse. The nurse is in route to Metro Memorial Hospital for the shift in ICU."

Andre rotated administrative call with Veronica, my Director of Nursing. They were two of the first people I'd hired when I started the nursing agency five years ago. Both were competent and professional. I was lucky to have their loyalty and friendship.

"Great. Follow up with the ER and Gail in about an hour. Also, let her husband know that we are aware of the accident and will check on her periodically." After hanging up, I headed to my bedroom to continue my morning routine.

After a hot shower, another cup of coffee and a small toasted whole-wheat bagel, I felt energized. An hour later I checked my appearance in the mirror. The long tresses of my auburn colored hair bounced smoothly past my shoulders. The makeup I chose today was by Dior in neutral brown which played off the dark grey color of my eyes. I slipped on three-inch pumps, elevating my 5'4" a little more.

Turning off lights in the living room and kitchen, I made my way to the garage of my townhouse. I was out the door and in my car hoping that traffic would play nice today. My phone rang again as I engaged the push-start button of the engine. The Bluetooth in the car picked up the call.

"Hellooo," I answered, grinning as I reversed the car into the street. It was my sister, Jenna, who called me at least twice a day to 'check on' me. I always give her a hard time for calling me so often, but secretly I was glad she did.

"Hi, sis; on your way to work?" Her cheerful voice always put me in a good mood.

"Yeah, just heading out and so not looking forward to traffic." I tried not to sound as annoyed about the Houston traffic as I actually felt.

"Well, don't let anything get you down today. I'm excited about this weekend! My baby sister is turning thirty." The excitement in her voice was contagious and I smiled.

Jenna and her husband, David, are hosting a birthday party for me tomorrow night at their gorgeous ranch in Austin. I didn't have the heart to tell them that I would be just as happy having dinner and calling it a night.

The two lovebirds met a year after Jenna graduated from the University of Texas in Austin. She was working for an advertising agency and snagged the international bank as a client that David worked for. David was smitten! They dated for a year and got married when Jenna was 25 and David was 28. She quit her job a few months ago and has been trying to get pregnant.

"Get the hell out of the way, buddy," I muttered at a motorist in front of me.

"Language so early." Jenna constantly reminded me that she was trying to get pregnant and I needed to clean up my potty mouth or I won't be allowed around the baby. Ha, as if! I was so excited about my prospective new role as an aunt. That baby will be so loved and spoiled. Jenna and David will be terrific parents.

"Um, Jen…thanks again for the party. Just don't ever feel obligated, you know?"

"It was no problem at all, Zoe. Really, I chose everything with the party planner and she took it from there. It will be a gorgeous event! I even sampled the cake and it is divine!" Jenna was very much a part of Austin's social scene and was also involved with several charitable organizations. Hosting and attending events came naturally to her. She has great people skills and loved to entertain.

"Speaking of cake, I've been running in Memorial Park once a week for the past month, in addition to my morning workout routine just so I can do justice to the spread."

Jenna does nothing on a small scale. She may have coined the phrase *anything worth doing is worth doing big.* I'm sure my party will be no exception. We ended our conversation a few minutes later with Jenna's promise of another call later today.

Our parents died in a boating accident when I was two and Jenna was seven. Aunt Suzette, my mother's only sibling, raised us. Her career as a sci-fi author was taking off with a series of popular books, but she took on the enormous challenge of raising two small girls as well. Although never lacking for male companionship, she never did get married nor have any children of her own. Jenna took on the role of being my protector and we have a very close relationship; she's always worried about me. I constantly remind her that she's done well as my big sister and I turned out just fine.

After graduating from Baylor University, I went to work for one of Houston's largest hospitals as a nurse. Three years later, I saw the need for nurses working in hospitals on a temporary basis, which prompted me to open a nursing agency. With money left over from my parents' life insurance, I started the agency in a small building not far from the hospital. The rent was affordable which allowed me to buy my town home in The Heights, one of Houston's older, but trendy neighborhoods.

I had my nursing degree to fall back on if the business didn't do well, but I was determined to make it work. Although the past couple years has been stressful due to the economy and hospitals cutting back and opening their own in-house nursing agencies, I was grateful for the opportunity to own my own business and worked very hard to keep it viable. Any money that I had saved from the first few years, I invested back into the business. Recently I took out a loan to expand the business in San Francisco. My market research showed the need for agency nurses there. Now I just needed to get contracts in the hospitals and keep every-one working.

My phone rang again. "Zoe here." My voice was clipped as I swerved out of the way of a metro bus.

"Good morning, Miss Caine." It was Grace, my recep-tionist.

"Hi, Grace, I'm almost at the office," I informed her. Mornings were busy and this one was no exception.

"I wanted to give you a heads-up, Miss Caine, that the air conditioner is out again. I got in a few minutes ago and put the fans in place. I called maintenance and they should be here soon to see what the problem is."

"Call Lenny and let him know as well. Maybe he will spring for a new cooling system." Lenny was the landlord and owner of several small shopping strips around the Houston area.

"Will do, Miss Caine." I hit the disconnect button as I pulled my car into the small parking lot.

CHAPTER 2

STEPPING OUT OF MY CAR, I TOOK IN MY ATTIRE, GLAD that I'd chosen a simple white shift dress with some floral design scattered along the bottom. The dress came just above my knees and complimented the Antonio Melani pumps quite nicely.

When I entered the office, Grace was on the phone so I mouthed good morning to her and headed into my office. I opened the door and took in its sparse decor of a small sofa, a bookshelf in the corner, and two chairs in front of my desk. A few personal photos and my diploma hung on the wall.

I set my computer bag and Coach purse on the desk and opened the blinds of the only window in the room. The heat and humidity was typical for Texas summers and this morning was no exception, but with no central air circulating, the warm air from the fans wouldn't do much to keep us cool.

Once again, I wished that I could afford to move the office to a newer or more updated building, but money was tight and I was in the process of expanding the business. I also offer more benefits to my employees, which is an added cost to my tight budget, but necessary for employee retention. I lifted the hair off the back of my neck, then rummaged through my purse for a ponytail holder.

"So, tomorrow is the big day." Veronica, my Director of Nursing, and one of my best friends, came in and sat down. Veronica was beautiful. Her mixed heritage from a Latin mother and Caucasian father gave her skin a light olive coloring and gorgeous caramel color eyes. She was wearing her long, glossy black hair in a fish bone braid today that hung down her shoulder and lay on one side of her well-endowed chest.

"Don't remind me. I don't think I'm ready and hope I still fit in the dress I bought a few weeks ago." I scowled at her from under my lashes, but my eyes were playful.

"Gaw! Get over it already." She blew an exasperated breath. "This party will do you some good. You have been totally dedicated to the company and hardly socialize or do anything fun anymore." She fiddled with the stack of papers in her hands. "But really, Zoe, we appreciate the sacrifices that you've made. Despite the stressful times, you work harder to make sure we all take a paycheck home. Much appreciated."

I was touched by her kind words and told her so.

"Yeah, you're right. I will be in the party mood by tomorrow. It will be fun, plus I have not had a taste of my favorite friends in a bottle for a while like Grey Goose and Don Julio." I grinned at her from across my desk. Like me, Veronica was a native Houstonian. We met in college, got our first nursing jobs at the same hospital and she was determined to be at my side when I told her of my plans for the agency.

"So, let's get some business out of the way then." Veronica opened the Apple laptop computer as Andre strolled in with Starbucks coffee for all three of us and sat in the other chair. We started our morning with the usual 30-minute meeting.

Andre reported that Gail was having some X-rays done, a couple more nurses that had minor issues he resolved, and other nurses that reported to the various hospitals in and around the Houston area who got to work on time. The morning was business as usual. Andre and I worked on two more contracts for hospitals in San Francisco. I was also looking at market analysis for hospitals and their need for temporary nurses in Atlanta.

Andre went to his office to finalize our travel plans to go to San Francisco for our meetings with hospital administrators next week.

During the course of the day I met with a few more nurses who were new hires and were going through the paces of exams and competencies with Veronica. After my standard boring lunch of Chobani yogurt, a banana and Vitamin Water, I headed back to my office when Grace notified me that I had a call from my boyfriend, Robert Royden.

"Hi, Robert. How are you? Is your mother more amenable with her new nurse? Did you get my text this morning about the limo that Jenna rented to take us to Austin tomorrow?" I usually asked all my questions at once, as Robert would rather speak uninterrupted.

He answered my questions and continued to tell me about his day, uninterrupted. "Hello, sweets. My day is going well although it could be better. I met with mother's attorney yesterday. He said mother will need to cut back on her traveling or do without her private duty nurse. She did not take well to the news and has taken to her bed again. I think he's being a little unreasonable and I told him so."

I looked out of my window at the busy street in front of the building as I listened to the latest dilemma of my possible future mother-in-law and tried to follow along. Since some of the hospitals had their own in-house nursing agency, several hospitals did not renew my contract. I had expanded my agency to private duty nursing a year ago. My clients were wealthy and able to afford private nurses, whether it was medically necessary or not.

"...Sadly, sweets, that includes you, too." Shit! I'd lost him somewhere in the one-sided conversation and tried to catch up as he continued..." Don't take it personally that she won't see you next Wednesday for dinner. She's upset but will revert back to herself soon."

I scrambled to interject something intelligent in the conversation as Robert paused as if waiting for a response from me.

"Don't worry about it, Robert. I, ah…that is, you will help her figure it out." Really! I can't believe that is the best I could come up with. Was it too late to make a New Year's resolution? I didn't care, I was making one anyway…pay keen attention to anything your boyfriend has to say. Yes, I can do that.

"Sorry about the limo, lovie. I will fly to Austin tomorrow evening. This ordeal with her attorney has upset her and I need to make sure she will be OK for the weekend."

"I understand, Robert. I will miss your company on the ride to Austin. Until tomorrow night then." I felt a little guilty for not insisting that he stay in Houston, but I also wanted him to attend the party.

"Thank you, sweets. Goodbye."

And just like that the conversation was over. I looked down at the phone and convinced myself that Robert was good for me, just what I needed in a companion. At 40, he seemed like an old soul. We'd met at a charity fund raising event six months ago for battered and abused women. He was representing his company law firm. On a very small scale, I donate an item for the silent auction like I've always done over the past few years.

Robert was very sweet that night and gave me a ride home. I had attended the event with one of my best friends, Mia Lambert, who swore she had the worst headache of her life and had to leave early. She then texted me and said that Robert caused her horrific headache due to his boring stories and my audacity to actually listen to them.

She was such a brat! But I loved her dearly and the following week she showed up at my office with lunch and asked my forgiveness for being rude and ditching me. Mia was from a very rich Texas oil family. Refusing to go in to the oil business, she'd defied her father's wishes and became a nurse. To her father's delight, upon graduating from college she decided to follow in her older brother's footsteps and work in the family business after all...but as the Director of Nursing in the company's employee medical clinic.

The afternoon was just as busy as the morning. At 6 p.m., I stood at my desk allowing the blood to flow into my now aching legs. The private duty patients all had nurses lined up for the weekend shifts, the hospitals that requested nurses were staffed and Andre and I had face to face meetings next week in San Francisco with several hospitals for possible contracts.

I powered off the Mac computer and the company name and logo scrolled across the flat screen...

Bluebonnet Nursing Agency.

My mind was drawn back to the gorgeous painting in my reception area. It was an original by G. Harvey, one of America's renowned Texan artists.

It had been painted from a photograph that was taken 10 years ago and housed in a rustic wooden frame. The painting was a field of bluebonnet flowers, with a girl in the distance walking in the field, her head turned to the side. She was looking back at the camera, a gorgeous smile on her face, her dress billowing in the wind around her knees.

I shook my head to clear the memories of the painting and its depiction of the 20-year-old girl, so much in love and full of hope. Thankful for the knock on the door of my office, I called for the person to enter as thoughts of the carefree, idealistic girl were pushed back into the recess of my mind as a sad unfulfilled dream.

The last one to leave, I made my way out to my car, an Infiniti G37 sedan, and headed Midtown to meet Mia and Veronica for a margarita at Cyclone Anaya's Mexican Kitchen. Pulling the keys from my purse, I handed them to the valet who winked at me. I smiled back at him and went into the restaurant to meet my friends. The place was packed which was typical for a Friday evening. I grinned as I saw them waving to me on the outside patio and headed their way.

"Not that you don't look great, chick, but you look like you need one of these." Mia greeted me with a hug and placed the frosty mug of frozen goodness in my hand. I took a long sip of the margarita and plopped down in my seat. We immediately started talking about the party, the limo for us, and a party bus that Jenna rented for several of my Houston friends that didn't want to drive to Austin.

All three of our phones were buzzing with texts, Facebook messages and tweets with news of the party tomorrow night. We giggled and flirted with some guys at the table across from us. One of them bought us a round of drinks for my birthday. He blatantly hit on Mia and charmed her the entire hour we were there.

We had a two-limit drink since we were our own designated drivers. The valet reluctantly handed over the keys to Mia while ogling over her convertible Aston Martin. I shook my head at the attention she drew. As if she wasn't gorgeous enough with platinum blonde hair, a petite size four, and baby blue eyes, she drove an equally gorgeous car. Outrageous in all that she does, Mia loved attention and got plenty of it wherever she went. Veronica and I grinned at her as she slid into the uber swanky car and sped off. The guy that was flirting with her on the patio stood up at the table and whistled. His friends gave him a hard time since Mia hadn't given him her phone number. More relaxed now that I had some time to unwind from my busy day, I headed home.

I called Jenna and chat about the party tomorrow night. She filled me in on the activities taking place in her backyard. Along with tending her magnificent yard, Rojellio, her gardener, tended to her botanical garden and greenhouse that has been featured in *Nature and Botany* as well as *House & Garden* and *Southern Living* magazines.

After taking a shower, I gratefully slipped into a nightshirt, poured a glass of chardonnay and sat on the small patio in my backyard. Reluctantly I allowed my mind to drift to my parents. I did not have the privilege of knowing or having any memory of them. I'm often told that I look a lot like my mother. I miss not having the structure of a traditional family that so many of my friends did have, but I was grateful for all the love and affection that Aunt Suzette showered on Jenna and me.

Since she was 7 when our parents died, Jenna remembered them well and took on the role of my protector after their passing. It seemed hard for her to give up that role in my life even now that I was an adult. When she was away at college, she called me every day and we would chat about our life and missing each other. She listened to me complain about boys that I liked who didn't know that I existed, or not fitting into the popular groups of girls that always seemed to date the entire high school football and basketball boys' teams.

Despite not being the most popular girl in high school, I managed to do well with grades and was on the track and field team and my tennis game wasn't bad either. I also made some great friends along the way, like Jeremy who was a math genius, who'd gotten a full scholarship to MIT. He'd covered for me more than once in my junior year when I dated a boy that Aunt Suzette did not approve of. I was thrilled that he would be coming to the party as he was living in San Francisco since starting his own IT company a few years ago.

I finally slid into bed between the cool cotton sheets a little after 10 p.m. My weary body, helped along with the alcohol, pulled me into a deep sleep. I dreamt of the girl in the field of bluebonnet flowers and how much in love she was with her boyfriend.

CHAPTER 3

SATURDAY MORNING I DRESSED IN A LONG COTTON summer maxi dress, with sandals, and pulled my long hair into a ponytail, sans make-up.

Mia walked into my bedroom and shoved a Starbucks Grande Caffe Latte with a shot of double espresso into my hand. I greedily gulped the hot, delicious liquid.

"You sure know your way to a girl's heart." I gave her a hug and took another sip from the cup.

"Seriously? I wish I knew what the hell they put in that cup for you to act so strange." Mia didn't drink coffee. I laughed as we headed out to her car.

"Happy birthday and all that jazz, friend." She looked across at me and winked. Her face held a smug smile. Her surprise gift to me was this morning's activities and I had no idea what she has planned. Her instructions were to dress casual with no makeup.

"OK, spill it. Where are we going? And could you try not to kill us before we get there?" I hung onto the seat for dear life as Mia hit the gas and the car sped onto the freeway.

"You snooze, you lose, baby girl," she yelled over the music of Lady Gaga as she weaved through traffic. "This is Houston. The traffic's always a bitch, but don't worry your pretty head about it, you will be just fine."

She had the top down on her convertible this morning. Mia was a spitfire. Her perfectly proportioned figure may be petite but she had a huge attitude that served her well to get her own way. Luckily, under that fickle and brash exterior, she was an extremely poised and polished person with a kind heart, but only a few knew that about her. She would much rather come off as a hard-ass.

By some miracle, we exited safely off the freeway a few miles later and seemed to be making our way to The Galleria Shopping Center. She pulled the Aston Martin up to the valet and jumped out before the guy could open her door.

"Yeah, it's a beast, my good man." Mia handed over the keys to the man who was grinning from ear to ear as he stepped back to admire the car. She shoved some bills at him but he shook his head and put his hands in the air.

"Lady, you don't even need to tip me for this one. Just a few spins around the block is all I need to make my day."

Mia laughed and shoved the money in his shirt pocket.

"Nah, just park him somewhere where he can be admired."

"It's a him? I thought it would have a name like Candy or Monique." He slid into the seat.

"It's only a car for Christ's sake," I said, shaking my head, although I should be used to the reaction of Mia and her car by now.

"Ah...did she just go there?" He looked at Mia with raised brows.

"Disrespectful wench," Mia replied as she walked up to me and pulled my neck in a hug. We laughed and headed into the mall, took an elevator to the 30th floor and stepped into the ultra-modern salon.

"Oh, wow! What a treat." I did a happy dance as I looked around the room in amazement.

"You like?"

"Like? No, I love! This is awesome. So you must know someone that knows someone to get in here, and so early;

it's only 9 a.m." Philippe Salon and Spa was the most exquisite, outrageously expensive and snazzy spa in Houston…in the country for that matter, with at least a three-month waiting list for the ultra-rich and famous. He also has one in New York, Chicago, LA, Tokyo, London, Paris and several other cities around the globe.

He was well-known for his signature skin and hair care products. All of his spas employ an impressive list of world-renowned dermatologists for those wanting more bang for a whole lot of bucks. Collagen, Restylane, Botox, peels and infrarey therapy are but a few among many other professional services offered.

"Um, I hate to break it to you, love, but I know Philippe personally." Mia winked at me as a handsome young receptionist greeted us.

"Good morning, Miss Lambert. So good to see you again." He slipped mimosas into our hands as Veronica stepped in the door behind us.

"Happy birthday!" she squealed, while pulling Mia and me in for a group hug.

"Thanks. It is indeed happy. I mean, how could it not be when I'm in one of the most prestigious spas in like, the world." I took a moment to gawk at the spectacular crystal chandelier hanging overhead, priceless art on the wall, floor to ceiling windows showing off the skyline of the city, and baroque paintings on the ceiling of angels and cherubs.

"Good morning, ladies. My name is Gish. Please allow me to take you to your first station." We followed Gish into the massive salon where we were met by an entourage of people ready to pamper us with wraps, facials, massages and everything that makes for a delightful morning of indulgence.

After our rounds of luxurious pampering we were sated and full due to being served endless decadent chocolate covered strawberries, Champagne and Sterling Caviar. Grinning like idiots, we headed back to the lobby where we were greeted by none other than Philippe himself.

"How is my Houston princess doing today?" He embraced Mia and gave her a kiss on the lips. "Lovely as ever I see." He held on to her with an arm around her waist.

"Flattery will get you everywhere with me, as you well know." A smile played on her lips. A delicate blush crept up to Philippe's cheeks.

"These are my besties...like best friends ever, Zoe Caine, the birthday girl, and Veronica Saldana."

Philippe kissed our cheeks and settled back in a friendly embrace with Mia.

"I've heard a lot about both of you from Mia and delighted to finally meet you. How was your time at the spa?" He was tall and handsome with dark brown hair and green eyes. An expensive grey lightweight summer suit showed off the dark striped pink button down shirt that he wore without a tie.

"We had a fabulous time. Four hours simply flew by," I said.

"Well, you must plan to stay longer on your next visit." He flashed us a fabulous smile and graciously escorted us to the elevator and down to the valet, all the while his arm never leaving Mia's waist.

"When will I see you again, lovely Mia? I'm only in town for a few days and I will be crushed if you don't have time for dinner. Better yet, how about a quick trip to New York?"

Veronica and I dropped a few steps back and looked at each other with our mouth agape. I whispered to her about Mia's charming admirer and being left in the dark about him.

"Philippe, I am so busy. You can't just pop into town and try to whisk me away. I have a job, you know." She pouted prettily and made excuses about how hectic it was at the office.

Veronica and I looked at each other and rolled our eyes. We couldn't wait to get all the details of her and Philippe. Why would she not tell us that she knew him? Like, personally and most likely intimately. We shared everything with one another, or so I thought.

We stepped outside to a beautiful sunny afternoon. There was a limo and driver waiting for us. Mia made plans for the limo to pick us up here since we had a few drinks and we would leave for Austin now. Our bags and clothing for the party were neatly packed in the limo. Someone would pick up Mia's car later and deliver it to her loft.

"Zoe, enjoy your birthday party. It was a pleasure meeting you and Veronica," Philippe said. He kissed Veronica and me on our cheeks. We slid into the luxurious vehicle with soft leather seats that enveloped our relaxed bodies.

Mia was about to get into the limo but was detained by Philippe. He pulled her into his body and swooped down to claim her lips in a long passionate kiss. Mia whimpered and slid her arms around his neck.

Veronica's slammed both her hands over her mouth and stared at me. I shrugged my shoulders at a loss for words.

A few moments later Mia slid onto the seat of the vehicle and Philippe closed the door behind her.

"Spill it, Mia." Veronica wasted no time getting to the details of her and Philippe.

"There is nothing to tell," Mia said, as she jutted her chin out in defiance of the question.

"Liar, liar…something is going on with that fabulous piece of man and we want to know what, when and for how long," Veronica went on as I nodded my head in agreement.

"Well, it was a long time ago."

"That's it? That's all we get?" I asked as the limo pulled onto the freeway.

"It was about a year ago. I met him in New York and we hit it off. Well, sort of...anyway, it was only once and now...well, I'm not sure; I mean, he wants more, but I'm way too busy," she blurted out and twisted the top off a bottle of water. This so not like Mia to be nervous or evasive, even on a matter intimacy.

"And why are we just finding out that you had a thing with the fabulous Philippe?" I asked, not satisfied with her answer. She seemed to be leaving some juicy details out and I wanted to know what one of my 'besties' as she'd called Veronica and me, was hiding from us.

"Look, Mia, there is obviously something going on. Like some chemistry and as for being too busy...your father owns the corporation. You always take off whenever you want to and I fill the position with a temp nurse from the agency," Veronica piped in. We all knew that she was a daddy's girl and used to having her own way. I saw that she was getting frustrated, and gratefully answered my phone that was ringing.

After a brief conversation with Jenna, we decided to put the topic of Mia and Philippe on hold. Snuggling down into the plush pillows and soft throws that Jenna requested we have for the trip, we all agreed that a nap was called for. I smiled as I thought of Jenna not missing even the smallest of details when it came to entertaining.

~ ~ ~ ~ ~

My eyes fluttered closed and I finally allowed my mind to drift back 10 years ago. I was twenty and a sophomore at Baylor University in Waco, TX, working on my nursing degree. For my summer break, I went to visit Jenna in Austin. Since she was getting married, I wanted to be with her until the wedding instead of me heading off to Houston to work at The Busy Bee Bookstore. I worked there during my senior year of high school and Mrs. Bailey took me back during my college breaks. The extra money came in handy and it kept me busy.

Jenna and David's wedding was a big deal in Austin since David's family was a part of the Austin social scene. The wedding was lavish and Jenna was an exquisite bride. I was her maid of honor. Veronica and Mia were bridesmaids along with four of Jenna's friends.

That was where I first saw Jordan. He was speaking with David during the wedding reception and there was an incredibly beautiful woman on his arm. She had one arm hooked around his elbow and her other hand running slowly running up and down his biceps. She looked bored while scanning the room, her blonde hair in an updo with flawless features and a dress that fit her like a second skin. I tried not to stare at him but my eyes kept glancing in his direction. After a while one of the groomsmen asked me to dance and I gladly joined in the festivities.

Another hour later and I was still following the gorgeous man with my eyes. I hoped that I was being inconspicuous. I sure didn't want him to see me checking him out. After Jenna and David cut the cake, they danced to one more song and headed out to the waiting limo that would take them to the airport. Everyone lined up to wish them farewell. Jenna pulled me in a tight hug and we both burst into tears. David finally pulled us apart and kissed me on my cheeks. He made some jokes about being my bother now so he could finally boss me around. We laughed and hugged some more, then they were gone.

I headed back inside and looked around for my date but he was off dancing with another girl, someone he found more interesting and fun, so I sat in my chair at the table making small talk with a couple I didn't know. Mia and Veronica were dancing as well. I decided to have more cake until my friends returned.

I kept glancing at the handsome couple as they made their way across the dance floor, but this time instead of going around again like they did before, they seem to have slowed down and were dancing in place not far from me. My eyes landed on the gorgeous man. He was watching me intently while listening to what the woman was saying. I quickly lowered my eyes and shoved another bite of cake into my mouth, which suddenly tasted like sawdust. I peeked at him from under my lashes to see that they moved on, but he was still looking at me.

My friends made it back to the table babbling about the dance and hot guys and what a beautiful bride Jenna was. I participated in the conversation, but wasn't fully engaged since I kept thinking of the magnificent, handsome man with brilliant blue eyes, dirty blond hair and an intense gaze that sent goose bumps across my body and a tingly feeling in places that had not yet been explored.

"Dance with me," a deep voice whispered in my ear, as a large hand enveloped mine and tugged me onto the dance floor. It was the gorgeous guy that I'd all but stalked for the past couple of hours. I was sure I was floating as he effortlessly guided me around the dance floor as the band sang "I Hope You Dance" by Lee Ann Womack.

"Hi," he said, as I stared into his face. I was lost for a moment in his lovely features. Sinful lips that were made for kissing, a chiseled jaw that accented his features and those brilliant blue eyes that I'd been staring at all evening.

"Hi," I replied and quickly averted my eyes to stare at his tie which was the same color as his eyes.

"My name is Jordan. You must be the sister of the bride."

"Yes. Yes, I am Jenna's sister."

"Does Jenna's sister have a name?"

My eyes flew up to his as a blush covered my cheeks but I saw he was teasing me and smiled. God, even his teeth were perfect.

"Zoe." I wasn't usually tongue-tied, but this guy had me in knots. I quickly looked around the room, anywhere but at Jordan.

"Hello, lovely Zoe. David has mentioned Jenna's little sister, but I thought you were a teenager."

"Um, so you're a friend of David?" I was curious that I hadn't heard of him before. Not that I knew all of David's friends, but I knew most of the ones that were in attendance.

"Business led us to friendship. I started my own business and David was instrumental in financing and finding investors for it. We're cycling buddies as well."

David was an avid cyclist. Since parts of Austin and its surrounding areas are hilly it makes for good and challenging bike rides.

"Do you live in Austin as well, Zoe?" We continued dancing and I wondered where his girlfriend was.

"No, I'm a nursing student at Baylor, but I visit Jenna often," I explained, but still curious as to why he was dancing with me. I spotted his girlfriend off to the side looking at me with daggers in her eyes and sipping on a martini.

"She's my date, not my girlfriend."

I was mortified! I wasn't aware I said my thoughts of his girlfriend out loud.

"Sorry...I... Did I say something about her?"

"No, but you looked curious. Just thought I would set the record straight." He grinned down at me and my breath caught in my throat. I felt a blush creeping up my neck.

"Me either…I mean, that is, I don't have a boyfriend," I blundered the lack of a male companion in my life. Wow. He must think I'm real loser. I was relieved when the song came to an end.

"Thank you for the dance, Zoe. It was a pleasure meeting you. I will see you again soon." Jordan kissed the back of my hand. I was mesmerized at his impeccable manners, flawless good looks and incredible charm. Really good reasons why I needed to never see him again. Anyone that perfect and gorgeous was bound to have major flaws; plus, looking at the type of women he preferred to date, I was certain I didn't measure high on his meter of fabulous hot women.

"Wow, Zoe. Who was the decadent, delish guy?" Mia and Veronica immediately pulled me aside to ask about Jordan.

"I'm not sure, actually. He said he does business with David and they've become friends over the past couple years." I looked around the room and saw that he was once again speaking with his date as they made their way out of the room. I wondered if they were heading to his place or hers? With a sigh, I turned back to my friends.

"He said he started his own company a couple years ago and David helped secure investors for him," I explained to Mia and Veronica. I feel a pang of regret that he left, but chided myself; it was for the best. I didn't even know him and would probably never see him again. No more contact with Jordan would be just fine with me, as I was sure he would be a heartbreaker.

"Well, he can take me to the dance floor anytime and I mean T. A. K. E.," Mia said, as we all giggled at her outrageous jokes.

"I wonder how old he is? He's probably about David's age, like late twenties?" Veronica answered her own question. I was wondering the same thing, but didn't want to seem too interested in Jordan.

We gushed over him for a few more minutes then went back to mingling and dancing again. By the time the evening came to an end, I was still consumed with thoughts of Jordan. No matter how hard I tried...his tall, lean frame, strong hands and brilliant blue eyes kept sliding back into my mind.

CHAPTER 4

"ZOE, WAKE UP, SLEEPY HEAD. WE WILL BE AT YOUR sister's house in about half an hour." I was gently shaken awake by Veronica who actually set her alarm on her iPhone. Veronica was the pragmatic one in our group. Mia and I jokingly call her our timekeeper. She was never late to anything and never forgets important details about anyone in her life.

I texted Jenna to let her know we were almost at her home and took a photo on Instagram of all three of us grinning in the camera and sent it to her.

The car drove down the picturesque driveway that was adorned on both sides with live oak, crepe myrtle and magnolia trees, then came to a stop at the circular driveway. We were greeted by Jenna who was laughing and shaking her phone at us.

"I can't believe you sent a photo of y'all wearing no makeup. See, that is just what I need for bribing," she laughed gaily, her sweet smile contagious, and we all joined in the laugh but the other girls were now blaming me for the photo.

"What? I think we look great. Unadorned and pure," I said, defending myself.

"Ah, speak for yourself on that one," Mia piped in, which led to more laughter.

"Makeup perv...I was talking about makeup." I hit her on her ass that she wiggled even more.

"I could simply spend days in your yard and not see all the plants and flowers you have growing here, Jenna," Veronica said looking around. Although I see Jenna more often than Mia and Veronica, I try to schedule a couple trips during the year for all three of us to visit and have Jenna spoil us senseless. She loves her girl time with me and my friends.

"Thank you, Veronica. Rojellio will love to hear that. He is an amazing gardener. I swear the man can find the most exotic and rare plants from all over the world and somehow convince them to grow in Texas." We slowly made our way up to the magnificent home and entered through the front door where we were met by Aunt Suzette who enveloped us in an embrace.

My sister's home is well appointed with a dramatic curved stairway leading upstairs. The massive foyer was adorned by an elegant chandelier hanging overhead. We walked through the house and entered the backyard where there was an air-conditioned white party tent with a temporary wooden floor in place for dancing. The band was setting up and caterers were busy preparing food.

Jenna told me to close my eyes and led me into the tent. When I opened them, I gasped in surprise. There was a huge screen with scrolling images of me from birth to my current age.

"Oh, Jenna. So many memories. I can't believe you have so many photos of me." I gazed around the tent that was beautifully decorated with plants, and flowers. Tables were set with dark pink and black tablecloths, white napkins, silver cutlery and white dishes. The centerpiece on every table was a gorgeous bouquet of pink and yellow roses. There were also several small chandeliers hanging from the ceiling of the tent. I was touched by Jenna's effort and the time my friends were taking to travel to the event.

"You're making me cry too," Jenna said.

The event planner came over to us while talking on her phone with last minute instructions.

"Everything looks great as usual, Pricilla. I think she loves it," Jenna said as Pricilla beamed with a smile.

Jenna used Pricilla for all her functions and the events were always a success. We chatted about the photos again as some of them were with my friends from high school. I played the cello in our high school orchestra and there were photos of me competing in tennis competitions and track as well.

"Well, we need to head in now. I see the hair and makeup team is ready for you girls." We went inside and got ready for the evening.

My dress was a Marc Jacobs' strapless red and flirty that swirled gently around mid-thigh. Veronica gave me jewelry for my birthday gift that I wore with my outfit. It was a lovely Swarovski crystal earrings and necklace set. I paired it with several silver bracelets of different designs that make for a chic look. My stylish Jimmy Choo wedge shoes showed off my calves quite nicely.

The girls whistled and clapped when I came downstairs. We complimented each other on our attire. Everyone was in a party mood. The party buses were arriving with friends and we headed outside to greet them.

"Zoe, you doll. You are the picture of perfection. I swear you are more beautiful every time I see you." My friend, Jeremy, was the first one off the bus and greeted me with his usual flair. His brown hair was stylish with blond highlights and his green eyes twinkled with laughter. He was voted most likely to succeed in high school and he did just that. Jeremy was beautiful, simply put, and always fun. Right at 6' tall, he always attracted attention wherever he went.

Jeremy always seemed to overcompensate for his intelligence. As much as he wanted to be popular in high school, most kids seemed to shy away from him since he operated on a different intellectual level. He sort of reminded me of the guy in the movie *A Beautiful Mind*. Sometimes he'd be in the middle of a conversation or doing whatever, and off he would go to figure out something else right then. He works in theory and is very analytical.

The others were slowly unloading and I was greeted with affection, kisses and birthday wishes. Someone reminded me that I have one more year that my age will be on the calendar, then I will be a full-fledged adult. The light banter and contagious party sprit was in full swing when I received a call from Robert that he rented a car and driver and would be here in five minutes.

The party was underway as the guests moved in to the cool air of the tent. There were two bars set up to serve drinks and the three-tier birthday cake was beautiful. I went back outside just in time to see Robert getting out of the car. I ran up to him and gave him a light kiss on the lips. Not one for public displays of affection, he held me at arm's length and complimented me on my outfit but noted that I may need a light sweater. I smiled, as it was mid-May in Texas, but he was protective of me and I appreciated his concern.

We entered the tent and I took Robert around to meet some more of my friends while the band started up with light dance music. I was delighted that everyone seemed to be having fun and the screen with scrolling photos of me and my friends was turning out to be a big hit. As the night wore on, the music and fun intensified. My head was spinning from the effects of a few shots of tequila. Jenna made sure I was eating since she reminded me of the extra workout I endured over the past month so I might as well indulge in the decadence of great food.

"Dance with me." My breath caught in my throat. I would know that voice anywhere. I have played this scene out in my mind countless times over the past 10 years. I often wondered if I would ever see him again. I was standing at the side of the dance floor catching my breath after dancing to a fast song by Beyoncé, while Robert fetched us a drink.

My body stood rigid. Unable to respond, I shook my head no, slowly. I could hardly breathe. He was back. Now what? Sensing my discomfort and inability to answer, he made the first move. His strong arms came around my body. Large, capable hands settled on my waist. Those hands, I remembered them so well, as they'd once glided over my body sending me into a frenzy for more of his glorious touch.

He propelled me to the left side of the dance floor and gently turned me around so that I was facing him. The band was playing Chris de Burgh's "Lady in Red." I was not aware of my hands resting on his biceps until I felt them flex in my palms through the expensive material of his suit. My eyes focused on the paisley design of his purple silk tie then tracked up to the broad expanse of his shoulders.

Try as I may, I could not avoid looking into his eyes. Gorgeous blue eyes were staring back at me. They reminded me of the deep ocean on a stormy day. Turning darker still with dilated pupils during his passionate lovemaking. He was sexy as hell! Luscious lips curled at one corner of that sinful mouth in what looked like the beginnings of a smile. His tall lean frame moved me gracefully across the temporary wooden dance floor. I felt like I was floating. Maybe I was, or maybe I was slowly losing my mind which is possible as this man can surely drive me insane with lust and need.

My pulse increased to a gallop as his arms around my waist pulled me closer into his body. It was an intimate stance that had my body leaning into the warmth of his. His cologne was intoxicating and I wanted to bury my face in his chest. My body knew his so well, it responded to his touch as if it were just yesterday.

Traitor! My subconscious yelled at me. *He hurt you once, he will do it again. Plus, you have a boyfriend.* My mind was trying to reason but my body was rejoicing in the reunion of this magnificent being holding me in his arms.

Drawing me closer into his embrace he lowered his head and placed a soft kiss on my left ear. His breath was warm on my skin. I gasped and tried to step back but his arms were like bands of steel, unmoving. His head lowered to my left shoulder where another kiss followed but this time the kiss lingered. Warmth rushed through me settling in my lower abdomen. I stumbled due to the response of my treacherous body, but he lifted me effortlessly and gently set me back on my feet.

"Hello, pretty girl." His deep husky voice washed over me like cool water going down my throat on a warm Texas day. He used the sweet endearing name he used to call me when I was in college.

"Jordan." My voice sounded foreign to me as I croaked his name. Clearing my throat, I looked away. I couldn't think logically when I was staring into his handsome face with gorgeous features that should only be found on the pages of a glossy magazine.

"Why...how...?" I wasn't sure what I wanted to say to him. I needed some air. His presence at my 30th birthday was a shock to say the least. My arms were around his neck. How the hell did they get there? He had this effect on me, making me giddy with his touch, and his voice with words that would make any woman swoon just to be closer to him.

Vaguely aware of being locked in an intimate embrace with another man, my eyes scanned the room looking for Robert. Thankfully, I saw him with his back to the dance floor engaged in deep conversation with Andre.

Move, get away. You don't do hurt and pain well. I was aware of the voice of reason trying to get through to my treacherous body but it was so not listening.

I willed myself to leave his warm embrace. Stumbling out of his arms, I bolted from the massive enclosed air-conditioned white party tent. Glancing over my shoulder, I saw that Jordan was following me. I quickly made my way across the perfectly manicured lawn. I was fuming! With deliberate steps, I walked to the east side of the garden and stood looking out into the night across the rolling hills in the suburbs of Austin. The glow of gas lamps on the property cast us in a muted light.

I took a few deep cleansing breaths and held on to the rustic wood fence. This can't be happening. Why now? Why was he back? I looked over my shoulder to see Jordan standing a few feet away from me. Hands in his pockets, he walked slowly toward me like a predator on the prowl. I turned my gaze back to the open expanse of land.

"What are you doing here, Jordan?" I asked, desperately wishing him away. Far, far away. I was getting over the initial shock of seeing him again. My words were a little slurred due to several hours of celebrating.

"Is that any way to treat an old friend, Zoe?" He was directly behind me now. His arms flanked me on both sides capturing me in a loose embrace against the fence.

"We are not friends. You made sure of that." I put an emphasis on sure so he would not miss my meaning. He was the one that caused our relationship to crash and burn.

"No, we were more, way more than friends. We were lovers. I have not forgotten you, Zoe; I never will." He lifted my long auburn hair away from my shoulder and placed an open mouth kiss on the exposed area of my skin. His warm lips slowly made their way up my neck. My breath caught in my throat. I bit my bottom lip to hold the moan in that was desperately bubbling to explode from my mouth. I arched my neck to one side giving him better access.

My eyes fluttered shut as I reveled in this moment. With skillful hands rubbing up and down my forearms, I was lost. I wanted his touch. Longed for his kisses again. This raging passion that I'd suppressed for the past 10 years was yearning to be set free. Free to glory in the way my body came alive from his caress and passionate kisses.

"I have a boyfriend," I blurted out, as if that would make Jordan suddenly disappear from my life again and leave me at peace.

"So I've heard." I turned my head to ask him how he knew about Robert. He must have known that I would question him and quickly filled in the blanks. All the while his mouth continued with soft kisses along my neck and shoulder.

"Look, Zoe, I did not crash your party. I was invited," his incredible sexy voice purred as he caught my earlobe and sucked gently against my Swarovski crystal chandelier earrings.

"Who invited…David?"

"Yes, David. I had some business with him for the past couple days and he invited me to stay for the party since our last meeting ran later than we thought today." OK, that was logical, I suppose. Although David knew how I felt about Jordan. I would have to ask him why he would invite someone I never wanted to see again. Like ever!

Liar. My treacherous body was still responding to his menstruation with ardent need that was building inside me like Mount St. Helens before an eruption.

One cognitive thought hit a part of my brain for a few seconds…I was so totally fucked! My eyes flew open at this realization hoping it was not true.

His skillful hands left my arms and traveled down my sides. My gorgeous, flirty dress did little to cover me since it fluttered around my thighs in the night breeze. Taking full advantage of my state of undress, Jordan slid one arm around my waist and his other hand under my dress as he caressed my thigh.

"Happy birthday, lovely Zoe. May all your desires be fulfilled, starting tonight." He placed his head at the other side of my neck and continued with his lethal kisses that made me all but melt right there at his feet. His assault continued on my other shoulder. He moved both hands right below my breasts but went no further as if waiting for permission to continue.

Of their own volition, my arms slipped around his neck. With my back still facing away from him, the motion pushed my breasts forward. He cupped them both in his hands as their weight settled in his palms.

I trembled at his touch. As if sensing that my defenses were slowly breaking down, he squeezed my nipples through the dress. I couldn't help it. I moaned and wiggled restlessly in his arms. I wanted more. His hand moved back under my dress as the other held me against him at my waist. He rubbed me at my point of need.

His hand slipped under the flimsy material of my thong. He stopped suddenly with palm open over my aching womanhood.

"Christ, Zoe, you're killing me, babe. Your beautiful sweetness is bare. I like that." I was coming undone as he stroked me. My female desire was dripping with juices onto his fingers. He dipped one finger into the slit of my opening and I was lost. Rubbing my body against his, I was unable to understand the unintelligible words coming from my lips.

I was craving his smell, his caress. My body was straining against his. I was lost in a sea of lust. I've been here before. With Jordan, only with him. There had been other boyfriends in the past few years, but I found excuses to break off the relationship or they got tired of waiting to get to second base with me.

I refused to let go with anyone else, to give over to the total abandon of this carnal need to be taken. Yes, that's it. I wanted to be taken by him.

"Jordan, please," I whispered as my body trashed in his arms. I don't want him to stop.

"What do you want, my Zoe?" His hands ceased their exploration as he waited for me to respond.

"I...I don't know...I need..." I was trashing and pleading at him for my release.

"Say it, Zoe. Tell me or I walk away." Hands with a demanding, masterful touch gripped my waist.

"No!" I bit my lip as I realized I all but shouted at him to leave his hands on my body.

"Say it," his commanding voice taunted me. We are locked in a battle of wills. I gave in. I didn't care. My need for him was too great.

"I want to come, Jordy, I want you to make me..." I used the name I used to call him. I heard his sharp intake of breath.

He plunged a long finger into my wet center then slowly pulled back out. Not sure if he would keep his finger there, I placed my hand over his to continue his sweet torture and he did. Adding his thumb to the pleasure, he rubbed it over my clitoris and I was helpless. With reckless abandon I rubbed my ass onto his front and felt his huge erection.

Like palm trees swaying in the breeze, we moved effortlessly against each other and I was coming fast. He added another finger to the deep, sweet torture and increased the tempo. Like a ballerina, I was on my toes gasping and begging for more.

"How long has it been?" he asked. I didn't pretend to misunderstand his question.

"Since you, Jordy. Only you." I gasped as he spun me around toward him and leaned me into the fence, his hand never leaving my sweet spot.

"Fuck. I can hardly get two fingers in, Zoe." He leaned down toward me and I couldn't wait anymore. I pulled his mouth down to meet mine. We kissed with a reckless passion I did not know existed. He quickly took control of the kiss and pushed his tongue in to conquer mine. His mind-blowing kiss could make any woman forget herself and beg for more, more of his glorious tongue and lips on any part of her body.

With one large hand he cupped my neck and continued with his assault on my mouth while his other hand reclaimed my slick sex. I couldn't last much longer; it had been too long. His finger glided in and out of me again and again. He lay his forehead against mine.

"That's it, my Zoe, come for me, babe." With his words of encouragement, I fell into the sweet abyss that was ours alone. My eyes flew open and met his looking right at me. The soft folds of my sex squeezed frantically on his fingers. The pent-up need and desire for him was so great, I was sobbing and grinding my pussy on his capable hand. I was chanting his name over and over like a mantra not soon to be forgotten.

He placed one hand over my mouth and I couldn't breathe. The explosion of passion was too great. I bit down with all my might. I needed to scream! To rejoice! My body was dancing with joy and in that moment I was lost. Slowly, I became aware of Jordan holding me against his body.

"Shhh, baby. Je suis revenu pour vous, Zoe. Tu es à moi." I was not aware of crying, but Jordan was kissing my wet cheeks and murmuring sweet words in a foreign language. I closed my mind from all the thoughts of anger I had built up against him over the past 10 years. For the loss of time and what could have been. I succumbed to the few minutes of pleasure I have dreamt about with him.

"I want more. Please, now." Frantic with need, I stroked him through his clothing. His desire was evident as I rubbed my hand against his hard erection.

"You need to get back to your party, Zoe, or someone will come looking for you."

Oh my God. My party! What in all that is holy have I done? I had a boyfriend that has not taken this privilege with me and he was in the tent along with another seventy guests and I was out here doing the unthinkable with…what the fuck!

Ya think? Now you try to reason with this shit. I have been yelling at you. Hussy! hissed my subconscious voice of reason.

Oh shut the absolute fuck up already! Was I crazy or did I just use the *F* word with my subconscious? I really needed to pull it together, like now. This man was capable of breaking down my defenses that I had painfully built up during the past 10 years.

CHAPTER 5

THE REALITY OF WHAT HAPPENED BETWEEN US NOW dawned on me. I needed to leave. Needed to say goodbye to Jordan, again, and get back to my life of normalcy. I'd been dating Robert for the past six months and he was getting serious about us. He mentioned wanting to make a commitment in our relationship and get engaged. Robert was considerate, never imposing himself on me or my time. I was proud of him and his accomplishments as an attorney at a prestigious law firm in Houston.

I pulled at my dress to get it back in some order before returning to the party. Jordan quickly adjusted the back and produced a handkerchief to blot my face and forehead of perspiration then tied it around his left hand.

"Oh God, Jordan, this cannot happen again. I had quite a bit of alcohol tonight and I'm not thinking logically. I…um, this was not in my plans at all." I was embarrassed at what I'd allowed Jordan to do with me. I blatantly responded to his every advance. Quickly walking across the lawn, Jordan guided me toward the front door of the house.

I pulled my arm out of his grasp, and all but ran up to the door, furious that I made a fool of myself with such behavior when I should have insisted he leave. Jordan came to an abrupt halt, grasped me around my waists and stood in front of me.

"Should we go at it again, Zoe? Or will you blame your response on the alcohol once again?" My pulse accelerated as I glanced up at him. There was a dangerous glint in his eyes and I knew better than to deny what he just said.

"Go inside and freshen up your makeup then go back to the party." Ever the gracious gentleman, he opened the door and I stepped inside. "Please tell David something came up and I had to leave but will be in touch soon." My eyes flew up to his. His eyebrows cocked and a wicked smile touched the corner of his lips.

My face suffused with warmth as I blushed all the way to my hairline. I ran across the opulent marble foyer of the magnificent home and made my way upstairs to my room. My racing heartbeat would shatter a cardiogram machine right about now. I heard the front door close.

Quickly I made my way to the bathroom and restored some order to my appearance.

Returning to the party tent was nerve racking. I was calmer now but guilty for my disappearance and lack of self-control with Jordan. Thankfully the party was still in full swing. Everyone was occupied with drinks and...well, almost everyone.

"Hi, birthday girl. So you decided to rejoin in your festivities." Mia sauntered toward me. Her shoulder length blonde hair was perfectly styled and blue eyes blinked mischievously at me. She pushed a dirty martini in my hand and took a sip of hers.

"So, do tell all the gory details of why the dashing Jordan Dawson showed up at your party and why you did not tell me you had invited him? By the way, you better calm the hell down. You look guilty as sin." Leave it to Mia to miss absolutely nothing. Locking our elbows together, we walked through the crowd of friends to the back of the tent.

"You can thank me later for covering your lovely ass too. I took your boyfriend on the dance floor and all but forced him to have a couple more drinks. I swear to God, keeping the man engaged in a conversation is a full time job." Mia, ever the socialite, continued to hug and kiss the people around us with easy banter while she talked and made sure I knew that I owed her, big time.

Not a fan of my boyfriend, she continued on with the many reasons why we were wrong for one another. "Really, Zoe, like he has nothing interesting to contribute to a conversation if it does not have to do with work or law, a courtroom, or his mother. And by the way, how many people understand his legal jargon in a regular conversation? I mean…"

I cut her conversation off about Robert. It never gets us anywhere. "OK…I get it already, but he is good for me and I am so not talking about this right now." I smiled at my friends that were still partying and tried to put the Jordan incident in the back of my mind. Like way back into the part that is like amnesia.

"…for the advice, Robert." I caught the last part of David and Robert's conversation but did not miss the guilty look on David's face. He avoided my dagger-throwing stare at him and he quickly made his way to my sister's side to claim her in a dance.

"There you are, lovely." Robert put a doting hand on my arm. "I had the most enlightening conversations with your friends tonight." Grateful that he did not say anything of my absence over however long I'd been gone. I leaned into him for a hug.

Try as I may, I couldn't seem to put Jordan out of my mind. I was scrambling to follow the conversation around me by pasting a smile on my face and nodding my head in agreement. Well, there is no damn way I will see him again. My life was perfect as it is, thank you very much. I'd worked too many long hours, sleep deprived, exhausted from troubleshooting and worrying about keeping my nursing agency afloat…I was just plain worn out, but apart from all that I was doing fine, just fine! The last thing I needed was a disruption like Jordan Dawson in my life.

"Darling, I think I will turn in now." Aunt Suzette gave me a hug. "It was a great party, dear. As always, Jenna has pulled off another beautiful event."

"Yes, Suzette, that's a good idea. It's almost midnight and this week has been most taxing. Why, I was just telling Zoe about what a dreadful week it has been for mother." *Oh God! He had? What was wrong with his mother now?* My eyes flew up to Mia's hoping that she was following the conversation. With a smirk on her face, I see that she had been.

"So sorry to hear about your mom not adapting well to her new medication and routine, Robert." The look on my face was of pure relief as I listened keenly now to what was going on with Mrs. Royden. "I am sure that Zoe will get a full report from your mother's nurse next week." I cleared my throat and mentally kicked myself for allowing Jordan to divert my attention from my almost fiancé.

"I will speak with her nurse on Monday," I said.

"Thank you, lovey." He was so sweet and understanding. I ignored the fact that his arm around my waist did not ignite the feeling of passion and possession that I'd felt with Jordan.

There you go again! Well so much for your promise to suppress any more time spent of thinking about Jordan. OK, fine...focus, focus.

"Goodnight then. Don't forget a couple ibuprofen, kids." Aunt Suzette winked at us and made her way out bidding others goodnight as she left.

As the band continued to wind down from the mind blowing, body gyration of dancing legs and winding hips, they started a series of slower love songs.

"Ah, now that is more like what music should be." Robert guided me onto the dance floor and held me an appropriate distance from his body; such a gentle and considerate soul. I placed my head on his shoulder. Around the dance floor once, twice...my eyes closed as I replayed Jordan's arms around me. His skillful moves and decadent hands moved across my body, my thighs, cupping my bottom. Bliss, pure pleasure, erotic and hot against the fence...I spun out of Robert's arms and bolted to the door, clashing into Jenna.

"Zoe, what's...?" Jenna's concerned look slowed me to answer.

"Fine, little headache...dance with Rob. Be right back." I bolted to the house and this time entered through the back door. I was panting as I made my way across the kitchen and through the living room, down the hallway, up the stairs... how big is this fucking house! I was about in tears as I yanked open my borrowed bedroom door again and slid the lock in place.

Panting for air to hit my burning lungs, I slowed my breathing and threw myself on the bed. My hands made their way under my flirty dress and yanked off the thong that was covering my wet pussy. My finger dipped into the warmth at the apex of my thighs and I gyrating my hips to the movement of blissful, capable hands I imagined as Jordan's.

In no time at all I was there. The orgasm hit me and I bit my lips from screaming his name. Silently, I chanted his name over and over. For the second time in less than an hour I had an orgasm with Jordan's name on my lips. Yes, way too much alcohol. I comforted myself with that thought.

Taking a deep breath, I got up on shaky legs and made my way to the bathroom. Slowly I collected what little sanity I had left and went back to the party that was just about over now. I was Robert's girlfriend, for Christ's sake. He has every right to touch me. So, if he touches me tonight, down there, then that would be just fine and I will enjoy it. As a matter of fact, I will instigate it as I know that he respects me too much to indulge in such intimacy so soon in our relationship. His words, not mine, but I'd readily agreed with him at the time.

"Ah, there you are. Feeling better? Although you look a little flushed." He placed a kiss on my forehead and continued to fuss over me. "My poor girl. This party has taken a toll on you." Glancing at his watch, he confirmed that it was after one in the morning. He looked at me sympathetically and rubbed my arms.

Feeling like a total pile of elephant dung, I mercifully leaned into his slight hug.

"You should have insisted that Jenna put a couple hours limit on the party." I was nodding my head in agreement as a full on headache attached itself to my aching temples.

"I'll walk you to your car." Like a good and dutiful girlfriend, I held his hand in mine and we made our way outside. I took a detour to the side where there were a few green oak trees and pointed out the nice night and great weather we had in May.

I purposely stood behind one of the trees and pulled Robert in a close embrace. My plan of seduction firmly in place, I rubbed my chest on his and looped my arms around his neck while kissing his lips.

"Um, Rob, I am feeling a little reckless right now." *How do I tell him he can, um…*

"My poor love. You are tired, sweets. We are just not into wild and crazy things." Well hell. So much for that seduction scene.

He carefully removed my arms from his neck.

"You will feel more like yourself tomorrow," he said. Such a good and considerate man. He took my hand and led me back to the party that had started to dwindle. I was met by more hugs and cheers. The party buses were lined up in the driveway. Most of my friends and acquaintances lived in the Houston area. Jenna, ever the party planner, rented limo buses to and from Austin complete with hotel rooms. Aunt Suzette, Mia, Veronica and I were staying at Jenna and David's home.

Robert gave Jenna a peck on her cheek while chastising her about the party that lasted way too long and wore me out. His concern for me was touching and I reassured him that I would go straight to bed. Jenna tried to suppress a smile. The caterers and cleaning crew were busy with the after party duties so we headed into the house. Veronica and Mia were singing out of tune and wobbled upstairs as I went to the kitchen for a glass of water.

"Great party, love." David came up behind Jenna and placed both arms around her while nuzzling her neck. Jenna giggled like a schoolgirl as he whispered something in her ear. It didn't hurt that Jenna is elegant and beautiful. She also has a doting husband who was completely in love with her. Our parents would have liked David; he's a good person and Jenna is deservedly happy. I rolled my eyes at them but was smiling as I took a sip of water. They both laugh at me as I teased them about too much public displays of affection.

"Thanks again for the party. I had a great time, and catching up with my friends was a bonus."

"Good, sweetie. That's what I aimed for. For you to have fun; since you work so much, it seemed like a good time to throw you a party," Jenna said, leaning into David's embrace.

"By the way, Zoe, it was good to see Jordan again. I knew he was in town to see David for business but I'm glad he could stay for the party." I looked over Jenna's head and squinted my eyes at David. Suddenly he was restless, shuffling his feet. He knew I wanted nothing better than to never set eyes on Jordan again.

"Sorry, Zoe. Look, the poor guy was dying to see you. He has tried many times over the past few years and, well, I just felt sorry for him. Don't hold it against me for not telling you he would be at the party. Please? Say you forgive me." I saw that he was honest and did feel bad to be put in this situation, so I nodded my head.

"OK, David. All is well. He did say he was sorry for leaving without telling you goodbye and that he will be in touch."

"So you did talk to him then?" asked Jenna.

"Yeah, I talked to him. Nothing resolved and good riddance to him and his endeavors but I am happy to move on with my quiet life as it is." They both knew that Jordan and I had been an item when I was in college and that he hurt me. Although he still did business with David in banking, I did not want to hear about him and what gorgeous women he had hanging on to him.

"Well, I'm glad you moved on. I just want you to be happy, Zoe. You deserve it," said Jenna.

"Keep an open mind. Sometimes the best things in life are right in front of us. Don't let hurt keep happiness and fulfillment away." David said in a quiet tone. He was looking at me and I tried not to read too much into what he said, but I knew what he meant just the same.

"Goodnight, you two," I said.

Jenna kicked off her shoes and bent down to pick them up. David spanked her on her ass. She yelped and giggled while running down the hall and up the winding stairway as he ran after her.

After a quick shower, I slid into bed. I pulled my iPad off the night stand and updated my Facebook status about the party. I saw that several of my friends had already posted photos of the event and chatted about it. At this moment I felt thankful that I had so many people in my life that loved and cared about me.

Again, I thought of my parents and knew they would be proud of Jenna and me, and grateful to Aunt Suzette for being steadfast in our lives while raising us as her own. I turned out the lights, but sleep eluded me. My mind drifted back to my past relationship with Jordan.

CHAPTER 6

TEN YEARS AGO

AFTER JENNA'S JUNE WEDDING, I HEADED BACK TO Houston with Aunt Suzette and settled into my job at The Busy Bee Bookstore. The weather was typical for this time of the year in Texas—hot and humid. I spent a couple days with Mia at her father's mansion in River Oaks, a ritzy area of Houston that reeked of old money.

Mia's mom had left her dad for a doctor from New York when Mia was 12 and her brother, Trevor, was a senior in high school. Her mother divorced the doctor after two years of marriage and came back to Houston. She convinced Mia's dad to take her back, but six months later she left again and went to Paris with another man. Her father continued to raise Mia and Trevor. He never remarried, although he was never lacking for female companionship.

Mia, Veronica and I settled down at the pool with ice cold drinks and lazily talked about friends, school and life in general when I got a text from Jenna asking me to give her a call. She and David had been back in Austin for a few weeks after their honeymoon and were settling into their condo as a new married couple.

"Hi. How's married life?" I asked as soon as she answered the phone.

"Loving it. My man is the absolute best! I am so in lust... I mean, in love with him," she said giggling. We chatted for a few minutes while catching up on the past weeks and memories of her wedding.

"Um...so, David asked me to tell you something." I sat up in the lounging chair wondering what the heck?

"OK. What's the something?" I asked.

"He's been doing some business with Jordan Dawson and I know you don't know who Jordan is. I've met him several times, but he always had a different girl with him so I thought he was like taken or something. Anyway, Jordan told David he danced with you at our wedding and now... ummm..."

"Whoa...slow down. I did dance with Jordan, but I think he felt sorry for me since I was staring at him like the entire evening. And yeah, he was with a drop dead gorgeous woman," I said.

"Well, he asked if David would give him your phone number but Jordan wanted to know if it would be OK with you first, which I think is rather sweet. So...?"

"Hmmm. I don't know, Jen...I mean, the guy is gorgeous, charming and sexy, that's for sure," I said as I recalled our dance and how mesmerized I was with him.

"But, I am not sure that I'm his type. We probably have nothing in common and I am way too busy with school." I tried to stay calm hearing that he was interested in me and silently doing a happy dance, but I was also trying to be cautious. I didn't have any desire to have a one-night stand, and since I'd only had a couple boyfriends in high school that only got as far as first base with me, I felt way out of his league.

I had been kissed and my last boyfriend went as far as rubbing and touching my breast. That was the extent of my sexual experience and I'm sure that someone like Jordan would not be satisfied with a few kisses. To put it mildly, he scared the shit out of me.

"As much as I'm flattered, I must say no, Jen."

"OK. You need to follow your instincts, although he is a very nice person and I wish you would at least go on one date with him. He lives here in Austin and Baylor isn't far away, but I'll tell David to let him know you're not interested," Jenna said. I think she thought I would change my mind, but I stood firm and changed the subject.

"OMG! You totally did not turn down that Jordan guy!" exclaimed Mia.

"Eavesdropping?" I asked and jumped in the pool to cool off. Veronica and Mia jumped in as well and peppered me with questions about the conversation with Jenna. Since we started college, Mia's had a couple boyfriends but she got bored with them quickly, and Veronica hadn't had a boyfriend since she was in eleventh grade.

"Come on, Zoe, live a little. Jordan could easily be on the cover of *GQ* magazine. He oozes sexuality. Honest to God, the man has all the right stuff!"

I ducked my head under the water and Veronica stop twirling around and looked at Mia.

"Why couldn't it be me?" she asked with a sigh. We continued our conversation about hot guys and the debate of who was the hottest of all our guy friends.

~ ~ ~ ~ ~

The summer passed quickly and I headed back to school in September. I was thrilled that I'd done well in college. I was a junior this year. This semester, I will start going to the hospital for clinicals, which is direct contact with patients. Mia, Veronica and I were living in a campus apartment now and we were thrilled that we had individual bedrooms and bathrooms.

Veronica was always the first one to get up in the morning so she makes the coffee for us and tea for Mia. We chatted for a few minutes while the coffee was brewing when the phone in the living room rang. Mia picked it up as she was on her way into the kitchen.

"Zoe...that was the front office. There is a delivery down there for you."

I arched my brows. "Really? This early? I don't remember ordering anything. Maybe Aunt Suzette sent me something or maybe..."

"How about, maybe you can go and find out what it is," Veronica said, rolling her eyes. Her long silky black hair hung over her shoulder past her perfect voluptuous breasts. Swear to God, the girl was blessed with an amazing curvy body.

"You don't have time, chick," Mia chimed in, looking at the clock on the wall.

"Oh, God. I'm so nervous and excited at the same time. I can't believe we're finally starting clinicals, hands-on patient care," Veronica said as she pulled bagels out of the toaster oven for us and I shoved a banana in their hands.

We gulped down out breakfast, showered and donned our student hospital scrubs with a huge patch on both arms with the word STUDENT sewn on just in case someone could not identify us from a real nurse despite the deer in the headlights look we were bound to have on our faces, especially during our first clinical semester.

We made our way to the hospital and met with the instructor. There was a pre-clinical conference, then we were paired with a nurse and observed her in action. The day flew by and we were convinced that we'd never achieve the level of skill that we observed today, but the instructor gently reminded us that it was only our first day and we had two more years before the state would trust us with a license.

Back at the apartment, I went to the pool to reflect on my day. Other students were milling around. Mia was passed out on her bed and Veronica went to the library. My phone rang.

"Hello," I answered.

"Hi, is this Zoe Caine?"

"Yes."

"There are two deliveries in the front office for you. Kindly pick them up."

I put on my cover-up over my bikini and went into the office. The girl at the front desk went around the corner and came back with two brown packages and handed them to me. She plopped back down in the chair and continued her assault on a piece of gum. I occasionally received care packages from Aunt Suzette and Jenna but they always come in the mail. Back in my bedroom, I opened the first package and furrowed my brows.

"What the hell is this?" I muttered, as I looked at the contents. Three tickets to Shakespeare's *All's Well that Ends Well* play at the Winedale Historical Center in Round Top, which is two hours away from my college. There was also a note. I quickly scanned the message.

What we have in common...Shakespeare. Enjoy a trip with your friends to Winedale. The students of the University of Texas will perform. I have seen them in action and they did a great job of Othello when I attended in my senior year at UT. I will send a car and driver as well and dinner will be provided. Enjoy. ~ Jordan Dawson.

There was also a phone number and an email address. The second package contained three small battery operated fans, three seat cushions and a leather bound book of Shakespeare's play *All's Well that Ends Well* along with three copies of the screenplay that we would be attending. Another note was attached: *Although lovely and appropriate for the play, it is an open-air theatre and I found that a fan may be necessary as the weather can be quite warm.*

I didn't know what to do. Stunned, I call Jenna.

"Hi, Zoe. How are your classes and your first day of clinicals?"

"Jen. Oh my God…so that Jordan guy, he sent a package for me here at the school and I don't know what to do. I mean, I don't know what it means or anything and there is a note too." I quickly read her the note. I was excited but scared as well, and if I was honest with myself, I had thought of him a lot over the past couple months.

"Really? He just won't give up. I told him what you said when he asked for your phone number. Not like verbatim, but I did mention to him that you didn't think there would be much in common between you and him. Guess he took it to heart and wanted to prove you wrong."

"Well, I will send him a text and thank him, but I'm not sure that I will accept it. I need to think about this, plus with something new like clinicals starting, I don't need any distractions." I walked to the patio and looked outside while twirling my long auburn hair, a nervous habit of mine.

"I can find out more about him if you like, Zoe."

I blew a long breath through the phone as I contemplated my response. "No. I will think about it. Thanks, Jenna, love you and say hi to David for me." We chatted about my day at the hospital and her settling into married life. I hung up the phone as Mia came out of her room. I told her about the packages and she flipped out with excitement. Veronica had the same reaction when I told her. I texted Jordan.

```
Thank you for the tickets. I love Shake-
speare, as you must know. I'm not sure I can
accept gifts from someone I don't know, but it
is a nice gesture. Regards, Zoe Caine.
```

I pushed the send button and in less than a minute my phone beeped with an incoming text.

Give me a chance to prove that we do have many interests in common, Jordan texted back.

I smiled at his quick response, but wanted him to know I was not playing hard to get and was not one for playing games.

I have a crazy, busy semester. Thank you for the kind thoughts. I will speak with my room-mates tomorrow about attending the play. No need to send a car. Where can I return the other items?

I was shocked at his response.

I will send someone to meet you at Starbucks on your campus tomorrow afternoon. Will 4 p.m. work for you?

I was little leery and responded with one word.

Fine.

I told the girls what I planned to do. Although disappointed, they were happy that I kept the three tickets.

After class the next day, I walked to Starbucks. The heat was unbearable and I was sweating. Luckily, it was only a 5-minute walk from my lecture hall. Happy to slip into the cool air of the store, I got a cup of ice water and a cafe latte. I turned around to look for a seat when I spotted Jordan coming toward me. I stopped and simply stared at him. He was just as handsome as I remembered him to be. His long lean frame came toward me as those brilliant blue eyes took in my appearance.

Suddenly I was aware of my worn jeans with holes on both thighs, my Nike tennis shoes, a grey Gap T-shirt, and my long hair sticking to my neck. There were two girls in front of me that were outright gawking at him but he is focused on me.

"Here, let me help you with that." His voice was low and maybe it's just me, but I thought even just those few words were sexy. We were attracting attention now and I quickly took the seat at the table in the corner where he'd been sitting. I tried not to stare at his brilliant white shirt, grey tie and dark blue slacks. He must have discarded his suit jacket due to the heat of the day. He looked nothing like a college student. I briefly wondered what the other students were thinking of us.

"I thought you were sending someone?" I asked, making it sound like a question. I was also a little annoyed since I was caught off guard meeting him again.

"I'm sorry, Zoe. I just wanted the opportunity to meet you under different circumstances. Am I forgiven?" His piercing blue eyes look honest and I gulped down the cold water while thinking of an appropriate response.

"So, why did you want to see me?" I asked. Since he went out of his way to seek me out, I felt that I needed some honest answers.

"Can we take a walk?" His eyes scanned the room.

"In this heat? It's 95 degrees outside," I said, as I had no intentions of strolling around campus unless I had to. I arched my brows and looked at him. He was smiling.

"You are aware that you are drinking a hot beverage and it's 95 degrees outside." I wanted to argue with him but it made sense, so I scoffed and took another sip of the super-hot liquid. He took a sip of what appeared to be iced tea in his cup.

"I'm addicted to their latte and I desperately need the caffeine," I said in defense of my beverage of choice.

"If I promise not to kidnap you or harm you in any way, would you feel comfortable with sitting in my car while we talk? I'll keep the air on."

I twitched my lips from side to side while considering his suggestion.

"OK, I'll text Mia and let her know I'm with you and that we're in your car. There's a small lake with some large oak trees about a mile from here. Is that OK?" I asked while texting Mia with my whereabouts. He got up and stood behind my chair. I was about to put on my backpack when he took it from me.

"Please, allow me." A+ for impeccable manners.

"Thanks," I said as I read Mia's incoming text that she wanted all the details later.

We walked in silence to his car...what a car! He stood beside the vehicle and opened my door. I was slightly embarrassed as there were several guys staring at the car. I felt a blush traveling up my neck. Quickly, I slid into the seat. The white luxurious leather seat felt like butter, creamy and soft to the touch. It rivaled something that James Bond would drive in the movies.

"Nice car," I commented. I was duly impressed.

"Thank you. Please note that we have something else in common. The appreciation of sport cars," he said and started the engine. It purred to life as he skillfully backed out of the parking space. I directed him toward the lake.

"What kind of car is it, anyway?" Curiosity got the better of me, I just had to know. It was an older car, but in mint condition.

"It's a 1974 Maserati Bora. It will reach speeds up to 170 miles per hour, 0 to 62mph in 6.7 seconds." He clearly loved cars. He said he'd bought the car two years ago when he made his first big commercial real estate investment deal in Miami with money that he had borrowed from his grandfather. David's dad took a risk on him by financing the deal, but Jordan proved that he was a savvy businessman and doubled the money.

We came to a stop in front of the lake. He put the car in park but kept the engine running with the air on high. He flipped off his seatbelt and turned in the seat toward me. I looked at the instrumentation since I didn't want to stare in his eyes, but I was aware that he was looking at me.

"I am intrigued with you, Zoe. I would like to know you better and I promise not to bite." My eyes flew up to his and I saw that he was smiling. "If I do, I promise you will like it." The blush that was fading on my cheeks deepened and I turned my head to stare out the window. My heart was beating in staccato and my subconscious was doing a happy dance on the hood of the car.

He put his finger under my chin and gently turned my face back toward him. I was deeply attracted to him. But, I wasn't sure that I was ready to have a boyfriend and I sensed that he was not one to be put off. What if he was demanding of my time? I needed to concentrate on school.

"I can see the wheels turning in your lovely head. Don't over-think it. I'm just a regular guy and I would like to know who Zoe Caine is. I do know that I haven't been able to get you out of my thoughts for the past few months." His voice was calm and comforting and I wanted to give in to his request, but called on my last bit of common sense.

"I just don't need the distraction right now, Jordan. I have two years of college ahead of me. I know you're probably a nice guy and all, but…" I couldn't seem to formulate my thoughts about all of my hesitations.

"So, that's a yes."

"Um…" I felt that I was losing this battle so I let my guard down and laughed.

"Great. I will work around your school schedule and study time."

I nodded my head, giving in to a trial date this weekend.

He leaned in to me for a kiss. Even if I wanted to move, I felt that I was unable to do so. He was like a magnet that I was drawn to and I gave in to the moment of the light sweetness of his kiss. He brushed my lips once, twice, my eyes closed and I exhaled the breath I was holding, into a soft moan. His tongue slowly slipped into my mouth and swirled gently as if though he was giving me the choice to stop the kiss or go on.

I went on. I was drawn to this man and now totally intoxicated by his kiss. He withdrew and ended the sweetest kiss I had ever experienced. I relaxed back into the seat. I was not aware of meeting him halfway across the console of the car for the kiss, but I guess I had and it was well worth it.

I looked at him and he was smiling at me. I returned the smile, slowly shaking my head. "You are a smooth talker, Mr. Dawson," I said.

"I think that is a firm yes. Dinner Saturday night then." He smiled and put the car in drive. We drove back to my campus apartment.

CHAPTER 7

"HELLO, SLEEPYHEAD." JENNA WAS GENTLY SHAKING MY shoulder to wake me up.

"Go away. It's like 5 a.m. or something," I muttered and opened one eyes to peek at her.

"Fine. I will take my coffee with me too," she replied. That got my attention real fast.

"Coffee? I love, love, love you. You are my favorite sister."

"I am your only sister, goofy." She handed me the cup of coffee that I sipped on as if my life depended on it.

"Fresh ground, Guatemala blend, black with one Splenda, no cream," I said, my eyes closed as I inhaled the aroma of the coffee.

"You are sick; you do know that, right? No one should know that much about something as insignificant as coffee," Jenna said as she pulled out clothes from the walk-in closet for me to put on.

"Hey, don't hate 'cause you can't have any." Since she was trying to get pregnant, Jenna has given up on most caffeine and alcohol as well. Which is why she was disgustingly sober today and I was sporting a dull headache.

"Oh, and take the ibuprofen on the nightstand," she said. I must give it to her; Jenna always managed to look gorgeous. It seemed to come easy to her. She is perfectly made up and in a gorgeous summer pantsuit. Her dark blonde hair was pulled back in a ponytail that made her look cool and sophisticated instead of drab and boring. I complimented her on all of the above and she smiled and blew me a kiss.

"It is well past noon. Mia and Veronica are down at the pool nursing a hangover. Aunt Suzette has had breakfast and about to have lunch, David is off golfing, and you need to get out of bed if you want to make it back to Houston today." Jenna laid out all this information and left the room while I shuffled to the bathroom for a shower and changed into the summer dress she decided on for me to wear. I shook my head. Still such a mother hen. No wonder I love her.

I phoned Robert on my way downstairs.

"Hello, sweets," he said. "Hope your day is going well. I'm almost back home. I just checked in with Greta, mother's nurse. She said that mother did well with her new medication and the physical therapist is with her now. I will see you on Tuesday for dinner at 7 p.m., since mother canceled on us for Wednesday. We can go to Fish since you like sushi. I can have a steak or something else." Yup. Thoughtful and accommodating. Such a sweet man.

"OK, Robert. Sounds good. Give my regards to your mother. I will head home shortly and will see you Tuesday evening." The phone went dead as he ended the call.

"She lives," Aunt Suzette said as she rose up to give me a kiss on the cheek. I pulled her into a tight hug.

"Good morning or afternoon, I think." I gave her a kiss and let her go back to eating her lunch. Jenna's housekeeper guided me around the counter to show me the spread of food she had prepared for lunch.

"Oh my gosh, Juana! This all looks amazing. I love your cooking. Are you feeding the Texas 1st Brigade, or what?" She laughed and shoved a plate in my hand. Not needing much encouragement with food, I dug into the scrumptious offering and sat at the table. Just then, Mia and Veronica made their way in, fresh from their shower.

"Hey, Juana... I think there is a conspiracy here. No one called us in for lunch," said Veronica, as she piled food onto her plate, grinning at Juana.

"It's Miss Jenna. Getting pregnant, she drives us all crazy around here," Juana said as she bustled around the kitchen. She loved to be complimented on her food and nothing pleased her more than to see everyone partake in what she prepared.

We all jumped on the bandwagon, blaming Jenna for just about any silly thing we could imagine. She ate it up too, and chimed in about how much fun it was trying to get pregnant, but that it had already been three months, and she was ready to get pregnant already.

We finally said our goodbyes to Jenna. I texted David and thanked him again for everything. We piled into the limo and made our way back to Houston.

"So, Jordan Dawson was at your party, huh?" Aunt Suzette asked. She was as sharp as a tack.

"Aunt Suz...leave well enough alone. I hope never to see him again, good riddance."

She chuckled. "So, I will have to be the one to tell you?"

"Tell me what?" I sat straight up in my seat. My eyes looked around at Mia and Veronica as if daring them to know something I didn't, but clearly they did not know much more than me since they were all ears as well.

"Sweetie, Jordan apparently is moving his headquarters to Houston from Brussels," she said calmly, as if though she were talking about the weather.

"What the f——"

"Manners, dear!" she admonished me quietly as I was about to let the F-bomb fly, which would have embarrassed her and myself greatly.

"Who else knows about this, Aunt Suzette, and when did you find out?" My tone of voice was frosty and I was trying not to take my frustrations out on her.

"I found out last night. David told me. He asked me to tell you and I thought that since Mia and Veronica are your best friends and you would tell them…well, I thought that it would be OK to tell you now." I saw that this has made her uncomfortable and I leaned over to her and squeezed her hand.

"I'm sorry for losing it. Really, I am."

"Understandable, dear. David said Jordan told him about the move a few months ago, but David didn't know how to tell you and he didn't want to get Jenna involved, so he asked me to tell you." Aunt Suzette had been there to hold my hand when Jordan's relationship and mine went south. I imagine she knew I was still pissed at Jordan and may never get over his betrayal.

I looked at Mia and Veronica and saw that they were concerned as well. Jordan and I dated for a little over six months and they were there to pick up the pieces when he cheated on me with his secretary. Someone I had only met a couple times, but she made it quite clear that she and Jordan had been around the block a couple times and they were still an item.

I looked out the window of the car in dismay. I didn't want to go through this. I didn't want to live in the same town as Jordan Dawson. Why was he moving to Houston? Why move his whole company? Why now, after 10 years… just as my life was about to be settled into a nice, quiet phase with a perfect gentleman? I took a deep breath. I have friends and family around me. Everything will be fine. Houston is a massive city and big enough for both of us.

I have my business and employees that I'm responsible for. We didn't move in the same circles and we have no friends in common. From what I tried not to hear about him, but inevitably did...Jordan lived a life of wealth, never lacking of gorgeous women on his arms, private aircraft jetting around the world and driving fast, expensive sports cars. We probably didn't even know the same people. I could avoid him. No, I must at all costs avoid Jordan Dawson.

"You have an incredible amount of support around you, Zoe. We were there for you 10 years ago and are here for you now," Mia said, squeezing my hand that was actually cold and numb now.

"Look, Zoe, Jordan will not be dealing with a young, naive 20-year-old girl now. You're an accomplished business woman. He's in for a big surprise if he thinks he can waltz back into your life and mess around with your head again," Veronica, ever the practical voice of reason, said.

"Yes, so true. I have a lot of back-up and reinforcements if I need to ward off Mr. Dawson. Thank you both. Aunt Suzette, I'm sorry you were the bearer of bad news, but I love you for being concerned about me, even though I'm an adult." Brave words when I actually wanted to burst into tears.

"No matter how old you are, you will always be my baby girl," she said, smiling at me. Those words of love and comfort washed over me, calming down my racing heartbeat. God, I can't wait to get home now. What will I tell Robert? He doesn't even know about Jordan. There was never a reason for him to know. Jordan was always a world away from Houston.

At some point we would discuss intimacy and I would let him know that there was once a guy...a jerk, in my life. I planned to tell him there had only ever been one guy with whom I was intimate with. Not that that was so important or that Robert needed to know any details of my past personal life but I wanted to be open and honest with him. Fuck! I didn't care at this point. I just wanted to be home and think, think... Why?

With great luck, and to my relief, I was the first one to be dropped off. We said our goodbyes, as the girls and Aunt Suzette help carry gifts from the limo into my town house. Although I'd told everyone to just bring themselves to the party, no gifts needed...I got many in the mail and those who did not mail gifts, took them to the party.

I went through the motions of settling back into the routine of a normal Sunday evening but my mind was not on the week ahead—it was on Jordan and his decision to move to Houston. More disturbingly are my thoughts of my response to his lovemaking, against a fence, in my sister's front yard, on the lawn, my begging and pleading... God! What a mess! I was mad at myself for betraying Robert. He loves me. He trusts me and I blatantly betrayed that trust.

Later in the evening, Andre texted me and reported that he took back the administrative duties from the two nurses that were covering calls for the weekend and all was well. Some minor issues with a couple of nurses canceling their shifts but other nurses were happy to pick up the shifts and make extra money. I thanked him and got on the treadmill.

Three miles later, I decided to keep my little sexual escapade to myself and not worry about what Jordan would do with his company and his move to Houston. I planned to stay clear away from him.

My head hit the pillow and again sleep eluded me. I decided to be brave, but to do so...I must face the demons hiding in my attic. I got back out of bed and headed to my garage, pulled down the lever to the attic and clambered up the ladder. Flipping on the light switch, my eyes adjusted to the intrusive brightness and narrowed on the brown trunk that was a few feet away from me.

Gingerly, I reached for the handle of the trunk and pulled it closer. Taking a deep breath, I wrestled with the enormous box and pulled it slowly behind me. I wasn't sure why I hadn't burned the contents. My conscience had not let me. As much emotional pain as he caused me, I had every right. But something, though I wasn't sure what, prevented me from destroying all the gifts he had sent me over the past years.

I managed to pull the trunk into my living room. In the peace and quiet of my sanctuary where I was able to think clearly...I slowly opened the lid. With a deep breath, I pulled out the first item on the top. It is the last gift Jordan has sent me one year ago.

Don't cry, I whispered, but my soft foolish heart would not listen. Tears gathered in my eyes as I opened the elegantly wrapped gift. My breath caught in my throat as I saw what that foolish man had sent me for my 29th birthday.

It is an 8x10 painting of me. How did he get this photo...I may never know, but will certainly try to find out since this picture of me was taken last summer. I was looking at the large structure of Hoover Dam, smiling with my hair blowing in the wind over Lake Mead. For my birthday last year, Mia, Veronica, Jenna and I went to Las Vegas.

There was a card with two heart intertwined with some sappy love words at the bottom. On the inside was a note that said: *Enjoy the Bellagio cabana, dinner and shows.*

I was pissed! That entire trip was paid for by Jordan. The chips were falling in to place now. I thought the first class airplane tickets and hotel came from David. No one questioned where the elaborate accommodations came from. I suppose we all assumed that each other knew. The four-bedroom cabana at the back of the hotel came with its own private pool, a chef and housekeeper, limo and driver.

Setting it aside, I opened the other package. I was sure my neighbors heard my explicits from their quiet bedrooms as I stared at the antique books that I'm sure cost a fortune. They were Shakespeare's *Othello*, *Macbeth*, along with *All's Well that Ends Well*, the first Shakespeare book he'd given me that I returned to him when he proved that we had many common interests.

Every year since we broke up, Jordan had sent me birthday gifts by express mail with no return address. I never bothered opening them, as I did not see any reason why he should be sending me anything. I always felt that the gifts were sent out of guilt. To me, they were a clear reminder of the pain and embarrassment he had caused me. Try as I might, I could not bring myself to throw them away nor give them to someone else. I mean, how would I even start explaining the whats and whys of such personal items? So I always took the gifts and placed them in the old trunk. I suppose now was as good time as any to open them.

The second gift would have been for my 28th birthday. It was simple, elegant and timeless...a gold Cartier Ballerine watch. Stunned, I stared at the perfection and beauty of the timepiece. I had a Cartier and all these other exquisite items in my attic. What a foolish, foolish man. Surely he must know I would not have opened his gifts. Foolish, gorgeous, definitely sexy, and still dangerous, man.

I couldn't open the other gifts. I was too emotional and his gifts evoked feeling in me that I no longer wanted to feel. I put it all back in the trunk and pulled it into my spare bedroom closet, but I took the watch and placed it in my jewelry box. I suppose at some point I must come to some conclusion about Jordan and what my true feelings are for him. I sat on my bed and turned my iPod music on to the soothing voice and sound of Enya. I allowed the music to take me back to more of my time with Jordan. To go forward, I decided that I must go back and relive the memories I have kept hidden in the recesses of my mind.

CHAPTER 8

TEN YEARS AGO

I WAITED ANXIOUSLY IN THE APARTMENT FOR JORDAN TO text or call and let me know he had arrived to pick me up for our first date. Mia was going out with some friends and Veronica's mom was in town visiting her. I paced back and forth in the living room, rearranging things here and there, anything to take my mind off the guy who had taken up permanent residence in the forefront of my mind.

"Girlfriend, you will totally wear some serious holes in the carpet," Mia said, coming into the living room and standing in front of me.

"Just nervous."

Mia pulled my finger from my hair that I had a death grip twirl going on. "You look totally mag and he will have the hot's for you all night." She looked over my choice of nice jeans minus the holes, three-inch slinky summer sandals, white silk top and light pink, short-sleeve summer jacket. Some dangling silver earrings and a couple bracelets completed my outfit. "I approve," she commented.

"You should, since the jewelry is yours and you chose the entire outfit." I took a sip of water and emptied the rest down the drain in the kitchen. Just then there was a knock at the door. Mia graciously opened it.

"Hi, handsome, who might you be?" she asked as if she had no clue who he was. I peeked over her shoulder to see

Jordan looking at me. A smile broke over his handsome face as our eyes met. He winked at me and mouthed hi. I grinned like a schoolgirl and blushed.

"Hi. I'm Jordan. You must be one of Zoe's roommates," he said in that sexy low voice that had me all but drooling. I walked toward the door.

"Yes. Mia. Well, come on in, Jordan. I was just on my way out. Have fun kids." Mia turned around and gave me a squeeze on my arm. We'd already had the talk that if the date does not go well, I would call her.

"These are for you." Jordan was holding a dozen yellow roses in his hand. I took them into the kitchen and placed them in a glass container that was under the sink. I inhaled the sweet smell of the roses and thanked him.

Jordan drove us in to town. All the while, we engaged in light conversation about my school. He also filled me in on some of his business acquisitions. He was venturing in to Asia and Europe with investors that were eager to work with him since he was doing so well in Miami, Chicago and Los Angeles.

He took me to a steak house where I tasted the most delectable and succulent steak that Texas is famous for. I relaxed in his company. I enjoyed our time together and could not believe when he said it was 11:30, and we headed back. I told him I had a study group at ten in the morning so he'd promised to get me back by midnight.

I was a little disappointed that our time flew by so quickly. Jordan was very attentive and charming, holding my hand and squeezing it gently every now and then. He made me feel beautiful and had eyes only for me the entire evening.

"Do you mind if we go back to your little lake for a few minutes, Zoe?" he asked just before we turned off the freeway and onto campus. My subconscious started that little happy dance again, and I told him that would be OK with me if we hung out for a few minutes, but my heart was racing in a gallop. Secretly, I wanted him to kiss me again and I was so ready for another of his breathtaking kisses, but I wouldn't tell him that.

Tonight he was driving a new red convertible BMW. If he was trying to impress me with cars, that was accomplished. I complimented him on his choice of car. He was too cute, gushing over all the details and the car specs. I had no clue what most of it meant, but he was having fun explaining it and I gave him my undivided attention. We pulled up in front of the lake and he killed the lights but kept the engine and air on.

"I am madly attracted to you, Zoe. I respect that you're honest about why you're hesitant about dating, but I'm glad you allowed me to take you out tonight and I hope it won't be the last time I get to enjoy your company."

Wow! OK, enough said, but he continued and I was enthralled and gazed unabashedly into his gorgeous blue eyes, while his long fingers gently caress my hand. Nothing forward, just comforting.

"I can't stop thinking about you and I can't help but kiss you again."

I leaned toward him and allowed the kiss to wash over me.

His hands moved up my arm and he gently cupped my neck while he slowly deepened the kiss. Both my arms reached around his neck and I pulled him closer to me. He groaned into my mouth and firmly took control. His lips were soft and moist as he pulled my tongue into his mouth. Retracting from my mouth, he placed sweet kisses along the side of my lips and sucked gently on my bottom lip. He went in for another deep and intimate kiss, slowly driving me insane with the need for more.

Wantonly, I pressed my body against his chest. He reached between us and stroked the side of my breast. As if not satisfied, he reached under the flimsy silk top and cupped his hand around my breast. I arched my neck backward and his mouth left mine to kiss along the column of my neck.

"Come here, baby. I need to feel more of you. God, you're so soft and sweet. I love the way you taste." His beautiful words washed over me like rain in a desert that had not had water over its coarse, dry sand for years. I was not aware of him pushing back his seat but he must have since he reached over and pulled me onto his lap.

"I need you, love your kisses. Your soft body is magnificent and I've thought of nothing but you for the past few months." His hands cupped my face and he looked at me like a man starved for his next meal while placing kisses along my jaw and lips, on my eyes and my chin.

"I'm sorry if I seemed forceful in getting to you. I just couldn't help myself. You are so gorgeous, baby. Your grey eyes, soft lips, gorgeous breasts…thoughts of you have consumed me," he whispered. Somehow whispering in my ear sent moistness to the center of my womanhood.

"Oh, Jordan, I feel the same way, but I'm afraid."

"Afraid of what, baby? I would never hurt you or do something you didn't want to do. You should know that. I will respect any boundaries you set. Just say that I can see you again." His kisses continued to break down my defenses.

"No, I mean…I feel way out of your league. I'm just a normal girl going to college. Nursing is not a glamorous job and…um, well you hang out with women that I have…what I'm saying is that they are gorgeous and rich and not normal." I felt foolish for blabbing on about his preference of women that he was often seen with, and being a realist, I didn't want to pretend that I looked anything like them.

"Baby, they are who they are and the reason I want to be with you is that you are nothing like those women. You are beautiful and wholesome, smart and funny. You have a body that is real and most women would die to have. It is perfection."

I looked at him with a smirk on my face, but quickly dropped the smartass comment I was about to make. He is dead serious. Wow. Is that truly the way he saw me?

"Yes. You are all that and more. Don't ever doubt the beautiful and passionate woman that you are. As long as the passion is directed toward me," he whispered and took my mouth in another deep kiss. Any minute now I would start squirming and make a fool of myself. I wanted to go further, yet I knew we need more time to get to know each other better and this was also not the place for that.

As if sensing my dilemma, Jordan hugged me to his chest and lay his chin on my head. He took a deep breath and asked, "When can I see you again?"

"I'll look over my schedule for the week and let you know."

He drove me to my apartment. A few more kisses at my door, then he was gone.

The next few weeks passed in a blur of activities. I was totally devoted to my studies and there was enough to keep me busy every moment that I was awake. True to his word, Jordan didn't take up my time unless I called or texted to let him know when I could see him. I wished I had more free time because I missed him so much, but I simply didn't, so I settled on seeing him once a week.

This went on for another month and we were well into the end of October. I told Jenna about Jordan and me. She said she and David had no idea but that they knew he was awfully happy when he was around them. He must have wanted me to tell my family about us. I felt there is some sort of balance between us.

I'd gotten a call on my cell phone during one of my classes and couldn't wait to listen to the message since I knew it was from Jordan. He usually didn't call me when I was in class so I was a little anxious and hoped all was well. I quietly stepped out of the classroom and returned his call.

"Hi, Zoe." His sexy voice greeted me but for some reason it sounded like all business. "Sorry for interrupting you during class."

"I have a first time slide policy," I responded as I walked down the hallway and leaned against the wall. His soft chuckle on the other end of the line brought a smile to my face.

"I won't keep you long. Just wanted you to know that I'm leaving for Singapore. An emergency meeting with some new investors that need some face to face time and reassurance that their millions will be secured and well invested. I won't bore you with the details but I'm leaving now."

"Oh…wow. OK, well safe travels, Jordan. I hope your trip is productive." I was saddened by the news that he was leaving and that I may not see him this weekend.

"Think about me while I'm gone, baby."

My heart missed a beat with that statement. "I will, Jordy. I'll miss you." I wasn't sure if I should ask when he would be back and hoped he would provide that bit of information but he didn't. He ended the call on an upbeat note that he will miss me as well. I headed back to my lecture, but I was unable to concentrate on what the professor was saying. I did write down the assignment for the following week and headed back to the apartment where I moped around and thought of Jordan.

I received several texts from Jordan over the following four days. It was good to know that he missed me as much as I did him and that he missed not going out on our Saturday date. I looked forward to Wednesday, as Jordan would be returning to Austin. He said he couldn't wait for the following Saturday to see me. Mia and Veronica teased me about my moping and said that he was getting to me with his charming ways and handsome good looks. I readily admitted that he was easy on the eyes and yes, what girl would not want to be seen with such a gorgeous human specimen? I was getting used to his time and attentiveness toward me. It was a good feeling. I could no longer deny that I felt somewhat carried away by his attention.

Jordan was making strides in the business world. He often appeared in global business newspapers as one to watch. His savvy business dealings were prosperous and growing along with his expanding wealth. Over the past few months, I'd followed his name in the business arena and he never disappointed his investors. We didn't speak of his business dealings when we were together and I didn't want to bring up the subject, as I didn't want him to think I was stalking him. If I were a business major it would be easier to approach him since I was intrigued that he's so focused on growing his company. It was easy to see he was a workaholic. Many times when I was studying after midnight, I would text him and sure enough, he was working in his home office with Asia and Europe. I swear the man must never sleep or require very little to function.

I rolled out of bed Sunday morning and made my way to the kitchen for coffee. Mia was staring at the TV and Veronica was pretending to read the newspaper. I knew she is pretending as she cared nothing about what was in the newspaper and definitely stayed clear of the sale ads since her funds were always low.

"Ah, hello, to you two as well," I said, as I plopped down beside Mia on the sofa. Mia glanced at me with her baby blues, then turned her stare back to the TV.

"What? Your date didn't go well?" I asked. Now I was getting curious about the silence so I turned to Veronica and raised a quizzical eyebrow toward her while I sipped on my coffee.

"Nah," Mia finally decided to speak. "All is well. Just a typical Sunday morning. Trying to figure out our day." She looked at me, blinking innocently.

"OK, so we can hang out in the library to study or go to the pool for an hour or so. We're also invited to Jenny's impromptu birthday party," Veronica chimed in as she picked at the newspaper. What's with the newspaper already?

"Ah, she speaks!" I grinned at her and got a smile that was too big. OK, something was up with these two but I wasn't in the mood to play fifty questions, so I said I would leave the day's activities up to them.

"Um, if you are quite through with the newspaper, I would like to take a peek at the business section."

Veronica's eyes went wide as she shot a look at Mia.

"Oh hell. Fine. Might as well tell her or show her." Veronica stretched her arms out to hand Mia the newspaper. Mia flipped through the sections and came out with the business pages. She folded it in half and showed me the photo they were trying to hide from me.

I gasped and my eyes went wide as I gazed at the picture of Jordan and a lovely young lady. Her blonde hair hung over her shoulder in beautiful curls that laid perfectly on her well-endowed chest. She was looking up at him. His arms were around her waist and the look of adoration for her was hard to miss, except if you were blind, that is. Another photo below was of them locked in an intimate kiss. What the fuck! I felt the tears gathering in my eyes. I didn't bother to read the headlines. The paper fell out of my limp hand as my breath caught in my throat.

I was vaguely aware of Mia and Veronica surrounding me. They were pissed! I wanted to go to my bedroom, to get away from the morning that could not possible get worse. I was hurt and angry. How dare he! I was still trying to digest the shock of Jordan, a world away with another woman. Someone he was obviously comfortable with and knew well.

God. I was so stupid. I let him sweet-talk me into falling for him, and all the while he was just playing me. Wait. Back up…and I mean back all the hell up! Did I just say that I fell for Jordan Dawson? That he meant more to me than just a gorgeous guy that I was dating? How did I really feel about Jordan? I looked at my friends in dismay. They were consoling me because he was cheating on me, but I was dealing with that, plus the fact that I had totally fallen in love with Jordan.

How could I not? He was handsome, charming, attentive, and kissed like…well, he made me feel emotions that I'd never felt before. I loved the fun side of Jordan. He was witty and made me laugh with his lighthearted banter. He left his business side in Austin, so I hardly ever saw him in action with business unless he had to take a call from someone in his company or needed to deal with an emergency overseas. I loved to hear him talk shop in the business world. He spoke in millions of dollars, which was mind boggling for me. I couldn't imagine dealing with that much money on a daily basis. He was constantly buying, building or merging companies. It was fascinating.

I squeezed the girls' hands as I tried to pull myself together and made my way back to my bedroom. Dazed, I stripped out of my oversized sleep shirt and stepped in the shower. I scrubbed my skin and hair until I was squeaky clean. All the while I was crying. Devastated.

I chided myself for being stupid, for allowing a smooth talker like Jordan into my life. He was at the pinnacle of making his name and power know in all the world financial markets. A workaholic by his own admission. In the two months I'd known him, I paid more attention to possible opportunities in the medical field, such as maybe someday owning my own business. I wasn't sure yet what it would be, but seeing Jordan committed and driven to succeed made me want to think about nursing in a different capacity. But right now I was crushed. I needed to get back to where I'd been, the pre-Jordan days, when my life was boring and normal. Just another nursing student.

I pulled on some running clothes and my wet hair into a ponytail. The fact that I just showered to go jogging did not make any sense at all, but I didn't care. Nothing was logical right now. I just wanted to put this all behind me and clear my mind, so I headed out of the apartment after reassuring Mia and Veronica that I was fine...just fine.

CHAPTER 9

WAS IT ME? OR DID MONDAY MORNINGS AUTOMATICALLY put everyone in a sucky mood? My early morning treadmill run was cut to twenty minutes due to my lack of respect for the alarm clock which I promptly turned off and slept another half an hour. Genius. Now I was rushing to work and hit every red light. Swerving through traffic had several horns blaring at me. Maybe I was the cranky one in a sucky mood. I so needed to work and get the memories of this weekend with Jordan off my mind.

I even packed an extra running outfit, as Veronica said she would join me in Memorial Park for a run after work. Nothing better than working to exhaustion then go jogging to drain the last bit of energy out of one's system.

I placed a call from the Bluetooth in my car to Jenna as I was in a hurry this morning and had promised I would call her back. We chatted for a few minutes, and bless her, she let me off easy with not too many questions of Jordan. Her main concern was that she was hoping I wasn't mad at her that Jordan was at the party. She hadn't known, and I was not upset at David either. I was a big girl and sometimes faced with difficult situations…well, I'd just have to deal and get on with my life.

Stepping into the office, Grace greeted me and shoved a Starbucks Grande coffee in my hand as she continued answering the phone calls that were coming in like the rapid fire of a gun. I gulped the coffee and made my way to my office. I instant messaged Veronica and Andre on their computer that I would be ready for our morning meeting in my office in ten minutes. I sat at my desk and booted up the Mac computer.

"Good morning," Veronica greeted me and sat across from my desk. She had her Apple laptop open and placed it on the desk.

"Good morning, Veronica. No coffee?" I asked, as she was fueled by the jolt of caffeine, much like myself.

"Had my two cups already. I don't want to end up with tachycardia. I'll need to wait a couple hours for my next fix." We laughed and chatted about the party, all the while avoiding the elephant in the room. I was grateful that it was busy, no time for lengthy heart to heart, not today anyway.

Andre sat in the chair beside Veronica as he ended a call on his iPhone. "Good morning. Hope all slept well and re-vived from our weekend of blissful partying." He pulled up the first order of business for the day on his computer. Ve-ronica and I groaned and told him to get on with business. He grinned and did just that.

"Well, overall, we had some hospitals cancel a few shifts over the weekend. Some of the nurses were not very happy about that and others were elated. Some nurses with con-tracts were floated out of their areas but got to work, so that is good. We had two of our own nurses call in sick, but their shifts were filled with other nurses that were more than happy to work."

"Thank you, Andre. As ever, you are thorough and con-cise. Veronica?"

"I will start off with Mrs. Royden."

I groaned inwardly. I just couldn't figure out why the woman did not like me. I send her flowers when she's not feeling well, provide a nurse to keep her company even if I need to pay overtime, call her on the phone when she cancels dinner with Robert and me. She never takes my phone calls, so I always end up talking to the nurse that is with her.

"How was her weekend?" I dutifully asked of my possible future mother-in-law.

"Well, she had a panic attack Saturday night but the nurse calmed her down by calling Robert who suggested Dr. Hollis be called, since Robert was heading to your party. The nurse finally persuaded her to take her Xanax or she would need to send Mrs. Royden to the ER. Her Sunday was better as Robert was there to see her and they had a late lunch together. She cooperated with the physical therapist and this morning she is going to brunch with some of her friends." Veronica finished her reports of the other private duty patients we had and reported that several other patients were going to be admitted to the agency for nursing care this week. Some patients requested a few hours a day, while others wanted a few visits a week. Since they were paying out of pocket and under the care of a physician, they were able to request nursing services whether it was medically necessary or not.

My morning went by quickly. Andre and I had appointments with several hospitals in San Francisco on Wednesday that would hopefully end with contracts. We also have several nurses that are signing on with the agency. Human Resources would be taking care of that end of the business. We already secured office space, hired a receptionist and an office manager.

"Miss Caine, Mr. Dawson is here to see...never mind, he's on his way to your office," Grace sounded breathless as she beeped my phone line.

There was a brief knock on my door then it swung open and Jordan walked in. Will this man never fail to put me in a state of hyperventilation? I worked on my breathing as I stared at him. He calmly closed the door behind him and walked slowly toward me.

"Why are you here, Jordan? I have no desire to see you." I picked up a pen and pulled a note card toward me. I didn't have any idea what I would do with it but it looks like I am official or something...I think.

"Hello to you, too, Zoe. I have this little problem." He calmly took a seat in front of my desk and took the pen out of my hand. Not missing a beat, he placed a soft kiss on my hand and placed the pen back on the desk.

"I am sure you have a number of people at your bidding to take care of your problems. I'm busy and you will need to set up an appointment with Grace if you want to take up any more of my time." Wow! I shocked myself. That sounded pretty good.

"No, you see, Zoe...you are the only person that can take care of my problem since it happened while we were to-gether locked against a fence in Austin."

What the hell? I looked at him, and try as I might, I was unable to resist being totally lost in his brilliant blue eyes twinkling with mirth.

"You were never one to play games, Jordan. Why start now? What the hell do you want?" I was anxious for him to leave my office. I needed him...I needed him to leave, right. I must try to sound convincing, so if I have to use some ex-plicit language, well so be it.

"No, no games. What I need from you, or rather what I want from you, are your skillful hands on my, um..."

"Out! Get out, Jordan, or by God I will call the police! I swear I will. It was a mistake. I was taken by surprise and it was all a mistake for me to...for us. So you need to leave." I stood up and placed my hand on the phone just as it rang.

"Miss Caine, there is a delivery here for Mr. Dawson. He said to send it straight to your office as soon as it arrived."

"Thank you, Grace." I placed the phone back down and glared at Jordan who was still sitting with his long legs crossed and dangling over his knee. He has the audacity to look innocent.

"What the hell, Jordan. You can't waltz into my office and give my staff instructions." There was a tentative knock on the door. Jordan sat silently. Christ, this man drove me absolutely fucking crazy.

"Come in." The delivery guy handed Jordan the package and bid us good day. Seeing Jordan in my office was anything other than a good day, but I smiled and thanked him politely as he took his leave.

The smile left my face as soon as the door closed. I was fuming! "OK, Jordan. What do you want? When did you start delving into the medical field? Is this a hostile takeover or something? Surely I am a drop in the bucket as far as you are concerned. I owe more than I'm worth and barely keep my head above water, but it is an honest business and keeps many employed so they can continue to take care of their families."

My chest was tight from all the information that just left in one breath. Why the hell had I just vomited my business to this person that I despised? As usual, when I was around Jordan, I lose all sensible thoughts. Not even the lapse of 10 years has changed that fact. I looked at Jordan expecting to see a smirk on his face but he was not smiling.

He got up, went to the door, and turned the lock. I opened my mouth to speak but since such nonsense had just come out of my blabbing mouth, I decided to sit back down in my chair and sulk.

Jordan swiftly made his way to my chair and knelt down beside it. My arms were crossed over my chest and I was looking anywhere but at him. He gently squeezed my arms while looking at me.

"Zoe, I will not insult you by offering to help you unless you ask for it. But I know that you're a smart woman. You have carved this agency in the Houston medical community and made it one of the most reputable and dependable. You will not see it fail and neither will others in your life that knows how hard you work to keep it going." His calm words of wisdom were quite unexpected and as much as I hate to admit, were much appreciated. "I am not here to buy you out. However, I would like to take you out to dinner."

"No. No, Jordan, I have a boyfriend. I respect him and I need to tell him what happened between us on Saturday." His hand gently grasped my chin and turned my face toward his probing eyes. I dropped my gaze to his tie which was the color of his eyes, and caught my lower lip between my teeth. Jordan took the opportunity to rub his hand along my jaw line. I desperately wanted to lean my face into his palm, but resisted.

"So, you have not told him yet. Why?" he asked as his fingers continued to caress my jaw and neck.

"Well...I mean, it's not something I can just calmly tell my boyfriend. I love...him. And anyway, he trusts me and I don't want to break that trust by hiding stuff from him." I sounded so lame. As much as I wanted to be convincing, it sounded like anything but.

"Do you respond to him like you do to me? Be honest with yourself, Zoe. Do you?" His voice was soft but commanding, as if he could see right through me and pull out the truth.

I took a deep breath and pushed at his hands to let me up. He did so easily and stood as well. I walked to the window and looked outside. I wasn't sure what I wanted to say or what I needed to tell him, but I decided to be honest.

"Look, Jordan. You are probably gloating now that you know I have not had sex with Robert or anyone else for that matter, since you. I get it. Robert is getting serious about us and he will be proposing any day now. I want a quiet life with someone that will be true to me. Someone that I can trust. Our relationship is not sitting well with his mother and he is having to deal with her as well. I am not sure she likes me, or maybe she wants someone else, someone different for her son. At any rate, I had no right to respond to you the way I did." I desperately wanted to believe everything I just said. I bravely lifted my head and looked at him.

He was leaning against my desk and staring at the Waterford crystal vase with the bouquet of bluebonnets that he'd sent for me as a college graduation present.

"Then she is a fool. And so is he," Jordan said as he turned his head toward me.

"The same can be said for you, Jordan," I replied. He got my meaning but did not retreat.

"You need to break it off with Robert." My mouth opened in surprise. I was speechless. Did he just say that?

"Excuse me, but you do not control my life. You don't get to tell me who I date and when to break up with him. You wander all over the world with gorgeous women doing God knows what with them. Those are the women you get to tell what to do." He had the audacity to chuckle.

"You find that funny? I am not joking, Jordan. Robert and I are going out Tuesday night to discuss our engagement plans, so there." Oh great! I just gave him more information than he needed to know about my plans with Robert.

Like a predator, Jordan walked slowly toward me. He reached behind me and closed the blinds. A chill went through my body as he placed both of his hands on the each side of my head and captured my mouth in a deep kiss. I gasped and he readily swallowed the soft sound that left my lungs while he skillfully assaulted my senses with the kiss.

My hands grasped the windowsill behind me. It was either that or push my hands in his sexy dark blond hair and pull him closer into me.

As if reading my mind, he put an arm around my waist and the other at the back of my neck, tilting my head to deepen the kiss. He left my mouth and nipped gently at my bottom lip again and again, then finally sucked gently. He finally ended the kiss, but not before briefly rubbing his erection on my abdomen. I gasped as he walked away to retrieve the forgotten package.

"I need a tetanus shot. My doctor was kind enough to send it via courier for you to administer it."

I was coming undone, trying to hold on to some thread of sanity and hanging on to the window for dear life, and he was talking about a shot? Was he for real? Yes, he was. He opened the package with the pre-filled syringe of medication and a note from the doctor asking me to fax the record back to his office so that it could be scanned and attached to the patient medical record.

"I don't know what this is all about, Jordan, but I am so not giving you a shot."

"You're a nurse, Zoe. Saturday night I sank my hand on a nail poking out of the fence. You bit my hand while I gallantly covered your mouth from screaming my name, and it just so happens to be time for my tetanus booster shot. Would you kindly do me the honor? You can take out some of your frustrations toward me with the needle."

I covered my smile by placing my hand over my mouth while shaking my head. "You do know I am a busy woman."

"I do know that you are a gorgeous, desirable and busy woman, yes. Forgive me for taking up your time?" He looked like a boy asking for forgiveness. I'm not sure how it happened, but we both chuckled. I felt the wall of defense that I had erected around my heart wobble a tiny bit. My emotions were all over the place since Jordan reentered my life a few days ago.

"And you must admit you are also ridiculous for bringing this shot here and giving my employee more work by taking care of your medical record," I said, as I prepared his arm for the shot and set out the necessary supplies to administer the medication.

"Yes, I am aware of that, but in my defense, I am also aware that you would not have agreed to see me under any other circumstances. Ouch!" he yelped, as I covered the area with a Band-Aid and threw the gloves in the trash.

"Ha. The mighty Jordan Dawson is such a baby when it comes to shots." I smirked at his childish behavior. He took the opportunity to pull me onto his lap. I wasn't sure what to do or where any of this is going.

"To be fair, baby, you need to break it off with Robert. He is not the one for you."

"Oh, and you would know that how?"

"By the way you want me and I need you. You know it's true. Say it. You feel the same way."

I took a deep breath and looked straight into his eyes. My olfactory receptors were succumbing to the faint hint of cologne he was wearing that was as sexy and desirable as the man wearing it. I was tempted to close my eyes and inhale his scent, his smell that I have committed to memory. It was seductive. I could easily lose myself in him again. As much as my body responds to his touch, I really need to keep a clear head around Jordan. But to my chagrin, I reminded myself that I am so totally fucked. For some reason, Jordan is back and his aim is at me.

I unclasped his arms from around my waist and went back to stand at the window. It did no good for me to continue to try and make my relationship with Robert something it is not and will never be. As I stood at the window I decided to make a decision that shocked even me. Being fair to Robert is something that he deserves. Maybe I am restless or I just need to reassess where I am in my personal life. Turning around, I made the announcement to Jordan.

"I will break it off with Robert. It's not fair for me to continue in a relationship in which I do not truly love him like I should. I do admire and respect him. He's a good man, but he does not deserve a cheating girlfriend." I finished on that note and felt terrible about myself, but I knew it was the right thing to do.

"Good. I will see you Tuesday night after the break-up then."

"Whoa, slow down. I may be breaking up with Robert, but that does not mean I am making way for you in my life. I'm doing it because it's the right thing to do for him and for me." Looking back at Jordan, he seemed deep in thought about my announcement. His fingers slowly rubbed his chin.

"You're doing the right thing, Zoe. There is no way in hell you would be happy living a life without passion. It is who you are and you would die emotionally by hiding in a shell. There is also the fact that we need to talk once and for all about what happened 10 years ago. We need to get it out in the open so we can move forward. There is a lot about that morning that you don't know because you will not listen to me or anyone else at what the truth really is. Please give me a chance to clear it up. Please, baby. I hate that you have avoided me for 10 years, all the while hating me. I can't take it anymore."

I wanted to believe him. I wanted to hear him out, but 10 years of steering clear of someone and trying to put their memories away is not easy.

"I know what I saw, Jordan. You did not deny nor did you correct that...that despicable person that was laying in your bed." Just thinking about it again made me angry and that is one emotion that I did not want to waste any of my energy on.

"You would not let me explain what happened. I was not in the bed with her. I slept on my sofa, for Christ's sake... take a minute to hear me out. You refused to see me, and when I broke into your apartment and bedroom to try and explain, you had me arrested. Give me this. Please." He stood beside the chair. His eyes never left my face, as if daring me to deny him the opportunity to rehash our past. I wanted to crumble, to weep and tell him yes. That I would listen and easily believe him this time...but I couldn't. Not now.

"I have a lot to do and even more to think about. I need to get back to work and I am sure you have an empire to run and some new investors to play world domination with," I said as I walked toward the door.

Jordan stood by the door and leaned against it. His gaze on my face was intense. I took a deep breath and looked at him, losing myself in the beautiful image of the glorious male that he is. His tall lean body erect, he leaned down and placed a sweet, soft kiss on my lips.

"I've missed you, baby," he whispered in my ear. Slowly, he opened the door and left my office. I walked to the window and opened the blinds. Looking outside, I saw him get in the back of a new black Range Rover. He looked up at my window as I pulled back, but I knew he saw me staring at him. His perfect white teeth flashed his gorgeous smile that had my heart racing again.

Thankfully, the afternoon was just as busy as the morning and I didn't have time to chit-chat with Veronica or Andre about my unexpected visitor, but I'm sure they were dying to know what it was about.

"Are you still up for a run?" It was 6 p.m. already and Veronica had changed into her running clothes. She sat in the chair in front of my desk with a smirk on her face.

"What?" I asked, as her smirk turned into a smile.

"Well, well. Our girl had a visitor that left her speechless. Hmm. Just tell me when we should all gang up on him and kick his handsome ass. I'm taking that kickboxing class twice a week and ready to try out my new skills."

"You would not even believe how twisted up I am about all this shit between Jordan and me. Then there are my dwindling feelings about Robert and me. I sure did not need Jordan to waltz back on the scene, like ever. Anyway, I have to deal, right?" I stood up and pulled my gym bag from the corner where I'd thrown it this morning.

"Be right back." I headed to the bathroom to change and ran right into Andre.

"Ah, drinks on me later this week if I get to hear what that visit was all about."

"Yeah. I may just take you up on that offer. I will need several drinks by the end of the week," I replied, as I continued my way down the hall. It felt good to have friends that cared about me. I needed to clear my head and sometimes talking about it helps. Stripping out of my dress, I pulled on my running clothes. I can't wait to burn off some of this energy that had my heart racing every time I think of Jordan and his motives for moving back to Houston. I thought it strange that he didn't mention moving back permanently, but there was no way in hell I'd ask him. His timing sucked! Not that it would ever be a good thing for Jordan and me to live in the same city, but I didn't need the distraction.

Veronica and I walked to the parking lot and got in our cars. My phone rang as I started the engine. I grinned as I saw Veronica's name flash on the screen.

"I can see you, goofy. What's up?" I asked, as she was sitting in her car right beside mine.

"Last one there is a rotten egg."

"Because that is not childish!" We laughed and set off for Memorial Park where we would run.

After a brisk two-mile run, I made my way back home and took a shower. I pulled out a chicken salad from the refrigerator and poured a generous glass of Pinot Grigio. Feeling sated and relaxed, I placed a call to Jenna. I needed her advice in this confusing turn that my life had taken.

After a casual chat, I mentioned the visit from Jordan. I even mentioned the kiss in my office and confided my concern about his move to Houston. I told her about my feelings for Robert, that I care about him and what a great person he is, just not the one for me. Liking and respecting was not enough when one is talking about a long-term commitment and marriage.

Jenna is a great listener and did not interject her opinion of my decisions, which was what I needed right now. She did, however, agreed with me about ending it with Robert if I did not truly love him. I just needed her to listen and she did. After our conversation, I lay on the sofa and listened to the music of Lana Del Rey playing on my iTunes. My eyes fluttered closed as I allowed in thoughts of the events that led to the break-up between Jordan and me.

CHAPTER 10

TEN YEARS AGO

I DIDN'T RESPOND TO JORDAN'S CALLS OR TEXTS. I KNEW he was on his way back to Austin from his trip overseas. Still hurt and confused about the photo of him and the woman in the newspaper, I told Mia and Veronica that I didn't want to see him and they went into protective mode.

Sure enough, Jordan landed back in Austin and headed straight for my apartment. I was walking from the library when his long lean frame easily caught up to me.

"Zoe. What the hell is going on? You won't take any of my calls answer my texts or emails."

"Seriously? How many girlfriends can you juggle at one time, Jordan?" I increased my pace but did not look at him. "Let me guess, you have one in every country."

"Please tell me what you are talking about. I don't have a girlfriend anywhere else but here. There is no one else but you."

"Don't play games, Jordan. Fine, let me refresh your memory. There is a photo of you and a woman in the Sunday papers and you sure look chummy with her."

He put his hand on my arm and stopped me from walking. "I did not attend an event on this trip. It was just business and even if I had somewhere to go that required a companion, I would have taken one of my employees."

I wanted to believe him but the picture was proof.

"I'm not dumb, although you're playing the part really well." I pulled my arm from his grasp and continued to the apartment. Mia was on the balcony and ran to the door when she saw us. She opened the door and pulled me in while glaring at Jordan.

"Back the hell off from her, Romeo," she said.

"Mia, please listen to me. I did not attend an event. I have no idea what is going on about a photo with me and another woman." Mia was trying to close the door but Jordan's broad shoulder was wedged against it.

"Here, let me refresh your memory." Mia went to the coffee table and picked up the newspaper. I took it from her and shoved it in Jordan's face.

"Remember now?" I yelled at him.

Jordan studied the photo as we glared at him.

"This photo was taken a year ago. Obviously I know who this person is, but she is no longer in my life. I have no idea why they would have reprinted this photo. I'm sorry it upset you, Zoe, but I'll find out why it was published and who is responsible for it."

I crossed my arms over my chest wondering if what he said was true. An old photo. After a few more minutes of negotiations to continue seeing me, Jordan decided to leave and was already making phone calls about the photo.

~ ~ ~ ~ ~

The next morning I woke to a knock on my door. I still had another thirty minutes of sleep before the alarm went off. This had better be good.

"Come in 'cause am not getting up yet," I replied to whoever was behind the door. Mia sauntered in with a huge bouquet of red roses and a card from Jordan.

I leaned up on my elbows and eyed the elegant bouquet.

"Open the card already," Mia said. Veronica came in yawning and complaining about all the noise.

'Babe, the person in the photo is the daughter of the family that owns the newspaper in Germany where the photo was taken. She's pissed that I have a new girlfriend and somehow got the photo printed again in hopes of causing distrust between us. I am sorry that it caused you to be upset, but it proves that there is no one else but you in my life. Yours, Jordan.'

I handed the card to Mia after I got through reading it. "OK, friend. Sounds believable, but where the hell did he get roses so early?" she asked.

We giggled, but all decided that knowing Jordan, he was sure to charm the owner of the flower shop out of bed at some ungodly hour this morning. We were laughing at what the explanation would have been to the shop owner when another banging sounded at the door.

"Regular Grand Central Station this morning," Veronica commented and went to the door. "Wait in the living room. I'll tell her you're here."

Right then I knew it was Jordan. I got up, pulled on a robe and went to the living room.

"Did you read the card?" he asked with an anxious look on his face.

"Yes. Makes sense, I guess," I mumbled and slid my arms around his waist.

"Good. Have time to go for breakfast?" he asked.

"If I hurry."

"I want to see you. Change quick." He pushed me toward my bedroom.

~ ~ ~ ~ ~

We got back in to our routine. Sometimes we didn't go out to dinner but rather stayed in and watched a movie. Jordan was fun and it was easy to be in his company. It was also easy to forget that he's an entrepreneur in the business world. His travels to Europe and Asia were more frequent than when we first met.

Thanksgiving was a welcome break from college. I headed to Austin since newlyweds Jenna and David were hosting Aunt Suzette and me, along with David's parents in their new home. Jordan was on his way back from Hong Kong. He'd been gone for five days and I was happy about his return tonight. He asked if he could steal me away for a few hours and I was more than happy to be in his company.

After a short visit with Jenna and David, Jordan took me to his penthouse in downtown Austin. I was impressed with his taste in modern art and elegant furnishings. I stood at the door of the kitchen admiring the stainless steel appliances and gleaming granite countertops when Jordan wrapped his arms around my waist. He gently rocked me from side to side.

I closed my eyes, savoring the feel of his strong arms around me and leaned into his body, inhaling his unique scent and a hint of his cologne.

"I missed you, pretty girl," he whispered in my ear and moved one hand to rub the side of my breast. Instinctively, my body arched and pushed my breast into his hand. Taking full advantage of my body posture, he pinched my nipple through the bra.

"Jordan, I..." Aware of my inexperience with sexual intimacy, I wanted to warn him that this would be my first time to go further than a few kisses, but his expert hands on my body was seductive. I responded to the onslaught of his delightful fingers that made me squirm against him.

My heart was pounding, I could hear the blood roaring in my ears. He turned me around toward him and tilted my chin up to meet his eyes.

"I want you. I want to make love to you. You are sexy and gorgeous. I am consumed with thoughts of you. What is it about you that has bewitched me?" His voice was low and seductive. His lips touched mine once, twice...

I closed my eyes for the onslaught of his mouth on mine. I gave in to the moment, this moment, this time. I wanted to be his. I wanted to know what it was like to be taken by this gorgeous man with brilliant blue eyes, bulging biceps, steel hard abs, narrow waist and long legs.

He swept me into his arms and headed to his bedroom. It was the first time that he had brought me to his place. He lay me on the huge king-sized bed and switched on a bedside lamp. The mattress dipped as he sat beside me.

"Look at me, Zoe." I turned my gaze to his face. "Is this your first time?" he asked.

"Yes."

"I can imagine you're probably scared. I will take care of you. We'll go slow and if you're not comfortable with doing this just let me know." His hand caressed my leg while he talked.

My breathing increased and I feel like squirming. I nodded my head yes.

"Are you on birth control?" His hand moved to my neck as he slowly rubbed his thumb up and down my now sensitive skin.

"No." I bit my bottom lip. It hadn't occurred to me to get on the pill. I felt foolish and my face warmed with embarrassment.

"It's OK. I'll use a condom, but I want you to get on the pill."

His hands slipped behind me to unzip my dress. I lifted my back to help with the process as he effortlessly slid the garment down my legs and off my body. My hands clenched in the bedding. The pink demur cotton undies and bra was all that was left on my body. His gaze was intense and I saw that he was as affected by me as I was by him. He slowly kissed his way up my leg. I shot up to a sitting position as he reached the apex of my thighs. Not missing a beat, he reached behind me and unclasped my bra. My arms looped around his neck and I drew closer to his body. His soft lips molded to mine and I opened my mouth to give him better access to explore.

I heard sounds coming from my lips. Soft moans of pleasure and need radiated from my body. Jordan's tongue covered my areola, teasing my nipple that elongated and begged for more.

"Please, Jordan, please." I wasn't sure why I was begging, but whatever this euphoric feeling was, I simply needed more.

"Yes, babe. I'll take care of you." He pulled away and looked at me, taking in my state of undress. "Gorgeous," he muttered.

He moved to my other breast and repeated the action. In one swift motion, he eased me back onto the bed and pulled off my underwear.

"All I thought you would be. So sweet," he said as if speaking to himself.

His hands reached down and he covered my mound. I jumped at the intimacy of his touch.

"Shh, lovely girl. Let me love you." His voice was raspy against my skin as he slowly moved a finger over my slit. I squirmed against him and made a mewling sound. My body was hot with desire and anxious with thoughts of having sex with Jordan.

He placed a soft kiss on my clit then pulled it gently in his mouth. My body rocked with need and my legs quivered below him. I whimpered softly. Jordan was now kneeling between my legs. His eyes darkened as he looked up at me.

"Look at me." His voice was firm.

I opened my eyes and complied.

"I will pleasure you with my mouth. Don't hold back your pleasure. You will have an orgasm. I want you to enjoy it. Take your mind off the anxiety of penetration for now."

"OK." I nodded.

He slid one finger in my pussy and my hips jolted. I gasped at the intrusion as he continued to move his finger in and out of me. My eyes flew open as he expertly added another finger, stretching me a little more. I felt a slight burn, but it quickly faded. His tongue joined his finger as he sucked gently on my clit. My hips moved in unison with his fingers. I pushed my head back into the pillow and groaned his name.

I was lost to everything but this man, and in that moment I was his. He drove me to experience something new; something that I'd only heard and read about, a new level of sensation that I hadn't known existed. My body thrashed against his hand and his lips were relentless on their assault of my plump, wet pussy. I gasped and pleaded. I didn't know what I was begging for. This was new for me, but he was taking me somewhere. We were on this path, taking this trip together. He was right there with me as his thumb centered on my clitoris.

"Come for me, Zoe," he whispered in my ear. As if that was my clue to release the pent-up tension from my body, I spun into a vortex. My inner folds contracted greedily on his fingers. I felt lightheaded with the release of my orgasm and delighted in the moment of pure unadulterated pleasure.

My eyes opened slowly and Jordan was over me murmuring sweet words of approval. He pulled my trembling body into his chest as I came down from the intense pleasure I experienced.

Jordan slid off the bed and quickly undressed. I looked at his gorgeous cock bulging with a massive erection. My lips caught between my teeth as I gasped.

A wicked smile slowly spread across his face as he arched his brow. "See anything you want, sweet Zoe?"

How could he be calm in such a time? When I was coming apart with a mind-blowing orgasm and seeing a beautiful male specimen with a true and glorious erection for the first time? My face reddened again with a blush that I was sure was spreading across my entire body.

He quickly slid a condom on his magnificent cock.

"I will take that as a yes," he said and slid his warm hard body over mine.

Aware of the need to go slow, I felt Jordan straining over me to maintain control. Instinctively, I opened my legs. He positioned his taunt body over mine and slid his shaft over my wet sex. I gasped as he entered me. We gazed in each other's eyes as he gently pushed his huge erection into my warm, tight space. I inhaled sharply and bit down on my bottom lip as I felt the invasion of his cock. The burn was intense and I let out a sharp gasp as my body strained to accommodate him.

"I have wanted you from the moment I saw you, Zoe," he whispered.

His body loomed over mine. His brilliant blue eyes darkened with pleasure and paused at my breasts. As if unable to resist, his head dipped to suck on my nipples, first one then the other. A groan escaped his lips.

I gazed in wonder at his powerful body embedded in mine. His pace increased above me, stroking the embers of fire between us. I felt the pleasure of another orgasm starting to build deep within my core, at the low center of my abdomen and my muscles began to contract again, pulling and sucking onto his cock.

"Now, beautiful. Come for me again."

I shattered with his words and held on to his arms as my vagina spasmed onto his cock.

"God, baby…what you do to me, ah." He convulsed over me, taking his pleasure. With a last powerful stroke, he came undone in my arms.

We were both spent and remained in a tight embrace. Slowly I was aware of the stubbles on his chin tickling my neck. His warm breath slowed to a more controlled pace. My body relaxed against his, and for a few minutes we basked in an incredible post orgasmic feeling of bliss.

"Are you OK?" His husky voice rumbled against my neck.

"Hm. Yes," I answered with my eyes still closed.

Jordan eased off me and I heard him discard the used condom. He produced a warm washcloth and cleaned between my legs. I squirmed with embarrassment, but he quickly wiped the evidence of my virginity away. Strong arms gently pulled me under the covers. I peeked up at him and smiled.

My limbs were lax against his lean waist. Sometime later, I stirred in his Jordan's arms, but he tightened his hold on me, keeping me in place.

"Zoe."

"Hmmm."

"Thank you for sharing your first time with me. As always, you take my breath away, beautiful lady."

I blushed at his compliment as he tilted my face up to his. His full sexy lips took mine in a sweet kiss that had me clinging to him for more. He didn't disappoint, as the kiss deepened and I felt his erection against my abdomen again.

I opened my eyes with raised brows.

"Yes. You do that to me."

My mind swelled with the realization that I affected this gorgeous, powerful man. A man who could have just about any woman he wants…but he wanted me, desired my body, and yearned for my touch. I gloried in the newfound knowledge that he found me irresistible.

As Thanksgiving night drew to a close, Jordan made love to me again. He rained kisses from my neck to each of my breasts.

"Beautiful. Mine, all mine," he said, as if memorizing every part of my body and marking it as his.

He suckled on my nipples, drawing them to hardened peaks, taking his time as I thrashed under him. His tongue drew moist circles around my belly button, then finally moved lower between my legs. My breath came in short gasps as I reeled from the orgasm that was building slowly inside me. He licked and lapped up my juices as if starved for more of my essence.

Jordan's lovemaking was slow and tender, but it had me spinning out of control. I convulsed above his head, screaming out his name again. He made his way back up to my mouth and kissed me, making sure I tasted the salty sweetness of myself on his lips. I held his face in my hands and licked the juices from his mouth. His lip curled into a smile.

"My girl is learning fast. Your taste is as irresistible as you are."

He rolled a condom on and sank into me again. My hands splayed onto his chest then moved to his bulging biceps. I moaned with pure pleasure as his hips plunged faster. My now sensitive pussy fluttered around his cock as the urgency of his strokes increased. Jordan's breath hissed above me as I exploded with another orgasm. He yelled my name as his powerful hips plunged one last time into my depths.

Later, he drew a bath for us in his sunken whirlpool tub. I lay in his arms, replete as he ran his hands slowly over my body. All too soon, it was way after midnight and Jordan returned me to Jenna's home with a promise to pick me up tomorrow morning at ten. He had a boat on Lake Travis and we would be spending the day on it.

CHAPTER 11

DESPITE MY LATE NIGHT WITH JORDAN, I GOT UP EARLY for a three-mile run to clear my head. I smiled at the memories of last night with Jordan. He was magnificent, and I was glad that he was my first sexual experience. I could not imagine being with another guy. I was totally smitten with Jordan Dawson.

Aunt Suzette would be heading back to Houston today while Jenna and David planned to join us on the boat for lunch.

Jordan picked me up in his car, then stopped by his office briefly to connect with an overseas conference call. He said it would only take about fifteen minutes or so. On our way to the elevator he paused to introduce me to a young woman that was leaning against the wall by the elevator.

"Celia, this is Zoe Caine. Zoe, Celia Fuller, my secretary," Jordan said.

She was beautiful with long black hair and green eyes that narrowed on me. "Hello," I said politely. I got the feeling that she did not particularly like me.

"How do you do," she replied, although her eyes were now on Jordan as she spoke.

"It's a holiday, Celia," Jordan said, as he walked to another set of elevators and placed a card in the slot. Evidently this elevator was private.

"Yes, but I came in to see if you needed me for the conference call to London. Just in case." She had a perfect smile pasted on her equally perfect face.

"Thank you, but that won't be necessary." Jordan held the door open for me to enter. Celia seemed put off by the dismissal, her smile slipping just a bit.

"OK, I will see you on Sunday for our flight to Tokyo then. I made plans for us to take a day off for sightseeing." She finally looked at me and the smile turned to a smirk. She turned around and made her way toward the exit.

The elevator ride to the 32nd floor was quiet. I didn't know what to say or if I had a right to be jealous. I wished Jordan would say something but he was reading some email on his phone.

My feeling of elation was turning into uncertainty. Maybe I was naive to think that Jordan would be content with just one woman in his life. I silently warred with myself as the elevator door opened and Jordan ushered me into a well-appointed lobby.

He headed down the hall to a large double door with his name and the word PRIVATE. I waited while he connected to the conference call, and true to his word, he ended his conversation fifteen minutes later. He then placed a call to Helen, his administrative assistant, and told her to cancel Celia's travel plans to Tokyo on Sunday.

Nothing more was said of the incident and we headed to the lake on a gorgeous boat on beautiful Lake Travis where we had a great lunch with several of Jordan's business associates along with Jenna and David.

And so began my love affair with Jordan Dawson.

~ ~ ~ ~ ~

"I don't want to take you back so soon." I was packing my bag at Jenna's to go back to college. Jordan sat on the side of the bed watching me.

"Jenna and David are leaving for a few days and Aunt Suzette went back to Houston. Plus, Mia and Veronica will be back, so I won't be there by myself." I placed the last of my toiletry items in the small case.

Jordan hoisted my bag on his shoulder. He leaned over and kissed me then led the way outside. I drove my car back to college and Jordan followed behind me in his.

Back at my apartment, Jordan said, "I have something for you." He pulled out a box and held it out for me to see.

"A webcam?" I looked at the box in his hand.

"Well, it's for both of us. For your computer." He set about installing the camera to my computer.

"We are not recording movies of ourselves in bed. No way," I said.

Jordan threw his head back and laughed. "No, we're not. How about we use it to chat when I travel?"

"OK. I guess we can do that."

"So, no movie, huh?"

I shook my head.

After installing the camera and testing it out, I sat on his lap with my arms around his waist while he talked about some more ideas he had for expanding his business.

"Break it up, you two, or I will get the water hose and I know how to use it," Mia said from the doorway.

"We're going to start sulking if we don't get some girlfriend time soon," Veronica yelled from the kitchen.

"He's leaving for Japan tomorrow, so y'all will get enough of my company."

"I wish you could come with me." He nuzzled his face in my neck.

"Maybe during spring break or next summer," I said, then pulled back and looked quizzically at him. "If we're still together."

"Look at me." His voice was serious and I pulled my stare from the floor back to his face. "Nothing will come between us. I won't let it. You mean too much to me."

"I want to feel as confident as you are about us, but sometimes...I don't know. School takes up most of my time and you travel. Can we really last until next summer, or will it fizzle away at some point?"

"Not on my part, it won't. You are all I think about. All the time. Always remember that when we're not together. Promise me."

"OK. I promise." I smiled at him.

~ ~ ~ ~ ~

The following weeks were an introduction of how to live a life of being in love with a boyfriend that was considerate, attentive and romantic. I was inundated with flowers and gifts, dined at great restaurants, met business associates of Jordan's at various functions. He insisted on taking me shopping for beautiful dresses and gowns to attend the events with him.

He made love to me every time we were together.

My head was spinning at how fast my life had changed from quiet and dull to crazy busy and exciting. I struggled to keep up with my studies and had to cancel some of our dates due to finals in December.

Jordan picked me up right after my last exam, took me straight to his apartment in Austin and we made love for the rest of the day. I was exhausted that night and slept for twelve straight hours.

The Christmas holiday was a blur, as I attended events with Jordan that he was either hosting or was invited to by business colleagues. There were also my own family functions and those with Mia and Veronica who were elated for me. We still kept our girlfriend times real, but I knew they were missing me as much as I did them.

Jordan's company Christmas party was held in the magnificent Austin Ballroom. The opulence of the venue spoke of Jordan's success. At age 28, he was a force to be reckoned with in the world of business. At the party, he announced another successful business acquisition in Hong Kong that solidified his company's viability and growing success.

The party led to my second meeting with Celia. Jordan was surrounded by some of his junior executives and other employees, so I sat at the table texting Jenna. Mia was supposed to be at the party too, but in true Mia fashion, she cancelled at the last minute due to a date with a hot guy.

Veronica was in Mexico visiting her mother's family over the holiday. I would not have minded having some company other than Jordan, since I knew he would be busy, but I was delighted to be his date and better yet, his girlfriend.

"What a nice little girl you are to just sit around and wait for Jordan." I looked over at Celia. She was gorgeous as usual in a long black backless gown with a slit up to mid-thigh. She was leaning on the back of a chair at the table looking bored.

"He doesn't need me to meddle in his business," I responded. I texted Jenna that a snake was slivering around me and had her fangs aimed at my jugular.

"Ah, not that you would understand the world of business anyway, and don't fool yourself thinking that you are the only candy in his jar. Jordan has an insatiable appetite for women and sex." Her hateful words were like ice water down my spine. I tried not to let her see how her malice affected me. I looked across at Jordan just as a woman whispered something in his ear, her hand running suggestively down his back. He looked down and smiled at her. Celia saw this as well.

"Tata, little girl," she said in a singsong voice and walked toward the group of people gathered around Jordan.

I so wanted to ask Jenna to come and pick me up, but I was determined to not let Celia affect me that much. I ended the conversation with Jenna and put my phone back in my purse.

The party went on for another two hours, but my feeling of bliss was fast replaced by despondency. I saw Jordan making his way to me, so I stood and slid a smile back in place determined that Celia's poisonous words would not get to me.

We danced to a couple more songs, then Jordan suggested we leave, which I readily agreed to. I wondered if Jordan's popularity with women was something I could deal with, or if jealousy and distrust would soon tear us apart.

CHAPTER 12

JORDAN DID NOT SPEAK OF HIS FAMILY, BUT SINCE IT WAS close to Christmas time, I wanted to know what his plans were. On our way back to his penthouse, I asked if he would be in Austin then. He pulled into the parking bay and leaned across the console of the car and nuzzled my neck making me ache and instantly moist between my legs.

"I am not quite sure what I will be doing but I most certainly know who I will be doing." He nipped my ears and I moaned as his lips traveled down my neck.

"Um, well, you haven't said if you will be with your family. I don't even know if they're from Texas," I whispered as I tried to keep my thoughts together.

He seemed to sense my curiosity. Jordan sighed and reluctantly pulled his mouth away from my shoulder. I felt that he was tense and would rather not discuss his family.

"I will be visiting my family sometime over the holidays. They live in Colorado. My mother died in a plane crash when I was an infant so my grandparents raised me. They had three children, one son who is the eldest child, then my aunt Vivian. My mom was the baby of the family.

"Unfortunately I don't get to see my family as much as I would like, but I visit when I can. My grandparents were great with me when I was growing up and tried to fill the void in my life as much as they could." He spoke kindly of his grandparents. "I'm not as close to my aunt and uncle."

"I'm sorry to hear about your mom. You probably know that my parents died when I was young as well."

"Yes. Something else we have in common. Raised by others due to unfortunate circumstances."

"Come on." I opened my door and Jordan hopped out to help me out of the car. "It's the holiday season. Let's go shopping or something fun."

He laughed. "I'm not sure many guys would admit that shopping is fun, but I on the other hand, have fun being with you, so shopping it is."

Jordan spent the rest of the holidays in Austin. I invited him to Jenna's home for Christmas dinner. We spent most of the holiday season in each other's company.

~ ~ ~ ~ ~

After the first of the year I headed back to college and Jordan was gone for a couple weeks to Europe for business. Despite mine and Jordan's busy schedules, our romance was blooming.

I could not quite wrap my head around the fact that this gorgeous man could not wait to be with me. He was burning up our phone lines with calls. To my delight, continued to surprise me with impromptu visits at my college apartment.

The last week in March, Jordan bought me a beautiful Nikon camera. We took a trip Saturday morning out of Austin to a beautiful spot filled with bluebonnets. I practiced my photography skills on the gorgeous flowering field. There was a pasture with cows grazing along the fence line and I got some great shots of that as well.

Soon, Jordan took the camera away from me and turned the lens toward me. I ran into the field of flowers and posed for the camera while laughing and singing out of tune to songs from the movie *The Sound of Music*.

We had a delightful day and basked in each other's company, momentarily forgetting about the stress of college and money to be made with mergers and acquisitions. Jordan did not miss an opportunity to make love to me when we were together. I craved his touch and his smell, the feel of his skin on mine and his groans of pleasure as he consumed my body with his tongue and his lips.

Even with little experience and being only with Jordan intimately, he was the God of lovemaking, of that I was sure.

That same Saturday night, I went out with Mia, Veronica and some other friends from college, so Jordan headed back to Austin.

I was telling the girls about the camera and photos, but remembered that I left the camera in Jordan's car.

Sunday morning I texted Jordan about the camera, and since he was leaving for Japan that evening, I wanted to get it from him. Although it was early, I headed to Austin. I thought of spending the day with Jenna and David after leaving Jordon's. When I arrived, I knocked on his door.

I giggled as I imagined he would be surprised to see me and we could have an early romp in his bed. The door opened and I froze as the smile fell from my face. I tried to take in the scene as nausea overwhelmed me. Hanging on to the door for support, I whispered, "What are you doing here? Where is Jordan?"

"Jordan is in the shower," said Celia. I took in her appearance. She had on one of Jordan's T-shirts; clearly there was no other clothing under it.

Oh God. No. No. This can't be true.

"Should I give him a message, or will you just stand there gaping?"

"No, I...I.... Oh, God." I could not find words to formulate a coherent sentence as my thoughts were racing, taking in the rumpled looks of Celia in front of me. I was such a fool. I felt so stupid. Dumb, dumb, girl. Oh, God. I turned toward the elevator when I heard Jordan.

"What's going on?" I heard him ask.

I pushed the elevator button willing it to open. Thankfully, it did and I stepped inside.

"What the fuck!" I heard Jordan yell as the elevator door swooshed closed.

I stumbled out of the building and ran to my car hoping that Jordan would not confront me. I don't want to see him. Ever! With tears streaming down my face, I jumped in the car and headed to Jenna's. I didn't even call her. I just showed up at her front door sobbing, ringing the doorbell. I fell in her arms when she opened it.

Jenna could not make any sense of my blubbering and fractured sentences so I sobbed some more. She led me into the den then ran to the bedroom to get David.

I immediately told them that I did not want to see nor speak with Jordan. Not now. Not ever. I finally calmed down enough to tell them why I went to Jordan's place and what I saw.

Knowing that David and Jordan were friends as well as business colleagues, I made David promise he would keep Jordan away from me if Jordan came to their home or called for information about me.

David was furious with Jordan. He said he never thought Jordan would do something like that. Much to my dismay, David headed out to see Jordan. I told him I didn't want him to go but he insisted, saying that's what a brother should do.

The rest of the day passed in a blur. I was totally devastated, wounded and embarrassed. Jenna called Mia and Veronica, who immediately drove to Jenna's and surrounded me with love. They vowed to keep Jordan away from me since we expected he would try to see me and lie about his relationship with Celia.

When David came back home from meeting with Jordan, he said I should think about talking to Jordan when I feel like getting some answers. He said it was up to Jordan to tell me what happened but I did not want to listen to lies. I was too broken.

Sunday evening, Jenna said Jordan was parked in the driveway. David went out and spoke with him, but I begged them not to let Jordan come in while I was there. I don't know how long he stayed in the driveway. I shut off my phone as well. I wanted to sever all contact from Jordan.

Monday afternoon I left Jenna's and went back to my apartment. I also got a new phone and changed my phone number. For the first time since starting college, I missed a day of class. Clinicals were important and I knew I would need to make up the hours missed on another day or on a weekend, but I could not think that far. Just one hour at a time.

Mia and Veronica hung out with me in my bedroom as they helped me study for the upcoming exam and filled me in on the missed day of class. Jordan came to the apartment but they would not let him in. He finally left after sitting outside for a couple of hours.

The rest of the week passed in a blur and Jordan made more attempts to contact me, but I made up my mind that he cheated on me once and he would probably do it again. I just needed time to get over him.

Friday night the girls went to a study group but I stayed in my room with a made up excuse of a headache. It was not entirely a lie since I'd had a dull ache in my heart and my head for the past few days, but I just wanted to be by myself. I was lying on my bed with a textbook, but must have fallen asleep.

I came to a start as someone was squeezing the life out of me. I tried to pull away but there was a death grip on my arms when I realized it was Jordan.

I yelled at him to leave, but he said he would not until I listened to him. Somehow I got to my phone and threatened to call 911 if he did not leave, but he refused to go and I refused to listen. We were yelling back and forth at each other and were getting nowhere, so I did call 911.

Jordan got arrested that night, but he did not care nor did he stop his harassing behavior, so I filed a restraining order against him. We went back and forth for another week before he would back off from trying to speak to me.

By the end of my semester in May, I was overwhelmed and exhausted. I was not quite sure how I passed all my exams, but Mia and Veronica helped cram information in my head until I thought it would explode. I could hardly retain any more information.

Thankfully, Jordan stayed away.

That summer I did not go to Austin to see Jenna and David and I did not work my summer Job. Veronica invited me to visit her family in Monterrey, Mexico. It was just what I needed. Her family lived in the suburbs of Monterrey where the mountains meet the sky or stayed shrouded in clouds.

I basked in the warm sun and enjoyed great food. Her family was very friendly and accommodating. Some of her cousins even tried to teach me a few sentences in Spanish.

We stayed there for a month then headed back to Houston. My family and friends were concerned about me, but they honored my one request that we would not speak of Jordan.

~ ~ ~ ~ ~

The fall semester of my junior year in college, Veronica told me that Jordan moved his headquarters to Europe and would not be in Austin very often.

As the months and years went on, I built a wall around my heart about Jordan. I avoided reading sections of the newspapers he would be in and avoided listening to gossip about his latest love conquest. It was not easy to forget him. As a matter of fact, he made it impossible for me to do so.

Despite not wanting to see or hear from him, Jordan continued to send me flowers and gifts. He never missed an occasion in my life, and much to my chagrin, most of the gifts were expensive. It felt too wasteful throwing them away, so I kept them hidden, most of them unopened, in a box. Gifts were sent for my graduation from college and when I started the nursing agency, along with birthdays. Every Christmas was yet another reminder of Jordan.

Try as I might, I could not get away from him. He always knew where to find me and have his gifts delivered. There was never a return address and most of the gifts were left in my living room or in my office.

I could have made a huge fuss about his invasion of my privacy, but that would lead to me contacting him, so I accepted that he was going to forever feel guilty, and his unopened gifts were to ease his conscience.

CHAPTER 13

PRESENT DAY

NOW THAT I'D RELIVED THE MEMORIES BETWEEN JORDAN and me, I realized that there is a chance, a possibility, that I may still have feelings for him. That thought scared the hell out of me. Ten years was a long time and I've changed. I was no longer the 20-year-old naive girl, but an accomplished business woman.

I'd kept the opposite sex far and away from my body and my heart. Although I have several male friends, they were just that, friends. I did try dating a few times during the past 10 years, but they soon lost interest due to my reluctance to engage in sexual intimacy with them and they moved on. Except for Robert, who was not crossing the line of intimacy any time soon with me, which is why I was in such a comfortable relationship with him.

With that thought, I got up and walked around my home, but avoided the room where the box of gifts from Jordan sat. I didn't want to see what else was in the box. Not now. I felt vulnerable at the moment and if I looked at more of his gifts I may break down and call him. So I turned in to bed for the night and dreamt of Jordan.

Tuesday morning I was inundated with work related issues including my accountant with whom I was wrapping up my monthly financial report.

"So, Miss Caine, your head is just above water for this quarter, but don't make any sudden moves or changes without consulting me first or you will be heading back to the bank for another loan." Larry Walsh adjusted his wire-rimmed glasses and placed his computer and files in his briefcase.

"I can always count on you to keep it real with my finances, Mr. Walsh," I responded.

"I imagine you don't want me to bullshit your time away, Miss Caine." Not one for small talk, we shook hands and he took his leave.

I slumped back in my chair and blew out a slow breath. It was not easy being a business owner but it was a great feeling of accomplishment and fulfillment for me. I skimmed over the financial spreadsheet on my computer from Larry.

I was always keeping just one small step ahead of the taxes paid to the IRS. Malpractice insurance for my business and employees, along with benefits for the full-time employees and loan repayment were just a few of the financial obligations that sometimes kept me up at night.

I did not consult Larry about expanding the agency in San Francisco. He was not happy with the decision to expand the agency at this time since I was taking a financial hit from all the changes going on in the larger hospitals, but it was too late to back out of the meetings in San Francisco. It was his job to keep me from going bankrupt, but it was my decision to keep the business viable and my obligation to my employees to make sure their checks cleared the bank.

With no warning the door to my office swung open. I rolled my eyes as Mia came in followed closely by Veronica.

"What? It is lunch time and you can thank me for bringing it to your office." Mia had a picnic basket in her hand that she put on the small table in front of the sofa in the corner.

"Thank you, friend." I walked around the desk and embraced her in a hug.

"Yeah, well this lunch isn't free. I heard Jordan was here yesterday and I want all the gory details."

I narrowed my eyes on Veronica who looked innocently at me with her huge caramel colored eyes.

"It wasn't Veronica. I do have other sources, you know, but I should not have to hear shit like this through the grapevine." Mia made fast work disassembling the basket of chef salads, crusty French bread and bottled waters.

"I was going to call and ask you out for dinner tonight, but since you're here..." I claimed one of the salads and dug in.

"Sure you were. So, I have some news about Jordan," said Mia as she picked invisible lint from her wrap dress that hugged her petite figure like a glove. I pretended indifference although my heartbeat sped up.

"For Christ's sake, stop the suspense already. Do tell." Veronica playfully kicked at Mia's ankle. She was always ready for juicy gossip.

I squinted my eyes at Mia but she ignored me and dug into her lunch.

"You are a bitch. You do know that, right? Fine. So let's say I am somewhat interested in your news." She had the audacity to giggle. Swear to god, I could simply choke her neck for making me ask for news about Jordan.

"Well, daddy said he had a meeting with Jordan a few months ago in Brussels. You see, daddy is on the board of directors for a European company and so is Jordan. Anyway, he said Jordan told him then that he was moving back to Houston to reclaim what was his. Daddy said he thought Jordan was speaking of business, but Jordan made it clear that he left some personal business unattended for far too long and he was moving to Houston to close the deal." Mia dabbed delicately at her mouth took another sip of her water as I stared at her, my mouth agape.

"What the hell, Mia! How is that of any interest to me?" I asked, but I knew this was leading back to me.

"First of all, the only personal business left unattended here for Jordan is you. Next, we need to confront him about that morning you caught him with Celia, who by the way, is divorced and living in Austin again," Mia said. She crossed her arms and tapped a staccato on the hardwood floor with her Valentino couture platform pumps.

"We don't need to confront him," Veronica piped in. "Zoe needs to do that, and the sooner the better for her."

And here I was thinking that Veronica was the one to come up with some sensible solution.

"Not like she is not able to defend herself," Veronica continued. "But he is Jordan Dawson. I mean, he can make any girl drop her panties, so he's likely to sweet talk his way right back…"

"What the fuck! Hello, I am still right here, not invisible." I packed up my lunch containers and got up, pacing around the office as I defended myself. "I am fully capable of making my own decisions and believe it or not, I am able to contain myself and retain my panties where Jordan is concern."

Lies, lies and more lies. My subconscious is forever holding my feet to the fire but I defiantly held my head high and faced my friends. "Yes, Jordan came to see me yesterday morning. I am not sure we resolved anything. He had a lot to say and asked me to hear him out about what happened between him and Celia." I confided in my friends since talking about the situation somehow helped to sort out this mess.

"I must admit, I felt sorry for the guy for the first few months after the breakup, but he was a jerk for playing you all along," Veronica said.

"Well, he did go to great lengths to speak to you about it, Zoe. Many attempts were made on his part to try and explain about a huge misunderstanding and things not being like they seemed. I just can't help but think that maybe you should listen to what he has to say." Mia was not backing down nor shutting up until I listened to Jordan and put it behind me.

I chewed on my bottom lip, deep in thought. Was I wrong about what I saw? Just too stubborn and hurt to listen to his explanation or excuse about Celia? Could it be something other than what it seemed? For months, he'd pleaded with my family and friends to give him a change to explain, but I refused to listen to anyone. So many questions and no possible right answers.

"I'm breaking up with Robert tonight." Now who would have thought my breaking up with Robert would cause such a reaction from my friends. They both high-fived one another and got up to do a quick happy dance.

"Told you. I knew it all along," Mia said to Veronica.

Obviously, I was not privy to what she knew about me. I raised my eyebrows in her direction.

"Mia always said you were not in love with Robert. I only recently agreed with her only because I could see that over the past couple months your heart was not in the relationship." Veronica gave Mia a hug and air kisses. "On that note, I must return to my office." She blew me a kiss and exited the room.

"Clearly as your friends, we are supportive of any decision you make in your personal life. Although we may not totally agree on everything, know that a phone call is all that separates us." Wow, flighty Mia as the voice of reason and understanding.

"Are you happy now? You're making me cry." I sniffled as my eyes blurred with tears.

Mia left my office and in true Mia fashion, leaving her discarded lunch for someone else to clean up. Shaking my head, I did just that then tackled the afternoon meetings starting with Andre.

"So far, we are set to depart Houston Wednesday morning at 7 a.m. Our first meeting is with San Fran General Hospital, then with St. Francis Memorial. Afterward, we'll head back to the new office to meet with some of the nurses that are new temp hires and the new office staff." Andre consulted his laptop while throwing out information about our upcoming trip. He had everything crammed in two days with more hospital meetings and setting up training modules and hands-on competency with medical exams, making sure our nurses were prepared to work under any situation and able to chart on various different types of electronic medical records.

"Thursday is much of the same, but with several interviews for the new Director of Nursing position." He consulted his records one last time. "Well, that just about covers every minute of your two days in gorgeous San Francisco. You will head back solo on Friday and I will spend a fab weekend with Ben. I am totally psyched to take him on a tour of Napa." He grinned like a Cheshire cat that just lapped up sweet cream. Andre, and equally handsome partner Ben, have been together for several years now.

"Sounds like fun, Andre. Stop by Domaine Chandon and have a glass of bubbly for me."

I was nervous about my dinner with Robert. I did not want to think about Jordan today. My mind was set on Robert and not wanting to hurt him. For the hundredth time I reminded myself that he will be better off with someone that loves him.

In true Jordan fashion, I got a hand written note on his personal letterhead that was delivered by courier at 4 p.m. that read: *Thinking of you. Yours, Jordy.*

I am not sure if he expected a response, but if so, he was so going to be disappointed. I slid the note in one of of my desk drawers, but not before reading over it several time. My pulse was doing that funny thing it usually does when I thought about Jordan.

By 6:55 that night my nerves were frazzled. Thankfully, I arrived a few minutes before Robert, so I decided to have a glass of wine.

"Hello, Zoe. Am I late or are you early?" Robert asked as he greeted me with a kiss on my cheek.

"I was a little early so I had a glass of wine." I wanted to add that it was much needed, but my stomach was twisted in knots and I was short on words. Grateful to be seated at a quiet booth, I gulped down the rest of my wine promising to do justice to the next glass of William Hill chardonnay I was sure to have tonight.

"Well, we seem to have a lot to talk about tonight, Zoe." My eyes glanced up to Robert but he was looking over the menu. I was guilty as sin and wondered if someone saw Jordan and me together on Saturday night and passed on that tidbit of information to Robert. Either that or he was going to propose to me.

"Sure, Robert, but before we go on..."

"Why don't we enjoy supper first, Zoe, then talk about our relationship," he suggested.

WTF? I guess I assumed that I was the only one with issues about our relationship but it appeared otherwise. Taking a closer look at Robert, I saw that he was as nervous as I was but trying to keep calm. Not one to drink, he shocked me by ordering whiskey on the rocks for himself and another glass of wine for me.

"I don't think I can enjoy supper when we need to talk about things affecting our relationship, Robert." I decided to take the bull by the horns, so to speak, and just delve into the issue of moving on with our lives, separately.

The waiter delivered our drinks and we both took a sip, eyeing each other over the rim of our glasses.

"OK, Zoe, if you insist. You see...well, I am just not the right person for you. I tried to make it work, but mother just has the most awful feeling about you and I trust her to have my best interest at heart," Robert said as he gulped down the rest of his drink and wiped his forehead with his napkin.

"Excuse me? What the hell, Robert! You are leaving your life and a woman you love up to your mother? You are 40 years old and should be able to make your own decisions. When will you stand up for yourself and take control of your life?" I fumed that Robert was letting his mother manipulate him.

Suddenly it occurred to me that Robert was breaking up with me and sparing me from hurting his feelings, although he didn't know that I'd planned to break up with him tonight, too. Internally, I laughed at the absurdity of the situation, although I was still pissed at his mother for controlling his life.

"Now, I know you are upset, Zoe. Mother said you are a strong willed woman and that you would not take this news easily. She was right and I am so sorry for breaking your heart." He gallantly clasped my hands on the table.

"For fucks sake, Robert, I know you love your mother and all, but when you find the woman that you truly love, make sure and stand up to your mom about your feelings. It's the right thing to do for you, and...well, it's just the right thing to do." I figured that I'd better shut up while Robert was still hell-bent on the break-up, but I still felt guilty as hell.

"True, so true. I will have another drink then and…"

"No, Robert. You usually don't finish one drink and you're driving. Better go home and tell your mom the good news."

Robert readily agreed. I told him I would pick up the check for our drinks and he all but ran from the restaurant.

"Thank fuck. I thought he was going to drag out the mommy shit all night," Jordan said as he easily slid into the seat Robert just vacated.

"What the hell, Jordan? What are you doing here? Did you follow me, and how did you know where…"

"To be fair, I will need another drink if I am to answer all those questions, babe," Jordan said with an amused smile on his face.

He was gorgeous as usual in faded jeans, T-shirt and a lightweight jacket. Christ, is there anything this man wears that does not scream sexy as hell? His blue eyes were brilliant even in the dim light. Not wanting to encourage his stalking tendencies, I threw some money on the table and got up to leave.

"You should never drink on an empty stomach," he said as he held onto my hand.

"You should never follow people around and stalk them," I replied.

"I don't make a habit of following people around, only you. Only for the past 10 years." Jordan got up as he laid that bombshell on me.

My eyes must have been the size of saucers with affirmation of the fact that he had been following me, or I assume had me followed, over the years, since he's mostly been overseas building his financial empire. He quickly propelled me down the hall and out of the restaurant.

"Why, Jordan? You know I don't want anything to do with you. I don't want to see you. I just broke up with my boyfriend." I walked toward my car when a limo pulled up beside us. Jordan opens the door and ushered me to get in.

"No. I have my car here and I will not be getting into a vehicle with you…" Before I could finish my train of thought, Jordan took the keys out of my hand and gave it to another guy that exited the front seat of the limo.

"I swear to God, I will kick you in the shin if you don't get out of my way. I mean it, Jordan." My heart was racing, as I could only imagine what being in a limo with Jordan would lead to.

"If that will make you feel better, then give it your best shot, but we will be talking tonight. Now, we can discuss us here, or you can go with me. As you can see, we have quite an audience." Not that Jordan was worried about the audience. He seemed to be enjoying the tiff as much as those observing it. I got into the vehicle and slid all the way to the other side. Jordan got in and stretched his long legs out as the limo pulled away.

"So, Robert gave you the easy way out and now you're mad at me," said Jordan.

"I am mad at you for totally different reasons, as you are so well aware," I huffed in my corner of the limo.

"It's time that we cleared the air and talk about us. I've waited 10 years. Ten years for you to come to the conclusion that I did nothing with Celia. Ten fucking years for you to listen to the truth from me," he said.

I turned my head and looked out the window.

Jordan slid closer to me and grasped my chin. "By God, you will look at me and listen to what I have to say."

"Fine. Say your peace, or more like lies, then leave me the hell alone." I stared back at him.

"Celia showed up at my place banging on my door at 4 a.m. She was drunk and crying. She said she was having an affair with a married man and he gave her the boot that night. Obviously, she said she had a thing for me, but I always kept our relationship strictly business. She knew she would not get anywhere in my bed nor get me in hers. Needless to say, she was pissed. I was going to call her a cab, but felt that if someone took advantage of her in her state, I would obviously feel responsible. I offered her the bed and I slept on the sofa in my home office.

"She was asleep on the bed when I went in to take a shower. I was going to play golf with some friends that morning. I did not know of her state of undress, nor that she had on one of my T-shirts. As much as she would like for you to think so, I swear to you, Zoe, nothing ever happened between Celia and me. The next day I transferred her to another department. A few months later, she was fired. I don't know why and I don't care."

CHAPTER 14

OH GOD. COULD IT BE TRUE? HAD I PUT US THROUGH THIS much agony for the past 10 years due to being hard-headed? Maybe it was the wine, or that I was just ready to listen and come to another conclusion. I shook my head slowly as the tears came. Unstoppable.

I wanted to believe Jordan. He'd tried time and again to prove his innocence to me and stayed in contact with my life despite my total disregard for his efforts. I lunged myself into him catching him off balance. He caught me easily and held me to his chest while I sobbed and molded myself further in his embrace. I wasn't aware of much more than crying and feeling sad for the lost time in our lives. Time we could never get back.

The limo came to a stop and Jordan picked up my purse from the floor where it fell. I looked through the car window and saw that we are at my townhouse. Gently, he dislodged me from his chest and opened the door, took me by the hand, and led me inside.

Jordan sank into the living room sofa pulling me on his lap again. This is my new favorite place to be. It revived memories that brought tears to my eyes again.

"Somewhere in all this mess, I always knew there was an explanation for what happened between us, Jordan. I should have listened to what you had to say, hear you out, but I bolted. I suppose things have a way of working out, and maybe this is no different." I leaned back in his arms and gazed in his eyes.

His hands were running over my body, caressing me, pausing briefly only to feather light kisses on my face and neck.

"Thank you for listening to my side and trusting your heart. It has been a long 10 years, Zoe, but you are worth the wait. I know what you saw hurt you, but I was hurting as well. Knowing that you thought I betrayed you. It was killing me. I had to leave Austin. I always thought I would leave, for a few years anyway, since most of my business was with Asian and European investors, but I wanted to wait until you were through with college."

His sincere words touched me. I could see the pain in his eyes as he spoke.

I slid my arms around his neck, running my hands through his dark blond hair.

He closed his eyes and leaned his head back as my hands explored his neck and face.

I kissed his neck sucking lightly on his skin.

Letting out a soft groan, his eyes were half-lidded as he looked at me. "God, baby, you're killing me. I want you. I want to make love to you, Zoe."

"Yes."

As if waiting on that one word from me, that word that told him I was ready to move forward, Jordan picked me up in his arms, and like a treasure, held me easily into his body. He made his way to the master bedroom and stood me by the bed.

With shaky hands I started to unbutton my silk blouse, but Jordan stopped me.

"Let me do this, babe. I have thought of this moment so many times." He slowly unbuttoned my top pulling it out of my pencil skirt. He unzipped the skirt and let it fall to the floor. He took in a sharp breath as I stood before him in pink and black matching lace bra, thongs and three-inch Vince Camuto stilettos. "More beautiful than ever," he whispered.

I was under his spell, but I didn't mind. His sexy voice enthralled me sent chills down my spine.

As if unable to wait a moment longer, Jordan quickly unclasped my bra. My breasts spilled out of the size C cups and into his hands. With firm pressure, he rolled my nipples between his fingers as the dusky pink buds puckered.

His head lowered to my breast. He suckled on the areola while his other hand paid homage to the other breast.

I watched, entranced, as he made love to my body like a man starved for days, deprived of food and water.

He pulled his lips off my breast with a light popping sound that left the nipple wet and elongated, begging for more of his attention. Lifting me onto the bed, Jordan quickly pulled at his clothes and threw them wherever on the floor.

My eyes feasted on his huge erection, his cock jutting upward toward his abdomen with the round dark head straining for release. I was unaware that I was worrying my bottom lip between my teeth until I felt Jordan gently rub his thumb across it.

I let it go as his mouth swooped down and claimed mine in a mind-blowing kiss that took my breath away. Pulling away again, he placed both my arms above my head and took off my shoes and thong.

I was trying not to squirm or pull him onto me, as my need to capitulate with his body was a raging inferno now.

Jordan spread my legs and brushed his fingers against my labia, pausing to rub his thumb gently around my clit. Two fingers were at my wet slit and he slowly inserted them.

I heard the faint noise of my moisture as his fingers continued the in and out motion. My pussy clenched as it begged to be taken.

As if not satisfied with feeling the dripping essence of my desire, Jordan put his fingers to his nose and slowly inhaled. My breath caught in my throat as he sucked his fingers into his mouth. He was still standing by the side of the bed, so with little movement, he leaned over and kissed me, making sure I tasted the juices from the center of my core.

The fragrant smell of my pussy was musky and tasted somewhat salty.

Getting on the bed, he knelt between my legs bent my knees up and looked at me.

"You are so fucking beautiful." His head ducked down between the apex of my thighs. He flicked his tongue from the bottom of my slit to my clit. My body jerked, bringing my ass off the mattress, but his hands were holding onto my thighs.

I was mewling with pleasure; my head tossed from side to side on the pillow.

Jordan swooped down again and did the same thing, only this time he did not stop. His talented tongue delved in my slit, in and out, as he fucked me with his tongue. His mouth clamped down on my pussy and his tongue concentrated on my clit.

"Please, Jordan, please, ah..." My hands went to his head, which was not moving from between my legs. I felt the orgasm bearing down fast on me. Screaming out my pleasure, I erupted in his mouth as he lapped away the juices of my release. My pulse raced and I panted for air, but Jordan did not stop.

His fingers were back in my slick pussy. As his thumb rubbed my clit to a hard knob again, with a swiping motion, he moved his thumb in me to pull residual juices and continued to assault my sex.

Vaguely, I was aware of chanting his name, begging for another orgasm.

"Come now."

On his command, I shattered, holding on to his shoulders for dear life as I trembled beneath him. My body rejoiced with the reunion of my lover, as my limbs went lax from the rush of orgasmic anticipation and the pleasure of the release.

Jordan crawled up my body, rubbing his steel hard cock on my abdomen and settled beside me. He pulled me into his arms.

"I missed you desperately, sweet lady. I could not stay away any longer. Watching you from afar has been like sweet torture. Get used to me being around, Zoe. I am not going away again, not without you."

His whispered confession in my ear sent goose bumps across my body. I turned my head into his neck and kissed him all the way up to his mouth. The light kiss turned into a union of tongues and teeth blended with lips. We pulled at each other with frantic hands, reclaiming the pleasure we once had.

"Condom; I need a condom." Getting off the bed, he located his discarded pants. With expert fingers, he sheathed his gorgeous cock.

With my legs open and bent at the knees, I welcomed his hard warm body into mine.

"Open your eyes. Look at me."

I did as he said and took in the glorious sight of this gorgeous man about to mount me. I couldn't wait for his gorgeous cock to slide into me.

"No one else, Zoe. This is mine." I nodded my head yes, but he was not satisfied with that. "Tell me it is so, babe."

"Yes, Jordan. It's only for you." My breath hitched in my chest as he rubbed his manhood at my entrance, although not penetrating. He leaned on one elbow above me and fisted his cock in the other hand while rubbing on me.

"I don't want to hurt you, Zoe, but it will since it's been a long time for you. Let me know if I need to back off some."

I nodded my head in understanding.

With slow but steady pressure, he pushed into my pussy, pausing only to readjust so he could advance further. There was a moment of fullness and burning as he continued, but I quickly adjusted to his size and wiggled my hips for better position.

Wanting more of his cock in me, I pushed into him with my hips. I pulled in a ragged breath as his length went all the way inside me.

"I'm OK, Jordy. It feels incredible."

He leaned his forehead against mine and began to move, slow at first, but with sure strokes that was driving me crazy already.

I locked my ankles around his waist and hung on as he picked up the pace and pounded into me. The perspiration on our skin mingled with our whispers and groans of pure pleasure as it built to a crescendo.

"Christ, you feel good. Warm and tight. That's it, baby. Move with me."

His words were drawing me closer to the edge.

"I'm close. About to fucking blow this condom to kingdom come." Jordan panted above me as I screamed his name again for the third time in less than an hour with passion that had been building in me and long overdue.

Shouting out his own pleasure, Jordan slumped on top of me. I licked his neck and shoulder with open mouth kisses. A few moments later, he rolled off and pulled us on our side facing each other. We made the slow descension together from our heightened state of pleasure.

I knew we needed to talk. So much time had passed, it was as if we were strangers, yet we had a history of intimacy. I didn't want to think about all that tonight. It was too much, and I was totally exhausted. My limbs were heavy and relaxed; slowly our breathing and heartbeats returned to normal.

"Stay where you are. I'll be right back." Jordan slipped out of the bed.

Curious about his exploration of my home, but too tired to care, I snuggled deeper in the pillows and welcomed the slight ache between my legs which reminded me that the cobwebs have been blown the fuck away. I smiled at the thought. It was something that Mia had teased me about over the past few years.

CHAPTER 15

"I MISS THAT SMILE. WHAT'S IT ABOUT?" JORDAN INQUIRED.

I opened one eye and peeked at him, seeing a tray of food in his hands.

"It's a silly girl thing." I told him what Mia said about cobwebs.

"Well you can happily report to her that upon my inspection, your beautiful pussy is cobweb free, since I totally obliterated anything trying to get in my way of claiming that sweet treasure." His wicked smile lit up his face and I took in his handsome features that were a sight for my sorely deprived eyes.

I giggled at his analogy of my anatomy, all the while gawking at his. He was naked and his cock nestled in short blond curly hair.

"Like what you see, pretty lady?" He winked at me and I could not miss the twitch in his cock that was getting ready for more action.

"Let me replenish your energy. Your refrigerator is stocked with great stuff, by the way. Reminds me of your great eating habits when you were in college, but good to know you still eat a healthy amount of junk food."

I laughed as he got back on the bed and fed me a sandwich stacked with deli meat and cheese. I took a handful of salt and vinegar potato chips and munched on them.

"So what were you doing at that restaurant tonight?" I asked.

"Darling, the object of my desire and reason for moving to Houston is you. I was not giving Robert another moment with you and I wanted to be there when you told him to take a hike." He wiped some crumbs from my lips and licked it off his finger.

"I did not break up with him. He broke up with me. Anyway, I may have let you off too easy. I mean, less than a week ago you showed up at my party and now you're in my bed." I took a swig of water.

Jordan picked up the bowl of cookies and cream ice cream and paused with the spoon at my mouth.

"Things have a way of working themselves out. I was hoping you would listen to me and give me a chance to explain, but it was also important to me that you believed what I had to say was true, and that you trusted me to be true to you."

I was surprised at his frank answer and it settled me even more.

After devouring the ice cream, Jordan put the empty tray on the night stand and reached for me again. He pulled me across his middle as I straddled him. Immediately, his erection was steel-hard and pushing against my bottom.

I slid backward onto his thighs and fisted his cock in my hands, sliding it up and down his satiny skin. His engorged cock beaded with pre-cum at the tip. I bent down to lick the droplet as Jordan gathered my hair that fell onto his thighs and abdomen. I looked up to see him staring at my mouth. I licked my lips and went down to lap up the sweet essence of him.

He inhaled sharply and his breathing increased.

Feeling empowered and naughty, I flicked my tongue out and circled the head of his cock several times. I went down on him, taking almost half of his shaft into my mouth.

With our gaze still locked on each other, I repeated the action again and again. With no warning, I increased the motion and let his cock hit the back of my throat. Jordan's hips came off the bed and I gagged slightly on his huge penis. Adding to his pleasure, I continued my mouth action and lightly rolled his balls in my hand.

"Zoe, fuck!" Jordan was close and I increased the suction of my mouth causing my cheeks to hollow as I exhaled through my nose. His balls pulled up and out of my hand.

"I'm going to come. Christ, babe."

As his warning of impending eruption neared, I added one finger to his puckered ass and pushed up.

"For fucks sake! Zoe. Fuck!"

His explicit language was music to my ears as his hot cum hit the back of my throat. I greedily gulped the warm liquid that readily slipped down my throat. Slowly, I felt Jordan's body go languid beneath me and I slipped his cock from my mouth.

He reached for me and cradled me to his chest. His heart was beating a furious staccato beneath my ear. Jordan tilted my chin up and took my mouth in a deep kiss.

"My beautiful woman. You take my breath away." He pulled me back into his chest as we snuggled against each other.

"Just brushing up on some tricks you taught me." I grinned as I remembered Jordan telling me how to please him during our few months of sexual intimacy.

"Just so you know, no brushing up needed on that one. You are officially at expert level. Any better, and you would be performing CPR on me."

I laughed as he swatted me on my ass.

"Come on, Miss Blowjob expert. A shower is in order." Jordan picked me up off the bed as if I weighed nothing at all and headed to the bathroom.

Leisurely we washed each other with a lemony body wash that was one of my favorites. Jordan inhaled deeply as he turned off the water and reached for a towel to dry me off.

"Do you remember this body wash?" I asked.

"How could I forget? You got a sample from one of your friends and insisted we try it together. You loved it, so I kept supplying you with L'Occitane." He grinned at me in the mirror.

"Um, if I remember correctly, you had a jar of it sent to me from Nordstrom every month." I rolled my eyes at him.

"They should be sending a different fragrance every month."

"They do. You know, we will have to talk about your obsessive disorder, right?" I threw my towel at him and hopped back in bed and under the covers.

Jordan followed close behind and pulled me in his arms as he nudged my legs apart and slid one of his between them.

"Don't get comfortable. I don't remember inviting you to spend the night in my bed," I said as my lids drooped.

He kissed the top of my head. "I waited 10 years to get back in your bed. You will pretty much have to get one of those restraining order you are famous for to keep me out," he murmured.

I pushed out of his arms to sit straight up in the bed.

"Christ. I'm kidding, babe," he said as he reached for me again.

I batted his hands away and glared at him.

"Your driver and limo are still outside my house. I need to pack for my trip to San Francisco tomorrow." I scrambled to get out of bed, but Jordan had a death grip around my waist inhibiting my movement.

He easily pulled me back down to his chest. "I sent the driver away when I made our snack."

"You went outside naked? Are you out of your mind?" I squealed.

"Or I used my cell phone. Relax, Zoe. Now about tomorrow—I will take you to the airport. The alarm is set, so I can even help you pack. Would you allow me to do that?"

When I did not answer right away, he put his lips to my ear and whispered, "Please, pretty lady?" Not missing a beat to seduce me, he pulled the lobe of my ear into his mouth.

Oh God. Why can't I resist this man? My pussy was wet and clenching with need again.

As if on cue, Jordan slid his hand down my body and slipped two fingers into me. He pulled out his wet digits and rubbed them across my lips, then lowered his head to kiss my lips, then nuzzled his head into my neck. I arched my head up to give him better access. He slowly made his way down to my breasts, feasting on one, then the other.

"I love your breasts. Plump and beautiful." He paid homage to the globes, pulling deeply on my nipples.

I moved my leg against his cock which was hard again.

"I don't have any more condoms, babe," he said.

"I have in an IUD."

"So I can't get you knocked up?"

"I'm 99.9% sure."

"Even if my boys swim like Michael Phelps?"

"Not even then."

"What if I gave you an unwanted present, say, like an STD?"

"You won't."

"How do you know that?" he asked.

"Because you love your cock way too much to take chances without a condom."

Jordan shouted out a laugh that shook both of us. We laughed at the old joke between us.

When we first became intimate and spoke of birth control, Jordan said that any guy that had sex without a condom must not love his dick very much.

"I don't want you to regret anything between us. You'll have a full report of my last blood work that was done a couple of months ago. I have not had sex…"

"I don't want to know," I said, covering my ears. It pained me to think of other women that had touched him as intimately as I have.

"I know you're clean, since there hasn't been anyone but me," he said, as he continued to kiss his way down my belly. He paused to dip his tongue in my navel.

"Don't gloat."

"Just sayin'." He pushed my legs apart with broad shoulders then ducked his head between them. His glorious lips latched onto my clit.

I fisted my hands in his hair and held on to his head. Jordan always told me to hold his head in place when he goes down on me so that he doesn't move if I don't want him to. It was one way of him doing what I liked without me having to tell him. So I held onto his head like it was my lifeline.

My orgasm knocked my knees from under me and I splintered into a million pieces. My head trashed against the pillow as I begged for mercy.

"Please, please, no more, Jordan, please." With a heaving chest and short puffs of breath, I whimpered for Jordan to let go of my clit.

"Not going to happen if you don't let me up, babe."

Unaware that my hands were still clenched in his hair, he was held firmly between my legs. I gladly let go as he reminded me, but he was grinning.

"Glad you remembered a few things about owning your pleasure. Now it's almost midnight and you need to sleep." Jordan pulled the cover over us.

"But what about you? I mean, you need..."

"Oh, I will collect. Goodnight, beautiful Zoe."

My lids fluttered shut. I fell into a deep sleep.

CHAPTER 16

I WOKE WITH THE SMELL OF COFFEE WAFTING IN THE air. Actually, it was right in front of my nose. Grateful, I sat up and took a slow sip of the hot, sweet liquid, then another and another. Finally, I opened my eyes and…

"What the hell? Jordan."

"Well, good morning to you, too. Drink your coffee. You have plenty of time to shower and dress before heading to the airport." Jordan's voice was calm, as I tried to grapple with what my eyes were seeing.

Jordan had showered and dressed in a grey tailored suit with a purple shirt and grey tie. He looked like the savvy man that he is. He towered over me as he put a tray of food on my lap. I snapped my mouth shut as I gazed into his gorgeous blue eyes surrounded by long lashes. He moved around my bedroom as if quite familiar with it. Hard to believe last night was the first time he set foot in my home.

"OK. Talk to me, because right now I am freaking out. I don't even want to know what time it is so I don't have to panic about that too." I had more to say to him. A hell of a lot more, but right now I was hungry, still sleepy and in need of some answers.

"What would you like to know?" he asked calmly as he walked to my closet and took down my suitcase, put it on the bed and went back to the closet.

"Would you get the hell out of my closet?" I almost yelled at him as I shoveled a piece of scrumptious toast with fig preserves in my mouth.

Jordan came to the closet door and leaned against the frame. With feet crossed at his ankle and arms folded over his chest, he cocked an eyebrow at me.

"Why are you dressed?"

"Because I can't stay naked all day." His smart remark did not help my anxiety level.

"I mean, where did you get clothes, and how come I didn't hear the alarm, and what time is it? Because I simply can't miss my flight. I have too much going on today." I moved the tray and got out of bed. My hair was hanging down to my breasts in disarray and I didn't have a stitch of clothing on.

"Zoe, trust me to take care of you. I said I would make sure you got up in time and I have. Now if you dilly-dally about your shower and doing your hair and makeup, you may have to miss seeing me pack your suitcase for your trip." He sauntered back into my closet.

I bolted into the shower, and in record time, my hair and makeup were done.

"I know you are not one for power suits, but I rather like this one. It will be perfect for the great weather in San Francisco." Jordan held up a gorgeous buttercup color pencil skirt suit with a baby blue silk blouse. The jacket was short and flirty but professional.

"Where did you get those clothes?" I eyed him wearily.

"From your closet."

"Yes, but I mean, I should know my own clothes...you know what, never mind." I grabbed the clothing from him and put them on. I paired the suit with a pair of Vince Camuto peony pumps from my closet. At least I knew these were mine. I bought them a couple weeks ago on one of Mia's shopping spree trips. Back in the bedroom, I slipped a long silver necklace over my head and put in matching earrings that complimented the outfit.

"Well, that should about do it for you. You look absolutely gorgeous." Jordan had my suitcase in his hand and headed to the door.

I rolled my eyes as he walked past me. I was so totally fucked for this trip. Why in the hell did I agree that he should spend the night? God only knew what he packed for me. I had no one to blame but myself, so if something was forgotten, I'd just have to buy it when I got there. I dashed in the living room and grabbed my phone, purse, and computer bag and headed to the garage.

"What the hell?" I muttered.

Jordan was standing at the front door waiting for me. His driver and black Range Rover was in my driveway.

Again, I was too rushed to care. I walked past him with a glare in my eyes.

He smiled and patted my ass.

I looked at the driver, but thankfully he was conveniently looking anywhere but at us. I slid in the back seat and Jordan sat beside me.

He reached for my hand, squeezing gently, then ran his thumb over my knuckles.

Grateful that I was on my way to the airport, I gave him a weak smile.

"I need to call Andre," I said and reached for my phone.

"Here, allow me." Jordan pulled my phone from the inside pocket of my purse and swiped the screen.

I must remember to use the zipper on my purse.

"I'm not sure he is available," Jordan said as he handed me the phone.

"How would you know anything about my staff and their schedule? He always calls me if there are important meetings or a trip coming up. It's just weird that he's not picking up." I pulled the phone from my ear and looked at the screen to make sure I was calling the correct number then put it back to my ear. "It went straight to voicemail. I better call Veronica to see what's going on." I pulled the phone from my ear again and scrolled through to find her number.

Jordan placed his hand over mine.

I looked up at him with raised brows.

"Babe. It's almost eight. Your flight was at seven. Andre is well on his way. I sent him on the flight," Jordan calmly said as he flipped down a sleek compartment from the back of the passenger seat in front of him and opened it to a computer with his company logo.

Jordan Dawson Enterprises.

I put my head on the headrest behind me. Jordan was consulting with something on the computer, but he sensed that I was looking at him. He had the audacity to flash his 'panty dropping smile' as Veronica calls it, and winked.

"Please tell me what else is going on. I don't have time for all these surprises. And how the hell am I getting to my meetings on time?" I asked.

"You will be taking my company jet and will make it there on time as it will fly faster than the commercial airline. A car will take you straight to your first meeting where you will meet up with Andre." He seemed happy to deliver the news flash for my change in plans.

"Here's the deal, Jordan Dwight Dawson." I squinted my grey eyes at him. "Before yesterday, I did not have a personal chef, slash personal groomer, slash person to pack my suitcase for me. Nor did I have someone to rearrange my schedule. And how the hell did Andre not freak out when I didn't show up for my flight?"

I'm not sure that I should feel relieved about him looking into all the details of my trip, but he did make me late by not waking me up in time.

"I got his number from your phone." He slid his large warm hand behind my neck and lightly massaged the area.

"I have a passcode on my phone."

"I hacked it."

"What? That's illegal."

"Sue me."

"No more surprises, Jordan. Promise?" I asked, as I answered an incoming text from Jenna saying that she missed chatting with me yesterday and hoped for success on my trip. She also said to check my email when I have time.

"The year you were born for a passcode. Really, Zoe? I could have hacked that in my sleep. I reset it with a new passcode. No one will hack into your phone now," he said as his thumb worked its way over my neck.

We pulled into the private terminal at Hobby Airport and did the whole security thing then headed onto the tarmac to board the airplane. A pretty middle-aged flight attendant greeted me.

"Good morning, and welcome aboard, Miss Caine," she said as I headed to the seating area of the plane.

I took in the opulence of the aircraft and could not be anything but impressed. The interior was dark beige with light cream leather seats. The top of the seats sported Jordan's company logo. There was dark wood throughout the aircraft, which complimented the elegant interior. It was obviously top of the line in comfort and had as many amenities as space would allow. I slid into one of the seats and Jordan took the one beside me.

"Let me guess. You're going to San Francisco as well?" I asked, since I had no idea that Jordan would be going with me.

"Affirmative," he replied as he secured my seat belt.

"Don't you have like a job, you know, a company that needs your attention instead of traipsing across the country with me?" I demurely crossed my legs and looked out the window.

"No, I don't have a job. I own the company which has its perks, such as traipsing across the country with my girl-friend."

I whipped my head in his direction and he looked right at me.

"Your girlfriend? When did that happen? Because I don't remember a conversation where we decided that this thing that happened last night between us will be repeated, much less agreeing to exclusivity in sexual intimacy." I responded. But then again, he may just have been kidding and wanted a rise out of me.

"Oh, make no doubt about it, Zoe. What happened be-tween us last night will be repeated again and again and... well you get the picture. And since you made a promise to me last night that you are mine, then I will do everything in my power to ward off any asshole that tries to make a pass at you."

There was a dangerous glint in his eyes but I was not ready to let this go. Hell no. He just got back from Europe, waltzed his way into my life and my bed, and now claimed that I was his girlfriend.

"I did not say that I was yours. I said that my pussy was," I said defiantly.

"Same difference. Every part of you is precious to me, but your pussy is precious and delicious." His hands reached over and rubbed my thighs pushing my skirt up to mid-thigh. "And now it is mine, so don't get any foolish ideas otherwise." His jaw was set and there was not a hint of smile or playfulness on his face.

"I'm sorry to interrupt, Mr. Dawson, but a package was delivered for you. On your instructions we were waiting for it, so now we can take off."

Jordan thanked her and put the large manila envelope on the seat across from us.

The plane taxied out to the runway and soon we were off with Houston growing smaller in the distance below us.

"Is there Wi-Fi on the plane?" I asked.

"But of course," Jordan said as if that was a silly question. He moved to the other side of the aircraft that had four chairs and a conference table. Touching buttons on a side panel, a flat screen TV and two flat screen computer monitors gently rose onto the table. He turned the TV channel to Bloomberg television and turned on the computers.

I moved to sit in a seat across from him, then navigated through to my email.

Just then the flight attendant wheeled in a silver tray loaded with food and drinks.

"Nice spread," I said, picking up a glass of juice and sipping on the cold tangy liquid.

"I ordered your favorite omelet," Jordan said as he took the silver dome lid off one of the plates.

My mouth watered at the site of the succulent food. I dug in to my omelet with bacon, onions, peppers and cheese. I took a few moments to appreciate the fine bone china plates and cups. Everything had Jordan's company logo on it. I looked across at Jordan to see him staring at me.

"What?" I asked.

"Nothing. I just like to watch you eat. I like that you enjoy food, like real food, and not try to pretend you're not hungry. I also love feeding you and sometimes even get jealous of the food in your mouth, wishing it were my cock you were sucking on."

Leave it to Jordan to discuss crude anatomy even around a dinner table. I smirked at him.

"I can't always have your cock in my mouth. There were and still are other useful things I need to put in there, such as food," I replied as I smiled at the silly conversation.

"Yeah, well a guy could wish, right?" he responded as he dug into his own breakfast.

Sitting back after doing justice to the great offering of food, I sipped on strong black coffee and took in Jordan's appearance once more. He was simply gorgeous. It was that simple and I was slowly realizing just how much he has accomplished. He was admired for his astute and aggressive business sense, making not only himself a load of money, but his investors as well.

Jordan was reading a page on the computer of the *Wall Street Journal*. Suddenly he looked up and caught me staring at him. A smile lifted the edge of his lips as he leaned back in his chair and sipped his coffee as well. We settled in a few moments of companionable silence, each lost in our own thoughts.

The flight attendant quietly picked up the plates, reloaded the tray and headed back to the galley. I went back to reading my personal email. I clicked on the one Jenna sent and gasped, my eyes going wide in surprise.

CHAPTER 17

"OH MY GOD. OH MY GOD," I REPEATED, AS I HOPPED UP and down in my seat. Looking at Jordan, I turned the screen toward him and showed him the image that caused this excited reaction from me.

"Look, Jordan!" I exclaimed, as he stared blankly at the screen.

"I'm sorry, babe, but I have no idea what that is, but it has obviously made you happy...or sad, since you're crying now." He got up and knelt beside me pulling me into his arms.

"Oh, Jordan. It's a photo of a positive pregnancy test. Jenna is pregnant! That's why she wanted me to read my email and call her." I sniffled as I explained what the lines on the stick meant. "I can't wait to land so I can talk to her." I blotted my eyes with the napkin.

"You can use this phone on the airplane." He indicated the small sleek phone at my elbow. "Or your cell phone. This is a private jet, so we get to travel and communicate a little differently from the commercial airlines. Not as many restrictions," he explained.

I immediately picked up the phone beside me and placed a call to Jenna, who answered right away. We were both laughing and crying at the same time.

"Jenna. You're going to be a mom and I will be an aunt." It dawned on me that I would have a niece or nephew and I couldn't wait.

"I know. I've been feeling off for about a week and this morning I woke up puking. I knew right then. So I took the test and showed David and we haven't stopped crying since," Jenna said. "I don't mind being sick at all because it means that I'm pregnant. David is calling the doctor. Hopefully I will be able to see her today or tomorrow. I think I'm about five or six weeks along."

Jenna made a three-way call with Aunt Suzette. Right away she was frantic with worry.

Between her bouts of joyful tears, Aunt Suzette said, "I will head to Austin today, Jenna. I want to make sure you take care of yourself."

"Oh, Aunt Suzette, your baby is having a baby," I said to her, and all of us started with fresh tears of joy again. Jordan sat quietly beside me but with a smile on his face as he rubbed my legs and held my hand. We parted ways with a promise to reconnect sometime tomorrow.

"OK, pretty lady. It's time for your nap. We still have a couple hour's flight ahead of us." Jordan led me to the back of the aircraft. We passed another set of chairs and a small sofa. The rest of the airplane had a wall with a door. Opening the door, Jordan ushered me in ahead of him.

The space was a small bedroom with a full size bed and a small bathroom in the corner. It was stocked with all the creature comforts one could imagine for traveling comfortably.

"This is nice; like exquisite, yet comfortable nice," I said.

"I'm glad you like it. I had it custom built a year ago with you in mind," Jordan said, as he took off his jacket and hung it behind the door.

"You had what made?" I asked.

"Why, the airplane, of course," he said nonchalantly.

"Wait. What?" I was trying to wrap my head around what he said.

"I had this airplane built a year ago and I thought that you would appreciate a soundproof cabin so I can fuck you and introduce you to the mile high club. I know you're a screamer, and you can scream all you want in here."

As if talking about buying a car with leather or cloth interior, Jordan continued. "Not only that, but I thought you would appreciate all the workspace it offers for trips we would be making and room for family and friends as well."

Jordan was slowly undressing me.

I was dumbfounded with all this information. I had a lot of questions, but then again, I was saving up for a come to Jesus session about how sure he is about me—us.

"You have a sinfully gorgeous body and I am shamelessly addicted to it."

I stood naked in front of Jordan as he kissed me. I looped my arms around his neck.

Easily he picked me up and placed me on the plush white down comforter. I sank into the cool bedding as he quickly undressed. Jordan stood at the side of the bed as I gazed unabashedly as his perfect manhood. His cock was long and hard.

He moved his hand up and down his length. I reached for him and he moved closer to my mouth. Flipping onto my front, I knelt in front of him, as he remained standing. I took his beautiful cock deep into my mouth, and unlike last night when I slowly pulled him to the back of my throat...I sucked him fast and hard. The taste of his essence was like an aphrodisiac on my tongue.

Jordan braced himself on the ceiling of the airplane as I sucked him off.

His velvety smooth skin slid in and out of my mouth. I increased my suction and held his dark pink balls in my hand, playing with them as I added pleasure to this moment of wicked ecstasy.

Jordan groaned above me as he took in the sight of my mouth, and my tongue on his cock.

"Ahh. Fuck." His breath hissed through his teeth. Jordan moved his hips toward me and held my head in place. He fucked my mouth with his cock. "I'm coming, babe."

I was more than ready to taste him. The pleasure he received from my mouth was music to my ears as he let out a low growl, emptying his load of cum into the back of my throat. Greedily, I swallowed and continued to suck him off, making sure that I got every drop from his generous cock.

Slowly, Jordan pulled out of my mouth.

I licked my lips and looked up at him with a smile on my face.

"Greedy little wench. You will be the death of me with your blowjobs, and what a way I would gladly go." Jordan lay beside me on the bed then pulled me into his arms and tucked my head under his chin.

I threw my leg over his hip as he slid a hand over my ass and between my legs. With leisurely strokes, he rubbed my pussy on the outside, enjoying the smoothness of my skin. Over and over he touched me as my body started to squirm, wanting more. Sensing my need, he pushed a finger inside the wet engorged lips of my sex that was begging for action. Adding another finger to the mix, Jordan continued with his slow assault on my sensitive flesh. He increased the tempo and my hips undulated with the actions of his hand.

I was getting mindless with need and about to tell him to fuck me already when I felt his hard as wood cock on my leg.

Suddenly, Jordan got up and put on a long white robe, saying he'd be right back. He left the small cabin and was back in a few seconds. He locked the door behind him. I saw that he was opening the manila envelope that the flight attendant delivered to him earlier before takeoff.

"These are my test results." He handed me papers with lab results.

I quickly scanned to see all negatives and reached for him. "You held up our departure to get your test results delivered?" I asked, although not at all surprise that he was able to obtain his test results from his physician.

"I have never had sex without a condom. You are the only person I ever wanted to go bareback with."

"Even when I was in college you used a condom."

"I didn't want to slip up and get you pregnant. I wanted you to finish your studies."

"Come. Make it happen," I said, reaching for him.

"I explained my reasons for requesting my records to Dr. Richards this morning."

I laughed at his ridiculousness. Trust Jordan to be totally unconventional and go after what he wanted, which was one of the reasons why he was rich and successful. If there was a way to make something happen that he deemed important, Jordan would do it.

"Knowing that I was getting ready to pursue you, I readied everything in my life to make sure you had no reasons to resist me. Having you back is of utmost importance to me, Zoe."

I blinked away the tears as he cupped my face in hands. Swooping down, he kissed me fast and fierce. I felt my pussy clench in anticipation of feeling his cock in me.

"Now, where was I?" Jordan leaned me back on the bed and knelt between my knees. Spreading my legs, he looked down at my smooth bare and now glistening womanhood. "Just fucking beautiful." Jordan took my hand and placed it between my legs. "Touch yourself," he said. His eyes narrowed to slits as he watched me slid my fingers over my warm bare pussy.

My breath caught in my throat as I looked at him above me.

"Play with yourself," he repeated again in a no nonsense voice as his hands ran slowly down the backs of my legs.

I rubbed along my labia and down the slit of my wetness as he instructed, all the while still looking at him as he gazed at my hand.

His pupils dilated and he drew in slow deep breaths.

"Put a finger inside and swirl it around." His voice had gone low and it made me hotter than ever causing my pussy to drip with my sticky essence.

"Now add another finger, then pull it out. I want to see it on your fingers."

I pulled out and lifted my fingers for his inspection.

He inhaled the scent of my pleasure. "Put it in your mouth and suck the juices off your fingers."

I brought my fingers to my mouth and pulled one inside, drawing in slowly. I paused at my lips and rubbed the other finger on the bottom lip, then pushed the finger into my mouth and licked it off clean.

Jordan took a sharp breath as his eyes followed my actions.

"That's just fucking hot," he mumbled. He came down to my mouth and took my lips in a deep kiss, sucking my bottom lip into his hot mouth.

My breath increased as I started to squirm below him.

Jordan made me repeat the action several times before he pulled me onto his massive erection. We both mewled with our own sounds of pleasure as he advanced into me, slowly at first, then increased the tempo of his hips. He pulled my legs together so they were pointing straight up and in front of his face. My bottom was hitting on his legs. Jordan continued to pound his shaft into me. The look on his face was fierce as he gazed down at our joined bodies.

My pussy was sliding on his cock, my juices dripping between our joined bodies. "Jordan!" I yelled out.

Following right behind me, he groaned as he filled me for the first time ever with his cum deep inside my body. He continued to move slowly in me as he emptied every drop.

We looked at each other and listened to the sticky sound of his cum mixed with mine. A huge smile broke across his face. I grinned up foolishly at him as 10 years later we experience another first together.

"Unbelievable," Jordan said. He stopped moving and put my legs around his waist.

My limbs were tired and all I wanted to do was snuggle into Jordan and fall asleep.

He detangled our bodies and got off the bed. Reaching in a corner compartment, he came out with a box of wet wipes and cleaned me off first, then himself. Jordan lifted me up and pulled the cover and sheet from under my body then slid us both under the linens.

I inhaled his unique scent and slowly fell asleep.

CHAPTER 18

"Babe."

I open my eyes and look up at Jordan. He was dressed and sitting on the side of the bed rubbing my back. I stretched and yawned. The past couple of hours came rushing back to my foggy brain. A slow smile crossed my face as my eyes fluttered shut again.

"Babe, you need to get up. Come on, lazy bones." Jordan pulled the covers off of me. "Sorry I kept you up late last night. I know you're tired, but we'll be landing soon." He handed me a large fluffy towel and inclined his head towards the tiny shower.

I got up, quickly showered off my body, then got dressed. I went into the main cabin. Jordan was sitting at the table working on one of the computers.

"She lives. I had some fresh coffee made for us." He pulled me down on his lap and nuzzled my neck with his face.

I poured some coffee into a cup and relaxed in his arms while I drank the hot liquid. "What are you working on?" I asked out of curiosity.

"I just purchased another high-rise building in downtown Houston," he answered, as he looked back at the screen with graphs, charts, symbols and numbers.

They all looked Greek to me, but he was quite interested in whatever they were.

"Another? I didn't know you hand one there in the first place."

"That is because you totally and completely cut me out of your life, including my business acquisitions that were sure to be on the news or in newspapers. But since you avoided business news of any kind…" he playfully tapped me on my nose.

"Hmm. So you moved back to Houston, bought a couple high-rise buildings. What else?"

Jordan threw his head back and laughed. I looked at him with raised brows. "Let me see…you want me to catch you up on my business dealing in Houston, or around the world? And I should do this in ten minutes?" he finished.

"Yup. Pretty much." I smiled at him sweetly.

"Smartass," he grumbled. "I have acquired several large commercial properties in and around the Houston area. I am building a condo with two hundred units in The Woodlands and bought a high-rise there that was going into bankruptcy. Let's see, there is also a hotel and golf course in Galveston and a couple other things I'm working on." He lifted me off his lap and led me to the seat across the isle, as we got ready for landing.

"Busy much?" I asked. My head spun with all that he has been working on over the past few months right under my nose.

"Oh, you know me. With time on my hands since you ignored me, I had to find something to do, and since time means money, I made some more while waiting for the right time to get you back."

The flight attendant came and cleaned the table, and shut off the computers and TV. A few minutes later the airplane landed easily. With renewed energy thanks to some great sex and sleep, I descended the stairs of the aircraft after thanking the captain and flight attendant.

We made our way to the new black Infiniti SUV waiting for us. The luggage was delivered in the back of the vehicle and we headed to my first meeting. Jordan made a few phone calls as I took in the lovely scenery of San Francisco.

The vehicle came to a stop at the main entrance of San Francisco General Hospital. Jordan placed a light kiss on my lips and got out. The driver opened my door and I walked around to the other side where Andre was waiting for me. He was chatting with Jordan about Napa.

I gave Andre a quick hug and waved goodbye to Jordan as he got back in the vehicle. I could not help but take note of several women that paused on their way in and out of the building giving appreciative looks at Jordan.

We walked to the professional building that housed the administrative part of the hospital. The sights and sounds of patients, doctors, nurses and other medical caregivers walking along the hallway or waiting in various offices reminded me of my own clinical nursing not that long ago.

The door to the elevator opened and we stepped in. Andre pressed the button for the 10th floor and looked at me with a grin on his face as if waiting for me to say something about our change in plans or the reason for such changes, but I didn't take the bait.

We stepped into the lobby. A woman at the desk informed us that the team we are meeting would be available in a few minutes.

Andre placed a call to the Houston office to check on the day's events and see if there were any immediate issues we needed to help with, but all was well and Veronica had the place running like a well-oiled machine. The only glitch this morning was Mrs. Royden, who requested we keep her on service and not take her nurse away since Robert and I were no longer together. Veronica said she reassured her that her nursing care would not be interrupted.

"Jordan seems to be a really nice guy," Andre said as we sat across from each other.

"Hmm," was the only response he got from me. Andre has heard bits and pieces of my past history with Jordan over the years, but had not met him until the night of my birthday party.

"Yeah. Must really suck to have someone chase after you for 10 years. And not just anyone, but *the* Jordan Dawson," Andre commented as he scrolled through his phone.

"Don't start, Andre, and don't go feeling sorry for him." I pulled my phone from my purse to check for messages.

"Oh crap!" I said, looking down at my phone. I still didn't know what the password was. I hadn't remembered to ask Jordan what it was and now I had no access to my phone or computer.

"What's up, boss?" Andre had a concerned look on his face.

"Um. Do you mind if I call Jordan on your phone? My battery seems to be on the blink." I made up the sorry excuse as Andre gave me his phone. I stared at the phone since it dawned on me that I didn't know Jordan's cell phone number. Think, think...

"So will you make the call or would you like for me to do it?"

I took a deep breath and handed the phone back to Andre. "Here's the deal, Andre. I, ah, I changed the passcode to my phone and computer and now I don't remember it." I avoided eye contact with him.

"So how do you propose to get access to your devices? I can try to hack into it, but am just not that good." He rubbed his chin as he tried to think of a solution to my dilemma.

"Please Google Jordan's company office in Houston and speak with his administrative assistant for me? Tell her I need to get a hold of Jordan on his personal cell phone." Yeah. I am proud of myself for being evasive and clever.

"Here you go. Helen, his assistant, needs to speak with you," Andre said passing me the phone.

Shit!

"This is Zoe Caine," I said.

"Miss Caine, I hope you had an uneventful trip to San Francisco this morning. I'm sorry, but I have strict orders from Mr. Dawson that if you ever call the office, I must speak to you personally to make sure you are well and whatever your needs are, I will endeavor to take care of them promptly." Ever the efficient administrative assistant, Helen was polite and professional.

"I'm fine, Helen. The flight went smoothly and all is well with me. I do need Jordan's cell phone number. I must have misplaced it somewhere." I knew that was a lame excuse but I was at an impasse.

Helen gave me the number and I jotted it down on a notepad. "Miss Caine, please allow me to call Mr. Dawson for you."

"That won't be necessary, Helen. I will call him myself, but thank you."

"I am so sorry, Miss Caine, but I have strict instructions from Mr. Dawson, that if you should call for him, I must call to give him a full report immediately to make sure that I have taken care of your issue to his satisfaction."

Really? I was trying to stay amenable with Jordan but this was just ridiculous. I thanked Helen for her help and told her I would hold on the line for Jordan. A few seconds later Jordan came on the line and Helen disconnected on her end.

"I need the passcode for my phone and computer." I got right to the reason for my call since I was feeling more than a little exasperated.

"The code for your phone is the last two numbers of the year I was born then the last two numbers of the year you were born."

My eyebrows shot up with the new code. I wanted to argue with him about it but I didn't have time.

"And the password for your computer is hotSexyZo30 with the s and z capitalized."

With that tidbit of information I got up and walked down the hall to have a few words in private with Jordan since I didn't want to do it with an audience.

"First of all, it is my phone, so my numbers should have come first, but more importantly, I cannot possibly use that password for my computer," I told him as I paced the quiet hallway.

"I want you to think about me as much as I do about you, so since you use your phone often you will do just that every time you make a call. Now why is the computer password a problem?" he asked.

"What if for some reason I need someone to access my computer? That is just not appropriate for me to tell my employees." My reason for not wanting to use the new password was plausible, but Jordan argued with me about it for another minute, all the while I could hear a hint of teasing in his voice. He finally told me that he could change my password to something more appropriate, but for today I would need to work with what I had.

I returned to the waiting area just in time. We were summoned to the conference room where we met with someone from the legal team, human resources, nursing services and accounting.

"Miss Caine, my name is Emma from hospital administration. I wanted to personally welcome you to San Francisco and thank you for expanding your nursing services to this area. As you know, nurses are in high demand and the shortage is great nationwide. We hope to form a partnership with your agency as we continue to serve the communities in our area." Emma seemed to be a few years older than me, but it was surprising that she is here from administration and seemed ready to sign my contract before the meeting even started.

"Thank you, Emma."

A middle-aged balding man nodded his head in Emma's direction and focused on me. "Miss Caine, I am Earl Newell from the legal team. We are honored that you have chosen San Francisco General to expand your agency and welcome you and your nurses with open arms. It is indeed a pleasure to be associated with such a stellar professional business owner as yourself. We have your file with accolades from many businesses including physicians from the Houston medical community about your agency, and the fine work that you have done to make so many hospitals run more efficiently as you provide much needed relief to full-time nursing staff."

I was thrilled that my agency's reputation is good and has always provided my nurses with training and education while expecting professionalism from every one of them, as they represented the agency in their workplace.

"Miss Caine, my name is Irene from Human Resources. I will be working closely with your office to maintain your employees' records, credentials and licenses. We are excited to work with your agency and look forward to have your nurses ready to work in our hospital just as soon as they are processed in our system."

And last, but not least, was the accountant that said he would expedite payment to the agency on a bi-weekly basis.

The attorney had our contracts ready to be signed and would be sending the signed documents via computer file to my office in Houston.

I looked it over with Andre as we focused on the most important part, such as protecting the nurses and agency in liability issues and other such matters. They had all the necessary operating and business licensing credentials for the agency. The meeting lasted a little over an hour and left my head spinning.

"Wow. So that went well." Andre sounded as impressed as I was about all the welcome speeches. My phone rang as we exited the elevator and made our way outside where the SUV and driver waited for us. Jordan's name flashed across my phone screen.

"Hi, pretty lady. How did it go?" he asked.

"Really good, actually. Better than I thought. I usually have to sell the agency and myself, then wait for them to get back to me." I sat in the back seat of the vehicle alongside Andre. "As a matter of fact, they offered me more than any of the hospitals in Houston. I think I am liking this city."

I laughed as I thought of the possibility of keeping my head well above water financially and that I'd be able to offer my employees better benefits and maybe, just maybe, an annual bonus.

"Great. Good luck with the rest of your day. A driver should be waiting outside for you," Jordan said.

"He was and we're on our way now, but please don't feel like you need to provide me with transportation. I could have easily rented a car."

"Allow me this," he said quietly.

"OK. Thank you. I'll talk to you later." I disconnected from the call.

Feeling less apprehensive now that the first contract was signed, I emailed my attorney and accountant regarding the contract so they could retrieve the file and keep for company records.

The second hospital meeting went smoothly as well, with the same welcome and happy to work with your agency speech. I was thrilled and phoned Veronica after the meeting to relay the news of our expansion with signed contracts.

Andre and I went to the new office where the receptionist and office manager met us.

"We had a great response to the ad for temp nurses, Miss Caine," Bianca, the office manager, said as she led us down the hall to her office.

We sat to discuss the past few weeks of operations.

"I pulled the files for the first five nurses applying for the Director of Nursing position. They have all the qualifications and work history that you requested in your email."

"I look forward to meeting with them. There are more interviews tomorrow as well?" I asked. I remember Andre mentioning two days of interviews.

She confirmed that there were three more applicants that I will meet with tomorrow. I felt assured that I would find the new DON and get the nurses hired and processed as soon as possible.

"We're going to lunch with Bianca at a new place down the street," Andre said. "Since we are in California, we might as well enjoy the great cuisine they have to offer." He grinned at me and I readily agreed.

The time simply flew by and I was surprised to see that it was 6 p.m. when we finally left the office to go to our hotel.

"Well, well. We have not one, but two, chauffeured driven vehicles. Hmm. Which one you will choose?" asked Andre.

My heart skipped a beat as I looked up to see Jordan leaning against the Infiniti SUV that we arrived in this morning. He was dressed in jeans with a button down shirt with a light blazer. His lean frame made my fingers twitchy. I couldn't wait to run my hands across his body. Magazines and billboard male models had absolutely nothing over this man. He oozed sexuality.

Jordan opened the SUV door as I approached and took my computer bag and purse from my hands. He placed a full-blown kiss on my lips. Lifting his head as if not satisfied with just one kiss, he kissed me again.

I avoided looking at Andre and the others and quickly slid into the car.

Although the day flew by and my brain was busy planning for the expansion and extra responsibility of the business, I found myself thinking about Jordan and the strange turn of events in my life.

I was surprised at how quickly my feelings of displeasure toward him had turned to desire to be with him. As I looked at Jordan, I realized that many things had changed about him.

Physically his shoulders are broader and muscles are more pronounced. His face and jaw has more of a chiseled look than 10 years ago and his demeanor is more serious, more assertive and aggressive. Even his lovemaking is more masterful and domineering. Just thinking of the way he handled my body made me shiver with anticipation for more. Jordan was so much more of everything than he was 10 years ago.

"Thanks for recommending the restaurant, Jordan. I can't wait for sushi tonight. Hell, I may even go for a Saki bomb with a bottle of Sapporo," Andre said.

"Ben should enjoy it. Try the sashimi as well," Jordan replied as we parted ways with Andre. I had no idea what plans Jordan had for us but we seem to be headed downtown.

Jordan pulled me into his arms and placed his chin on my head.

"I had some business to discuss with David today. He told me about the pregnancy and I told him about us being together again," he said.

He seemed a little uneasy since I have literally not had time to tell anyone that we've been in each other's company since last night. The only person that knew the extent of the relationship thus far was Andre, and I knew he wouldn't say anything unless I did.

"So, I thought you may want to tell your sister before he does."

I raised a quizzing eyebrow at him, surprised that he would be talking about us being together so soon. I was not sure that I knew where we were going with this thing between us or how long it will last. Maybe I was just kidding myself and might as well face the fact that Jordan was hell-bent on everyone knowing about us.

"OK. I will call Jenna and the other girls when we get... By the way, I have no idea about my plans anymore while I'm here except for tomorrow during the day," I said.

My body curled into his chest and I lay my head on his shoulder. He kissed the top of my head and ran his fingers along my side, slowing the action as he approached the side of my breast. He lightly rubbed the side of my breast through my clothing and my body immediately responded. My nipples puckered up which did not escape his attention.

One side of his lip lifted in a sexy smile as he continued to touch me. I lifted my face to his and he bent down to kiss me.

"I missed you, baby. Glad you had a productive day. I just want you to relax this evening, and although I have a few things planned for you, we will stay in."

All right then. Well, that settled any questions that I had about going out or staying in tonight.

"Hmm," I replied and he laughed huskily, taking my one groan for contentment and he was right. At this moment, I felt at ease and peaceful.

CHAPTER 19

THE VEHICLE CAME TO A STOP AT THE RITZ CARLTON hotel. The doorman opened the door and ushered us inside. I took in the opulence of the lobby with marble floors and elegant chandeliers. A young man met us inside the door and escorted us to a private set of elevators.

"Welcome back, Mr. Dawson. Miss," he said. He used the key card to open the door.

"Thank you, Robbie," replied Jordan. He kept a possessive arm around my waist. I motioned that I can help with my computer bag and purse, but Jordan would not let me.

"Have a great evening, sir," Robbie said as the elevator came to a stop.

We stepped into a lobby that seemed to have been converted into an office. There were at least five people buzzing around on phones and computers.

Jordan took my hand and led me down a hallway and toward a set of doors.

"Sorry to bother you, Mr. Dawson, if I may have a minute." A short balding gentleman addressed Jordan.

"Sure. James, this is Miss Zoe Caine. Zoe, one of my attorneys, James Moore." We shook hands as Jordan made the introduction and I stepped inside the door that Jordan opened while he spoke with his attorney.

"You wanted a report on unit four in Houston. There are actually two more with another holding company and they want an additional fifty million for those two which brings the total to a hundred and fifty million."

The difference between Jordan's business and mine is that I speak in hundreds and thousands when it comes to money, whereas Jordan... Well, I was more enlightened about his financial status as the hours goes by.

They walked into an office, but Jordan left the door open.

I looked around the area and noticed that we were in the penthouse suite. It was plush and extravagant. The decor was expensive from floor to ceiling and once again, I was reminded how much life has changed for Jordan, but he seemed to take it all in stride. I was starting to appreciate all the sacrifices he had made in his personal and professional life. Many times he acquires companies in a hostile takeover or outbid others for prime commercial real estate.

They were only in the office for a few minutes when Jordan and James walked back to the door.

"Have Jeremy look over the documents tonight. Tell him to use his judgment about their demands and we will work more on the deal tomorrow." He showed James out of the suite and joined me by the window.

"My company budget could easily afford such humble accommodations," I teased him and absorbed the view of the magnificent city below. The suite had several rooms with elegant furnishings and decor.

"Glad you approve," Jordan said as he step behind me and circled my waist with both arms. Clasping me in a tight embrace, he rocked us gently from side to side. I felt his warm breath on my neck.

"Hm. You get E for effort and A+ for comfort."

He laughed softly against my neck. "You have always been easy to please."

"Who would not be pleased with all this?" I responded.

"You would be surprised, but I'm glad you're relaxed. You work way too many hours."

Now it was my turn to laugh. "Say's the kettle..." Ever since we met when I was in college, Jordan has pushed himself to achieve his goals and that meant working an insane number of hours in any given week.

After a few moments of light banter and caressing, Jordan led me to the sofa where he sat me down and took off my shoes. He propelled me to lie down while he massaged my feet and calves.

Bliss. Pure bliss.

"This will be the end of our evening." I peeked up at him then closed my eyes again.

"Nah. I won't let you off so easy, but I want you to regenerate your energy. I have big plans for you tonight." I opened one eye and looked at him. His wicked smile lit up his face.

"By the way, you don't need to have your administrative assistant call you with a report if I need to get in touch with you through her. It's a waste of her time." I needed to put down some ground rules with Jordan since I didn't want his employees looking after me.

"No problem at all. I need to know that you are OK and taken care of. Of course I will make sure that you never need to go through anyone to get to me starting tomorrow. I'm sorry that I didn't give you the codes. It won't happen again."

I saw that he will not budge on this issue so I let it go. "I do need to call Jenna," I said, feeling guilty that I hadn't taken the time to do so already. A smile crossed my face as I remembered that she was pregnant.

"Here is your phone." He pulled my phone off the coffee table where I set it earlier. "Or you can Skype, FaceTime, Tango...whatever works. Let me know," Jordan said. He got up to give me some privacy and headed to the bedroom area.

I called Jenna and we chatted about her pregnancy all over again. Aunt Suzette was with her like a clucking mother hen and Jenna loved every minute of it.

"So, Jordan and I are back together."

I figured the best way to let those closest to me know was to get to the point and fast. I have zero interest in being in the social media and they had zero interest in me, but I was well aware that being with Jordan was going to make the headlines sooner or later. When we were dating, everyone thought he was with Celia or Tara since they were photographed in public often. He made sure to keep me out of the limelight for many reasons, and as I look back, I appreciated that only those close to us knew we were an item.

As much as our breakup hurt me emotionally, it was also embarrassing, but at least I did not have to do the whole hiding and changing my lifestyle due to the media. Whatever emotions I had to deal with were done in private and among friends and family.

"What? Jordan Dawson? I mean, I can't believe it happened so fast." Jenna was shocked, but not as surprised as I thought she would be. Hmm. Interesting.

"Well, funny thing happened the other night. When we talked earlier this week and I told you about me planning to break up with Robert... Well, Jordan was already coming on the scene. I suppose I didn't want to resist him in the end. I mean, I just...I believe what he had to say. It all happened so fast and now we are in San Francisco together."

Jenna momentarily forgot about her nausea and was relaying our conversation to Aunt Suzette. It was weird having to wait and listen to what could have been a three-way conversation but they were both happy that we worked it out and were together again. I finally ended the conversation after about fifteen minutes later and made another call. This time I made it a three-way call since I was feeling very much like a recorder.

"OK, y'all. I am in San Francisco with Jordan." I was not one to use southern slang, but this time called for just that.

"Oh. My. God," were the first words out of Mia's mouth.

"I knew it," Veronica chimed in.

"Unlike someone else that Veronica and I know, I will totally kiss and tell. I won't do the TMI thing but..."

I did not get much of a rise from Mia other than a huff and her saying that this was about me, not her and Philippe.

"Well, let's just say I am now a proud member of the mile high club." I started off with that bit of information as the girls squealed and wanted more details than I was going to divulge with Jordan being in the other room.

"So, our girl got some great loving and now she is not holding back. Will there be some naughty spankings on the way like in *Fifty Shades of Grey*? You know, the Christian dude? 'Cause that shit is totally hot," said Mia.

Trust her to take conversation to another level. She had never been one to hide her sexual fantasies and was always complaining that there were more vanilla guys out there than girls.

Mia and Veronica were excited about the changes I was making in my personal life and were asking so many questions that I threatened to cut the conversation short if they did not settle down. We talked for another ten minutes about Jenna's pregnancy before signing off.

I went in search of Jordan in the well-appointed suite and wondered again how he had time to make all the changes in my travel itinerary. He was working on his laptop computer but closed it as I entered the bedroom. A chill went down my spine as he advanced toward me. I could not help but think that he looked like a predator, lithe and graceful.

"All done?" he asked. That's all it took for my pulse to accelerate. Hearing his low sexy voice propelled me into a sensuous state of need.

"Yes. So now they know that we are traveling companions."

Jordan growled as he pulled me into his broad chest and tilted my chin. "Traveling companion, my ass." He delved into my mouth with his tongue. The kiss quickly became carnal between us.

Unable to deny the passion that was fast building deep in my core, I whimpered as sexual arousal quickened between us.

My hands trembled as I loosened his tie and unbuttoned his shirt. The shirt opened to expose his broad chest and I had no misguided notion that this man could not make me forget everything about myself or take down any barrier I ever had against his advances.

Jordan stripped me of my clothing in record time. I stood in front of him in my shoes and underwear as his eyes roamed over my body.

"Absofuckingdelightful."

"Is that a word?" I panted.

"It is in my book," he replied.

My hand rubbed the erection tenting his pants. He groaned as I pulled his huge cock toward me. No longer able to deny myself his body, I pulled off his belt and unzipped his pants taking it down to his ankles along with his boxers.

His gorgeous cock bobbed up toward his belly button. I fell to my knees and took him in my mouth. With one swift motion I pulled him in to the back of my throat. Jordan moaned above me as I started to move my mouth and tongue to pleasure him.

"Damn, baby. Damn," he said through clenched teeth. He held onto my head and guided my mouth over him, taking control of my movement.

I pulled on his length, paying close attention to the dark purple tip of his cock. I inhaled the smell of his manhood, as the soft warm skin of his cock glided easily across my tongue. I pushed my face into the small patch of dark blond hair above his penis as I concentrated on his pleasure.

Jordan's head was thrown back, quick breaths puffing through his clenched teeth. I gently scraped my teeth along the length of his cock when he shattered and come apart in my mouth.

"Fuckkkk! Ah." His cum shot to the back of my throat. I gulped the warm salty fluid and swallowed. I released his cock which was still hard as Jordan pulled me up into a hug, backing us up to the bed. We both fell onto the soft mattress. His labored breathing returned to normal while we cuddled.

Jordan recovered and sat up slowly in the bed. He pulled off the rest of our clothing and we settled in the middle of the king size bed. A few minutes later, he sat up and straddled me at my knees.

"Well, well. My pretty lady has an insatiable appetite for my body," he murmured as I squirmed beneath him.

He leaned over to take one of my nipples into his mouth and rubbed the other between his fingers. His hot mouth slid over my skin as he paid homage to my body.

I felt his erection between my legs, which excited me even more. I reached between us and wrapped my hand around his cock.

"Tell me what you want, babe," he whispered at my ear as he placed light kisses along my neck.

"I want you," I gasped as he nipped my earlobe.

"What would you like me to do?"

"I want you to fuck me."

"Say it again, Zoe."

"I want you to fuck my pussy, Jordan." I was frantic with need as I urged his body to capitulate with mine.

"Is that pussy mine?" All movement stopped and my eyes opened to see him looking at me.

"Yes," I whispered.

He sank his hard cock into my wet folds now drenched with need. Pushing mercilessly into me, Jordan's cock went deep into my core leaving no question of his ownership of my body.

I was aware that I was guarding my heart. I wasn't ready to deal with the emotional aspect of our reunion, but the physical part was oh so sweet. I moved in union with him, striking a perfect cord of balance between passion and fulfillment.

Jordan pulled one of my knees over his arm as he continued to push me to the edge.

My pussy quivered just thinking of his masterful cock dominating me.

Sensing that I was close to erupting, Jordan told me to touch myself.

I reached between us and slid my finger over my clit. The hard little knob was swollen and seeking attention. My orgasm was quick and fierce as I come apart below him.

Jordan followed moments later as he reached his climax. He rolled on his side and pulled me to his chest. Our limbs were sated, heavy and content in post-coital bliss.

"Much better than I could have imagined." Jordan seemed to be talking to himself as he mumbled those words above me.

I smiled in agreement and listened to his heartbeat thunder in my ear as it returned to normal.

"Now that I have totally depleted you of your energy, I think food would be a good thing right about now," he said.

I nodded my head in agreement but made no move to get up. With the mention of food my stomach growled causing both of us to laugh.

A few minutes later Jordan got up and cleaned himself off in the bathroom. He came back to the bed and gently wiped me off with a warm wet cloth.

"You have the prettiest pussy."

I blushed at his blatant appraisal of my anatomy and tried to close my legs but he would not let me.

"Seeing my cum drip from it is fucking hot, babe."

"Oh my God. Jordan!" I yelped and covered my head with the pillow. His low husky laugh vibrated through the pillow as he smeared the liquid around my labia.

"Are you through with the observation and inspection of my lady parts?" I peeked at him from under my cover.

"I have not even started with the inspection but I will, soon." He waggled his eyebrows and tickled me.

I squealed with laughter. I tried to push off the bed but he would not let me up.

"Now for some food." Jordan consulted me about what I wanted to eat. We decided on sweet corn and lobster soup, grilled lobster tail and grilled asparagus with hollandaise sauce followed by molten chocolate lava cake. He entered our food and wine selection into the bedside tablet and hit send.

"Come on. I ran us a bath." Not missing a beat, Jordan picked me up and deposited me in the whirlpool tub that was bubbling with sudsy hot water. He got in behind me and pulled me between his legs.

"This bath is delightful. Just what I needed."

He massaged my shoulders and neck.

I sank further into the tub and he pulled me back up.

"Now see, the selfish bastard in me would let you go diving in the tub and hold your head under until you suck me off again, but the right thing to do is save you from drowning."

I laughed at this light banter as he hugged me at my waist to keep me from sliding away from him. "Let me guess, somehow I owe you for saving me from drowning."

"Damn straight. And I will collect, baby."

Somehow I knew that he would. "Tell me, Jordan, why did you decide to move back now?"

"Being away from you was killing me and Robert was trying to get serious with you."

"How would you know that he was getting serious?"

"Honestly, there is not a lot that I don't know about you, Zoe. But I do know that he was looking at engagement rings about a month ago."

I knew that Jordan never completely left my life and somehow I just accepted that he would gather information by any means possible. I tried not to think of what those means were, but I was curious and wanted to hear about it.

"How did you get into my house and office? I mean, all the years of delivering gifts at both places and knowing my whereabouts?"

"Please tell me it will not upset you if I tell you how I got my information." His hands were running lazy circles on my body as I listened.

"Well, since I know about your stalking and invasion of my privacy... OK. Promise."

"I hired a private investigator to keep me informed." He took a deep breath. "I am not saying I'm proud that I had you followed now and then and I didn't do it all the time, but, well, you are important to me and I had to make sure no one else was moving in on my girl."

"Robert and I dated for six months."

"I did not consider him much of a threat until he went to a jewelry store. Now the guy from the Houston Texans football team, I had to let him know to take a frigging hike."

I spun around to face him, sloshing water over the edge of the tub. "Jordan! You did not! I liked that guy," I said, poking him in his chest with my finger.

"Yes, well he was a little prick and had a reputation with women, and I mean not in a good way. There was no way I was going to let him get any closer to you than having dinner."

I shivered as I listened to Jordan talk about me. Was I an obsession? A possession? Did I really want to know? Was I OK with this information?

"Forgive me for meddling in your personal life, but I could not let you go. I did not want to let you go or forget about you, Zoe. Of all the women I have ever known, none has made me feel the way you do. Not one."

I leaned back and relaxed in his arms as I mulled over his words and our conversation.

CHAPTER 20

WE FINALLY GOT OUT OF THE TUB AND SLIPPED ON white robes. Jordan went into the closet and came back with a beautiful cream colored lacey baby doll negligee with matching gown and mules.

"What is this?" I held it at arms length admiring the sexy see through garment.

"Just a little something I picked up," he said.

"Did you not have enough to do today?" I pulled him in for a kiss.

"I did a little shopping," he said as he took off my robe and helped me slip on the gown. It fit perfectly, hugging my breasts and barely covering my ass.

"This is from an exclusive shop in Paris. Agent Provocateur. You went to Paris today?"

"Didn't say I got it today." His eyes roamed over my body making me feel a little naughty. I spun around in a circle and did a curtsy.

"A little too sure of yourself. Unless it was not meant for me?" I continued to tease him as I walked slowly around him.

"I was hopeful is was for you. Everything I do has you in mind."

I stopped in front of him and ran my hands over my body pausing at my breasts.

Jordan swung me up in his arms just as a knock sounded on the door announcing the arrival of dinner. He put me back down with a low growl in his throat.

The delicious meal was served on a round table with a bouquet of beautiful yellow roses as the centerpiece. We ate and talked some more about our day and I could not help but tease Jordan with the flirty little gown.

I retreated back to the bedroom and answered emails that were urgent.

Jordan went to the office and was on the phone with his attorney.

When he came back to the bedroom I crawled on the bed and looked over my shoulder.

He shrugged out of the robe and pulled me toward him. With one swift motion, he hooked both my knees around his shoulders, lifted my bottom in his hands and buried his face between my legs.

My body convulsed as he continued his assault on the point of my need.

Closing on my clit, he licked and sucked the tight nub.

My breathing heaved with anticipation. "Please. I can't wait, I need…"

Jordan rose above me and sank his engorged cock inside my tight passage. He went balls deep into me and I mewled with pleasure, welcoming his hard, warm body against mine. He moved above me slamming into my core again and again until I begged for release.

"Now. Come now."

His commanding voice spun me into the vortex of sweet pleasure as my pussy clenched down on his cock. With heaving chests we clung to one another, gasping for air. I was spent even as Jordan cleaned me off and pulled me into his embrace. I fell asleep in his arms.

~ ~ ~ ~ ~

I opened my eyes to an unfamiliar room. A moment later a smile touched my lips as I recalled last night's events and where I was. Jordan was talking on his phone as he placed a cup of coffee on the bedside table beside me. He was dressed in a light grey trim fit suit, white shirt and a dark blue tie. His brilliant blue eyes were deep in concentration.

Jordan bent over me and kissed me lightly on the lips then went to the office area.

I stretched and sat up slowly in the bed, taking note that I was deliciously sore all over.

I moved to the table that was loaded with breakfast food and found that I was famished.

Jordan joined me as we enjoyed eggs benedict and English muffins with butter and fresh fruit.

Noting the time, I got up from the table and made a beeline for the shower.

Jordan caught me around my waist and pulled me into his body for a hug.

I hopped up onto his waist.

He stumbled backward but caught me easily. His hungry eyes took in my breasts in the flimsy gown and moved lower to the apex of my thigh. Seeing my bareness with no underwear turned him on immensely as I felt his erection poking through his pants, but he was dressed and already conducting business, so I decided to stop taunting him and get on with my day.

"Little minx. You won't be teasing me later. I have a conference call to Houston in a few minutes and a meeting with James after that." He kissed me on the tip of my nose and set me down.

"Why, I wasn't teasing at all. Just saying good morning." I fluttered my eyelashes at him.

He spanked me lightly on my ass.

I giggled and jumped in the shower to get ready for my day. There was another smart outfit and shoes on the bed when I came back to the bedroom. Again I didn't recognize the clothing, but looking at the tag I saw that it was a Betsey Johnson creation. I slipped into the grey and black dress that was fitted at the top and flared from the waist to just above my knees. The shoes were Salvatore Ferragamo black pumps with a bow on top. Chunky gold tone fashion jewelry completed the outfit that was chic and professional.

"My woman beautiful." Jordan slipped an arm around my waist and escorted me to the private elevator. "Erik, my driver, will take you to the first hospital meeting, and Andre will be there."

The door opened and I stepped in followed by his driver. Jordan winked at me as the elevator door closed. My heart gave that now familiar jolt.

Andre was waiting in the hospital lobby when I arrived. He was on his phone with Veronica in the Houston office. I walked up to him and tapped him on the shoulder. He acknowledged me by nodding his head. From the look on his face and tone of his voice, I could tell this was not a courtesy call to the office, so I paced in the lobby waiting for him to complete the call.

"Zoe is with me now. I will update her on the situation with Luke," he said, ending the call.

"Good morning. We have about five minutes before our meeting with administration." He picked up his briefcase and we made our way down the hall to the suite of offices where we were meeting.

"There is a situation with Luke Hastings. He had an ER shift last night. I suggest we go to our meeting then we can discuss the issue?"

I agreed and we stepped into the waiting room of the office where the receptionist announced our arrival.

Three members of the hospital met us and the result was about the same as yesterday. I signed the contract. There were four hospitals in this group and the contract covered all four. The nurses would be busy and I looked forward to the increase of applicants in the coming weeks.

Andre and I headed back to the new office, but did not discuss Luke due to privacy issues, so we looked at the interview info and meeting schedule for the afternoon.

"Good morning, Miss Cain," Bianca greeted us. We moved to the conference room where I asked her to give me a few minutes with Andre.

She closed the door behind her and went back to nursing applicants that were taking computerized exams or doing last minute prep, getting their badge, welcome package, and asking last minute questions before starting to work for the agency on Monday.

Andre began filling me in. "Luke Hastings worked ER in North Houston last night. Several nurses reported that he was acting strange and out of character for him so they reported it to the ER manager on duty. He was submitted to a drug test and tested positive for opioids. Incidentally, several patients that he cared for during his shift had orders for Demerol from the ER physician. He was relieved of his shift and sent home by taxi. The nursing supervisor notified Veronica this morning and requests a meeting with you Monday morning."

"Wow. OK. Did Veronica speak with Luke today?" I asked.

"She called, but he didn't answer. Probably sleeping, but she left a message and will try to reach him again."

"We will need to conduct our own investigation. Notify the state board and offer TPAPIN program to assist him in recovery from substance abuse. Until then, have Veronica clear his work schedule and ask him to report to the office at 8 a.m. Monday morning then ask the ER supervisor for a meeting at her office or mine at 10 a.m."

"Also, Angie Mata's grandmother died last night. She has been ill for a few months. Angie requested a week off for bereavement. Veronica said she approved the time off and has already filled the shifts in ICU."

I saw that Andre was not done with his report a he consulted his computer, and I was making notes of my own.

"Mr. Grant fired his private duty nurse. He said his nurse was too bossy and he's requesting a male nurse this time. We do not have a private duty male nurse, so I posted an ad online and in the *Houston Chronicle* for a full-time male nurse."

"Good. In the meantime, call some of our male nurses that work in hospitals and ask if they can help out by filling in those shifts until we're able to hire a full-time nurse for Mr. Grant. Call Veronica and ask her to notify Mr. Grant of our plan to fill in temp male nurses until we can fill the position with a full-time one."

He jumped into action with my instructions and I answered my most urgent emails.

Bianca ordered lunch to be delivered to the conference room so we had a working lunch. She also updated me on the progress of the office and applicants, hospital needs for available shifts, and the growing need for our new DON.

"I anticipate this office will be busy when the ad's hit the Internet and newspaper," I told Bianca. I wanted her to be ready for the onslaught of applicants and shifts that would be available.

"We will be ready, Miss Caine. If for some reason it is more than we can handle, I will let you know."

"If you feel that more office help is needed to process applicants, answer phones or take hospital calls, you can hire another office assistant."

The afternoon was busy and productive. My last interview ended at four o'clock and I wrapped things up with Bianca and Andre. I knew whom I wanted to hire for the DON position, but I needed to take a couple days to look over their applications and my notes before my final decision. I finally had a minute to speak with Veronica myself.

"I got your email about the hospitals. Six hospitals under contract should keep us all busy for quite a while," Veronica said.

"Very much so. I'm anticipating an influx in nursing applicants by next week. I may need you to come to San Francisco next week to help conduct interviews and process new nurses and whatever you think needs to be done."

"Great."

"Hmm. Have plans for the weekend?" I asked.

"Going to Monterrey with mom. My grandmother has not been feeling well for the past few weeks. It's hard to convince her that she needs to see a doctor and I'm not sure what else is going on with her except for pain in her back."

"Sorry to hear about that. Keep me posted about sweet Gaga then. I hope it's not too serious." I had met some of Veronica's extended family the first summer that Jordan and I broke up. They were friendly and accommodating, especially Gaga.

"Me too. How are you and Jordan doing?"

I got up to look outside and saw that the SUV was pulling up at the front of the building.

"Delightful. Incredible. Delicious."

"Are we talking about Jordan or food?" She laughed.

"Jordan is food."

"You've got it bad, girlfriend." We giggled like teenagers. "Can't say that I blame you. The man is smoking hot."

"I'm not sure what time I will be landing tomorrow..."

"No rush to come into the office. It's busy but I have plenty of help. You may want to take the afternoon off since I will be gone a few days next week."

I had no idea what Jordan has planned for us tonight or what time we'd be leaving tomorrow, but decided to start my long weekend off now.

Jordan was waiting for me outside as I exited the office. He held the door open for me to enter and slid in beside me. I flopped beside him and he pulled me to his side as the vehicle pulled away. I gratefully drank from a bottle of water that Jordan handed me.

"I missed you today," Jordan whispered in my ear. I smiled and looked up at him. He brushed his lips against mine.

"Hmm. Don't have enough to keep you busy in your empire?"

He tickled me and I yelped.

"Did you accomplish all you needed to?" he asked.

"And then some. The office will be very busy. A few of the Houston nurses said they would be interested in working here if I housed them since I may end up with way more available shifts than nurses, so I will think about that as well."

"Good." He rubbed my shoulder with one hand while the other kept a possessive hold at my waist. Jordan got a phone call but kept holding onto me.

A feeling of nostalgia came over me as I remembered our cuddling days, but I decided to build on new memories now and see where our rekindled romance would take us. Thus far, we engaged in easy flowing conversations and he can't seem to keep his hands off me. No complaints there. I intertwined my fingers with his hand that was holding me. It felt great to have a close physical connection, but was it too early to think of the emotional?

"I don't mean to be presumptuous about tomorrow, and I should have asked if you need to get back to your office. If you do, I will hire a private jet to take you back to Houston. I have meetings until early afternoon." He looked across at me.

"I'll take the day off so you can save your money for the private jet." I smirked across at him. He grinned at me and shook his head.

"This is a beautiful city. Plenty to do. You will have the vehicle, driver and a tour guide to take you wherever you wish to go."

"Goodie, cause I want to go to Alcatraz, but you can call off the tour guide."

"OK, no tour guide. That's one of the movies we saw when you were in college."

"Yup. Clint Eastwood was awesome in that movie. Have you been?" I asked.

"No, but I can't wait to hear about it after your visit."

"I may even have lunch with Jeremy," I said, as I scrolled to Jeremy's contact information.

"This Jeremy guy…"

"Is a very good friend of mine," I said with no hesitation.

"His IT company is doing very well. He has an impressive portfolio and financial statements."

"Is there anyone in the business world you don't know? Don't try to buy him out, please. He's a friend."

"Not at all. I already own an IT company in Silicon Valley."

"What a surprise. Not." I laughed.

CHAPTER 21

BACK AT THE HOTEL, JORDAN'S STAFF WAS WRAPPING things up for the day in the lobby slash temporary office. He stopped to speak with his attorney, but continued to hold onto my hand.

After a couple minutes we entered the suite.

"Would you like to take a bath or a shower? We're meeting with an investor and his wife for dinner. Would you do me the honor and accompany me?" he asked.

"Certainly. Do I have something to wear?"

"But of course." He raised his brows at me.

I shook my head as Jordan went to set the bath. I slid out of my clothes and yelped as he picked me up from behind and lay me on the bed.

He splayed my legs open and buried his face in the apex of my thighs.

My underwear dampened with desire as he rubbed his face in the fabric. I moaned and lifted my hips to his face.

Jordan slipped the flimsy fabric from my body and licked my slit.

I whimpered above him. My body trembled with need.

"You like this, baby?" he asked, as I fisted my hands in his hair.

"Yes. Yes. Yes."

He brought me quickly to orgasm.

I lay replete on the bed with my eyes closed.

Jordan chuckled then took off my shoes and bra. He carried me to the tub and I sank in the aromatic suds. Jordan slid in behind me. We stayed that way for a few minutes until he pushed me away and massaged my shoulders.

"Come on. Let's shower and get dressed. We're meeting them at 8 p.m.," Jordan said.

I sipped on a glass of J Rochioli Chardonnay that Jordan handed me. The Nicole Miller red V-neck lace dress fit perfectly as did the four-inch ankle cuff Sam Edelman stilettos.

Jordan ran his hand under the hem of my dress and over my ass.

"The only thing that should be between this dress and your skin is my hand. Lose the underwear," he whispered in my ear.

"Jordan. I am so not going with my ass hanging out..." I yelped as he pinched my ass.

"Either you take it off or I will. We are the only two that will know what you don't have under the dress."

"Fine. But you are some kind of kinky."

He had the audacity to chuckle as I slipped off the offending underwear.

"I will have fun fondling you. I may even cause you to orgasm right there at the table while our unsuspecting guests are with us."

"No, Jordan. I...you can't...I..."

"Well, well. You like the idea." A corner of his lip turned up in a smile. "Come on, my beautiful Zoe."

"Where are we going?" I asked as I grasped his hand in mine and we walked to the elevator.

"Saison. You will love it."

I texted Jeremy about lunch tomorrow and he said he would go with me to Alcatraz.

"Jeremy will be able to go with me tomorrow. We will lunch on the pier after Alcatraz," I said.

"Is that so?" He cocked a brow at me.

"Yes. It will be good to spend some time with him," I replied.

The food and ambiance of the restaurant was exquisite. Our guests were among the elites of San Francisco and the gentleman readily agrees to invest in Jordan's business overseas. They discussed business as I entertained his wife. She was my age and her husband was 30 years her senior. He was doting on her, but her eyes were glued to Jordan.

Despite her heavy glances toward him, Jordan managed to caress my legs and work his way to the apex of my thighs. I hurriedly excused myself to the ladies room.

I stepped into the restroom when my phone beeped with a text that read: 'Don't wipe it all off. I want to smell you.'

I blushed with the blatant sexual message from Jordan and stayed a few minutes longer than was necessary to calm my erratic breathing.

We finally left around midnight and I was frazzled from Jordan's hands on my private parts.

He jumped me as soon as the door to the limo closed. "I have been hard for hours. I can't wait any longer. I need you." He hiked up my dress and slammed into me.

The breath left my body for a moment as he fucked me.

I tried to match his strokes, but he was merciless as his hips pushed into my slick pussy.

"Fuck. Need to..." He didn't finish his broken sentence as his body shuddered against mine.

A few minutes later, Jordan pulled slowly away from me and grabbed some tissue to clean us off. He then pulled me into his arms and we reached the hotel in silence.

After getting ready for the night, I lie in the bed, sated and relax.

"Are you OK? Was it too rough?" he asked.

"I'm fine. I loved it."

"Your body, it's, um, I can't stay away, needing you…"

"Jordan. Come to bed. I loved every minute of if."

He slid into bed and we fell asleep.

~ ~ ~ ~ ~

The next morning I got up early to work out in the private gym with Jordan. We showered, he made love to me, I showered again, then we went our separate ways.

"You don't need to go with us," I told Erik, Jordan's driver, as Jeremy and I walked toward the ferry that would take us to the small island.

"I have strict orders, Miss Caine. Mr. Dawson also rented a private boat to take us. Faster that way. I am not to leave your side, ma'am," he said without a crack of smile on his face.

I was fuming, but did not want to yell on the phone with Jordan, so I decided to enjoy my time with my friend.

"I would not trust another man with my woman either, Zoe. I am fine with the extra company. Come on," Jeremy said and held my hand as I boarded the sleek speedboat.

"My woman? Really, Jeremy?"

"Um, hey, have you looked in the mirror lately, Zoe? You have really come into yourself. Successful and relaxed in your own skin."

Erik cleared his throat and gave Jeremy a cold stare.

Despite Erik's babysitting, we had a fabulous time and took in the history of the old prison.

Back at the pier we had lobster and a beer then headed back to the hotel. I bid Jeremy goodbye.

Jordan met Erik and me downstairs. He was holding the elevator door open. We stepped in and I squinted my eyes at him. Jordan looked at me sheepishly, then looked down at the floor.

"Don't do it again."

"I'm sorry. But I can't promise that I won't..."

"It's called trust."

"Understood. I will work on that."

"OK."

He pulled me to his chest and kissed the top of my head. I leaned into him and all was forgiven. Another step in the right direction for us.

"One more meeting, then I will be ready to leave."

Jordan walked into the suite with me.

Our luggage was packed and some clothes lay on the bed for me to wear. I sat in the living room and pulled my computer toward me and went through my email until it was time for us to head back to Houston.

The SUV took us to the private airport, and pulled in front of the door where we check in and board Jordan's company jet.

About an hour after takeoff we were served a delicious seafood meal of clam chowder in a bread bowl and grilled California White Sea bass with roasted vegetables.

"I won't be able to fit in my clothes if you continue to feed me all my favorite foods at once," I commented to Jordan as I dug into the hot creamy soup.

"Like I said, I love to watch you eat. I ordered food from the Pier since we didn't have time to eat out. I thought you would enjoy another meal of fresh seafood. Have some more wine."

I smirked at him, but he just grinned and refilled my wine glass with chilled Francis Coppola Chardonnay.

"Now you're trying to get me drunk?"

"Let's make this a memorable flight. I get you tipsy on wine, then you can have your wicked way with me." His mischievous smile was in place, and I was imagining myself all over Jordan's hot body.

"Now that would hardly be fair taking advantage of you and all."

"But I insist." He rose from his seat at the table and picked up the bottle of wine.

"Well, in that case…"

Jordan wasted no time and pulled me to the sleep cabin.

"I have an insatiable appetite for your delectable body." His hands slid over my shoulders and down my back, coming away with my dress and bra.

I held his face in my hands, all the while nibbling and kissing his lips. I quickly unbuttoned his shirt and threw it on the floor then started on his pants.

"Fuck. You don't have any underwear on." Jordan looked down at my naked form.

"Less clothes for you to deal with."

"If I knew that, we would have skipped dinner altogether."

He sat on the bed. Naked. My eyes immediately went to his beautiful penis.

I climbed onto his lap and took his cock inside me with one smooth motion.

Jordan threw his head back and groaned.

I lifted my hips, then slid back down on his steel hard cock.

His hands held on to my waist, pushing me to go faster.

My lips kissed a path from his neck down to his shoulder.

Jordan's wet mouth found my breast and latched onto a nipple. We were moving together in unison, each complimenting the other to bring pleasure to our now glistening body, as the sheen of sweat dampened our skin. Neither of us wanted to give over to the final pleasure that is inevitable in our climactic release.

Jordan flipped me onto my back on the bed and continued to slam into me. He pulled my legs over his shoulders which deepened our connected bodies even more.

I screamed Jordan's name as I came with a jolt, my body shaking against his.

Jordan moved above me a few more times, then emptied his essence of pleasure into me. He rolled to his side pulling me with him. Our bodies were still connected as our lungs filled with much needed oxygen.

"God, babe. I can't get enough of your body. It's like a fine Cognac, smooth and exquisite. I could die a happy man now." His hands moved slowly over my body.

I chuckled at his analogy of my body and snuggled closer into his chest.

After a few minutes, Jordan got up and cleaned us both off then pulled me back in his arms. "What are your plans for the weekend?" he asked.

"Haven't thought that far. But I took today off."

"Spend it with me." He did that sexy whisper thing in my ear that made it hard for me to think of anything else but pleasing him. Did he know the effect he was already having on me?

"Yes," I whispered back.

"Great. Now take a nap. We still have a little over an hour before landing."

Sated, my eyes fluttered shut and I slept in the cozy cabin of the airplane.

Jordan woke me up and as usual, already dressed. He'd changed from the business suit to faded jeans and T-shirt and wore brown Italian loafers. His casual look was stylish and sexy showing off his broad chest and narrow hips. Yummy.

"I'll leave these hanging behind the door for you."

"Again, those are not my clothes."

"They are now." He hung the clothes on the hook and closed the door behind him as he exited to the main cabin.

I got up and eyed the clothing. I had no idea where he got the clothes, but I didn't question it. The Miss Me jeans fits perfectly as did the top and sandals that he chose.

I will address the issue of all these mysterious clothing he magically produced for me to wear, but not now.

CHAPTER 22

JORDAN HAD A CAR WAITING FOR US WHEN WE LANDED and the driver gave him the keys to the impressive vehicle with its sleek elegant lines. I arched my brows at him but he smirked at me and opened the door of the new red Jaguar convertible.

"Admit it. You love boys with fast toys." He patted my ass as I slid into the luxurious leather seat and secured my seat belt. Jordan got in and pushed the button to start the engine. It revved to life and we took off on Interstate 45.

"What's there not to love about this car? I would look really cool behind her wheels."

"Did you just call my car a she?"

"Didn't know it was a him."

"He thunders and roars like a beast, babe."

"Hm. Does he have a name?"

"Dick."

I threw my head back and laughed at our ridiculous conversation and Jordan joined in.

"Fuck me! I'm getting a ticket. This is so your fault," Jordan said.

Sure enough there were red and blue lights right behind the car. Jordan pulled over to the shoulder of the freeway. We sat there until the cop walked up to my side of the car due to traffic whizzing by on Jordan's side.

"What is your emergency, sir?"

"Sorry, officer," Jordan mumbled as he took out his license.

"Zoe? Zoe Caine! Well, I'll be damned."

I looked up to see Lee Drummond from high school smiling at me. "Hi, Lee. How are you? I didn't know you were with HPD now." I'd seen Lee at our 10-year high school reunion two years ago. He said he was with the Dallas police department then.

"Yeah. I transferred back to Houston. My dad isn't doing well and I moved back to help my sister out with him. Say, let's have lunch sometime soon. Catch up and all." He got out a pad and scribbled his phone number on it.

"What the hell, buddy? I'm sitting right here beside her so you can see that she has a boyfriend, right?" Jordan growled at Lee with a no nonsense look on his face.

"Look here, buddy! I can ticket your ass again like I did last week. This is a freeway not the Indie racetrack. You were going 85 in a 65 mile an hour zone."

"Wait. You ticketed him last week?" I looked at Jordan who was looking anywhere but at me now. Busted!

"Oh, yes. He has all these fancy car's driving around Houston like a speed demon."

"Can I go now? And by the way, no, she can't have lunch with you."

"That's it! You can have another of these pink slips here and I'll see you in court where I hope your driver's license gets revoked." Lee was busy scribbling again.

"No! No, please, Lee. Just let us go and yes, I will have lunch with him if I want to." I squinted my eyes at Jordan who now had a real pissed off look on his face, but thankfully kept his mouth shut this time.

"Just for you I'll let it slide, Zoe. But I have your number, buddy; next time…" Whatever Lee was saying got lost in the wind as Jordan took off on the freeway.

"Are you out of your frigging mind? He can still give you a ticket, Jordan. Don't make it worse and you need to slow the hell down. You're back up to 70, for Christ's sake."

Jordan slowed down to the posted speed limit but was clearly not happy. "Dickhead. I was sitting right beside my girlfriend and he asks her out on a date. Who the hell does that?"

"Your girlfriend?"

"Yes." He lifted his chin in defiance, not backing down.

Fine, two can play at this game. "I don't remember you asking me to go steady with you."

"Go steady? Like we have to talk first then go steady, then I ask you to be my girlfriend?"

"Yeah. Something like that."

"Zoe, will you be my steady girlfriend?"

I could not help but laugh again.

"Good. I will take that as a yes and I'll call Dickhead and tell him to fuck off." Jordan took the paper from me and stuck it in his pocket.

"You will do no such thing. He is a friend. Plus, it's always good to know a cop."

"I know the chief of police."

"I know the mayor." *Were we really doing this?*

"I know the governor of Texas, so there," Jordan responded.

"You do?"

"No."

We laughed at the silly banter between us and I was struck again at the handsomeness of the man beside me.

Pure eye candy. His dark blond hair played off natural highlights from the setting sun and his smile lit up his face. Dark aviator sunglasses hide his brilliant blue eyes that I know were twinkling with mirth.

"Fine. You can go to lunch with us if you behave yourself."

He sat back in the seat and sulked but didn't turn down the invitation.

I was pretty sure that he'd go, despite hating the idea of having lunch with Lee. I turned my head, looked out the window and smiled. He was totally possessive and a little jealous. That was not such a bad thing as long as it was just a little.

Jordan pulled the car into a parking garage of a high-rise building in downtown Houston and parked beside an elevator marked Private. We got out of the car and were met by an attendant who held the elevator door for us to enter. Jordan's driver pulled up beside us in a new black Land Rover. Jordan spoke with him briefly then got in the elevator.

He chatted with the young man who caught him up to the latest weather that was the same when we left a couple days ago, hot and humid. We exited and walked down the hall to another elevator. There was only one button in this swanky elevator, which I assumed was also private for Jordan only.

We arrived on another floor and stepped out into a large room with elegant furnishings. It had a fully stocked bar at one side of the room and a small wooden dance floor off to the side. Floor to ceiling windows showed off the twinkling lights of the city below. We walked through this area to a double wooden door. Jordan pushed some numbers on the keypad and used his index finger for ID. A green light blinked and he opened the door.

"Thanks, Mike. Have a good evening, man." Jordan tipped the young man that escorted us.

"Let me show you around." Jordan took my hand and led me into his penthouse. I was stunned at the sparsely decorated space of his living room. There were marble floors throughout the space and again massive floor to ceiling windows allowed a spectacular view of the city and its surrounding areas.

"Did you get robbed?" I asked, since there was only a TV and sofa. The high ceiling of the room made the furniture look like toys.

Jordan laughed. "No. I am only just moving in here. This building is new and they're still working on parts of it." We walked through the living room to the office that was elegantly furnished with modern cherry wood furnishings. "I haven't had much time to work from home, so I've not used this home office." He showed me the guest bedroom, which was a suite in itself, but void of furnishings, then the master bedroom suite that was fully furnished.

"The space is gorgeous," I said. "You just need a decorator to fill it with equally gorgeous furnishings."

He led me back to the living room and into the kitchen. I paused to admire the beautiful gourmet kitchen with state of the art appliances and granite countertop. The adjoining dining room was completely empty.

"Actually, I waited to get the place decorated because I wanted you to sort of put your Zoe touch on it. I remember you used to love art and decorating. You went nuts shopping for stuff with Jenna when they bought their first home."

I was stunned at his request and touched that he remembered my love of art. I did love to decorate and had a keen sense of decorating style.

"That is so sweet, Jordan, but I'm not sure I have the time and this is a massive project, like professional huge and I don't feel that I have the knowledge to do it justice." Which was true. I could see that he knew it would be too time consuming, but then he smiled and I knew he had it figured out. "What?" I asked.

"I have an interior designer, but I would like her to get your approval on everything she does. I want you to choose as much of the furnishings and art as your time will allow. She will have all that you need, and if she does not, then tell her what you want and she'll find it. You can shop from Italy, to South America, Africa.

"Everything is possible with the Internet and her knowledge of where unique pieces can be found. She will make appointments to see you. I know you don't have a lot of extra time, but just think about it. I'm in no hurry. I have the bedroom, kitchen and office, which is all I need for now."

I swear to God, the man thinks of everything. Nothing is done or even suggested without a plan a, b and c.

"Well, maybe I can help her choose some of the furnishings and art. She will do a lot better than I ever could."

"Great. No rush." He took my hand and headed back to the door. "Wait till you see the pool. It's on the roof one level higher but it won't be ready for another week."

"This is a beautiful room. What do you use it for?" I asked.

Jordan stood looking around the room. His hands were in his pockets and sunglasses perched on his head, with his legs spread apart. I had an urge to be jumped by him right then.

I quickly looked away from him hoping he would not see the lustful need in my eyes.

"I plan to have some private parties here soon. It can hold about fifty people or so. Just close intimate friends or business colleagues. The decorators just finished up last week. I think we should break it in soon. What do you think?" He held out his hand to me. I grasped his fingers, a little confused that we seem to be heading out again.

"Um, where are we going?"

"To my estate in The Woodlands. There is not much here. I have a housekeeper for here, but she doesn't start until Monday, so I have no food and there's not much for her to do yet."

"How long have you had your place in The Woodlands?" I was not aware that he had another home here. Come to think of it, I don't know much about Jordan's living ar-rangements, nor his homes.

"I bought it a couple years ago when I decided to move to Houston."

We were back in the elevator. It just dawned on me as we are leaving, that his penthouse was on the 50th floor.

"Do you still have an office in Austin?"

"Yes, but it will be moving into this building in the next few weeks. My other offices in Asia and Europe will con-tinue with business as usual. The only difference is that I will not be there as much as I once was. I hired two vice presidents to oversee business in those areas but every major purchase or transaction must be cleared through me first. The changes have been coming slowly over the past few years."

Interesting.

Jordan walked toward another car not far from the Jaguar that we rode in from the airport. The attendant came running over to assist him. He gave Jordan a set of keys. Jordan pulled the car up to where I stood. Hopping out, he came over to my side and opened the passenger door. I couldn't help myself. I ran my hands over the luxurious leather. It felt like butter against my skin. A sleek black convertible Maserati.

"Nice car." I mean, what else could I say. I was totally speechless by his cars. They were gorgeous, obviously expensive, and all built for speed.

"Not just any car. This is a Maserati Grancabrio MC. I could give you the stats, but right now I'd rather talk about how totally hot you look in my car." He winked at me and peeled out of the garage.

"How many cars do you have?"

"In Downtown Houston there are two, and three more in The Woodlands. This one does not have a name. Would you do it the honor?"

I smiled at the way his face lit up like a teenage boy. The man loved cars.

"I will need to think about it. I'm not sure what kind of personality it has yet."

"I want to fuck you in all my cars."

My breath caught in my throat. I felt the heat slowly rising. His hand reached over to hold mine. I leaned my head back and closed my eyes, because if I looked at him right now, I just may beg him to take me back to his penthouse and fuck me senseless.

"It's that look. The look that you have on your face right now reminds me of how you look when you have my cock in your mouth." He put my hand on his jeans and I squeezed his growing erection.

"You would so be in my mouth if the top was up." The words had just left my mouth when Jordan exited the freeway, pulled over on the side and put the top up.

I laughed at his lack of patience.

"You have a wicked mouth, babe. I love when you suck me off." I slid his zipper down and his cock sprung out of his jeans.

"You're commando!" I laughed and licked my lips in anticipation of tasting him, in a hot fast car, on the freeway. Unbelievable.

"Surprise."

"Naughty boy. Keep your hands on the wheel and eyes on the road. And make sure no one sees me going down on you."

"Ah, sure, babe, but do it now, please, before I make a fool of myself in front of you and a mess in my new car."

I leaned over and flicked my tongue over the top of his cock. His musky smell was erotic and I pulled the round bulging head of his penis into my mouth, rolling it around on my tongue.

Jordan inhaled quickly, his breathing increasing as I licked the tip of his penis with my tongue. He tried to push his hips, up but I pulled away and took his shaft in my hand, smiling wickedly up at him.

"Little tease," he said with a strained look on his face.

I went down again, and with one swift motion, took him in my mouth until his cock hit the back of my throat. I keep pulling on his length and increasing my tempo.

Jordan started to groan and strained his body toward my mouth.

I let him this time. I sucked and pulled on his cock with a frantic pace as I tasted his pre-cum. He was getting close and I keep up the sucking and pulling motion that had my cheeks hollow. I pulled his balls from the jeans and dragged my nails along the bottom side of his globes as he erupted in my mouth. I gulped down the thick, slightly salty liquid and held him in my mouth until his legs stop shaking. Slowly, I let his cock out of my hot, wet mouth and zipped up his jeans.

"Fuck, baby. Your mouth is magic." He reached over and squeezed my hand. "I owe you and just to let you know, I always pay up." His grin was contagious.

"We're even. You did save me from drowning in the tub last night."

He smirked, lifting one side of his luscious lips that were made for sucking.

I squirmed in my seat as the center of my core pulsed with need. Delightful.

CHAPTER 23

WE WERE EXITING OFF THE FREEWAY AGAIN DUE TO OUR arrival in one of Houston's most prestigious suburban neighborhoods. Jordan filled me in on building his home in this area. He said he wanted to settle down somewhere where he could relax and not just have his penthouse in Houston, though he'll use the penthouse during the week and for entertaining.

He'd asked his deceased mother's best friend and next-door neighbor by the name of Becky Ross to be his house-keeper. Her husband had died shortly after they got married and she never remarried nor had any children. Jordan said she had periodically babysat him when she was in high school as well. She had worked for several families as a housekeeper and nanny in Colorado and she welcomed the chance to live somewhere different, so when his grandfather told him she was looking for a job, Becky welcomed the opportunity to work for Jordan.

"I would like my grandfather to move closer to me but he refuses. It would be good to see him more often. Although we do talk on the phone about once a week and I visit when I can." He had a wistful look in his eyes speaking about his grandfather who he calls 'pops'.

"I can imagine it would not be easy for him to move since he's always lived there, right?"

"That, and the fact that my aunt and uncle and their family live in Colorado as well. He sees them a hell of a lot more than he does me, but that's on me. I've neglected to keep in touch with my family except for my grandfather, but no one else has really tried to reach out to me, so I kept building my company and made more money."

I felt sad for him growing up as an only child and leaving home with no strong friendship ties. Although he has friends now, they are from his college days at UT and business associates.

"Your grandmother passed away about five years ago, right?"

"Yes."

"Sorry to hear about her passing. Jenna told me about it. She said you took some time off to be with her."

"I'm glad I did. She died of cancer but she did not suffer. She passed away a few months after being diagnosed."

"What about your mother? You never spoke much about her."

"That's a long story and I only know what my grandparents told me happened."

I didn't ask any more personal questions. I sensed that he did not want to go into details of such sad part of his life. Especially since like me, he had no memories of his mother and he never spoke of a father.

Jordan drove a few miles through the streets, navigating his way to a gated community on a lake. There were not more than twenty homes here and they all sat on a few acres each. Manicured front lawns enhanced the look of sophisticated homes that nestled among trees. Jordan drove around the impressive lake with a massive waterfall running over huge rocks and boulders recreating a natural scene that could be found in a forest. The homes were impressive and all seemed to be fairly new and custom built. No two homes were alike here, but their basic architectural theme was of a rustic, but charming, craftsman style.

"So, this is it. What do you think?" Jordan asked, driving down a curved driveway that led to a stylish house. He parked in the circular driveway and opened my door. It looked like something from a magazine with a huge porch that wrapped around the front and one side of the house. The fabulous decor of huge clay pots in various sizes and colors overflowed with different types of flowers and greeneries leading up to the home.

"It's spectacular, Jordan. A perfect depiction of a Texas style home." I looked around the home and yard, admiring the tranquility of the area that was surprisingly quiet.

"Your approval is the only one that counts. I'm so glad you like it." Jordan took my hand and led me to the front door. "Come on. I'll give you a grand tour of the outside tomorrow." He opened the front door to reveal a stunningly beautiful interior.

Hardwood floors complimented the rustic charm of the house. A gorgeous chandelier hung from the ceiling of the entryway. The living and dining room were visible from the entryway due to an open concept floor plan.

"Stunning." One word summed it up for me and Jordan smiled as he took me around his home pointing out beautiful pieces of art that he collected from Asia and Europe.

"Ah. Our favorite painter." I stood in front of a painting by G. Harvey, admiring the painting that the artist named *1600 Pennsylvania Avenue*. "From The Treasury collection. I know it well."

"You loved this painting, but wouldn't let me buy it for you when you were in college, so I bought it, but didn't tell you. I always hoped you would someday be reunited with it. I have a few more throughout the house," he said, still holding on to my hand.

My eyes misted with emotions. I flung my arms around his neck. "God, Jordan, you say the sweetest things. Now you will have me crying." I sniffled on his shoulder. "Yes, I remember you took me to Texas Art Depot. You sneak, but I'm glad that you bought it."

He tipped my chin up and placed a soft kiss on my lips. "Glad you feel that way. Come on, pretty lady." He led me further into the living room where the view of the backyard and pool was spectacular.

"I love all the trees. It's like you have your own private forest. You must have a hell of a gardener too." What was there not to like here? The house and grounds were simply superb.

"The kitchen and office have the same view. Speaking of kitchen, Becky left it well stocked for the weekend, so we actually have food here." He walked into the kitchen that was nothing less than divine.

The state of the art appliances were a cook's dream. "I love that refrigerator. Looks like an armoire."

"Wish I could take credit for choosing it, but the interior designer did. All the appliances are handmade in Italy."

"Meneghini. Hmm, never heard of the brand, but it is lovely, very unique. Nice touch with the chandelier in the kitchen."

Jordan was opening some of the many drawers of the appliance, pulling out fruits, cheese and a bottle of chilled Champagne.

"Becky didn't like the idea of it in here at first, but I think it grew on her. Here, let me feed you," he said.

We pulled out swiveled bar stools and sat at the counter.

"Open that pretty mouth."

I complied and was rewarded with a sweet, juicy strawberry. "Yummy, and by that I mean the guy feeding me the fruit," I teased Jordan as he plopped a plump grape in my mouth and gave me a glass of Champagne. We continued to tease each other as we ate the tasty, succulent treats.

Jordan placed the plates in the sink and grabbed the bottle of Champagne.

"Now for the rest of the house. There is a bedroom suite over there past the office." He pointed to the area of the house where I saw the office and further down the hall toward the front of the home was a bedroom. "And across the hall from the bedroom is a library which I'm sure you will love. I have some of your favorite books in there. Further down the hall is a music room with a baby grand piano and other instruments."

Again, he remembered that I love to read and I'm sure he has some of Shakespeare's work on the shelves. I couldn't wait to delve into the collection of books I was sure he had in his library. And a music room? I wonder if he'd taken up music in the past 10 years, or if he played some kind of instrument that I didn't know about?

"Feel free to use the office when you're here. The password for the computer is the same as yours."

I looked at him with a quizzical eyebrow, but he just smiled. Well then, that would be easy to remember.

He led the way to the stairs. We stood at the landing as he pointed to different areas of the impressive home.

"There are two bedroom suites up there plus the master bedroom and a media room for movies, another office and an art room were I keep a collection of fine arts from all over the world. I'll give you a proper tour, but right now I can't wait any longer to get you in my bedroom,"

Yes, please. My inner woman was doing a happy dance.

After going up the stairs, he pulled me to the opposite side of the house and away from the other rooms he was talking about, to open the door to the master suite.

Holy shit! And what a room. A massive cherry wood sleigh bed with matching dressers and armoire were not the only furnishings in this charming room. There was also a sitting room toward the back with a view of the yard. I peek at the bathroom with yet another chandelier, huge glass enclosed shower with five showerheads and an adjoining dressing room with lights, mirrors and more dressers.

"Jordan."

I stood at the door of the huge customized walk-in closet. An array of dressers lined one wall. Dressers with glass drawers displayed incredibly beautiful and sexy underwear, negligee and other clothing. Another wall had a floor to ceiling rack of shoes all color-coordinated; beside the shoes were the latest in designer purses. The other wall displayed short and long evening gowns, and professional clothes. In the middle of the room there was a glass armoire with jewelry.

"What do you think, Zoe?"

"I think you are out of your mind."

"That does not answer my question. Is it OK that I did this? I had a professional shopper, but I chose everything in here for you before he bought it."

"A 'he' bought my clothes?"

"Yes. I flew him in last week from Los Angeles to purchase and organize your closet. He's some kind of fashion guru and fashion adviser to many Hollywood stars."

"He has great taste and sense of style." I looked around the room again. "Jordan, we need to talk. Really, I mean all this...I don't know what it all means."

"Let me run a bath then we can start talking. I know you have doubts about me, about us, but what I feel for you is real and I would like to know if it means something to you as well. Will you give me that? Let's start at the beginning. But first a bath."

Jordan went off to start the bath as I continued to stare in the closet with a hundred different thoughts flying through my mind. Was it too much, too soon? Could I handle a committed relationship with Jordan after 10 years of having my mind set again him? Was he just trying to prove a point that I was wrong about him?

"Come here." He lifted me into his arms and took me to the bathroom where he stripped me of my clothing and set me in the tub. His clothing followed mine on the floor then he stepped in behind me and pulled me into his body. We sipped on the crisp Champaign that he'd brought upstairs with us.

"Now. Ask me anything," he said.

"I have too many questions, and I truly don't know where to begin."

"Then I will start by telling you that I never got over you. I left Austin because I couldn't deal with you breaking up with me. I needed to put some distance between us. I figured as time went by you would either get over me and move on, or you would call and we would work things out, but you didn't contact me. I thought it best to leave you alone, and I did for a few months, but soon I wanted to know how you were doing, so I hired someone to report to me once a month."

He took a deep breath as the water around us bubbled from the whirlpool tub. "Anyway, I tried to date, but just didn't have emotional feelings for any of the women I went out with, so I decided that I wouldn't date. By that, I mean I felt no emotional ties to any of the women I went out with, but I was up front by letting them know that I was not interested in an emotional or committed relationship. They got what they wanted from me and I scratched an itch, so to speak. They knew the score and I never disrespected them in any way, but the emotion thing did not happen."

"So all those photos with the drop-dead gorgeous bomb-shells were for what? An itch?" I bristled at the thought of Jordan with other women now, but had no reason to be mad at him.

"It was sexual, but that was all. I took some of them on a few trips now and then, especially when I was traveling for business and needed a hostess or companion."

Ouch, now that just plain fucking hurt. I drew away from him, but he pulled me back.

"I didn't mean to upset you. I just needed for you to know what went on with me, and especially with other women, because I don't want any grey areas in my personal life with you. No gory details, but all this is to let you know that no one could ever hold a candle to you. They could never fill that void in my life nor my heart that you did. I tried to move on with others, but it was just simply impossible. Emotionally, I had nothing to offer them."

"So you continued to have me followed and sent me countless gifts for just about every occasion in my life."

"Indeed. I figured since you did not want to see me, you would soon forget about me and I couldn't deal with that, so I sent gifts and made sure they could not be returned. Some of them were quite valuable but I didn't care what you did with it, just as long as you would remember that I still existed and was thinking about you. I even enlisted the help of David now and then with the understanding if you ever found out he helped me with information about you, he would kick my ass from Europe all the way back to Houston where I would come clean with you."

Silent tears streamed down my face with his confession, falling into the warm water in the tub like rain. It felt like the past 10 years my life has only know rain, forever rain, but now there was a glint of sunlight breaking through the clouds and maybe, just maybe, I would allow my head to turn to the sky, listen to my heart and stop the rain from falling. I'd caused that rain, no one but me.

Jordan got out of the tub and quickly dried off then picked me up like a prized treasure and wiped me off, led me to the bed and tucked me under the cool covers. He then slid in beside me cradling my head to his chest. We held each other as he stunned me by sharing what he knew of his mother.

CHAPTER 24

"AS YOU MAY REMEMBER, MY GRANDPARENTS HAD three children. One son and two daughters. My mother was the youngest of the three. By the time my mom was 16, her brother was married and her sister was in college. Both of my grandparents worked so there was no one at home when my mom came home from high school. A couple months after she turned 16, she came home and was attacked by a man. He raped her and almost killed her.

"My grandparents said she withdrew and did not go back to high school. She went to counseling but would not talk about the horrific incident and if she knew who raped her... well, she never said if she saw the man's face. Anyway, what I'm saying is that I am the product of rape. I don't know who my father is."

"Oh my God. Jordan. I am so sorry to hear that. Raped at any time in one's life is horrifying, but pregnant as well." I reached up to kiss his face and ran my hands down his arms comforting him as he continued.

"I'm glad I don't know who he is or I may just commit murder if he's still alive."

"You were an infant when she died." He'd once told me a little of his childhood and living with his grandparents, but never went into any details about it.

"I was about a year old. My mother would not leave the house from the time of the rape and she never went out in public again but she took great care of me. My grandparents said she would not let me out of her sight."

"I am sure she was a good mother."

"Yes. I feel that there is a connection between us even though she's gone. I feel the love she had for me."

I looked up at his face and saw that his eyes were closed as he spoke. As if though talking about the memories was painful for him and I almost asked him to stop. "Jordan, you don't need to tell…"

"I want to. I want you to know more about me. I'm asking you to give us a chance at a relationship and to do that you need to know about me."

I sighed and settled back down at his side with my arms wrapped around his waist protectively.

"One day my grandmother got home from work and my mother was gone. She said she was leaving for South America with a man that she loved and did not want anyone to look for her. That she was happy with him but could not take me along with her. So she chose him instead of me. I was home crying in my crib when nana got home and found the note. They filed a police report and the authorities started an investigation since my grandparents did not believe that my mother would have done this."

"They thought she was forced? Like kidnapped?" I asked.

"Yes. They never believed for one moment that my mother went of her own free will. A day later, there were reports that a plane went down over the ocean heading to South America and that there were two passengers. My mom and some unknown guy. They both died. Supposedly he may have been the guy that raped her. Seemed like he had threatened her not to speak of the rape, then kidnapped her and was taking her to South America."

I was dumbfounded by the information and my heart ached for his mom and the courageous man beside me.

"I feel guilty for destroying her life. Maybe she could have healed emotionally, but then she was pregnant and that further inhibited her from dealing with the rape, because now she had to live with the product from the rape."

"Oh, Jordan, you can't think like that. She would not want you to blame yourself about any of what happened to her. You were innocent in all this." I tried to ease his burden but I wasn't sure that I got through to him. He continued to talk and I decided to just listen, glad that he was able to talk about the ghastly emotional ordeal of his early life.

"No one knows who he was or how he hid his identity so well. He may have even changed the way he looked during the year my mom was pregnant and the following year after I was born. He was a pilot or learned to fly during the two years since he was supposedly flying the plane that went down."

"How did he buy a plane and not reveal his identity?"

"He stole it. Radar did not pick up the airplane since he was flying very low. There were reports in the investigation that he stopped and refueled in Mexico and again in Nicaragua, but he was in disguise."

I slid one of my legs over both of Jordan's, securing us in a tighter bond as he continued to share with me. I was hurting for the infant crying in his crib for his mother who'd adored him and did all she could to protect him, and for the man in my arms that was still trying to find closure to a part of his life that he was clearly still struggling with.

"The plane went down before they got to Venezuela. There was a distress signal picked up by a fishing vessel but it was very hard to understand what the pilot was saying. They did, however, tell U.S. authorities that the pilot mentioned my mother's name and that she was a passenger along with him." Jordan let out a long slow breath as if ridding himself of the haunting memories.

We both remained quiet and after a few minutes I placed light kisses on his chest. I wanted him to know he was not alone. Part of me understood the need to know the parents that others speak of but you never had the opportunity to meet, would never have the memories of their hugs and kisses, nor them tucking you in bed and reading yet another bedtime story.

"She would have been so proud of you. Of the man that you are and the way you care about her parents in her absence, sitting at her mother's bedside...yes, you have made her proud."

"Thank you. I think the same of you. You are a special and incredibly smart woman that has accomplished so much. Your parents would be proud of you indeed." Again, we fell into another silence, each in our own thoughts.

"Go to sleep, pretty lady."

I listened to his slow, strong heart beating in his chest. The cool dark room contributed to the calm that surrounded us as we lay in each other's arms. Deep in my heart I was aware that something changed for us tonight. Jordan's pain reached into my soul and I longed to help him heal emotionally. The more I found out about the gorgeous man beside me, the more he tugged at my heart that was now open for love.

Sometime during the middle of the night I was in a slumber and tried to turn over in the bed but our limbs were tangled in a convoluted state.

Jordan moaned and pulled me closer to his body.

My eyes popped open when I heard his husky laugh. He was awake and sporting an erection that rubbed against my belly. My body responded to his immediately. I reached down between our bodies and took his length in my hand, slowly pumping his huge cock.

He rewarded me by slowly pushing two fingers into my now moist folds. Jordan flipped me over on my back and with one slow fluid motion, entered me and did not stop moving until I felt his balls against my ass.

I wrapped both my legs around his hips and he started to move over me. As our body mated, our erratic breathing and groans were the only sounds in the room.

He increased his pace and my legs fell from his hips giving him more freedom to move. Jordan placed my knees over his arms pulling me closer into him as he knelt between my legs. Our bodies were longing for the moment when we reached the climax of our mating. I reached down to touch my clit and Jordan hissed above me as my folds clamped down on his cock sending him into a frenzy of need to release his pleasure into me. My hand flew over my clit again and I rocked into the moment of ecstasy as my orgasm slammed into me. With trembling hands I held onto Jordan's shoulders. His powerful body jerked above finding his moment of bliss.

A few minutes later, Jordan eased off me. We settled back in each other's arms. Sated and relaxed, we slipped into blissful sleep again.

~ ~ ~ ~ ~

"Nothing pleases me more than to find you in my bed."

I opened my eyes to see Jordan standing beside the bed with a cup of coffee in his hand. I reached out to take the cup, but he held it away from me.

"Oh no. You don't get this yet. Show me a peek of your sexy body first then you can have your crack coffee."

"God, you're mean. Fine." I shoved the covers to my knees. It was hard to be shy around Jordan. The way he ogled over my body…well, the man knew how to make a woman proud of herself. I grabbed the cup from his hand and sipped in the blissful hot liquid.

"My feelings are hurt, babe. I thought I would be the only one to make you moan like that, but you do it for coffee, too. May just have to buy out Starbucks."

"Why are you wide awake and sweaty?" I asked, taking in his disheveled appearance.

"My trainer was here at 6 a.m. and worked me over in my gym."

He had a trainer? No wonder his rock hard body was in incredible shape.

"Thought you may want to have breakfast before it's time for lunch."

"What time is it?" I looked around the room for a clock but didn't see one.

"A little after nine."

"I would love to go for a run, or I can use a treadmill if you have one in your mini mansion."

"My mini mansion does have one indeed. Come on, I'll take you." He turned to leave.

"Wait! I don't have any clothes."

"Sure you do. Let me show you around your closet."

We walked to it where he showed me a couple drawers with everything I needed to go to the gym. I could work out for a couple weeks without wearing any of the clothing twice. I quickly chose some running clothes and tennis shoes.

Jordan took a hold of my hand and led me downstairs and toward the back of the house.

"Good morning, Jordan. And this must be Zoe."

I looked across the kitchen to see a woman walking toward us. Her brown hair was pulled back in a bun and her amber color eyes were kind and friendly.

"Morning, Becky. Yes, this is Zoe Caine."

Becky shook my hand then patted Jordan on his arm. "She is just as lovely as you described her, Jordan. You did well with this one."

I looked at up at Jordan and he was smiling. I shook my head ruefully at him but he paid no attention to it.

"You are off to the gym then." Becky said, taking in our appearance. "I'll have a nice hot breakfast ready when you get back. I make a mean eggs benedict."

"Thank you, Becky. I look forward to it then." I smiled across at her.

Jordan took me outside. I stood for a moment and took in the beautiful morning. Birds chirped in the trees. A warm breeze was blew and the humidity caused a glint of perspiration on my skin. The pool had three water features with water cascading over the sides and a waterfall with rocks that added to the natural forest feel of the place. There was a four-car garage detached from the house and an adjoining building at the back of the garage.

"This is the gym," Jordan said as he keyed in some codes on the keypad. We stepped into a modern gym with state of the art equipment. "I have a brief meeting with my security detail, but take your time. You can listen to music on the individual equipment or on the surround sound system. I also have a virtual screen on the wall that goes through different terrain with magnificent scenes from all over the world. Here, take a look."

He picked up a remote control and clicked some options while looking at the blank wall in front of us. It came to life with images from the majestic scenes and I was in the middle of the scene. "There are TVs with the same options."

Jordan showed me the music features and choices, but I asked him to leave it on and program it for an hour of running. Jordan swooped in for a quick kiss on my lips then took his leave.

It felt good to get back to working out my weary muscles. I enjoyed the feeling of having a strong body and did not like to go more than a few days without some cardio. Soon the sweat was trickling down my chest and back.

I looked up to see the wall was a virtual TV screen that was showing me running on a track, then me jumping on the top of a rock in the Grand Canyon. The scenes changed every few minutes taking me through a forest, down hills, and back up to mountaintops, as if setting the pace of my workout with just enough cardio for me to not hit the wall so to speak, and I thoroughly enjoyed the routine.

The session ended and I started the cool down by walking on the treadmill as the screen displayed glaciers with an eagle soaring above the ice, then taking off over the icy waters of the ocean. "Fragile" by Sting played as I admired the magnificence of the colossal stationary ice, some giving way slowly and breaking off into the ocean. The song ended and I stood for a minute taking it all in then stepped off the machine.

I turned around to look for a towel. Jordan was standing at the back of the room, legs apart and arms across his chest with a remote control in his hand. We stood across the room in silence, our gazes locked, grey eyes gazing into blue, intense and real. He had taken a shower and changed into a grey T-shirt and cargo shorts with casual summer sandals.

Jordan turned off the screen, picked up a towel and slowly made his way toward me.

A shiver went down my spine as I felt like hunted prey that would welcome being captured by her captor because she knew he would mark her as his. I held my breath as he stood in front of me.

He ran his thumb across my bottom lip. I closed my eyes as he wiped off the perspiration with the towel. His lips replaced his thumb as he pulled my bottom lip into his mouth nipping it lightly then drawing away. Jordan looked down at me.

"Magnificent. Pure manna from heaven. That is what you are." He took both of my hands in his and held them to his lips. "Yes, I will have more than your body. Soon you will give me what is mine."

His words sounded like a promise. A done deal. That it was only a matter of time before I stopped denying what I really felt for him. I could lose my head and heart to this man that will stop at nothing to claim me, mark me as his.

"Come on, beautiful lady." He led me back outside and we went upstairs where he started the shower and got some clothes from the closet that he insisted were mine.

I showered and washed my hair. In record time I was back out and slipping into the gauzy cream colored summer dress Jordan chose for me with some sandals. I looked around for underwear but didn't see any.

"You don't need it."

"Excuse me?"

"Underwear. Rule number one...no underwear when you are here with me. It is the only piece of clothing you do not have here."

He was joking, right? "I can't possibly walk around your house with my ass hanging out when you have your staff here."

"I promise to fire them if they look under your clothing. The only one seeing that fine ass is me." He walked up to me and pinched me there.

"Ouch!"

"Now be a good girl and finish getting ready so we can eat. I'm starved."

Deciding not to argue about it, I went to the dressing room to dry my hair and pull it into a high ponytail.

Back downstairs, Becky had two places set at the breakfast nook that was the size of my dining room in my house.

"Look's great, Becky," Jordan said.

Becky beamed as she served the scrumptious food. "Enjoy. Let me know if you need anything else." She went back to the kitchen.

"What does your staff do when you're traveling or in Europe for an extended period of time?"

"They travel with me. Well, some of them do, like George, my personal bodyguard, and then there is my driver. I also have a personal assistant, Helen. You know, Helen, right?"

I nodded my head. She was very protective of Jordan and knew the ins and outs of his company.

"And one of my attorneys travels with me, and others if needed. I have a domestic management company that takes care of my residents along with gardeners, housekeepers and the like, except for Becky. She goes through me."

"Hmm."

"I will be going to Brussels next week for a few days," he said.

"When are you leaving?"

"Monday evening. Should be back on Thursday. I wish you could go. Brussels is beautiful, you would love it." He held one of my hands on the table then brought it to his lips and kissed my knuckles.

"That is on my bucket list of places to visit. Along with Italy, Sweden, Germany, Bora Bora...my list is long." I smiled at him, but he was serious.

"I want to take you to all those places. I want to show you the world. Will you let me?"

God, this man was killing me. The sincerity in his eyes and his words made me want to give over to his request and do anything he asked. I squeezed his hand and let it go. We continued eating in silence.

"Just give me some to take it all in."

"OK. I can do that." He smiled at me, satisfied that I was not totally against thinking about a relationship with him. We finished our meal and got up from the table. "Time for the tour then." He reached for my hand again and took me to the downstairs office.

CHAPTER 25

"THE FURNISHINGS ARE BEAUTIFUL." WELL-APPOINTED pieces of gleaming furniture showed off intricate details on the legs of the desk and matching chairs. An impressive stand-alone wet bar was off to one side of the room in the same wood as the other pieces.

"They were custom made for this room in Belize. The wood is mahogany."

"Were you deep sea fishing or scuba diving?"

"Well, I did both when I was there but my main purpose was business. I bought an island."

"Is that a joke?"

"I never joke about real estate."

We were standing at the windows overlooking another area of the backyard with views of a gazebo and some type of stream with water running over rocks and into a pond filled with beautiful blooming lilies.

"Is it for your own personal use or investors?"

A couple weeks after graduating from college a group of us went to Belize where we learned to scuba dive. We had a blast and some of us had been back a few times since then.

"Personal. I will have a home built on it soon and a small golf course."

Holy shit!

"Wow. That is a great accomplishment, Jordan."

"Hmm."

That's all he had to say about buying an island? OK then.

"Use the office any time you need to, and anything else here for that matter. Now on to one of my favorite parts of the house that has nothing to do with work."

He grasped my hand again and we went further down the hall where he opened a door to the downstairs bedroom suite. Like the rest of the house, this room was elegantly decorated in cream-colored French country weather furnishings and white linens on the bed.

"Um, Jordan. I have a funny story to tell you. About 10 years ago you took me to a winery in east Texas. We toured parts of the wine trail, so we decided to get a room at a bed and breakfast in the area. I loved the furnishings in the room. I thought it was the most romantic room. Anyway, the bedroom was very much like this one. Is that just a funny story, coincidence or..."

Jordan silenced me with a kiss before I could finish my sentence. "Neither. I have a confession to make," he said as we stood in the middle of the room. "There is not much in this home that was not done with you in mind."

"What?"

"Jenna and David's first home, although much smaller than this one, was of similar design on the outside. I remember you loved the rustic charm of the wood and stone with huge beams and a porch. You said if you ever had a home custom built it would be of that style. I even remembered that you love high ceilings. I bought this land five years ago, but did not want as much land, so I divided it into three-acre lots. There are thirty homes in this subdivision. Mine was the last home to be built."

I was flabbergasted and not sure if I should be happy or mad. If I got upset at him for going to extreme measures to please me, then I should tell him and walk away. Yet he was willing to live with all these memories of me in his life even though he wasn't sure that I wanted to be with him in any kind of relationship. Well, except sexual at this point.

If I was happy…I just needed more time. I reached up on my toes and pulled his head down to my lips and kissed him softly. Letting go, I turned around and held my hand out to him to continue the tour.

We walked across the hall to the library. Jordan opened the glass doors leading into the room.

I stopped short at the door and gasped as I took in the room. Bookshelves lined every wall except for the area at the back of the room with three huge floor to ceiling windows and the two glass doors on this side of the room. There was a small sitting area to the right of the room with two wing back chairs and a coffee table. In front of the windows was another sitting area with two matching Denver leather chaises sitting on what was surely a Persian rug. There were several books that were artfully displayed in various areas of the library and a collection immediately caught my eye. I headed straight to them.

Could it be?

Yes.

They are.

"The works of William Shakespeare."

I looked at Jordan and this time I couldn't help it. Tears gathered in my eyes blurring his image. I blinked and they fell on his hand. I was lost for words, so I just let the moment of silence speak for my appreciation of the works of one of my most beloved writers. I collected myself and ran my hands reverently across the light brown leather books. First editions, seven books in all.

"You didn't miss a trick, did you?"

"When it comes to you, no."

"You did good, Jordy," I whispered.

I held on to his hand as we walked slowly around the room. There were hundreds of books. Some rare and collectable, others current. He pointed out books that I've read and some that he thought I would enjoy reading. I sat on one of the lounge chairs and took in the sunny day outside, again taken by the beauty of the place, inside and out. Jordan knelt on the floor beside me and kissed me, taking my breath away. I felt the urgency in his kiss as if he thought I would disappear from his life again. The kiss ended and I held his beautiful face in my hands to gaze in his eyes.

"I am here. Right here with you. I'm so proud of you, not just for your financial accomplishments and mega millions that you have, but also for the person, the man, that you are. I could not be more proud of you. Equally, I'm honored that you want me in your life and that you didn't forget about me or allow me to forget about you," I told him.

"You are it for me, Zoe. I have traveled the world over, but my heart stayed with you." He put his forehead on mine, our faces so close together that I was inhaling the air he exhaled.

It was sweet agony. What was I waiting for? Then I knew. I knew what I needed to do and I would do it tomorrow. The feeling of rightness that would bring me to the realization of what I needed to do had dawned on me and I suddenly felt at peace with myself and with all that Jordan had done.

He got to his feet and swung me easily into his arms. We went further down the hall to the music room.

"This is a lovely room, and I didn't know you played so many instruments. Such a talented man," I teased him as I looked around the room with gleaming instruments. The black baby grand piano was the focal part of the room.

"Smart ass. Remind me to spank you later." He set me in front of the piano and slid onto the bench beside me.

"No, I don't play all these instruments. I play the piano and saxophone, but I hope to have kids that take an interest in music." He waggled his eyebrows at me and I rolled my eyes at him. He ran his hands across the keys and played a few seconds of a lighthearted melody, then started playing *Fleur de Lis*. At the end of the tune, he started chopsticks and I joined in this time.

I didn't play the piano very well, not having had enough time to practice, nor confident enough to play what I do know, but I knew *Chopstick*. By the end of the playful tune we were laughing in stitches as our fingers raced across the keys.

"Now for the grand finale." We headed upstairs and turned to the right of the stairway and down the hall. Jordan opened the door to one of the two bedrooms at the end of the house.

"Unless they are invisible, there is no furniture in here."

"Nope. These two rooms are for you to decorate as you wish. Put your Zoe touch all over them."

Seriously? I decided to keep the moment light although I was touched by his never-ending thoughts of me. I walked over to the window and sat cross-legged on the window seat.

"I say we leave them like this. One can definitely be your time out room, you know for those speeding tickets you are collecting all over Houston."

"You have a smart mouth, you know that? Come here and let me put something long and hard in there." Jordan was still at the door but I was feeling a little naughty, or maybe I was just horny.

"Is it just me or is this room warm?" I used my hand as a fan to my face.

Immediately sensing that I was in a playful mood, Jordan leaned against the doorframe and smiled at me.

Really? He wasn't moving, so I upped the ante by pulling up one leg and resting the heel on the edge of the window seat. His brows shot up but he stayed where he was. *Fine!* I hiked up the skirt to my waist and let my knees fall apart exposing my smooth pussy. I looked at Jordan and he was staring intently between my legs. I let my eyes travel slowly down his body and stopped at the zipper of his shorts. It was bulging, the zipper straining against his erection, but he still did not move. I dropped my hand to my wet heat and inserted a finger and pulled it back out. It was wet with my juices and I slowly sucked it off in my mouth.

"Holy fucking Christ," Jordan growled. He quickly locked the door behind him and pushed a button on the wall beside the door. The blinds behind me came down as Jordan pushed me onto my back. In one deft motion, he was at my wet need and his mouth clamped on my slick folds. My ass came off the seat as he grasped me and pulled me further toward his mouth.

I squirmed and bucked against his talented tongue seeking more. I gasped with need. With hands in his hair, I pushed his face into me.

He complied and rewarded me with his tongue flicking my clit. He went from my clit to the slit of my vagina and pierced me with his tongue.

"Oh God, Jordan, that feel's so good. Yes, baby, just like that." I was overcome with need and not embarrassed to ask for what I wanted from him.

"Please, please…I need it. I do, Jordy, I do." I was withering and moaning for more.

"Greedy little girl today. You want to come?"

"Yes, yes, I do. I want it. I need it."

"Hmm. Not very convincing."

"Fuck me already."

He laughed huskily between my legs. He blew on my pussy and took my clit in his mouth again and continued fucking me, faster now.

"Jordan, I…I, it will be in your mouth."

"Hmmm," was his only response, as the suction on my clit increased.

I teetered on the brink, my slickness oozing onto his tongue as I splintered in his mouth. My juices coated his lips as he lapped it up. My legs quivered and I groaned above him.

Jordan pulled me onto the carpeted floor. I grabbed his shorts, fumbling with the button as he pulled at the zipper. His cock sprung free and in one swift motion he was in me. He pushed his huge penis in my wet vagina again and again.

I held onto his arms as he neared his release. My pussy clamped down on his cock as I came again. I threw my head back with closed eyes as his powerful frame shuddered above me.

"Ah. Christ, baby." He groaned above me as his orgasm ripped through him. He shoved one last time, emptying the contents of his sac into me. His face was on my neck, both of our harsh breathing filling the quiet empty room.

I was humbled at the realization that I affected this man this way. This powerful, rich, yet sensuous and caring man, buried deep inside me.

Jordan reversed our position and I was now lying on top of him. We stayed on the floor for a few minutes, our bodies replete.

"Your tour isn't over yet. Let's get you cleaned up so I can show you the last of the inside tour." He got up and grasped my hand to help me stand. We headed down the hall to the master bedroom when my phone rang.

"Jenna. How are you feeling?"

"A little better today since I had medication. I try not to take it, but I hate feeling icky and the medication does help."

"Good. Aunt Suzette back home?"

"She went home yesterday after I promised to call her at least twice a day. She will be such a good grandmother, and David's mom is over the moon happy."

"A baby is always a good reason to be happy." I sighed as I thought of my own biological clock that was ticking. I shocked myself with that random thought. *It was random, right? Right.*

"So how are you and Jordan doing? And yes, I want all the details."

I laughed at her nosey remark. "Well, we are taking it slow, but it's going well, like holy hot hell we are...well, let's just say I'm making up for lost times in the sex department."

Jenna let out with a hooting laugh and told David what I said. I heard him whistle in the background followed by a, "Go, Jordan. That's my boy."

Now it was my turn to laugh. I couldn't believe I was sharing my sex life with my brother-in-law.

"We need to get together soon and catch up. Like in a couple of weeks. Hopefully I will be feeling better or you and the girls can come here to Austin for another visit."

"Sounds like a plan. Love you, sis."

"Love you too, Zoho." We ended the call, and I freshened up then went in search of Jordan.

He was on his phone as well in the hallway. From the sound of it he was turning down an invitation for tonight. He ended the call with a, "Later, man." Then he turned toward me.

"Jenna doing well?"

"As long as she takes her meds. The first trimester is the hardest for most women. Maybe she will be over the nausea in a few weeks."

We went back down the hallway and past the two empty bedrooms. We came to a heavy glass door and Jordan stopped to key in some codes then used his index fingerprint for identification. He opened the door and turned on the lights by remote control on his phone.

The room was exquisite and adorned with incredibly beautiful paintings. In the middle of the room was an easel. I walked slowly toward the painting on display. It was of Jordan and me dancing at Jenna and David's wedding. It was a side view of us. I had my right hand on his shoulder and my left hand in his right. His left hand was around my waist and we were looking at each other, smiling. I stood in awe and turned toward Jordan.

He cupped my face in his hands. I closed my eyes, willing the tears away.

"I wanted a photo of us together, so just before I asked you to dance, I asked the photographer at the wedding to take one of us. I asked him to send it to me and not the bride and groom. I never got around to showing you the photo. Five years ago I asked a painter to paint the photo into a portrait."

I placed my head on his chest and he slipped his arms around my waist, rocking us slowly from side to side.

"I'm speechless. A painting of the first time we met. Truly, I...of all the paintings you have in this room, you display this one in the middle of the room?"

"Of all the paintings in this room, this one is the most valuable to me. I wanted a picture of you because I was not sure that you would want to see me again. Sure enough, you turned me down. When I met you, I was quite impressed that you were so appreciative of art. Sometimes when we had cuddling time on your sofa, we used to talk about courses you were taking. Remember your art appreciation class?"

"Yes. I loved that class, and the next semester I took the advance course just because I wanted to know more about art. I see where you're going with this. You must have some of the paintings that I 'appreciated'."

"So right you are."

"So this is your art room. Yesterday, when you said that you would show me the art room, I thought you took up painting or pottery. I'm astonished at the pieces you have here."

Jordan turned me around and started on one corner of the room. We walked slowly around, discussing each piece and its creator. There were paintings from Omar Chkhaidze, Francois Mathieu, Andy Warhol, to African and South American sculptors. The room had no windows and looked like a museum with professional lightings that was placed strategically enhancing the paintings, pottery, precious stones and other rare antique and pricey pieces.

"This is a beautiful collection, Jordan, and an incredible testament of your financial success and love of art."

"It pleases me that you like the collection. I hope to continue to add to it with your help."

"I would like that," I replied.

"Would you like to go for a swim in the pool, maybe lay out and catch some rays?"

"Great plan. Do I have a swim suit?"

"Do you ever."

Back in the closet that I was quickly becoming familiar with, Jordan pulled out a drawer with an array of bikinis.

"Holy shit. I might as well go topless. These threads barely cover my nipples."

"That would suit me just fine, but I suggest not today since I have a few staff around."

"Jordan, I was kidding."

"Zoe, I'm not."

"Perv."

"Totally."

He grinned that mischievous boyish smile that was sure to make me give in to any of his demands. If I had panties on, they would be soaked.

CHAPTER 26

I CHANGED INTO THE FLIMSY AND QUITE REVEALING two-piece bikini then went in search of Jordan. He was waiting for me at the bedroom door. He growled and made a grab for me but I dodged him and ran to the stairs. I took the stairs two at a time and ran to the back door but he caught up to me.

He tickled me and playfully pushed me through the door. We jumped in the pool and swam a few laps. My limbs were relaxed and I felt more rested than I had been in weeks.

"Out with you. I need to get some sunblock on that delectable skin of yours. I don't want you to burn, then I wouldn't be able to touch you and that just won't do." Jordan led me to a padded lounging chair. I plopped down. He dried me off and applied the lotion.

We lie side by side enjoying the afternoon sun. Becky brought us some freshly squeezed lemonade with a plate of fruit. I was more curious about her now and asked Jordan to tell me more about Becky.

"I know that she was my mother's best friend in high school and she was one of the few people that mom would see besides her family. They spent a lot of time together when mom was pregnant with me and the following year as well."

"I'm glad that your mother had someone her own age to keep her connected to the outside world, like what was going on in school and with other friends. She must have been a great source of comfort at a very painful and confusing time for your mom. Do you think you mother ever confided in her about the rape?"

"I often wonder that myself but I have not asked her. I would like for Becky to tell me on her own."

"I suppose she may be waiting for you to ask her. Maybe she thinks that it would be too painful for you to hear, if she knows anything, that is."

"It's possible. My grandfather still thinks that mom is alive. He's in denial of her death."

"Sounds like he needs closure, like some kind of evidence that she's really gone." I reached for Jordan's hand, needing the tactile connection to let him know that I cared.

"Unfortunately, that is impossible but if it help's him to get through his day by thinking of her as alive, then so be it and I will not discourage him."

"I can't begin to imagine the pain that he feels. You and I are in a similar situation since we didn't know our parents, therefore we don't miss who we don't know, but this was his child. No wonder he's still hanging on to the hope that she's out there somewhere, still alive. I suppose I would do the same."

"There just seems to be no leads or evidence that she is. No plausible explanation for who did it and if someone knows, they sure as hell aren't talking. You would think that it wouldn't be easy for people to disappear, but whoever did this to my mother..."

"It's been thirty-seven years since she disappeared, right?"

"Yes. Becky has shared photos of her and my mom when they were teenagers. Maybe that's why I like having her around. It's one of the few connections that I have with my mother."

We fell into a companionable silence then Jordan said we needed to get out of the direct sunlight, but I suggested a stroll around some of the backyard and he happily obliged by pulling me to my feet and pointing out the obvious.

"This is the pool." He made a grand gesture with his hands.

"Never would have guessed that one, Sherlock."

He laughed that low, sexy as hell laugh that sent butterflies flying in my stomach.

Palm trees and foliage that were indigenous to Texas adorned the beautiful contemporary pool and hot tub. Blooming flowers overflowed from massive decorative pots. A pebbled path led into the woodsy area of the estate. Live oak and other trees and plants filled in the landscape.

"I don't recognize some of these plants and trees," I commented, looking around the tranquil landscape.

"Some are imported from different parts of the world and carefully tended by my gardener. He's a member of the American Horticultural Society and takes great pride in the garden. There is a butterfly garden on the other side of the property."

Numerous water features were scattered throughout the estate.

Different species of orchids bloomed in the trees providing a natural habitat for the treasured flowers. A Japanese garden was at one corner of the estate surrounded by vibrant green bamboo trees and other plants that flanked a pond.

"I could sit here all day and watch the butterflies." We sat on a bench under a tree and looked at the insects with beautiful vibrant colors going from flowers and plants to fresh fruits.

"We have plenty of time to stay as long as you wish."

We made our way back to the pool on a different path with blooming roses, hibiscus, cactus and other plants and flowers. The ones that I did point out on my tour with Jordan were my favorites, and of course he knew that, which was why he specifically had them plentiful throughout the estate. When we got back to the pool we were met by Becky.

"The masseuses are ready when you are."

"Thank you, Becky."

"You're getting a massage?" I asked.

"We are. This way." He led us toward the gym where there was an adjoining building that housed a spa fully equipped with a sauna, hot tub, four massage tables and a full bathroom with shower. A soothing eucalyptus aroma permeated the air as we entered the ethereal room elegantly decorated with bouquets of fresh flowers, paintings of Texas landscapes, plush seating and a chandelier that complimented the bamboo wood ceiling and tile floors. There were glass windows with black-out screens throughout.

"Mr. Dawson, Miss Caine."

We were greeted by two women that owned 'Our Hands, Your Home Spa'. "My name is Claire and this is Angie. Please let us know when you're ready, sir. We'll be in the waiting room; just ring the bell." Claire provided us with fluffy white robes and a tall glass of cold water with a splash of fresh squeezed orange and lemon slices. They stepped out to give us privacy.

"You've thought of just about everything, Jordan. This is heavenly. I just may fall asleep."

"I think falling asleep is a compliment to a masseuse. It means you're totally relaxed by their hands." I drank the entire glass as Jordan instructed. "Don't want you getting dehydrated."

We lay on our stomach with white towels across our bottoms.

"Hmm. I love the music. Yo- Yo Ma?"

"Correct. Should have known you would recognize that piece which is why we're going to his concert tonight in Houston. I have box office seats and invited one of my investors and his wife that are in Houston from Belgium."

"OK, you did think of everything."

We were lulled into silence as hands moved over our bodies. An hour later I was barely awake. Jordan and I looked dazed but relaxed.

He led the way to the hot tub that was bubbling with a wonderful minty aroma. We slid into it for a few minutes and sipped on cold water.

"Out with you, before you drown. Time for a shower."

I could so get used to this. The shower was stocked with everything I could think of including my favorite shampoo and conditioner. *Now why didn't that surprise me?* Jordan washed my hair, his magic hands on my scalp totally delightful.

His hands ran over my body with L'Occitane citrus shower gel. Suddenly his hands stop moving. He cupped my breasts in his hands and squeezed my nipples. The dusky pink buds perked up responding to the tactile stimulation that had me immediately responding to his erotic touch.

I leaned back into his hard body that was slick with water as the showerheads beat down on us.

He pulled me closer to him as one arm hugged me around my waist and his other hand slipped between my legs.

I immediately opened my legs and two of his fingers slipped in to assuage my soft, wet folds. I pushed my ass against his cock. The steel hard erection pushed against my body, seeking entrance to my pulsing womanhood now puffy with need.

Jordan pulled us further back in the shower. He sat on the shower bench and pushed me forward. Fisting his cock in his hand, he lifted me onto his erection seeking my slit as he lowered me down on his glorious cock. My ass nestled to his lower abdomen as a moan escaped my lips.

"Move with me, baby." He lifted me up and down and I joined in the motion. Our slick bodies moved in perfect harmony.

"I won't last long, babe." We slammed against each other. "Need you to come with me." Jordan panted behind me as my pussy slid over him.

My inner folds clenched on his cock. His body went rigid and his hands grasped my hips as I flew over the pinnacle, my orgasm crashing into me. I bit my lip from screaming out his name, but I am unable to control the sound mewling in my throat. I gasped as he pulled me into his chest, his cock pulling out of me, still semi-hard. Our breathing struggled to return to normal.

"You totally undo me. I can't keep my hands off you. Can't get enough." He bit my shoulder gently. After a few minutes we showered off, again.

"I'll head inside. Claire and Angie will help you with your hair and makeup in the dressing room."

"Really, Jordan, they don't need to do that. I am perfectly capable of doing my own grooming."

"Just humor me. I delight in pampering my lovely lady."

I rolled my eyes but he just smiled and took his leave. I put on my robe again and went in search of the ladies. They were in the adjoining dressing room waiting for me. I gratefully sat in the chair. Claire started with my hair and Angie did my manicure and pedicure.

Another hour later and I was pampered, puffed, fluffed and ready for a night at the symphony. I made my way back to the house where Becky met me. She said Jordan was in his office so I went in search of him.

He was dressed in a dark blue suit, white shirt and a dark pink striped tie. His face looked impassive as he focused on the computer monitor where he was engaged in a videoconference.

"Just get it done, James. They are in dire straights and can't afford to keep their doors open for more than six months."

"They're looking for funding and more than likely will get approved by a bank that is willing to take some risk. They're in the red and struggling, but not ready to give up." He paused as his attorney spoke quietly back to him.

"Then we do a hostile takeover. I own the majority of the shares and have permission from the board of directors."

"When did that happen?"

"I bought all the shares I could get my hands on last week which gave me majority."

I didn't want to eavesdrop any longer, so I slipped upstairs.

There was a gorgeous cocktail dress lying on the bed. The metallic dress by Hervé Léger was elegant and sexy with narrow shoulder straps and a moderate plunging neckline. The body created an hourglass effect and flared gently just before the hemline. I slipped into the dress that swirls at mid-thigh. A pair of strappy four-inch sandals by Fendi was beside the dress so I slipped them on.

"Beautiful lady." Jordan was leaning at the bedroom door.

He was looking some kind of hot, with legs apart and both hands in his pants pocket. His incredibly blue eyes seemed to look right through me. I felt a blush creep up my cheeks. I could not help the total admiration I felt for the gorgeous man now approaching me. My hands fluttered and I grasped the edge of the dress totally aware that I had no underwear on. Just as Jordan instructed.

I felt naked as air from the ceiling fan overhead swirled, sending cool air up my legs and beyond. I chided myself that after all the hot sex that we've had, and I was shy? *Really?* I am not sure why the hint of anxiety set in, but looking at Jordan was making me feel restless, edgy and horny again. *Damn!*

"Turn around, lovely."

I stumbled as I turned in the super sexy high shoes. Jordan steadied me and zipped up the back of the dress.

"Did this fashion guru guy consult Mia by any chance?"

"No. Why?" He kissed me softly on my neck.

"Because these 'fuck me' heels are just her style."

"You are wearing those heels because I absolutely intend to fuck you in them later on tonight."

Oh God! I was so not going to be able to think of anything else tonight but Jordan fucking me in these gorgeous heels and nothing else. I laughed at his blatant admission of what he intended to do to me. I could only imagine and I couldn't wait.

"Now for a little something extra." Jordan walked to the closet that he insisted was mine and came back with two blue boxes.

Now, I knew that color to be Tiffany's signature color. I mean, every woman on the planet knows, has, wanted or needed something…anything from Tiffany's.

Jordan slid a platinum and diamond bracelet on my left wrist. The other box was a matching necklace and earrings.

He clasped the necklace around my neck and I clipped the earrings to my ear lobes.

"I hope they're insured."

"But of course. Even if they were not, they are yours to do as you wish."

"You could have invested the money it took to buy these, you know. Like maybe buy another island or better yet, a small country."

"Like I said, your smart, delectable mouth, Miss Caine..."

"You like my smart mouth, Mr. Dawson."

"That I do." He kissed me soundly, effectively shutting off my quick retort to his teasing.

"Come on. I need to feed you. Dinner first with Niels and his wife, Eline."

CHAPTER 27

WE LEFT IN THE LIMO AND SETTLED IN THE BACK SEAT. Jordan opened a bottle of Champagne and we sipped on the cold bubbly liquid. Jordan pulled me beside him and filled me in on his investor from Brussels.

"Niels invested in several ventures with me in Europe and is keen on expanding his wealth here in the U.S.," Jordan said. "I have several opportunities that may interest him. We've been doing business together for several years."

I listened and sipped on my drink. We kept the conversation light and spoke of some of his travels during the past few years in Asia and Europe. I shared some of my struggles with the agency and the possibility that I may venture into home health nursing since the private duty nursing was doing well. Before long we pulled up to Vic & Anthony's Steakhouse where we met the couple.

"Niels, Eline, allow me to introduce Zoe Caine." Jordan shook the hand of the gentleman and kissed Eline on both cheeks.

I was surprised to see that Niels wasn't much older than Jordan. He is a handsome man with light brown hair, blue eyes and a few inches shorter than Jordan. His wife, Eline, was tall and elegant with straight brown hair that she wore in a fashionable cut above her shoulders. We were shown to our seats in a small private room toward the back of the restaurant.

"Zoe, you must come to visit us in Brussels soon. It's a beautiful city and I think you will enjoy it. There are many theaters and art museums, fine food and fabulous shopping. If you're a coffee lover, we have some of the best in the world."

"Thank you. I look forward to visiting soon. You're very kind." I smiled across at her. "How long will you be in Houston?" I asked.

"Another day is all we have. It is a beautiful city. Very international and welcoming," she replied.

"Have you been to The Galleria?"

"I love it very much. Very different stores from what we have in Brussels but beautiful things just the same. I found some alluring wedding gowns and will fashion some of mine with a little of their ideas."

"When you come to Brussels you must stay with us, of course, Zoe," said Niels. "Jordan, you must bring her soon."

"Thank you. That's a kind offer and I look forward to a visit."

"I would like to take her with us tomorrow, but she's just expanded her office in San Francisco. You do need to see my penthouse in Brussels, Zoe, and if you like it there we'll can keep it," Jordan said.

"You look very happy, my friend, more relaxed," Niels said.

Jordan smiled and looked across at me.

"I do think the beautiful Zoe has much to do with his happiness." Eline looked at Jordan and patted him on his shoulder. I got the impression that the couple was his friends as well as business associates.

"We will miss your brilliant mind in Europe, Jordan, but you will continue your success here in America as well. Of this I am sure, which is why we are eager to join in the opportunity of investing along with many others."

"Thank you, Niels. America continues to be a canvas. The financial opportunities are endless." Jordan discussed a few more minutes of business but steered the conversation to more generalized topic. Niels and Jordan had meetings on Monday morning, then the couple would return to Brussels with Jordan Monday evening.

After dinner, we all rode in the limo to the symphony together. Upon arrival, an attendant accompanied us to our seats.

I was about to step into the seating area when Dr. Charles Rivas greeted me. He's a young cardiovascular surgeon that is making a name for himself in the medical community. We'd met several times over the past few years at different medical and charity functions.

"Zoe, great to see you. How have you been?" He kissed me on the cheek. I turned around to introduce him to Jordan who was staring him down. *Really?*

"How do you do, Jordan? I think you met with my dad earlier this week."

Jordan shook his hand but kept a possessive arm around my waist. Charles' father was also a physician and the medical director of a group of privately owned hospitals in Houston.

"Let's do lunch soon, Zoe. I'm interested in hearing more about your idea for home health. Dad said you tossed the idea around with him the last time he saw you. For what it's worth, I think it would be a great move."

"Thank you, Charles. It would be a huge undertaking and I will keep that option on the table. I would also need a physician as medical director."

"Even more reasons to meet sometime soon then." Charles flashed a charming smile at me.

Jordan's finger dug a little tighter on my waist.

"I believe Zoe will be quite busy during the next few months. She just expanded her office, so do call and make an appointment to see her," Jordan interjected.

WTF? Did he really go there? I so don't need a personal time-keeper.

Charles' brows shot up. "Congratulations, Zoe. That is great news. I am very proud of you."

"Nice meeting you. Charles, is it?" Jordan said smoothly.

"Yes." Charles was about to lean in to kiss my cheek when Jordan spun me around. We took our seats beside our guests.

"Make sure you take Andre with you to that lunch," Jordan whispered in my ear. I elbowed him on his arm. "Lunch is not all he wants to have with you."

I squinted my eyes at him but he was looking at Charles as if sizing up the competition. Thank goodness Charles was looking elsewhere.

"A couple inches of these stilettos are going in your foot if you don't stop acting like a caveman," I whispered back to him.

He had the audacity to smile and wink at me.

The concert started and Yo-Yo Ma and the incredible Houston Symphony that accompanied him wowed us. Niels and Eline seemed to have thoroughly enjoyed the event and were gracious and complimentary guests. Eline and I promised to keep in touch. Jordan escorted them to the car and driver he hired for them while they were in Houston.

Jordan slid into the limo after me and the door closed behind him.

I yelped as he pulled me onto his lap.

He nuzzled my neck and slowly ran his hand up my leg. His large warm hand paused on my body. My chest heaved as I waited in anticipation for more of his touch. Jordan bit me lightly on my neck and a delicious shiver ran down my body settling between my legs.

I wiggled on his lap trying to get him to move his hand higher. All night I had been totally aware that I was not wearing a thread of underwear, and several times during the show, Jordan ran his hand casually up my thigh, but not high enough to be blatant of his intentions. He'd even whispered that he was turned on knowing that I was naked under my dress, which had me squirming in my seat since his wicked suggestions did blissful things to my body.

Suddenly Jordan set me on the seat beside him and reached for a bottle and two glasses. He poured two finger of bourbon in each glass and handed me one.

"That was just a little warm up, pretty lady."

I glared at him. "Did you really just do that?" I was now totally turned on and for a moment I considered attacking him with another kissing session, but I sipped the amber liquid instead. The decadent liquid burned down my throat and settled warm in my stomach.

"Patience, my dear Miss Caine."

"Not one of my virtues."

He chuckled and sipped on his drink.

"Tell me more about your idea for the home health division you wish to start."

"Are you frigging kidding me already? I can't keep my mind off sexing you right now."

"Maybe this is a test."

"I hope I fail miserably then." I sat in the corner sulking.

"So who are you considering for your medical director?"

"Why, Charles, of course," I answered, knowing full well that I had no intentions of asking Charles.

"Like hell you are. He wants to fuck you." Jordan's eyes glinted dangerously in the dim light of the limo.

"Well, someone needs to!" I yelled at him.

Jordan growled, tipped the glass to his lips and gulped down the rest of his drink. He slid closer and held the glass to my mouth.

"Drink," he commanded.

I gulped some of the contents and choked on it. The liquid burned down my throat as I continued to cough and sputter. Jordan finished my drink and threw the glass on the seat across from us.

He pulled his jacket off and threw it on the floor. He was pissed, and for some weird reason that turn me on even more. Jordan slid to the floor and pulled me in front of him. His hands reached for his belt and zipper of his slacks. The sound of his zipper caused a rush of goose bumps across my skin.

Pushing away from the seat, he pulled me on his lap. With perfect aim, his cock pierced my pussy.

I screamed his name in lustful need as he pushed forcefully inside me. My vagina clenched lustfully on his erect penis as my juices coated his cock. I leaned my head into his neck and moaned his name begging for more pleasure. My breasts lay heavy and full, wanting his touch as well. Every square inch of my body begged to be handled by Jordan's masterful touch. His grunts mixed with my moans of pleasure vibrated in the quiet vehicle. I held onto his shoulders with both my legs straddling his body. The force of his movements crushed me against the seat and I welcomed the weight of his body against mine. My breath was sporadic as it landed on Jordan's neck. I kissed his neck and sucked gently on the taunt skin. I wanted to mark him so badly as the incredible feeling of carnal erotic pleasure washed over me.

My orgasm rose and crashed into me quickly. My fingers dug into his shoulder as I found my release. I screamed his name and milked his cock that was pounding against my hot need.

Jordan's slammed his shaft in me one last time. His body shuddered as he came.

We lay spent with ragged breathing and erratic heart rates that slowly returned to normal.

Jordan lifted me up then pulled out of me. He lay his head on my lap as he continued to kneel on the floor. I ran my hands through his soft hair.

"Fuck. I'm sorry, baby. I didn't mean for it to happen that way."

"I hope you're not apologizing for making love to me. I begged you to do it and I would have been super pissed if you hadn't."

"I shouldn't have done it because I was jealous."

"Jordan?"

"Hmm?"

"I yelled at you to fuck me and you did."

"OK."

"I like what you did just now. It was hot. It turned me on. Enough said."

He pulled back and looked up at me. I eyed him warily, not sure if he was going to drop the subject.

"I just need to say one more thing about Charles."

"What about him?"

"He's a surgeon, right?"

"Yes. An excellent heart surgeon." Now I had no idea where he is going.

"I may just have to readjust his fingers if he even considers touching you. I would hate for him to sit behind a desk for the rest of his career pushing papers."

Now I laughed and Jordan joined in.

"That goes for any other man as well," he added.

"Got it." I giggled at his boyish jealousy.

"We're almost home." He kissed the top of my head.

A few minutes later the limo pulled into the circular drive in front of the house and George opened the door. We entered the house and Jordan gripped my hand and took to the stairs. He closed the door behind us after we entered the bedroom and led me to the bed.

"Take only the dress off. I want to fuck you in your shoes and jewelry." He unzipped the dress at the back. It fell at my feet silently, then he pulled off his clothing.

"Lie on your back at the edge of the bed." His voice was low, commanding. I complied.

He stood at the side of the bed and fisted his cock, pumping it slowly. I gazed unabashedly at the beauty of his body.

His other hand ran slowly up my leg to my mound. His finger ran down my slit then slipped inside my pussy. I was wet and ready for him again. He pulled his finger back out and lifted each of my legs by the heel of my 'fuck me' shoes.

I felt my legs quiver, my ass lifting off the mattress silently, begging him to take me again.

In one swift motion he pushed his erection deep inside me. I arched my neck and groaned his name, ready to ask for more, but he immediately started pumping his cock inside me. I felt the pleasure soar deep inside me.

"Look at me."

I opened my eyes which were glazed with sexual desire and looked up at him.

"See how beautiful you are. Sexy as hell with these 'fuck me' shoes. Remind me to fill up that closet with more."

My chest heaved and my body responded with needy greed to be taken by Jordan. I ran my hands across my legs and up my torso to my breasts. I rubbed them and squeezed both nipples as my back arched off the mattress. I was mewling and pushing my bottom toward his huge cock that pumped deep in me now.

Jordan stopped and I looked up at him again.

"Lie on your stomach and put a pillow under your chest."

"I want to come. I need it so bad," I implored.

"Not yet. Not until I tell you or we don't finish this tonight."

"But, I can't…"

"I will fucking jack off with you watching me if you don't do as I say and you still won't get what you want tonight."

I scrambled up to the top of the bed with my body begging for release. I felt my throbbing pussy and the juices running down my thighs. I grabbed the pillow and lay on it as he instructed.

"Now, kneel and spread you legs but leave your chest on the pillow." He positioned my ass in the air and came up behind me. I felt his erection on my bottom.

The broad head of his cock sat at the entrance of my pussy.

He pushed in slowly and groaned as he slid further into my wet folds.

I readjusted my legs and pushed my ass toward him.

His huge cock slid all the way in.

I felt his balls hit my pussy again and again. He held onto my hips as he controlled his strokes.

"God, baby. I wish you could see how fucking sexy you look. Your long hair over your back and the pillow, ass tilted up in the air, legs spread open and your glistening pussy begging to be taken. Absofuckinamazing."

I giggled at his made-up word.

He spanked my ass twice. "No laughing when I'm about to fuck you senseless." He demonstrated just what he had in mind for me by pulling out and slamming back in, repeating the motion countless times.

I held onto the pillow as he pushed into me.

"I want this pretty puckered ass, babe." He pushed a finger in the tight entrance of my ass.

I inhaled sharply with the sting of the intrusive finger. That would be new for me. We'd talked about it, but Jordan wanted us to wait since my sex ed with him was on a steep learning curve.

He pulled his finger back out. "Soon, but not tonight," he said.

His hands gripped my hips again. With each slam of his cock, I groaned as pleasure washed over me. His balls continued to slap my pussy making an erotic sound. Jordan pushed me further to the headboard as he continued with his sensuous assault on my body.

My body rocked with the pleasure of his magnificent body over mine. I wanted this. I wanted more. My inner walls of pleasure clenched onto his shaft as if promising never to let go. His manhood swelled inside my hot center as he drove further in me.

"Ah, Christ. Come with me, Zoe. Come now!"

My body convulsed as Jordan guided us to the pinnacle of ecstasy where we took a leap into oblivion together calling out each other's name. I fell on the bed with Jordan on top of me.

Our bodies were slick with the sheen of perspiration and our lungs pulled in air to grateful bronchioles that were starved for oxygen. Slowly, we became aware of our positions.

Jordan rolled over and pulled me into his chest. We stayed in that position until his cock softened and slid out of me.

"Are you OK?" he asked.

I nodded and smiled up at him.

Jordan took off my shoes and jewelry, then pulled the cover over us.

I nestled into his chest contentedly and my eyes fluttered closed.

CHAPTER 28

I DON'T KNOW HOW HE DOES IT. JORDAN WAS BALL OF energy that doesn't seem to slow down. Sunday morning I woke to God-awful singing. I wobbled out of bed and leaned into the bathroom door to see him vigorously washing his hair while singing, "Treasure" by Bruno Mars.

He looked through the glass shower at me and grinned.

I shook my head and went back to bed. He was totally hilarious with his singing and just wouldn't shut up. A few minutes later he was standing by the side of the bed.

"Don't you like your song that I chose for you?" He was naked in all his gorgeous glory. I pulled the covers over my head. Jordan jumped on the bed and tickled me through the comforter. We wrestled and played until I pulled a pillowcase off one of the pillows and waved it like a white flag.

"Just don't ever be tempted to give up your day job. You would not make a dime as a singer," I teased him.

He laughed, jumped off the bed and pulled on some shorts and a T-shirt. Commando. *Oh yeah!*

"I need to get going. I have totally neglected my house." I scrambled out of bed.

"I'll take you, but first shower and breakfast."

I saluted him and went to the incredible shower, turned it on full blast with all five shower heads beating down on my sore muscles.

Becky had homemade waffles with maple syrup and fluffy scramble eggs ready for us.

Jordan took me home in his sexy Maserati. During the ride home I texted Jenna to check on her but David texted back saying she was still sleeping from the Phenergan that she took earlier.

A visit with Aunt Suzette was long overdue so I texted her asking if we could meet for dinner tonight. I needed her advice and wisdom, plus I missed her company and I wanted to talk with her about planning a baby shower for Jenna in a few months.

Jordan came inside my house for a few minutes, and then I remembered that I forgot my luggage at his penthouse, which I told him. All I had with me was my purse and computer.

"I don't think I packed much from your house anyway. I had my driver bring some of your clothes from my penthouse the morning we went to San Francisco."

"Which is why I didn't recognized any of the clothes that I wore but I was way to busy to argue about it, you sneak."

He pulled me in a kiss and nibbled on my lips.

I broke off the kiss and shoved him through the door just as my phone started ringing. It was Mia on Skype.

"Have you been with Jordan the whole weekend or what?"

"Well, hello to you, too." I grinned at her. She was sprawled delicately on a lounger at her father's pool.

"I miss you, biotch."

"Yeah, I miss you too, but don't you have someone else to harass?"

"Wouldn't be as much fun. Plus, you are in the papers this morning."

"What the hell? Why?" Curious, I opened my computer and navigated to the *Houston Chronicle* online edition. "What section is it and what does it say?"

"Lifestyle section, and you are looking all kinds of sexy with Jordan and another almost equally gorgeous couple."

"Here it is. I didn't know there were photographers. Well, I knew they were around, but I thought they were taking photos of other people."

"Hate to break it to you, chick, but wherever Jordan is, well, the man is news in the social and business scenes. Nice dress, by the way. Totally hot. I approve."

"I wasn't wearing any underwear."

Mia jumped up into a sitting position at this news and pushed her sunglasses up on her head.

"You naughty girl! Thought I was the only one doing that. Although I have had like no action in forever, so no reason to leave off my undies lately."

I laughed at her complaining about her sexless life. She was a total flirt but very selective when it came to a sexual partner.

"I wasn't thrilled about the idea at first, but let's just say it had its rewards. I mean, I felt totally sexual and Jordan was winding me up all night long. He couldn't wait to get me in the limo."

"This fucking blows, you know? I mean, I'm happy for you, but I need some real action soon. My BOB is totally not cutting it." Mia's blue eyes stared woefully into the camera phone.

"You have my sympathies, but I'm happy to report that I am deliciously sore in areas that have not seen any such action, well, since Jordan was last there 10 years ago."

"Lucky bitch. He is really incredibly hot. So, are you all into him now? Like, everything is OK in Zoe-land with Jordan?"

"I am thinking yes. We've had the most incredible few days."

"I'm happy for you, but don't go neglecting your friends. We need some girl time soon."

"What about tomorrow night? We can go for a run after work then come back here and have some takeout. Catch up. Veronica will be going to San Francisco to help with the new office on Tuesday." We chatted for a few more minutes and Mia agreed to meet the following evening.

I grabbed my purse and car keys. Soon, I was on my way to the one place that I visit often. Although I had no memory of them, I felt the deep spiritual connection between us just the same. I sat cross-legged on the ground and pulled small weeds growing around their shared grey marble headstone.

"Hi, Mom and Dad. Jenna has some great news for you but she will be coming to see you soon and I'll let her tell you herself." I smiled at the news of Jenna's pregnancy and knew that my parents would have been thrilled with the news of their first grandchild.

"I know that I told you I would never let him in my life again, but Jordan had a totally different agenda. He moved to Houston and has pursued me. He's taking down just about all the walls I had set up in my heart against him." I looked down at my ankle where a brilliant red ladybug was crawling on me. I put my finger against my ankle and it moved onto my hand as I continued to speak to my parents.

"You see, I'm at an impasse. I want to tell him how I feel about him, but he has not said the words that I need to hear. He has not actually said that he loves me and I need to hear that from him. Well, I would like to hear him say it first.

Maybe that's silly. I mean, he's told me so many things I want to hear. He says that I'm the only one for him and that he's never felt that way about another woman. He pampers me and I feel so incredibly alive when I'm with him." I paused as if waiting for one of them to give me the answer I sought. A warm breeze blew, rustling some leaves across the lawn of the cemetery. Knowing that I would not audibly hear their words of advice or wisdom, I continued to tell them of the past week with Jordan and the care and attention he has showered on me.

"I always wondered what I would do if I ever saw Jordan face to face again. So much has happened in both of our lives, but if I'm honest with myself, I must admit that my feelings are stronger now toward him than they were 10 years ago. I am tired of running from him and it feels good that he has finally caught up to me. He gave me no choice, just moved back and plowed his way into my life." The heat of the summer sun and humidity had my hair sticking to my neck and I wiped at the perspiration with my hand.

"Anyway, I wanted you to know that he's made me very happy and my love for him grows deeper everyday." I touched the headstone then stood slowly. I wiped the tears from my eyes as I bid my parents goodbye and promised, as always, another visit soon.

That evening, Aunt Suzette and I sat across from one another at Churrascos restaurant snacking on crispy plantain chips.

"You look well, Zoe. How are you and Jordan getting along?"

I knew this would be the first topic of conversation and I was anxious to share my emotions about Jordan with her.

"I feel that we're at a great place right now, Aunt Suz, but things have happened so fast with us. I'm trying to be cautious-like, and get to know one another all over again."

"It's normal for you to feel that way. After all, 10 years is a long time. A little self preservation is just good common sense."

"Well, that's just it. Jordan did not completely disappear from my life. He admits that he had a private investigator keeping an eye on me. Now that's just creepy to me, but when he explained it and why he did it...I don't know, I just didn't over-react like I thought I would. Does that make sense?"

"Completely. Knowing Jordan, I think he knew that Robert was getting serious about you. We all thought that he was and Jordan was not going to let you go without a fight. Actually, dear, I always thought he would come back. David has hinted to me several times over the past few years that Jordan was talking of great investment opportunities here in the U.S. and his next move would be Houston. Jordan would not let you forget about him, with all the gifts, flowers and God knows what else he has sent your way. I think that he made a bold move to come to Houston without you knowing. Sounds like a man that knows what he wants and will not let anything get in his way."

As usual, Aunt Suzette's capacity to listen to Jenna and me seeking out her advice is priceless. We could always count on her to balance out the listening with a healthy dose of wise counsel. We talked about Jenna being pregnant, but we were concerned that she was experiencing hyperemesis due to the pregnancy.

"David watches over her like a hawk and is in constant contact with her physician," Aunt Suzette said with a huge smile on her face. "I've been thinking of names that I want the baby to call me."

"What's wrong with grandma?" I sipped on the glass of water.

"I will leave that for David's mom."

"You will think of something." I patted her hand as she looked over my head and squinted her eyes.

"GG."

"The alphabet starts at A, Aunt Suz."

"Gorgeous grandma. GG. That's what the baby will call me."

I laughed, but she was not laughing. I saw she was serious so I cleared my throat. "Yes. I can see that name is fitting for you."

"OK. I'm glad you agree with me." She smiled and we ordered our meal.

After dinner, we went our separate ways. I looked forward to the coming workweek. I will miss Jordan while he was gone, but I also had plenty to keep me busy, especially with Veronica's absence in the office for most of the week.

After a shower, I settled down to read when my phone rang. It was Jordan. Although I had a busy afternoon, I missed being in his delightful company.

"Hi," I answered as I set the unopened book back on my nightstand.

"There is someone missing from my house." His sexy voice coated my ear like honey dripping from a spoon, sweet and slow.

"Better call 911." I stretched out on my bed with my head propped up on two pillows.

He chuckled on the other end of the line. "That won't be necessary. She is running, but won't get far. I won't let her go this time."

I giggled, but my heart thumped faster in my chest. "Maybe she needs a little more time."

"Ten years about killed me, baby. The past few days proves that the greatest pleasure was missing from my life."

"Wow. Do tell."

"There is this incredible woman that has graced me with her company over the past few days. Her company would have been enough for me, but I was honored to experience the gift of her touch on my body." He paused and I wanted to hear more of his thoughts.

"I must take lessons from this woman."

"The pleasure of her mouth on me brought me to my knees and I readily admit that I am totally addicted to her incredible, talented tongue." I squirmed in my bed at his seductive words. He laughed as if knowing that he had me turned on. "You missing me, babe?"

"Yes."

"I miss you like hell. Do you want me to come over? I'm at my penthouse downtown."

I almost caved for a moment, but I thought a little time away was due, so I told him that I was exhausted and needed a clear head in the morning. We chatted for a couple more minutes before ending the call, but not before Jordan promised to see me before he left for Europe tomorrow evening. I was already counting the hours before I would see him again.

CHAPTER 29

I ARRIVED AT MY OFFICE EARLY MONDAY MORNING. THE most pressing issue was my meeting with Luke Hastings followed by another meeting with the ER supervisor that was on duty on the night of the incident with Luke. Shortly after 8 a.m., Veronica came into my office followed closely behind by Luke.

"Good morning, Veronica, Luke." I was seated at my desk reading the incident report that was emailed to me from the nursing supervisor. This report would follow Luke all the way to the Texas Nursing Board. I motioned for them to sit in the chairs in front of my desk and got up to close my office door.

"How are you doing, Luke?" I asked.

"Not too good, Miss Caine. Um, I am a drug addict and I was clean for two years, but for the past few months I fell off the wagon. Just lots of stress with my life and all." Luke sat with both elbows on his knees ringing his hands. He had tears in his eyes as he explained his current situation.

"It's not up to me to decide what happens to you long term, Luke. I am sorry to hear about the addiction. It is a disease, as you are aware, just like any other. I will speak with the nursing board this morning and they will let me know what I should do as your employer. For now, I must suspend you, but I know you have a family depending on you, so I have decided to pay you two weeks salary while you comply with the state board. Veronica?" I looked to my

DON for her input on the situation facing Luke and the agency as well.

"This is difficult for everyone involved, but ultimately we all want for you to be well. More than likely, you will need to go through drug rehab. We will cooperate fully in whatever capacity required by law and the state board. I'm sorry we don't have more to go on right now, but we will let you know as soon as we hear from the nursing board." Veronica took Luke to her office where they would meet with human resources and file a written report from Luke.

The nursing supervisor from the hospital met with Veronica and me about the incident and possible actions that Luke would be facing. The morning continued with more meetings and plans to hire the nursing director in San Francisco. I called the candidate that I'd chosen for the position. She was excited to join the agency and will start in two weeks.

Right at 5 p.m., Jordan walked through my door and locked it behind him. I abandoned the financial report from my accountant. My heart quickened to a gallop in my chest at the devastatingly handsome man standing in my office.

Jordan walked slowly around my desk and pulled me out of my chair and into his arms. I tilted my head back as his mouth crashed down on mine. His hands ran feverishly over my arms and back. Both of my arms were looped around his neck.

"My day just got a whole lot better," he whispered in my ear, then ran his lips down my neck.

I gasped as his hands rubbed the side of my breast.

"Not fair." I pouted as his hands continued to move lightly over my body. "This is a terrible thing to do."

"What is so terrible about what I'm doing?" He ran his tongue lightly over my ear.

"You're getting me turned on then…well, you won't finish what you're doing and I will be…"

"You will miss me while I'm gone."

It was a statement and I readily agree by nodding my head.

"I will miss you as well, pretty lady. Think of all the ways I will fuck you when I get back."

My breath caught in my throat as moisture gathered between my thighs.

"I will see you Thursday evening." He tugged on my bottom lip sucking it into his mouth. With a pat on my ass, he left.

I flopped down in my chair totally breathless with a silly smile on my face. What a great way to end my day. My phone dinged with an incoming text. I slid the indicator across the flat screen and grinned as I saw the message from Jordan.

`Are you wet?`

`Soaked.`

`Take off your underwear, put it in a manila envelope and send it down to me. George is on his way to your office.`

`What?` I texted back.

`Now!`

I ran to my door and shut it. I pulled off my underwear, and for good measure, I swiped it between my legs that was indeed slick with need. I scrunch it up and pulled a manila envelope from the shelf, shoved the undies in the envelope and sealed it. The knock on my door came just as I pulled down my dress. Calmly I opened the door and gave the envelope to George and turned back to my desk. My pulse ratcheted up a few more beats as I thought of my panties being taken down to Jordan. Oh God! The things I did with this man. I pulled my bottom lip between my teeth as thoughts of what he would do with the underwear hit me. The man was kinky as hell! A few minutes later my phone dinged again with another text.

`Delicious!`

`You are a wicked man.`

`You love it.`

`Yes.`

`Call you later, babe.`

"What are you grinning about?"

I turned to see Veronica propped up against my door. I shook my head at her, as the smile grew bigger.

"We better go for that run before I change my mind." She was already in her running clothes. I picked up my gym bag and went to change in the restroom. Thanks to Jordan, I would have to run with no panties on.

The run was just what I needed after the busy day at the office. Sweat dripped down our bodies as our feet pounded the trail. Back at the car, we cooled off with Gatorade and cool wet towels, compliments of Mia, who'd met us for the run.

"I've missed my girl-time," I said, looking at my friends. We were back at my townhouse and were now sprawled on the comfy furniture in my living room after taking turns with the shower. My housekeeper made baked ziti and we dug into the casserole served with a fresh summer salad.

"Yeah, yeah. Get to the good stuff already." Impatient Mia kicked at my calf as Veronica threw a pillow at her.

"I am in love." The girls squealed at my news and I laughed at the sound of my voice admitting the feelings of pure pleasure Jordan has brought to my life. "But I haven't told him yet."

"Why ever not, girl?" Veronica asked.

"I would like him to say it first." Mia and Veronica looked at each other and shook their heads. "I mean, I know he loves me and all, but he hasn't said it to me yet. Another thing bothering me is that everything is happening so fast with us."

"Don't waste time, Zoe. Go after what you want. Listen to your heart."

Veronica was right. I knew she was, so I agreed. "Yup. I will. I think I'm being too proud and love should not be proud."

"So right you are, Zoe," Veronica said.

"Now for all the delish details, and I do mean A-L-L."

I laughed at Mia's enthusiasm to delve into my love life.

"Well, I do hate to spoil your fun, but some things will have to be experienced when you're with your own guy. However, I can share this much with you."

I told them of the penthouse that he wants me to help decorate just so he can have some things around that I chose. They were both excited about the estate home in The Woodlands and I promise a girls weekend trip at his home. The closet full of clothes was Mia's favorite part, which did not surprise me at all. She was a self-proclaimed shopaholic. We were all in tears when I recounted Jordan's conversation regarding his mother and why Becky is now his housekeeper.

"That is heartbreaking for him. I mean, it is one thing to lose your parent, but to know that you were conceived from rape...although he is innocent in all this," Mia said, wiping the tears from her eyes.

"No, you're right, Mia. Jordan said he does feel a lot of guilt. In some ways, I think that is why he's so driven. It takes his mind off the pain. His mom would have been so proud of all his accomplishments." Talking about Jordan's personal life made my heart ache for him even more.

"Veronica, how is your grandmother?" Mia asked.

I was so consumed by Jordan for the past few days that I hadn't remembered to ask her about Gaga.

"About that." Veronica inhaled deeply and pursed her lips.

"Not cooperating?" I asked. Gaga was almost eighty-five years old and was rarely ill.

"I think it has something to do with her kidneys. Mom agrees too. We're hoping she doesn't go into renal failure. Gaga is just so stubborn, she won't budge one bit. She's in pain, but won't even go to the doctor to get diagnosed."

"Where would she go? Like what town is close to where she lives?" Mia asked.

"Monterrey." Veronica's family is close-knit and she followed in her mother's footsteps by becoming a nurse.

"If there is anything I can do or if you need time off, you know what to do," I told her.

"She's very opposed to being under the care of a doctor and would rather endure her ailments or take home-made remedies. She insists that the family not interfere with her method of treating herself."

The time with my friends flew by when they took their leave. I was sitting up in bed about to watch the news on my flat screen TV when my phone rang. It was Jordan.

"Hello." My voice sounded breathy. Jordan definitely had a delicious effect on me.

"How was your run with the girls?"

"How do you know about that?"

Jordan chuckled on the other end of the line. "I have my ways. Are you in bed?"

"Yes."

"Ah, unfortunately I can't be as naughty as I want to with you right now since I have guest on board. They are, however, in the bedroom taking a nap."

"So we can't Skype. Hmm, pity, since I'm naked on my bed with my busy hands…"

"You don't play fair, Miss Caine."

"I'm learning fast from you, my dear Mr. Dawson."

"My lovely Zoe wants to play tonight. Don't worry, we will have ample time when I get back and I expect you to deliver," he said and I giggled.

"I love that sound. Sexy as hell. There is not much about you that does not turn me on, Zoe. I am fast learning that I will be in agony when I'm not with you."

I looked up at the ceiling, wanting to tell Jordan I loved him, but I'd rather do it face to face. Excitement curled in my belly as I thought of what his reaction would be.

"You know the saying, absence makes…"

"That's bullshit, babe! Not having you with me right now is simply torture." He pulled in a ragged breath and I got it.

I got that he really did miss me and wanted to be in my company as much as I wanted to be in his. Too bad he had to go back to Europe so soon, but business obligations are important and I get that too.

"I do miss you, Jordan." I closed my eyes with the sweet admission. He was slowly stealing my heart piece by piece and I was so ready to give it all to him.

"Stole my line, pretty lady. I'll be back soon and intend to take up all your extra time."

"Promise?" I was being silly, but sometimes life called for silly and I have a guy that understood that.

"Promise. Dream about me. I will call you sometime tomorrow. Helen emailed you all my personal and company contact information before she left the office today, so if you need to get in touch with me for any reason, don't hesitate to call. OK?"

"OK. Night, Jordy."

CHAPTER 30

ANOTHER EARLY MORNING IN THE OFFICE LED UP TO A busy Tuesday. Vanessa was on her way to San Francisco. I was anxious to hear her report since the office was new and we were operating without a nursing director. Luckily, Bianca, the office manager there, was competent and managing the applicants effectively. She was also interviewing for a general office position. I was gearing up to start staffing the hospitals by next week.

"Skipping lunch today?" Andre asked. He came into my office and sat in one of the chairs in front of my desk.

"Didn't notice the time." I glanced up from my computer.

"Just say, 'Thank you, Andre'." He slid a bag across my desk with what looked like a sandwich in it.

"Thank you, Andre." I bit into the crusty French bread with cold cuts then took a long sip of my water.

"Let me guess, no breakfast this morning?"

"No time, but I did have my coffee. Skipped yoga as well."

"Hmm. Jordan is a bad influence."

I smiled at the mention of his name and for the hundredth time thought of him again today.

"So, did you love Napa?" I asked.

"Absolutely. Can't wait to go back. Jordan had some good suggestions for Ben and me. Oh, I invited your friend, Jeremy. He's a great guy. Lot's of fun."

"Good. I'm glad he could go. He loves the West Coast. Hard to believe he's a Texan."

"We had a good time on the wine tour. Ben needed a break anyway and he is already planning our next trip." Andre flashed that handsome smile that lit up his face showing off his dimpled cheek.

"Work hard, play hard." I grinned at him.

"Hey, did you hear that we will be under renovation soon?"

"Define 'we'," I said.

"Like this building. Lenny said he will be renovating and putting in a new cooling system. Even repaving the parking lot." Andre picked up our trash and sat back in the chair.

"When did he tell you that? Don't get me wrong, I'm thrilled that we will have a facelift and not have to worry about the air going out when it is a 100 degrees outside, but Lenny has always been low on funds."

"Don't know and don't care. Just glad that we will have a little more updated accommodations around here." He got up to leave.

My cell phone rang just as Andre left. I motioned for him to close the door since I recognized Jordan's number on my screen.

"Hello." I leaned back in my chair.

"How is my pretty lady doing today?"

"Missing you."

"Good to know you are not busy then."

I laughed at his statement. He was chuckling on the other end of the line.

"How is business in Brussels?"

"Going very well. I had a meeting with the two new VPs. They are earning their keep with me being in the U.S. I have plenty to keep them busy. Lots of new investors. Even have a couple new high-rises under construction."

"How about the office in Asia?"

"Even busier than in Europe, but a lot less costly since most of the building material that we use in Asia is made in China."

"Sounds complicated."

"It is, but good for the world economy."

Jordan asked me to call him when I got home this evening, although it would be past midnight for him, but he insisted. We bid goodbye since I had a call waiting.

"This is Zoe."

"Zoe, it's Veronica. I just landed and checked my email. There's one that's important so I forwarded it to you and Andre."

I opened a new tab on my computer and quickly scanned for her email.

"Forest Grove Hospital Systems?"

"That's the one. Let me grab my bags and regroup. I checked my voicemail and they left a message asking me to call the director after I read the email. I'll call you back on my way to the office."

After we hung up I read the email. Their DON wanted a meeting with us ASAP to discuss an exclusive contract for their four hospitals in Houston. They're a mid-size hospital group that is privately owned. That would be perfect since my agency had nurses in those areas. It was not unusual for hospitals to offer a contract to one nursing agency, but it was rare. I jumped out of my chair and ran to Andres' office.

"Great news. Forest Grove wants us to sign an exclusive contract with them. Can you come to my office in about ten minutes? Veronica's calling back and we need to plan."

Andre high-fived me and I grinned from ear to ear. When Veronica called back we decided to meet with their DON on Friday. Veronica would be back in the office and all three of us could attend the meeting.

I went back to my office and left Andre to arrange the meeting. A few minutes later an instant message popped up on my screen. It was Andre asking if we could possibly be there tomorrow. Glancing through my calendar I saw that I am available so I agreed to the meeting at 8:30 a.m.

Back at home that evening, I texted Jordan and asked if he was awake due to our time difference. My phone rang with a Skype call just after I sent the text. His gorgeous face was smiling on my screen. I sat on my sofa and curled my legs under me.

"There's my lady."

God. That voice did it for me.

"Hi." I smiled at the screen.

"Long day?"

"The usual. Busier since Veronica is out, but manageable."

"See, you never complain, just get the job done, which in turn makes you a successful and savvy business woman."

"Why, thank you. Your evening went well?" I asked. He'd said he was meeting with other investors that would be coming to America soon in hopes of finding more commercial real estate opportunities.

"Very well. I have plenty going on in the U.S for them to choose from, but enough shoptalk. I want you to go to your room and take off your clothes."

Oh yes, please.

I smiled in the camera phone and headed to my room peeling off my clothes as I went. I giggled like a teenager.

"I hear that sexy little laugh. I have a little surprise for you," he said.

I complied with his instructions and now stood naked with the phone in my hand.

"Ah, there she is. Now pull out the bottom drawer of your nightstand. There is a small white device that looks like a spider."

I reached down and pulled out the plastic device.

"Place one of your pillows at the foot of your bed then angle the device to stand on the pillow and place your phone inside."

I quickly did as he said.

"Now go back to the same drawer and take out the wooden box that is tied with a black ribbon and open it."

"Jordan!" I gasped as I looked in the box. It was a LELO vibrator. I slipped it from the pouch and gazed at the artful design of the instrument of pleasure.

"Not even close to the real deal, but it will do. Lie on the bed and let's play a little."

I hopped on the bed and lie supine, holding onto the sleek pink vibrator. "I have a perfectly good vibrator, you know," I said looking at the camera.

"I found yours and it needed serious upgrading. This one is charged and ready to go. Turn it on."

I pressed the ON button and it hummed softly and vibrated in my hand.

"We will start with that speed for now. Place it on your areola lightly, going from one breast to the other."

I slid the smooth device over my skin. My nipples beaded to tight knobs, pleasure slowly uncoiling in my abdomen.

"Good girl. Now, move it down slowly with your right hand and continue to squeeze your nipple with the other."

I slowly pushed the device to my pelvic then stopped.

"Lower, then lightly run it over your pussy. Start at the clit and go down to the end of the slit."

I closed my eyes imagining Jordan's hands on my body. I moved the vibrator up and down slowly as Jordan guided my movements. My legs were bent at the knees and I was spread out on the bed with my camera phone aimed between my legs. I felt sensual in this position.

"Such a nice view of your beauty, oozing your pleasure already. Now turn up the speed."

I did.

"Another level."

I complied and placed it back on my clit and ran it down my folds again. My breathing increased as I ran over my pleasure knob that was hard and getting more sensitive with every movement.

"Look at me, Zoe, and don't stop moving the vibrator."

I opened my eyes and gasped. "Oh my God! My underwear," I gasped

Jordan grinned as he sniffed my panties that he'd confiscated off my body yesterday. He moved his camera phone lower and his other hand was pumping his cock. It was the most erotic thing I've seen.

"That is, well, it's just kinky and hot," I said.

"Fuck, babe, wish it were you here. I must admit, taking your underwear was a brilliant idea. I love your smell, just pure Zoe."

I muffled a laugh as my pleasure kept building and I got slicker with every movement now.

"Jordan, I… Oh, this is feeling really good, like I need…" I gasped the words as I continued to rub the vibrator over my core.

"Don't come yet. Put it in your pretty pink pussy then push in and pull it out. Pretend it's me inside you."

I started moving my hips with the motion, all the while looking at Jordan. My breath was choppy as I tilted the vibrator upright at the spot that made me ache for more.

"How does it feel?"

"Amazing!" I gasped.

"Increase your pace. Push faster now. Eyes on me," he said, as my lids were about to flutter shut with pleasure.

"Jordan, I don't know how much longer…I need it. I do, please…"

"Back on your clit, now!"

I pulled it back out and slid it up my sex. The faster speed drove me wild and I bucked under my hand as I rode the vibrator hard. I wanted to pull it away but the pleasure was too great and I couldn't. I wouldn't. The promise of release was incredible as I moaned Jordan's name again and again.

I was about to erupt, so close…

"Back off. Place it back in your pussy!"

I did as he commanded and the need to orgasm was instantly less. I squirmed, but the feeling of fullness from the vibrator was a pleasure of its own. I mewled and begged for release again as my hips came off the bed. My hand was frantic and pushing the device in and out.

"We'll come together." he said.

I was moaning and griped the vibrator, willing it to slide up to my clit when Jordan said, "On your clit. Come now."

I quickly move it back. As it touched my clitoris, I orgasmed and screamed out my pleasure. I heard Jordan groan my name, then silence. My legs were shaking and my hands ached but the pleasure was so great.

I closed my eyes and swam in a blissful state of euphoria. My legs fell flat on the bed and the vibrator lay beside me, still humming softly, but I was too relaxed to turn it off right now. As if sensing that I needed a minute to calm down, Jordan quietly praised me with soothing words that I vaguely hear but didn't comprehend.

"Not a bad way to end the day," he said.

I took my phone off the pillow and positioned myself higher in the bed. "Hm. That was some surprise, and you are a sneak, getting that stuff in my drawer."

He had the audacity to chuckle. "Your BOB was way outdated. You needed a new one."

"Invasion of privacy. Hello!" More chuckling from him, but I smiled as well and we ended the call and planned to reconnect sometime tomorrow. God, I missed him.

CHAPTER 31

SINCE I'D GONE TO BED EARLY LAST NIGHT, I WAS energized this morning and used the treadmill. My morning routine was the same except that my mind was constantly on Jordan. I giggled as I thought of last night. He was cleaver, I must give him that. Even my long auburn hair had more bounce to it than normal.

I went through my closet and chose a simple but chic pink Antonio Melani Elise dress and paired it with three-inch nude summer pumps from the same designer.

I was going to the hospital for our meeting this morning then to my office. An hour later, I pull into the parking garage adjoining the hospital. Andre walked up to me as I parked and we headed into the administration office.

"Miss Caine, so nice to meet you. My name is Karen, secretary for the nursing office. I have Starbucks coffee with Splenda for you and cafe latte for Mr. Fisher."

"How kind of you, Karen, but how did you know our preferences?" I asked, as I took a sip of my favorite blend of coffee.

"I called your office this morning and spoke with Grace." She grinned at me.

"Nice gesture. Thanks," I replied.

We followed Karen to the conference room and took a seat. The usual people were present for the meeting as introductions went around the room. Everyone was very welcoming and polite. I thanked them all for the opportunity to be their temporary nursing agency provider.

"There are many changes going on around here, Miss Caine. Happening fast too, but the first order of new business was to get you under contract," the nursing administrator said. She was polite but never once looked directly at me. I'm sure not everyone was happy with whatever changes she spoke about. That was normal in any business reorganization so I didn't take it personally.

I signed all the paperwork with their attorney and handed them my agency's credentials. The meeting was a huge success and I couldn't wait to share it with my employees.

Back at my office it was business as usual. My office staff was busier than ever now with more employees signing on to work for the agency.

"Miss Caine, Lenny is here to see you," Grace beeped on my phone.

"Please send him in, Grace."

"Hi, Zoe." Lenny shook my hand and I asked him to take a seat.

"We will be starting some renovations on the building in a few weeks. Your suite of offices will be the first, so I wanted to let you know that we will move you across the hall where there is a vacant area."

"Wow, Lenny. I'm happy to hear about this but how much will it cost me and how much will my rent increase?"

"No, no, Zoe. Nothing at all. We will do the move. Just have your employees pack up their desk stuff. The new place will even have new furnishings as well."

"Whoa! Did you by any chance win the lottery? How can you afford to renovate the building and put in new furniture with no cost to the tenant, not to mention the rent staying the same?"

"Stroke of luck really. Right place at the right time. An investor bought me out, strip centers, this building and all. Asked me to oversee the whole thing for him and paid me quite a bit of money too. This building is the first to be renovated, then the others and he is paying for all of it along with the new furniture."

That just sounded too good to be true and I immediately made an educated guess of who this 'investor' was.

"Hmm. By any chance would this miracle making man happen to be Jordan Dawson?"

A flush creeped up Lenny's face. "Ah, well you see, Zoe, I'm not supposed to discuss anything of this nature. It's in our contract and I can't disclose it."

"Don't worry, Lenny. I won't ask for any details and you did not tell me who it was. I heard that Mr. Dawson was investing in Houston. Lucky guess is all."

We chatted about the changes that will be taking place soon then Lenny took his leave. I was fuming. I got up from my desk and paced in my office. I couldn't believe he was meddling in my business, as if I have not proven myself without his help, I might add. I looked in my email and punched in the many numbers for Helen, his assistant, who was in Brussels with him. She answered on the first ring.

"Helen. I need to speak with Jordan."

"Sure, Zoe. Is everything OK?"

"No. Just get him on the phone."

Helen put me on hold.

I was so mad that I kicked my desk.

"Zoe? Babe, what's going on?" His voice was deep with concern.

"I have done quite nicely without you since I opened my agency and I sure as hell don't need your meddling." My chest was heaving as I hissed at him.

"What has you so upset? I would not meddle in your professional life. I absolutely admire and respect you as an astute business woman."

"Then why is Lenny swimming in money with some crazy story about an investor that bought property in Houston and he is managing them? And said investor just gave him lots of money to spend on this building where I just happen to have my office... I know it's you, and don't you deny it, Jordan Dawson. Why?"

He inhaled a deep breath and I settled back waiting on his response.

"I worry about you in that building and you won't move out. I know you. You're stubborn and won't move into one of mine that is just a couple miles from where you are. So I'm keeping you safe and more comfortable. Is it OK for me to do that for my girlfriend? I did it all for you, babe. Please allow me this one thing. It will make me feel better," he said quietly.

I let out an exasperated breath and squeezed the bridge of my nose. The man was driving me crazy and he has only been back in my life for like two weeks.

"Look. Just stop throwing money at people like that. Lenny was doing just fi—-"

"No, he was not, Zoe. The bank was about to seize his property and I bailed him out. It's a small investment for me. He will keep working and make a great living doing what he's good at. He just needed some help and was more than happy to be relieved of the building that is in dire need of repairs."

"How would you know all that, Jordan?"

"Because it has to do with you. I offered to buy the building from him and was going to demolish the piece of crap, but I knew that would upset you even more."

"For God's sake, stop meddling in people's business. You can't save the world."

"I'm not trying to save the world. Just trying to make your life...ah, hell, babe, give me a break, pretty lady. It just makes me feel better doing this one small thing that has to do with you."

"I will think about how you will redeem yourself over this, but no more funny business around me."

"Can't promise that."

"Bye, Jordan."

"Zoe...never mind. I will see you soon," he said.

I had another call waiting so I didn't ask what he was about to tell me. As usual, the day simply flew by and I found myself back at home where a warm casserole was waiting. My housekeeper was a gem. I sat in the living room and ate while I listened to the evening news. I called to check on Jenna again, who is feeling a little better today, but was thrilled about the pregnancy that actually took up most of our conversation.

I spoke with Jordan again but we avoided the subject of our earlier conversation. Jordan said he would not have phone sex with me tonight and forbid me to use the vibrator on myself. I didn't think he could tell if I did use it, but he said he has a way of getting the truth out of me. I was excited to see him tomorrow evening and had another early night to bed.

~ ~ ~ ~ ~

The next morning, I decided to skip my workout routine. I made scrambled eggs and cinnamon raisin toast. It was delicious and I didn't feel one bit guilty. I was stacking dishes in the sink when there was a knock at my front door.

Who the hell could be at my door at seven in the morning? I looked through the peephole and saw Andre and Aunt Suzette. I swung the door open knowing that this was not good and my mind went immediately to Jenna. But what did Andre have to do with Jenna? Veronica? She should still be asleep on the West Coast.

"Oh God. What's wrong?" I asked as I pulled the silk robe around my body, securing it in a knot.

"Zoe. Let's go to the living room and turn on the news," Aunt Suzette said.

Andre shuffled his feet behind her. His clothes did not quite match up and his hair looked like he'd forgotten to comb it.

"Andre? I'm about to freak out here."

He steered me to the sofa as Aunt Suzette turned on the television.

"Now I know you did not come over here to watch morning television with me, so one of you better tell me what the hell is going on." I was about to get off the sofa when Aunt Suzette spoke up.

"It's about Jordan and some business he has invested in. I don't think you will like what you hear, unless he has told you about it?"

"What? The building that my office is in? I found out about it yesterday and decided that it was not worth a huge argument."

"No, Zoe. It's the hospitals that he bought here in Houston. Forest Grove Hospital Systems," Andre said. He took a seat across from me.

"I still don't get what that has to do with Jordan or me." Just then the news came back on.

"Once again, breaking news about Jordan Dawson and Forest Grove Hospital Systems. The commercial real estate giant decided to go solo on this investment and purchased the four hospitals last week. The news was apparently supposed to be released next week, but our sources came to us with news of Mr. Dawson's girlfriend, Zoe Caine, of Blue-bonnet Nursing Agency that acquired an exclusive contract to staff all those hospitals with her agency nurses. The two have been seen around town over the past week. Some are crying foul on this one since Miss Caine's agency has lost several contract renewals due to hospitals opening their own nursing agencies. Dating a financial mogul does come with benefits, it seems." The reporter sat back with a smug smile on her face.

"There is more to report on the two doing business in San Francisco just last week. Tell us, what you know about that, Sabrina?" another reporter asked.

"Yes, Jeff. Mr. Dawson and Miss Caine went on a secretive trip to San Francisco last week where she met with several hospitals in the area. Our sources found out that Mr. Dawson is on the board of those hospitals. Miss Caine's agency obtained contracts with those hospitals as well."

"Will Miss Caine be moving her agency to the West Coast?" the other reporter asks.

"The two are keeping their dealings to themselves and the general public in the dark, Jeff," she replied and smirked into the camera.

"Off. Turn it off!" I yelled and ran to my bathroom where I threw up the contents of my stomach. I was at loss for words. I knelt on the floor dry heaving as I hugged the toilet bowl. Aunt Suzette came to the door but I yelled at her to leave me alone. I was humiliated, angry, confused, and totally embarrassed. I had worked so hard to keep my agency's reputation spotless and trustworthy, and in less than two weeks, Jordan has brought it down.

I went back to the living room. I needed to get my shit together. I had a business to run and I didn't have a minute to spare. I can imagine that my employees will be wondering what is going on as well since I just sent out a mass email and signed up numerous shifts at the four hospitals where many of my nurses will be working as soon as this weekend.

"Andre. Head to the office and start drafting a press release of our own that the agency signed an exclusive contract with the hospitals with no knowledge of the hospitals' new owner. Get our attorney in the office as well. I don't know where to go with this and I need his advice. I can't fight Jordan and obviously he is punishing me for keeping him away for 10 years, but I can keep my agency going and I won't stop fighting for my employees. Ease the mind of our nurses and other employees as well by sending a mass email that it is business as usual for Bluebonnet. I will be in as soon as possible. Aunt Suzette?"

"Anything I can do to help, honey."

I gave her a quick hug and headed to the shower. No more time for tears. I had to make sure my employees believed in me and my abilities to deliver good on my promise that I was a responsible employer and had a great reputation for doing the right things for the Houston medical community.

Thirty minutes later, I was on my way to the office. I wore my hair in a tight bun, very little makeup and a lightweight summer suit. I looked like I was ready to kick some ass, but the only one that I really wanted to kick right now was Jordan. How could he do this to me? He was ruthless and this proves that he was heartless as well. He started on the building that housed my office and now he is controlling where I do business. Well, fuck him! I was not a little, lost girl that would curl up and cry. I was fuming as I answered the incoming phone call.

"Zoe, here," I just about bellowed in the car as the Bluetooth picked up the call.

"The press is outside in the parking lot and some at the door. Sorry, Zoe. I will look out for you and run to your car when you pull in. Grace and I will try and shield you best we can when you get out of your car," said Andre.

I wanted to say the F word again so bad, and as many expletives as I knew, but Aunt Suzette was sitting beside me and I won't lose respect from her over anyone, especially over Jordan Dawson.

"I will call Lee and see if he can send a cop over. I can't think of anything else right now. See you soon." I pushed the end button, then pulled off the street into a CVS parking lot as I Googled the Houston Police Department and asked to speak with Lee. After a couple minutes of grief, the receptionist got him on the phone.

"Let me get this...we went to Vegas over the weekend and got married?" Lee chuckled.

God, it was so good to know Lee right at this moment. "Sorry. She would not let me speak with you since I didn't know your extension. Only immediate family, like parents or spouse, or some shit... Sorry," I mouthed at Aunt Suzette who smiled at me.

"I'm flattered that you remember my invitation for lunch and yes, I can make it today."

I sighed as I thought of the invitation and felt guilty about what I was about to ask. "Lee, I need help getting into my office this morning. I guess you have not heard the news...anyway the press is waiting in the parking lot for me. Do you think I can have a cop with me to muscle his way through them?"

"Sorry to hear about whatever is going on, Zoe, but I can do better than that. I will be there in five minutes," he said.

I ended the call and got a text from Andre that he has had several calls and emails from my nurses that are supportive of me and believe in the agency's integrity. In the scheme of things, all that matters are that my employees know they can trust me to do the right things on their behalf. After a few minutes, I headed back on the street and sighed in relief as I saw the state trooper car with flashing lights in the parking lot and Lee standing beside it. He had another cop with him as well. In that moment I was reminded of the honor it was to have good people in my life that had my back.

I pull up beside his car and he opened my door and gave me a quick hug as the other cop opened Aunt Suzette's door and guided her by the arm. The press ran up to us barking questions and remarks about shady dealings and contracts being obtained unfairly. They also knew about the new office in San Francisco. It seemed like it took forever for us to make it to the door.

Thank goodness for Andre's quick thinking by calling Lenny to stand at my office door and keep it locked so they could not get closer. I was shaken but kept the stoic look on my face. I rather looked pissed off than fearful. I was relieved to make it into my office. My employees were totally professional and carrying on with business as usual. I appreciated that there were no pity talks or chitchat going on. I needed to stay busy and I knew somehow we'd get through the day.

"Zoe. I will tell David what's going on if you want me to and I can help with phone calls or whatever you need me to do."

"Thanks, Aunt Suz. That would be great. There is another desk in the office next to mine that you can use." She squeezed my hand and went down the hall.

"Thank you so much, Lee." I hugged him and felt the bulky armor beneath his uniform. He looked totally badass and I felt comforted with his presence. So much so that I asked if I could possibly hire an off duty officer while I was at the office and probably 24/7 for the next week, since I did not want Jordan anywhere near me.

Not that he would want to see me anyway. The damage that he set out to do is done. His mission of a personal blow to me was accomplished. My bad for trusting him, his charming ways and good looks, his incredible lovemaking and the way he pampered me and made me believe he truly wanted me in his life...no one else would do. God. I am so stupid. Fuck!

"No need, Zoe. I will take care of it. I'll be with you today and have someone at your house tonight and every night until you don't need us, but I will be with you during the day. I have a three-day weekend starting tomorrow and will take some vacation if needed. I never take time off, so they won't question it."

"You are too good to me, Lee. I'm sorry about all this and wish I could turn down the help, but I do need it right now. Thank you."

"I will be at the reception door. Don't worry, no one is getting in here unless you say so." I felt like crying, I really did, but I way too furious to do so.

CHAPTER 32

DAVID CALLED JUST AS I SAT AT MY DESK.

"Zoe. I'm speechless. This just can't be happening. I know Jordan, and there is no way he would do this maliciously, but I swear to God, if I ever find that he was out to hurt you in any way I will rearrange that pretty face of his. I'm on my way to Houston now. I have also hired a media team to go to your office. They will take any statement you wish to convey to your staff and the public. My attorney is speaking with yours right now and they will look into the acquisition of the hospitals."

"God, David. How could he do this to me? I had no idea that Jordan wanted anything to do with the medical industry. He set this up so smooth. I feel like a butterfly caught in a web." My breath hitched in my throat and tears gathered in my eyes.

"Don't worry. This will soon pass, but before it does, we will understand what the motivations were for Jordan. I spoke with his office in Houston. He's on his way in from Europe. Swear to God, he had better have his shit together."

I smiled at David's words. There was no way he could take on Jordan but I loved his protective nature toward me.

"This sure as hell makes me look like an opportunist and out to make a buck at any cost. I hope those who truly know me know that I would never deceive anyone. I would not jeopardize my business in any way."

"I'm sure your employees and business associates believe in you. We will figure this out."

Andre came in just as I hung up with David.

"My phone is on mute, but I have Jordan holding. He said your phone was turned off and Grace won't put his calls through to you."

"Damn straight. I don't want to hear shit from him and tell him to stop calling. Better yet, block his number from our phones."

Andre saluted and left for his office again.

I turned on my computer and read emails from my employees that were working in various hospitals. Most said that they were way too busy in the nursing world to gossip with anyone and it was business as usual for them. I took a call from Jenna and reassured her that she did not need to come to Houston. I had great support and demanded that she stayed at home and rest. She finally agreed to it and promised to keep in touch later today. We continued to conduct business in the office and refused to listen to the news. Some of the press had left since they had noting to report with no comment thus far from my camp.

My attorney came in and we discussed some strategies going forward. I told him I had a legal and binding contract with the hospitals that I staffed, and nurses ready to work. Jordan be damned! I owed him nothing. The media team that David hired spoke with my attorney. They would release my statement for the four o'clock news today. Nothing like fury to give one courage. I felt empowered with all the support and reinforcement around me. I may not be able to take on Jordan's financial empire, and I didn't want to, but I would fight like hell to keep what I have going and would settle for nothing less.

"Sorry to bother you, Miss Caine, but Mr. Dawson has all our lines tied up right now and he won't get off the phone. I don't know what to do," Grace said. She was standing at my door.

I only thought I was mad before. I was breathing fire now. I told Grace to forward his call to me. The phone rang and I snatched it from the base.

"Get the fuck off my phone, Jordan, or I swear to God I will have someone kick your ass when you land at the airport. You fight dirty, but I am not taking this laying down, you hear me? Let me make this clear to you—you can't break me. Ever!" I yelled at him. All the while I was speaking, Jordan was trying to calm me down. I heard bits and pieces of what he was trying to say but I didn't stop yelling. He asked me to hear him out...another misunderstanding, not what I think it is, he is sending his attorney to my office to speak with me now.

"Do not send any one of your douchebag people to even try and enter my office or I will have them arrested for trespassing. Lee is at my door and swear to God, I will tell him to fucking Taser their ass."

"Lee, the dickhead cop? You called Lee?" he yelled at me. "I will kick his ass when I get there. I don't give a fuck if he is a cop and don't care if I get arrested. I went to jail for you once, and I will do it again. Fucker was just waiting for me to leave before he marched in like some superhero..."

"Get lost, Jordan! Oh, and David will kick your ass as well if there is anything left of you when Lee is through with you." Ha. There.

I felt like a child calling on all my friends and family to come to my aid but I didn't care. They were all I had and he needed to know he was taking on more than just me. I slammed down the phone as he continued to yell about Lee. I went to the reception area and told Lee not to let any of Jordan's people in my office. He was standing right in front of the door, legs apart and hands on his Taser. I didn't really know if he was allowed to use the Taser while protecting me but that was up to him. Mia heard of the mess going on and came to my office with a promise to hire someone to work Jordan over in a dark alley.

"First, they have to get to him. He has bodyguards that are like pitbulls."

"I also told daddy to stop all dealings with Jordan immediately, but he said he has to back out slowly. In the meantime you have Veronica and me." She looked at me with huge baby blue eyes. We busted out laughing as we thought of the hilarious picture we would be, facing Jordan and his posse.

"God. I needed a good laugh today. Thanks, Mia. You're the best, but I know you must be busy too..."

"I am not going anywhere. I called your scheduler this morning and asked her to send a nurse to my office and fill in for me until further notice. Perks of being a brat." She winked at me and got on her cell phone to Philippe.

"I need you to blacklist Jordan Dawson. Leave no stone unturned," she told him.

Was she ridiculous or what? Anything that will help me feel better, that was Mia for you. No wonder I cherished her friendship.

"What do you mean he is a good man? Let me tell you what is going on in Houston and then you can tell all your rich buddies to do the same. Pretty please, Philippe?" Now who could say no to that voice? Certainly not Philippe. So Mia went on to fill him in on Jordan's dirty dealings and the effect it was having on my business reputation.

"Thanks, Philippe. I knew I could count on you. See you in a few hours."

Really? Just like that she makes a call and he is on his way. Christ. She was so spoiled and everyone in her life was to blame, including me.

I sighed and she made yet another call to her brother this time. No surprise there. Trevor promised to deal with Jordan himself and would pass the word around to all his friends.

"Look, Mia, I know you mean well, but I don't want to even try and bring down Jordan; not like I can anyway. I want him to leave me alone and pick on someone his own size. I need to spend my time and energy on my business."

"So far, I have five massive guys that will beat him to a bloody pulp. Teach him a lesson."

"Have you not heard a thing I just said?"

"Yes. But you are not making any sense. So I will take care of the bodily harm and you will take care of your business."

Again, I could only laugh.

I placed a call to Veronica and filled her in on what was going on. She would be coming in tomorrow and I told her to continue doing what she was doing. We would be fine and had ample help in the office.

"She will be OK," Mia piped in over my shoulder. "I am not leaving her side. Of course, it will be better when you get back tomorrow. Until then...Jordan Dawson will be sorry he crossed our path again."

Spoken like a real friend. I felt better, even stronger as the minutes went by.

David came into the office with his attorney. I showed them into the conference room where the team was working and trying to gather as much information about the acquisition that they could. The media team David hired arrived and released a short statement from me at noon on a major TV network. A longer statement would be released at 4 p.m. that will be repeated until the last news broadcast ended tonight.

I went back to my office and sat at my desk. Christ. What a mess. I certainly hadn't seen this coming. At this point I was in survival mode and refused to think of my emotions. The feelings that I had for Jordan that were blossoming into love were too painful to think about now. I had given him my body and was going to give him my heart. I blinked away the tears that threatened to fall and quickly got back to work.

Mia, my constant companion, was on the phone with Jenna now, checking on her and asking her if she needed a nurse. Mia did not do well with illness, which was hilarious considering she was a nurse. As far as being a patient, she was the absolute worst.

Someone ordered sandwiches and salads. I ate, but didn't taste a thing. Aunt Suzette came to check in with me and updated me on the calls of support from the community that were too numerous to count which solidified my faith in the city that I knew and loved so much.

David, his attorney and mine, left around 2 p.m. for a meeting with the group of investors, mostly physicians that had owned the hospitals that Jordan purchased from them. Right around 4 p.m. there was a commotion at the front office and Grace came running down the hall and stopped short at my door.

"Miss Caine, Mr. Dawson is trying to kill Lee!" she exclaimed, her eyes big as saucers.

Mia and I jumped up and ran into Andre and Aunt Suzette who were already on their way to the front office.

"Beat him to a pulp, Lee." I palmed my hand over Mia's mouth. She was jumping up and down like she was at a boxing match.

Through the glass door, I saw Lee and Jordan locked in a fierce fight. He was by himself and I wondered where his bodyguards were, but I was terrified for Lee. Jordan had

him in a lock with his huge arm around Lee's neck. He towered over Lee by at least five inches but Lee was not giving
in and head-butted him. Jordan ducked and Lee's head
slammed into Jordan's shoulder. I heard him grunt as they
continued to engage in the fight. I felt guilty about Lee as I
could see his face was beet red and perspiration ran down
his neck.

I tried to open the door but Andre held onto me and
Aunt Suzette wouldn't let me out. I was yelling for them to
stop, but of course they couldn't hear me and even if they
did, neither was giving in. Lee was reaching for his Taser
and I just could not let him use it on Jordan. I finally pulled
away from my entourage and unlocked the dead bolt to the
door.

"Jordan! Lee! Stop, stop now!" I yelled, but to no avail.
They continued to throw fists and grunts, when one would
land a punch. So I did what I had to do.

I ran into the mass of muscle and sweat and threw myself
in the middle. A blow landed to my head and another simul-
taneously to my left arm. I screamed with the jolt to my
body as my eyes fluttered shut, the darkness taking me into
oblivion where the pain ceased and I fell to the ground.

CHAPTER 33

"THERE SHE IS. OPEN YOUR EYES, ZOE. WE ARE RIGHT here, honey."

Darkness again, too tired to keep my eyes open.

"Zoe, it's Jenna. I know you want to hear my good new. I know you do, but you need to wake up, sweetie."

Bright lights hurting my eyes. Still so sleepy. What was going on? Why was Jenna at my house?

"Well, you have managed to fill several waiting rooms in the hospital, Zoe."

That was Mia. I couldn't formulate a coherent thought. I slipped into the darkness again.

"...will be OK. The CT scan shows a concussion. Her arm is bruised but not broken so we will..."

Who are they talking about and where was I? Darkness again.

"I will stay with her." That was Jenna. I recognized the voice but too tired to ask what was going on.

"No way in hell. You are going to her townhome with Aunt Suzette and stay there until she is awake or until tomorrow morning." David. Was I in Austin?

"Well, I am not going anywhere, just so y'all know." That was Mia.

I probably should tell them I will go too, or should I stay...not sure what to do. Darkness engulfed me again.

"...Don't give a fuck with what Jordan wants. The answer is still no and why is he not in jail?" Mia sounded pissed.

I wanted to tell her to leave him alone. Jordan must have pissed her off. Crap. He was in for it now. I was so thirsty. I flicked my tongue but it stuck to the roof of my mouth.

"I think she want's something. Get the nurse. Quick!" Andre. I must be at the office. Doesn't make sense.

"Ah, Andre, I am a nurse and she needs water, but yes, please ask her nurse to come in." Mia.

I squinted my eyes and closed them again. Someone lifted my head and dropped some water on my tongue. I lapped at the water. It felt like heaven on my tongue and I was rewarded with more when I swallowed the little I was given. Stingy people. Must be a shortage of water. Probably in the desert somewhere which was why it was so bright, daytime in a desert.

My head hurt and I moaned. There was a lot of movement around me and everyone talking at once. What was the big deal? I just need to get some ibuprofen. I tried to move my legs but they were heavy. Darkness.

"Mia?" I thought I yelled her name but Mia was holding my hand and didn't budge. Her head rested on the side rail. So I tried again. She must have a hangover or something. She couldn't hear me yelling.

"Mia." I coughed out her name and the room erupted in a frenzy of activity again.

"She's awake."

"Get her nurse."

"Oh my God, Zoe."

"Someone call Aunt Suzette."

"No, I want Jenna to rest."

"My head hurts. Thirsty," I croaked again.

My nurse took over and immediately brought order to the room full of people. She did a full neurological assessment and vital signs on me and I had no idea why but I cooperated. When she asked me my name and I told her, everything came rushing back to me.

I suddenly lost it. Mia pulled me into her arms and was crying too. David and Andre stood at the foot of the bed rubbing my legs.

"Oh, you guys. I'm a mess." I hiccupped and sniffled on Mia's shoulder. Just then, Veronica and Trevor walked in escorted by Lee who was now out of uniform and sporting a black eye and his other cheek was swollen but he was smiling and I cried all over again.

"My girl." Veronica pulled me out of Mia's arms and hugged me to her chest while kissing my head. I feel like a rag doll being passed from one to the other. More talking and lots of relief settled in the room. I hated to think about it, but I wondered what happened to Jordan and I want to cry all over again, but I held it together this time.

"How'd you get here, Veronica? Thought you were coming tomorrow?"

"I was wrapping up business in LA and Mia said Veronica needed a ride, so I made a detour to San Francisco, picked her up and came home," Trevor answered. I saw Veronica glance at him and pull her bottom lip between her teeth. Interesting.

Trevor was moving up the corporate ladder and was already a vice president in the family business. His father was giving him more duties, setting him up to one day take over the company which meant that they had their own corporate jet.

I was thrilled to see Veronica and was just saying that when Philippe walked in. Mia made a beeline for him and almost knocked him over when she slammed into his tall frame. He picked her up easily and placed a long noisy kiss on her lips, ignoring the occupants of the room.

After a few minutes of visiting with everyone, the nurse came in and broke up the gathering, but Mia and Veronica insisted they would stay right at my bedside.

"Maybe one of you gentleman can update Mr. Dawson about Miss Caine's condition. He's burning a hole in the carpet in the waiting room, not to mention he looks a mess." My nurse was standing at the door.

The room was silent. They were all looking at me and again I wanted to cry but I did not have the energy to do so.

"Due to patient confidentiality, I can't give him any information. He's already threatened all of us and I had him taken away by security, but he's back."

I just wanted to sleep so I asked David to deal with him. The girls made a makeshift bed and said they would take turns with naps while the other kept watch over me. I wanted to tell them to leave but was so happy they were here. I sighed as I noticed a cop stationed at my door as well.

I slept off and on during the night. The nurse woke me every two hours and performed her exams and took vitals. She called and reported my condition to the doctor who came in to see me twice during the night. He was the hospitalist and was on duty for the in-house patients.

I was discharged the next morning and David took me home. Veronica and Mia left for their own home when I signed my discharge paperwork.

Andre and Veronica would be in the office as usual but Mia insisted on going to help them. We couldn't change her mind so it was decided that all three of them would deal with the press and employees.

I was still tired but happy to be in my own bed. Aunt Suzette and David fussed over Jenna and me. Trevor came over with flowers and had a late lunch delivered for us. Philippe sent flowers and said he would come by this evening with Mia. Jeremy sent chocolate and flowers with a note that he would be coming to visit from San Francisco this weekend. Veronica's mom, Neena, and Julie, my part-time housekeeper, were cooking up a storm in my kitchen with the promise of dinner tonight for everyone, while David and several attorneys continued to gather as much information on Jordan and his investments in Houston.

I took some ibuprofen for the dull headache that I still had and was sporting a hematoma on my left upper arm. My bedroom was cool and quiet which was great since I wanted nothing more than to rest. After a shower, I slid into bed and Jenna lay beside me. I finally settled down, put my head on her shoulder and cried. She soothed me by rubbing her hand over my head and shoulder as I sniffled on her clothes. After a few minutes I collected myself and decided to bare my soul.

"I love him," I whispered.

"I know," Jenna replied.

"He hurt me again."

"Terrible man without a conscience."

"I was going to tell him how I felt when he got back yesterday evening."

"Hmm."

"Why are you not more upset for me?"

"All's well that ends well, Zoe."

"I don't understand that response from you."

"Let's see what David finds, then we will pass the proper judgment."

"Must be the pregnancy."

"What?"

"That makes you wise." I don't know how long we would have continued the conversation but it felt good to not think too much about the dreadful situation.

My heart swelled with gratitude as I thought of all the people that are close to me and how much concern, love and support they have shown toward me. Just then, David and Aunt Suzette came in the bedroom and closed the door. I eyed them wearily, not sure that I wanted to hear what they had to say.

Aunt Suzette sat at the foot of the bed and rubbed Jenna's feet and mine with a sweet smile on her face. I loved her so much and in that moment I knew that I would not ever have to wonder again what it would have been like to be raised by my own mother. She was the only mother I had ever known, and I couldn't ask for a better one.

"We don't have to talk today, Zoe. If you're not feeling up to it. We can talk tomorrow."

"God. I hate to know what you've found out and I never want to hear what all his shoddy dealings are but I need to know so I'm ready. What's going on?"

"Jordan has bought several hospitals in different parts of the country over the past six years. He outright owns twenty so far. They were all about to go into bankruptcy, but he bought them out and did what renovations were necessary to keep them competitive. He does not have investors, it's all him, but what is stunning is that he also opened a rehab unit in every one of the hospitals for battered and abused women and children, rape victims and displaced families. They offer counseling and family support as well as place-ment for the family if they need somewhere to live while they regain their lives."

"What are you saying?" I was a little lost about where David was going with this and I felt my head begin to throb again.

"His motivations were to help the ailing hospitals from going under and save jobs for those that worked for them. In the meantime, he offered new services for those in need, like his own mother was, and he bought these medical facilities before you even thought of opening your agency. In the contract with the hospitals here in Houston, they were supposed to disclose the information to you before you signed, but Jordan wanted to tell you this weekend, which is why he wanted the hospital to meet with you next week, not this week.

"So, who...why was I called for a meeting ASAP to sign the contract?"

"The Director of Nursing pushed for it to happen while Jordan was gone. Incidentally, she happens to be Celia's aunt."

"What?" I whispered in shock.

"Celia was taking her last shot at you for getting her transferred from Jordan's office then fired. She blames it all on you. Said that you told Jordan to get her transferred. Jordan never had any intentions of you signing anything without consenting that you agreed to the exclusive contract and if you did not want to do it then he was going to leave the temporary staffing up to the administrator of the hospitals. Here is something that would be of some interest to you as well. The new wings of the hospitals are named 'Greta Dawson Rehab Unit'."

"That was his mother's name. Oh my God. Jordan." I started a fresh stream of tears as I thought of what Jordan must be going through. How could this happen to us again and where was he right now? I needed to speak with him. Needed to see him. I just needed him. I grabbed my phone from the nightstand and turned it on. With shaking hands I scrolled to his name.

Jenna, Aunt Suzette and David left the room and closed the door quietly behind them as the phone rang.

"Zoe." His voice was hoarse and he sounded tired and weary.

"Jordy," I whispered.

"You know what happened then? The truth?"

"Yes. David told me. I need to see you. I need you, Jordan."

"My darling Zoe."

"Hurry, Jordan."

"Yes."

I hung up the phone and lay back on the pillow as I waited for Jordan to arrive. I couldn't wait to tell him that I loved him, make plans to be with him and help heal his heart. My eyes fluttered shut as I thought of Jordan on his way to me. There was so much that still needed to be done and said.

"Jordan," I whispered. His name floated across the room and I turned toward my lover as he made his way to me. I put my hands in his as he led me to one of the chairs in the music room of his home. He set me down and went to the sleek music equipment where he quickly programmed some songs. Walking to the door of the soundproof music room, he slid the lock on the door as the music started. The voice of Justin Timberlake singing "LoveStoned" vibrated in the room.

I turned around to see him slowly making his way toward me as he started to dance to the music. I was dumbfounded at the incredible moves that he had. His hips gyrated to the fast-paced music and his legs joined in the movement. His hands went to the buttons of his shirt. He stood in front of me as he performed a strip tease with his shirt and slowly unbuttoned his pants.

The music continued and I couldn't help but tap my feet to the sound. I wanted to join in the dance as his lean muscular body moved above, then around me. He moved back to face me and unzipped his pants. I wet my lips with the tip of my tongue and reached out to touch him but he danced just beyond my reach. Sweat beaded on his lithe body as the song reached a crescendo and his body twisted and turned into a seductive move.

God, I wanted to touch him. Run my hands across the muscles of his long lean legs. I held my breath as he reached for his underwear and pulled it off, baring his gorgeous sex which was pulsing with desire.

The song came to an end. He pulled me from the chair and whispered, "Your turn." He sat in the chair I just vacated as the voice of Nelly Furtado rang through the room singing "Maneather".

My body started a slow, seductive dance as I moved across the room. His eyes were on me as I lay on the chaise lounge and ran my hands across my body starting at my neck then slowly down to my breasts. I squeezed my nipples and moved lower still, pausing at my mound. I rubbed my womanhood but did not stop. My hands moved from my legs to my ankles then back to the apex of my thighs. I stopped now and looked at him then looked down at my hands as I parted my legs wider and pushed a finger in my hot, wet slit. In and out, again and again.

Slowly, I reached up to my lips and tasted the pleasure of my body then got up off the chaise. I made my way back to him, all the while moving my body to the seductive music. I stood in front of him as I slowly stripped off my clothing. I was naked now with only my four-inch stilettos. I continued to dance, my hands in my hair then trailed them to my breasts. The song ended and I straddled him in a lap dance with my chest to his. Lenny Kravitz' "I Belong to You" pierced through the room.

My lover's erection was steel hard and the head of his cock round and plump, straining toward his abdomen. He tried to enter me, but I moved a few inches away from him. He pulled my ass toward his cock but I moved a little to his left leg and rode it as if I were fucking his leg. We moved in the erotic motion for a few minutes in erotic play until our breathing was choppy and we were both needy with sexual desire.

He finally placed both of his hands on my hips, lifted me and impaled me on his massive cock. With one swift motion, he penetrated my dripping vagina. I threw my head back and screamed in ecstasy as I rode him. Harder and harder my hips gyrated on his penis. He pushed out of the chair walked with me impaled on his manhood. My back hit against the nearest wall and he fucked me.

I begged him for more, more please, and he obliged. Our bodies were drenched in sweat as I held onto his broad shoulders. My knees were locked around his waist as he slammed into me. We reached a climactic union together. I screamed his name as he groaned into my mouth taking my tongue in a fiercely hot kiss.

His hips jerked as he spilled his seed deep in my body. We held onto each other and gasped for air. He gazed into my eyes and I was unable to look anywhere else but at him.

CHAPTER 34

A GENTLE HAND AWAKENED ME ON MY SHOULDER AND for a moment I wondered why I was asleep during the day. I wasn't even sure what day it was. My left upper arm was sore and I had a dull headache.

The setting sun was streaming into my bedroom through white wooden shutters casting muted shadows on the floor. The curtains swayed slowly from the air vent above on the ceiling.

I turned over on my back. Jenna was looking at me with concern in her eyes. I wasn't sure how long I'd been asleep, but the erotic dream I had caused a light sheen of perspiration on my skin and jacked up my heart rate more than a few beats. I still felt the touch of my lover's hand on my body. A smile touched my lips as I remembered the erotic dream.

"I wanted to check with you before I let him in," Jenna said.

She grasped a hold of my hand and I reluctantly let go of the memory of the dream I just had about Jordan.

"Let who in?" I stifled a yawn.

"Jordan. He said you called and asked him to come over," she rushed on in a whisper.

I shot up to a sitting position in the bed as I remembered the nightmare that was all too real over the past forty-eight hours.

"Oh God. I look a mess," I said, hoping that Jenna would disagree with me.

"Well I like the glow on your face and there is a nice pink to your cheeks."

I cupped my cheeks in my hands and felt the warmth of the blush due to the intense sexual nature of the dream.

She smirked. "If it makes you feel better, he looks worse for the wear, but I imagine you didn't asked him to come over so that you can critique his appearance."

I pushed my long auburn hair away from my face and cringed at the now crumpled cotton sundress that I wore.

Jenna was patiently waiting at the side of my bed for my answer.

"Send him in," I said.

I propped myself on pillows as Jenna opened the door. Jordan was leaning against the doorframe and pulled away when it swung open. David was standing beside him. They were obviously in deep conversation about the situation.

Jordan's eyes darted toward me. My heart swelled with the feeling of love and admiration I felt for him. His tall lean frame straightened. He was looking intently at me.

I could not miss seeing the shadows beneath his eyes from worry and lack of sleep. His hair was disheveled as if he was constantly raking his hands through the dark blond locks, and his brilliant blue eyes were dim.

I held my hands out to him and Jordan quickly made his way across the room. In one fluid movement he sat on the side of the bed and pulled me into his arms. The feeling of rightness washed over me as I snuggled into the warmth of his body.

I was vaguely aware of the door closing as I reveled in Jordan's strong embrace. He easily held me to his broad chest. His heartbeat strummed a constant staccato beneath my ear which brought a feeling of serenity to me despite the stressful situation of the past couple days.

Jordan angled his head to one side and tilted my chin up to face him. We stared into each other's eyes and I was aware of a deep spiritual connection between us. The palm of my hand ran over his chiseled jaw and met with stubbles from two days without shaving.

Jordan leaned his face into my hand and I pulled his head down until our lips locked in a sweet kiss. I flicked my tongue and ran it gently over his mouth and nibbled on his bottom lip. He inhaled slowly as I covered his lips with mine sucking in his exhaled air.

We breathed as one for a few moments before he took over the soulful kiss. Jordan pulled away reluctantly and gazed into my eyes. I lay back on the pillows but kept our fingers entwined as if unable or unwilling to lose the physical contact between us.

"I'm sorry about the stress you have endured over the past few days, Zoe. It was uncalled for and unfair to you." His lips covered my face with light kisses that sent a delicious tingle over my body.

"My attorneys are dealing with the nursing director from the hospital that leaked the information to Celia. Celia was more than happy to go to the media with incorrect information as a way of getting back at me."

"She said that I was responsible for her getting transferred and losing her job 10 years ago," I said.

"Never mind what she said about blaming you. We both know it's not true. The law will be involved as well due to the breach of confidentiality." His eyes pleaded with me to understand the unfortunate situation that propelled us into the media spotlight depicting us in a negative way.

"I thought you had betrayed me," I said, my eyes not leaving his face. "That you were punishing me for avoiding you for the past 10 years. That your pride was wounded and you were seeking some kind of revenge. I'm relieved that none of that is true," I rushed out to assure him that I now knew the truth.

"It will all be resolved quickly. My media team is working on a news release that will run on all the major news channels about why I purchased several hospitals in different states and the reason for adding rehabilitation wings onto the hospitals. Incidentally, the reporter that broke the story is Celia's cousin. He was relieved of his job for falsifying reports as soon as I found out."

"I am so proud of you and what you have done, Jordy. Busy as you are with other aspects of your business, you took time to offer others a place of solace and healing in desperate times in their lives." I gently squeezed his hands and rubbed my thumbs across his knuckles.

His face remained somber as I expressed my admiration for what he has done and continued to do on a personal level.

"David just found out about the hospitals. What you are doing for these communities, well, it's admirable and shows what a good person you truly are." My heart broke with sadness as I was reminded through these acts of kindness that he was honoring the memory of his mother.

"I want to give a little to those less fortunate, and keeping those hospitals open does just that. Many would be without a job if those institutions closed. Patients in need of help would be at a great disadvantage trying to get to another hospital for medical and emergency care."

"So true. I'm sure so many would lose their pensions and benefits as well."

"The news release will end with your staffing agency and focus on the incredible job you have done in the greater Houston medical community. By offering hospitals nursing services when their own nurses are sick, take vacation or have other emergencies, you are able to step in, therefore the patient gets uninterrupted medical care."

"Jordan, I don't need to prove anything to anyone."

"You have been active and give generously to food banks and homeless shelters. Only the organizations that you help to support know of your generosity. That will be the highlight of the newscast. Therefore disproving why you would do any underhanded dealings for personal gains."

"What I do for our community comes from my heart and does not need to be broadcast..."

He silenced me with a light brush of his lips on mine.

"The public will know of the mean-spiritedness of Celia, her aunt and cousin and what they meant to do to your spotless reputation."

I couldn't help but notice the change in his demeanor that seemed to be holding off the aggravation he was feeling.

I gently squeezed his hands affirming our concordance in this ordeal. "I don't need you to fight my battles."

"I understand and respect that. But this attack was meant to tarnish me as well. In the meantime, I will clear your name from all the untruths."

"Well, it is not necessary. I can do that, plus I have had incredible support from family, friends, employees and the public. There is, however, the issue of my agency staffing your four hospitals."

"What about it?" Jordan cocked an eyebrow at me.

"I will withdraw my contract and have my attorney rewrite it." I saw that he is about to interrupt so I placed a finger over his lips to silence him.

"This is what will happen, Jordan," I said, giving him no room for argument. "I will provide nurses only in the event that the hospitals are unable to find nursing staff from other agencies."

"Why the hell would you do that?"

He was not happy about that bit of information, but I would not back down from my decision.

"Let's not discuss this right now. You are just recovering from a blow to your head and I'm sure you are tired from all the stress," he said, although I knew he was not about to contend with me walking away from a contract that could indeed benefit my agency and myself financially.

"Waiting to talk about it won't change my decision. This will happen and I want it in effect as soon as possible."

"It's business. Not personal. Your agency was given the opportunity of an exclusive contract. That has nothing to do with us," he said.

I knew he was right, but I also knew that I would feel better if I didn't have this issue hanging over my head. It was just not the way I operated and Jordan would have to understand and accept it. I arched my brows at him.

Jordan sighed and placed a kiss on my forehead. "Fine. I will inform my attorney of your decision and change the contract."

"Good. Plus my new office in San Francisco is getting very busy and I will be making a profit on that end so I won't be quite as strapped for cash flow. This brings me to another issue. Did you have anything to do with me getting contracts in those hospitals last week?"

"I did not. They were given incorrect information from Celia's cousin. He forged a note to them saying that I was involved with you, and your agency was seeking contracts in San Francisco. They may have been overly polite to you when you met with them, but ultimately you will be serving their needs with temp nurses. My attorney found out this information and has been in touch with the hospitals. They are sending you a letter stating that your agency's credentials and reputation was the only reason for them giving you that contract. It had nothing to do with us being together."

I pulled in a ragged breath with this new information but was relieved that Jordan already addressed the issues with the hospitals.

A few moments of silence passed between us with each caught up in our own thoughts. Suddenly I giggled as I thought of what I looked like propped up in bed.

"What is so amusing, pretty lady?"

A look of relief passed over his facial features and his body relaxed with the lighter mood in the room.

I ran my hands up and down his arms enjoying the firm muscles rippling under my hands. The tactile sensation of my hands brought a smile to his face.

"I feel like an invalid lying in bed in the middle of the day."

"It's well into the evening now and you have good reasons for being in bed. I am still shaken about the blow you took to your head and knowing I did it…"

"Jordan. It was an accident. You would never have done that on purpose. The blow was meant for Lee and I jumped between the two of you to break up the fight. By the way, you could be in a lot of trouble for assaulting an officer."

"I am well aware of that. Lee is a good man. He is not pressing charges against me. I was determined to see you and anyone that was in my way…well, it did not end well."

I smiled at him as I thought of the fight that ensued between him and Lee.

"I couldn't bear the thought of your anguish and that I was responsible for you and your business being tarnished in any way." His eyes searched mine again for signs of distress. "I had to get to you, to see you and explain in person that the information was not correct. That I would never do anything to hurt you."

He could not seem to keep his hands off me. His hands gently cupped my cheeks and I rubbed my face in his palms as his thumb ran across my lips.

"How are you feeling?"

"Much better, Jordy," I whispered.

He leaned in and placed a sweet kiss on my lips.

My eyes fluttered shut as I savored the feeling of his warm beautiful lips on mine.

"Come away with me. Please. I want to take you away for a few days."

"I am too busy at work."

"Veronica and Andre can step in like they always do."

"But I have a lot going on with the new office and all."

"I understand, but three days away will do you good. It's not overseas."

"What about all the drama here?"

"I hire people to deal with drama."

"I'm not sure."

"Good."

"How is that good?"

"It's not a no."

I laughed at our quirky banter and Jordan swooped in for a kiss.

"When and where?"

"Tomorrow, and it's a surprise."

"How will I know what to pack?"

"I will pack for you. You just need your essentials. I will do the rest." He flashed a sexy smile and his blue eyes lit to their familiar brilliance.

"Fine, fine."

"Thanks. One more thing." He sat on the side of the bed and pulled me onto his lap. "I love you, Zoe Caine," he whispered.

My breath caught in my throat as I gazed into his eyes.

"I want to be your best friend. Your lover. Your partner in life. In other words, darling Zoe, allow me to be your forever man." His gaze held mine, unblinking.

I wound my arms around his neck.

"I love you, Jordan Dawson. Always have. Always will."

CHAPTER 35

THE SMELL OF FOOD COOKING WAFTED IN THE BEDROOM and my stomach growled reminding me that I hadn't had lunch and it was now suppertime. I laughed and Jordan crushed me to his chest.

"Time to feed you, pretty lady," he said and stood with me in his arms.

"Wait. I need to use the restroom and make myself presentable."

"OK. I will get something out of your closet for you to wear." He took me to the bathroom and set me on my feet in front of the mirror.

I looked in the mirror and gasped "It's worse than I thought." My disheveled features stared back at me in the mirror. My hair was in a tangled mess, my nose pink from crying and my eyes were a little puffy.

I pulled a brush through my hair and secured it in a loose bun then splashed water on my face and brushed my teeth.

I wobbled back in the bedroom.

Jordan pulled off my crumpled dress and held me at arms length. His eyes roamed over my body as he took in my state of undress. His hooded gaze caught me off guard.

I wanted nothing more than to throw myself in his arms but with the last bit of self-control I had, I reached for the bra and top he held in his hand and slipped into the clothing, and then my slacks.

Jordan pulled me into his arms and gazed at me with a hunger that shook me to the core.

I squirmed against him and felt the fullness of his erection straining against the zipper of his jeans.

A gasp escaped my lips and he took the opportunity to slam his mouth against mine assaulting my senses with a deep kiss that had me wanting to beg for more.

"What you do to me. You take my breath away," he whispered in my ear.

"You most definitely have the same effect on me," I replied.

He kissed the top of my head and stepped away adjusting himself. He caught me gawking at him and winked at me.

I quickly turned around and walked toward the door with a smile on my face.

Jordan slipped his arms around my waist and we exited the room together.

The room was buzzing with friendly conversation and the aroma from the kitchen filled the house with the promise of great food. I took in the sight of those I cared about most in my life and my eyes misted with tears, grateful that I had such love and support.

Jenna was sitting in the recliner. David stood behind her rubbing her shoulders.

Mia was perched prettily on the side of the sofa with Philippe beside her, his hand on one of her knees.

Veronica looked across at me with her brandy colored eyes and smiled. She sat in the middle of the sofa with Trevor beside her.

Lee and Andre sat on chairs from the dining room, deep in conversation. Lee winked at me. It did not go unnoticed by Jordan; his hand tightened on my waist and pulled me closer to his side.

Aunt Suzette and Neena were busy dishing up the delicious food in the kitchen.

I sniffed the air appreciatively and smiled broadly at everyone, reassuring them that all was well in my world now. I moved around the room hugging and thanking everyone for being at my side during this awful ordeal.

"So, we're cool with Jordan or what?" Trust Mia to pipe up to address the elephant in the room right away.

"Yes. Jordan and I are cool." I looked up at him and smiled.

"Just making sure I can call off my boys." She grinned.

"Can we eat now? I'm starved?" asked Jenna.

"Oh good. You're getting an appetite then. Less nausea?" asked Veronica.

"Finally feeling a little better. The meds help. Great to eat normal food but I'm taking it slow," Jenna said, beaming from ear to ear.

"Then you're first in line," David said as he helped her out of the recliner.

Jordan gently squeezed my arm and excused himself. He made his way over to Lee and shook his hand. They spoke in a low voice and relief washed over me as I saw they were both smiling.

Soon we were all scattered in the dining room and living room as we ate and conversed.

Aunt Suzette and Neena were beaming with compliments on the food from all of us.

An hour later the group slowly dispersed.

Aunt Suzette fussed over me for a few minutes. Her eyes took in my appearance and she commented on the color that was coming back into my cheeks. She placed a glass of water and a couple ibuprofens in my hand and insisted that I take them.

I sighed with contentment and I relaxed against Jordan on the living room sofa. My feet were tucked under me as Jordan held the glass of water to my lips. The cool liquid slid easily down my throat and contributed to the placid feeling that I easily succumbed to.

I yawned and leaned into the leather sofa as Jordan went into the kitchen. He returned and picked me up. I giggled as he navigated his way back to my bedroom and lay me on the bed.

"I love that sound," he said. "I'll never tire of your giggles and laughter. Among other sweet noises that you make. It's…well, I hope to hear a lot more of it. I missed you like hell, my love."

My breath caught in my throat at the sincerity in his voice and I paused for a moment with the realization that I missed him too. We'd been apart for five days (not counting Jordan's brief visit before I left my office Tuesday) and it seemed like an eternity.

"I'm glad you made it back safe from Europe. Business was good I presume?" I asked.

"All went as planned. Just business as usual, but we will not discuss the details of acquisitions. You need to rest." He chuckled as I pouted. "Now, let's get you undressed."

"Why, Jordan Dawson. My doctor would not be pleased that you want to have your way with me soon," I said and laughed as he tickled me.

With quick movements he rummaged in one of my drawers and produced a tank top and matching bottoms.

I slipped them on and lay demurely back in the bed.

"Don't look at me like that or I will forget my good intentions and have my way with you, Miss Caine."

"Would you like to spend the night with me?" I asked.

"I insist on it." He pulled off his shoes and jeans. I unabashedly stared at the absolute perfection of his chiseled body. "Turn around, or so help me…"

I quickly scooted to the middle of the bed and lay on my side facing away from Jordan. I felt the bed dip as he got in beside me.

He pulled the cover over us and scooped me against his chest.

I reached around my body to touch him and came in contact with his shirt. "You're almost fully clothed," I said.

"Keep your hands in front of you and go to sleep." His voice was stern and I couldn't help but tease him.

I should behave myself. I knew I should, but why? I wiggled my ass against him and came in contact with his growing erection. I gasped and my eyes flew open. Oh, God. He felt delicious and divine.

Jordan pushed me gently away from him and something cool and soft hit my backside.

"Did you just place a pillow between us?" I squeaked.

"I did." His deep no nonsense voice sounded above my head.

"Honestly?"

"Go. To. Sleep."

I grumbled and took in a loud woeful breath but refrained from plucking the pillow from behind me and tossing it against the wall.

Jordan's arms held me steadfast and I wondered if he was smiling or cringing at my behavior.

After a few minutes, I settled down and drifted off to sleep.

CHAPTER 36

SATURDAY MORNING I CALLED VERONICA AND ANDRE TO tell them I would be out of the office on Monday. As usual, they stepped up to the plate, so to speak and urged me to relax and enjoy my time with Jordan.

Jordan wasted no time whisking me away to the airport where we boarded his jet.

"Mimosas for both of us, please. Then breakfast," he said to the flight attendant.

After reaching cruising altitude we sat at the table and sipped on the cold beverage.

Jordan pulled a folder from his briefcase and pushed it toward me.

"Lake Tahoe Shakespeare Festival. Oh, Jordan. Thank you." I flipped the pages and scanned the information.

"I thought you would like it. I planned it a few weeks ago, but I was waiting for the right time to tell you about it."

"I have always wanted to go but never took the time."

"I know and was hoping you wouldn't visit over the years. I selfishly wanted it to be with me." He smiled, pleased with himself.

"I will absolutely love it. The place looks beautiful."

"We can experience it together," he said.

"Will we have time to take a canoe or boat on the lake? Maybe swim?" I asked.

"Will we ever." He chuckled. "Can't wait to show you what I have in mind for us to do over the next two days."

I got up from the chair and flung myself into his arms.

"I love, love, love you. Thank you." I rained kisses over his face and neck then settled in his lap for a kiss.

"Remind me to surprise you more. I love the rewards of your appreciation."

After breakfast, Jordan took me to the private sleep cabin.

"This is fast becoming one of my favorite places to be," he said.

"Mine too. I mean, how many women can say that they get laid at thirty-five thousand feet?"

"Anything to keep that smile on your face." Jordan quickly stripped me of the summer dress he chose for me this morning. His clothing followed mine on the floor.

Jordan paused and settled me gently back on the bed. He stared into my eyes then slowly ran his hand down my neck.

"I love your neck. You have the cutest little brown moles on one side but not on the other." He ran his tongue over the moles.

I bit my bottom lip gently as he continued his exploration of my body.

"Then there are your arms, long and graceful with a light dusting of freckles." He lips followed his hands.

"Your breasts are perfect with yet a few more moles." He swooped down and licked the moles then pulled his head back and gazed at me again. His head went back down to my breasts. He took a nipple in his mouth and suckled gently on it. First one, then the other.

"I love the soft curve of your hips and your pretty belly button, but your legs drive me insane." He picked up one of my legs and kissed along my thigh all the way to my calf.

My breathing slowly increased with his touch and I moaned. Delicious chills ran across my body as I anticipated more of his touch on my skin. My hands were restless. I wanted to pull his head down to my body but I was captivated by his touch.

"Then there are your delicate feet that always have just the right color nail polish on every pretty little nail." He kissed my toes and blew on them.

I jolted from the erotic sensations playing across my skin.

Jordan smirked at me. "Oh, I have not even started to worship your gorgeous body, baby. I will unlock every erogenous zone on your body until you are completely and totally senseless with pleasure."

"Jordan..." I gasped.

"Shhhh, babe. The best part is yet to be explored, but not with words. No, words could not suffice what incredible pleasure awaits me... But, we will take a nap and continue..."

"Jordan Dawson, I swear I will hurt you..."

Jordan splayed my legs apart and swooped down straight between my legs. My pelvis rushed up to meet his glorious mouth as he delved his tongue in my pussy. I screamed with pure unadulterated pleasure as he added two fingers in my slit. His tongue moved up to my clit and he sucked gently. My body rocked with pleasure below his as Jordan assaulted my senses with ecstasy.

He pulled away from the apex of my thighs and slid over me. His erection pierced my vagina. I moaned as his mouth claimed mine in a kiss. I lapped at his mouth tasting my essence on him.

"I love you. I could stay in your sweet body forever. Your gorgeous pussy is like nectar for my soul. Please, please, let me love you forever, Zoe," he whispered.

"Anything, whatever you want," I said, and held his face above mine as I looked into his eyes.

His hips picked up the pace as he rocked his powerful body against mine. I held onto his arms and latched my legs around his waist crossing my feet at my ankles.

Jordan drove further into me, his hips relentless as he slammed into my body again and again.

I shattered below him in euphoric bliss.

Jordan followed behind me.

We lay in silence holding on to one another. Jordan slowly rolled to his side and pulled me into his body.

I settled beside him as he ran his hand through my hair.

"I hope that wasn't too much for you but the doctor said we could resume usual activities including sex."

"You called my doctor?"

"First thing this morning. I wasn't taking any chances."

"You are like a fussy mother hen. What will I do with you?"

"Anything you want." He smiled above me.

After an hour of talking and snuggling, we pulled our clothes back on and got ready for landing. A limo was waiting at the curb for us, and soon we were on our way toward Lake Tahoe.

After an hour of admiring the breathtaking mountain views, the limo pulled up to a beautiful rustic house nestled in the woods. The crystal clear turquoise water of the lake sparkled like gems below, and across the lake were mountains that seemed to touch the sky.

"This place is simply perfection." I walked up to the huge porch with hanging baskets of flowering plants and stop to admire the huge planters that lined the walkway.

I plopped down in one of the rocking chair and smiled up at Jordan.

"I bought it last year. All part of my plan to get you back in my life."

He pulled me up and took me on a tour of the house and grounds. Then he took me for a walk on the trails.

"How did you ever find this place?"

"I told my realtor what I thought you would like. I must let him know you're pleased with my choice then."

"How could I not love this? Nature at it's best. Trails to hike, lake to swim, mountains to scale, skiing in the winter. It's the perfect place for just about any time of the year."

"And it's yours."

"What do you mean, 'it yours'?" I stopped to take a picture of wildflowers on my phone.

"I had it put in your name," he said nonchalantly as he continued to stroll on the path with his hands in his pockets.

"I won't even address that issue right now." I sighed. I decided to choose my battles with Jordan.

"Wouldn't do you any good to argue. It's on twenty acres. Heavily wooded so I had a fence erected around the property. That way, if you get lost, I know where to look."

"My phone has a GPS. It gets a great signal," I replied, holding up the phone for him to see.

"So it does. Come on." He held his hand out and I slid mine in his.

We turned back toward the house and continued down to the lake.

"Love the boat." I stood on the dock beside Jordan and admired the blue and white *Cobalt Boat* that bobbed gently on the water. Its cream and brown leather interior promised a comfortable and luxurious ride.

"I had her delivered here last week."

"Her?" I asked.

"She's yours as well. Look at the side."

I peeked at the side of the boat where her name was in a stylistic cursive writing. Miss Zoe

"She is a beauty," I breathed as we boarded the vessel. Jordan showed me more of what was onboard.

Below deck housed a small cozy bedroom and bathroom. There was also a small kitchenette and table seating for four.

"We'll spend the night on her soon, but I want you in a huge bed tonight."

I laughed and shook my head at him.

Jordan started the boat with the push of a button on the instrumentation panel. The powerful engine roared to life and a few minutes later we were skimming across the surface of Lake Tahoe. After pointing out homes nestled along the lake, he drove further out to a secluded cove, anchored the boat and cut the engine.

Jordan sat on the long leather seat on the back of the boat and pulled me onto his lap.

"This is pure bliss. Thank you. I haven't taken time away to relax for, well, too long."

Jordan slid me off his lap and knelt in front of me.

"Marry me, Zoe Caine. Make me the happiest and luckiest man in the world. Please, marry me," he whispered.

I saw a bit of apprehension in his eyes and the pensive look on his face as if his life depended on my answer.

"Jordan." I reached up to cup his face in my hands. "Yes. Yes, I want you to complete my life. I want to be your wife."

Jordan let out a relieved breath and threw his head back and let out a whoop to the sky. He pulled me into his arms. We were both kneeling as we rocked back and forth for a few moments.

"My love. My life. All I am and all I do are for you. I want you to have the wedding of your dreams, but I am not willing to wait longer than a few months."

I laughed and sat down again. He slid me back onto his lap.

"I'm not sure how long it will take to plan, but…"

"I will hire as many wedding planners as necessary to make it happen. Four months. That's all the time they get. What do you think?"

"If that's what you want, then let's make it happen." I grinned up at Jordan. It was so good to see him happy and carefree.

"What I want, is you as my wife. To love you always and put a baby or two in your belly." He laughed when I elbowed him in his stomach.

"You are incorrigible. But I would love to be your wife and have your babies."

"Come on. I want to consummate our engagement. Which reminds me, we need to shop for a ring next week. I will arrange for an engagement party at our penthouse."

We made our way down the small stairway of the boat. Jordan led me to the bedroom. We quickly pulled off our clothes and threw them on the floor.

Jordan's erection was straining up toward his abdomen and I licked my lips in anticipation of the silken feel of his penis in my mouth and the musky scent of his body that I've come to crave.

He pulled me down to his long, lean body. Our limbs tangled together. A soft moan escaped my lips as Jordan's warm tongue sluiced up my neck and sucked gently against my jaw. I jolted with pleasure and melted in his strong embrace.

Jordan claimed my lips in a toe-curling kiss and my arms slid around his neck. My legs straddled his waist as I slid my moist heat along his massive erection. I gasped as he penetrated me.

"All for you, my lovely Zoe," he muttered.

"You have a perfect, um, beautiful cock." I giggled as he tickled my side.

"Why, thank you. I aim to please you with my, um, perfectly beautiful cock." He chuckled.

"I *am* pleased, and your aim is perfect and accurate as ever." My breath caught in my throat as he moved below me. His finger stroked my clitoris and I mewled above him.

I moved my hips and rode him hard. Our bodies danced like the lovers we have become. Giving and taking, back and forth, up and down. I held onto his biceps for leverage and lost myself in the moment of pure sexual bliss.

Jordan pulled me down toward him and laved a nipple with his wet tongue. The sound of his mouth against my breast and our bodies mating bounced off the walls of the cabin. He pulled his tongue from my nipple and it made a soft popping sound. Jordan moved to my other breast and did the same.

I lost myself in the joy of this moment. This pure love and ecstasy that we were sharing was a long time coming and we delighted in the treasure that was our commitment to one another.

I threw my head back as I continued to pump my body on Jordan's cock. My hands reached behind me and I held onto his thighs. The movement pushed my pelvis forward and Jordan wasted no time landing his fingers on my clit. He stroked and rubbed the elongated bud until a violent orgasm smashed into me. I cry out his name, again and again then shuddered in sweet release above him.

Jordan gently reached for me and enfolded me to his chest. He flipped me over and climbed over my body. My chest pressed to the cushions, and I was on my knees with my ass in the air toward Jordan. He held my hips in his big hands and mounted me. With swift strokes, he pumped his shaft into me, relentless in his pleasure. With one last push into my slick vagina, he shattered.

His body shuddered above mine as he emptied his release into me. His body crushed mine as he slumped onto my back. A few moments later he flipped our still joined bodies onto our sides.

We lay in each other's arms as Jordan drew lazy circles on my belly.

"We're going to the festival this evening where you can browse and indulge yourself in everything Shakespeare," he said.

"I would like that."

"Then stay for the play."

"Awesome."

"Then I will take you back to the house and ravish your body good and proper."

"This was good and proper."

"Good and proper again." He chuckled. "Tomorrow morning I am taking you on a hot air balloon ride."

"I would love that, but can you like handle one of those things?'

"I can if I need to, but I hired someone. I want my attention on you."

"OK."

"You are mine, Zoe Caine. Always and forever mine."

"Yes. Yours always," I whispered back to my lover.

RAIN OVER ME
BOOK 2 IN THE
'RAIN WILL FALL' TRILOGY

Mia Lambert is beautiful, rich, and used to having her own way. When it comes to intimacy, she makes her own rules. Convinced that she is selfish and self-centered like her mother, she stays away from matters of the heart. Mia's rules leave her empty and unfulfilled, but she is too stubborn to change until Philippe strides into her life and challenges her to let him fulfill her wanton body's desires.

Philippe Colson is every woman's dream. Handsome and charming, he shows Mia passion beyond her wildest dreams. He has come to play, and when he does, he plays for keeps.

Will Mia allow her fears to rule her heart and leave her with an empty, guarded life or will she accept the challenge from Philippe and trust her heart to him?

A Note from the Author

Dear Reader,

I thought of you as I wrote this book. I am equally delighted and humbled that you have purchased your copy today. My wish is that you will cloak your heart in love and live your happily ever after with the person of your dreams.

All the best,
Cindy Lou Moldovan

ABOUT THE AUTHOR

Cindy Lou Moldovan graduated from Lee College in Texas with a nursing degree. She is a certified PADI Scuba Divemaster, loves the outdoors, spending time with family and friends and traveling extensively. An avid reader and book lover, she is the author of her memoir *Growing Up Third World*.

Cindy creates strong characters in her steamy novels that her readers will fall in love with and leave them panting for more.

She lives in South Carolina with her husband.

Forever Rain is her first romance novel.

Cindy is a member of Romance Writers of America, Georgia RW, and Low County RW. She would love to hear from her readers. If you enjoyed this book, please consider leaving a book review on a retailer site.

Website: http://www.cindyloumoldovan.com
Facebook: https://www.facebook.com/cindyloumoldovan
Twitter: https:livepage.apple.com//twitter.com/cindylmoldovan
LinkedIn: https://www.linkedin.com/in/cindymoldovan
Goodreads: https://www.goodreads.com/cindyloumoldovan

www.ingramcontent.com/pod-product-compliance
Lightning Source LLC
Chambersburg PA
CBHW020331180626
46812CB00001B/145